Aveline

by

S. J. Carson

Cover Art by *Kristian Norris*

The Wild Rose Press, Inc.
PO Box 708
Adams Basin, NY 14410-0708
Visit us at www.thewildrosepress.com

Publishing History
First Edition, 2024
Trade Paperback ISBN 978-1-5092-5751-5
Digital ISBN 978-1-5092-5752-2

Published in the United States of America

Dedication

For my mother and in memory of my father.

Chapter 1

She heard them before she saw them.

"Hey, Fatsoline!"

Aveline froze. It was Quintana, and close behind, her lieutenant Cynthia. She knew that if she turned she was giving them the power to call her that awful nickname, yet she feared the consequences if she didn't.

As she turned, Quintana gave her a shove from behind and she fell onto her knees with a thud, all her books flying from her arms. The two girls surrounded her.

"I hear you were swilling the garbage pail again," said Quintana. "What'd you think you'd find in there? Leftover meatloaf?"

Cynthia snorted. Aveline averted her eyes.

"I-I don't eat from the garbage pail." Aveline bit her lower lip to prevent herself from crying.

Just then, she heard the sound of heels clacking on the marble floor. The three girls stood immediately to face Sister Harriet, their Language Arts teacher. A member of the Sacred Order of the Monnag, Sister Harriet was dressed in a black habit, with prayer beads around her waist. At the end of the prayer beads was the charm of Monnag, a fleur-de-lis with the head of a dragon turned to the left. Sister Harriet was young and the girls were not afraid of her, but they stopped teasing Aveline when she walked over to them.

But as soon as the Sister passed, they began their cruel game again.

"Hey, stop!"

Aveline looked up and saw her best friend, Bruno Page. Like Aveline, he was thirteen years old. He had sandy brown hair that fell into his eyes and a round, freckled face.

The bullies turned.

"Oh, it's only Doggo," said Cynthia.

"My name is Bruno." He gritted his teeth.

"Well, Bruno's a dog's name," said Cynthia.

"You'd better leave her alone—"

"Or what?" said Quintana, hands on her hips. "Gonna tell your daddy on us? He's just a commoner, not even a member of the Party."

This was a sore spot for Bruno, and Quintana knew it. Only the wealthy and well-connected could join the National Democratic Party of their own volition; the poor needed Sponsors to vouch for their integrity. Bruno hated to be reminded that he was from a lower-class background, that the only way he could attend a private school like Belfort Academy was on scholarship.

He lifted his fist as if to strike her, and she laughed.

"You wouldn't hit a girl."

"You bet I would."

Quintana waggled her fingers in his face. "I'm so scared, I'm shaking."

Cynthia gave Aveline's books a kick, sending them flying. "We'll be back, so don't get too comfortable." With that, the two girls sauntered down the hall, their heels clicking on the floor.

Aveline trembled, her face red. Bruno gave her a

hand and helped her to her feet.

"Thanks," she said sheepishly. This wasn't the first time he'd had to rescue her from the bullies.

He shrugged. "No need to thank me."

Bruno picked up Aveline's books and carried them for her. They exited the school building and went into the courtyard, a large square of grass surrounded by big shade trees, at whose center was a tall marble statue of the Leader—Aveline's grandfather, Alfred Fleur.

Fifty years ago, Alfred had founded the National Democratic Party and led a coup to overthrow King Reuel IV and take control of the country's government, installing himself as its Supreme Leader and establishing the various ministries: the Ministry of Law and Peace, the Ministry of Civic Enlightenment, and the Ministry of Health among them. He had also established the state religion, the Sacred Order of the Monnag, named after the sigil of the Fleur family.

"I don't understand why you don't just use your grandfather—or your mother or even your uncle—to get Cynthia and Quintana off your back," said Bruno.

Aveline's mother was Allyn Monnag Fleur, Minister of Civic Enlightenment, or Lightminister for short. Her uncle Simon, Allyn's younger brother, was Minister of Law and Peace, also known as the Lawminister. It was true that Aveline could have mentioned one of her relatives to the bullies because it was high treason to speak ill of a public figure, but there was no law against making fun of one of their descendants. Besides, the bullies knew exactly who Aveline was. They bullied her precisely because she did not look like a Fleur. She was tall and big-boned, with frizzy blonde hair and freckled skin and an upturned nose wide at the bridge. The rest of the Fleurs were small and dark-haired, with sharp features and paper-pale skin.

In response to his question, she shrugged. "It wouldn't do any good."

"If my grandfather were Leader, I would be shouting his name from the rooftops and nobody would ever mess with me."

They both looked up at the statue. Alfred had been a strapping man in his youth, with a barrel chest and a mustache and a look of absolute determination in his eyes, which the sculptor had captured perfectly. Posed in the Salute of Loyalty, his right hand over his heart, he gave the salute back to the country he had saved from a tyrannical monarchy. Aveline and Bruno both saluted the Leader, lest any of the Sisters come out and find them staring idly at the statue without paying proper respect.

The two friends sat on a bench together, sharing the chocolate muffins they'd taken from the cafeteria at lunchtime. The Ministry of Education ensured that every school was well-stocked with food for its students. Even though Aveline's mother had her on a strict diet at home, she could eat whatever she wanted at school, and thus never lost any weight—much to Allyn's chagrin.

Aveline often wished she had been born into Bruno's family instead of the Fleurs. How wonderful it would have been not to be scrutinized and judged at every moment! How wonderful not to be compared to the other members of her family and to her forebears! But she also knew that Bruno would have given his right arm to have been in her position as the so-called luckiest girl in the entire country.

"Want to play a game of cricket?" asked Bruno.

Aveline sighed. "I'm afraid I've got riding lessons today."

At three thirty, a car came to pick her up and take her from school in the City Center back to the Fleur Estate. The driver, Elton, smiled at her in the rearview mirror. Aveline smiled back, though she'd never been entirely comfortable with being driven around in one of the black Party cars like a celebrity while Bruno and the lower-class kids from school took the bus or walked.

The driver caught her eye in the rearview mirror. "How're things, Miss Aveline?"

Elton was a burly man in his early fifties with a heavy mustache and kind eyes. He'd been driving her and her family around for as long as she could remember.

"Not so bad, Elton. And yourself?"

"Can't complain. It's a beautiful day. I've got air in my lungs and my favorite gal in the back." He winked at her. "But I can tell something's on your mind. What's eatin' at you, Miss Aveline? It's not those bullies again, is it?"

She sighed. "You guessed it."

When he stopped at a traffic light, he caught her eye again and smacked his right fist into his left hand. "Boy, I'd just like to—"

"It's okay, Elton. Bruno and I will figure out a way to handle them. I appreciate it, though."

The car stopped at the top of a wide brick drive, each stone of which had been hand-laid, with the largest stone nearest the Great House bearing the Fleurs' dragon sigil. Aveline exited the car and walked up the elegant marble stairs leading to the House where she lived with her family.

Four stories tall, with nearly two hundred rooms, the House sat upon a hill and was the most opulent structure in the entire country of Alterra. Behind the House, as far as the eye could see, sprawled the emerald grounds of the Estate, with lawns and meadows and forest and ponds and a creek and a hamlet built especially for Aveline's late grandmother Marie, and rolling hills all along the perimeter. A tall iron fence followed the curves of the hills, sealing off the Estate from the rest of Calador, the capital city.

Aveline followed a dirt path a quarter of a mile down behind the House to the large stone stables situated by a pond patched with water lilies. After quickly changing into her riding clothes in the carriage house, she proceeded to the stable.

Her horse was a brown shiny Dutch Warmblood called Paintbrush, for the dusting of white across his snout. In the stall beside Paintbrush was a black Oldenburg called Pacer, her mother's horse. A champion dressage rider in her youth, Allyn had since given up the sport to work in the Alterran government.

Paintbrush's reins in her hand, she stopped to watch Jem lead a new horse in a circle around the corral and hold his hand above its head and command it to lie down, docile as a puppy.

Jeremiah "Jem" Caslon was twenty-eight years old and had started his job only recently. From the Province of Lystra in the southern part of the country, Jem had never been to Calador before, much less to the Fleur Estate. He was tall and well-built, handsome and soft-spoken, a true horse whisperer. He had olive skin that tanned easily, the sun bringing out the gold beneath it. The sun also streaked his dark brown hair gold, and he wore it long, so that it moved gently when he turned his head and he tucked it behind his ears when working with the horses.

"Hi, Jem!" said Aveline brightly, waving.

"Well, hello, Miss Aveline," he said, giving a nonverbal command to the horse to make it rise.

Aveline mounted her own horse. As Jem guided her through a series of exercises, she couldn't help but feel a bit sorry for the young man who had left everything, his family and friends and hometown. She also knew that he desperately wanted to be a member of the Party but could not find a Sponsor. He wore a crimson ribbon on his lapel to signify that he was an Aspirant.

"Since my mother is Lightminister," said Aveline, "perhaps she can be your Sponsor."

He shook his head, laughing softly. "You have no idea, Miss Aveline, how badly I wish she could."

"I could just ask her."

"Oh, no, please don't trouble her on my account."

After her lessons, Aveline returned to the House and ran upstairs to her room. She saw that Jossie, her lady's maid, had left out a black dress for her. She changed quickly and dashed downstairs and into the dining room, taking a quick sniff under her arms and hoping she didn't stink of body odor.

Just as she was conducting her sniff test, her grandfather Alfred marched into the room. He never walked anywhere; he always marched, a vestigial motion of his soldier days. He was only about five-foot-five and had lost weight and musculature as he'd aged, but he retained the same powerful, dignified air of his youth, and looked much taller than he was. Now, instead of a mustache, he wore a salt-and-pepper beard, and still had a full head of white hair. With his sharp nose and thin lips, he didn't even have to open his mouth to seem intimidating. Aveline immediately straightened up when she saw him.

"Good evening, Grandfather," she said, just as the old Monnag clock chimed six, echoing throughout the dining room.

"Good evening, Aveline," he said in the upper-crust accent of Calador, which Aveline had never truly mastered. "No time to bathe?"

"My apologies, Grandfather." She looked down at her feet.

He lifted her chin with his forefinger. "Always look at me when I'm speaking to you. And thank you for your honesty. But please do be sure to bathe after your riding lessons. We don't want our home smelling like a stable now, do we?"

Aveline, trembling inside, shook her head no, trying not to break away from his gaze.

But he was no longer paying attention to her; his focus had shifted to his daughter, Allyn Monnag Fleur.

"Ah, Madam Lightminister," he said.

"My Leader."

They liked to play this game, calling one another by their public titles in private. Alfred also liked to address Allyn as "Monnag," to emphasize that he had given *her* the family sigil name, as opposed to her younger brother Simon.

Aveline studied Allyn as she walked in. She was thirty-five years old and stood five-foot-two. Slender to the point of being almost emaciated, she existed on little besides coffee and pills. Her thinness was more a political statement than a lifestyle choice—as if to demonstrate that, living in a land of plenty, she would not indulge.

Allyn was beautiful in the way of the Fleurs, with a straight nose, high cheekbones, and large gray eyes that seemed never to blink. Dressed in a skirt suit and stilettos, she wore the Monnag sigil pin—a gold dragon's head with the fleur-de-lis—on her left lapel, signifying that she was a member of the Party. At the end of her long chestnut braid she wore the crimson loyalty ribbon. Despite seeing her mother every day, Aveline never failed to be struck by her beauty.

Allyn leaned down and gave her daughter a kiss on either cheek.

"How was school today, darling?" she asked in the same clipped accent as Alfred.

"Wonderful," lied Aveline. She made it a point never to trouble her mother with her problems.

Just then, her uncle Simon and his wife Lilia entered the dining room, smartly dressed. Simon, aged thirty-three, was short and dark-haired and slightly plump. Lilia was strawberry blonde and pretty in a bunny-rabbit sort of way. Their children, six-year-old Lilia (called Lily) and four-year-old Simon Junior ("S.J." for short), followed close behind. Aveline found it funny that her aunt and uncle had duplicated themselves. And they doted on their miniature selves, making sure they had the best of everything, and turning them into entitled little brats. Aveline was sometimes forced to babysit her little cousins, who treated her like the bullies at school.

The family members were seated in their usual spots, Alfred at the head of the table, Allyn to his right, and Aveline to her right. To his left sat Simon and his family.

Aveline felt her mother's hand on her back, reminding her to sit up straight in the presence of her grandfather.

The footmen began serving supper, beginning with pea soup. Aveline, who was hungry after her riding lessons, wolfed hers down. Under the table, Allyn nudged her foot, reminding her to eat more slowly and gracefully.

Allyn herself simply stirred her soup with her delicate spoon, lifting it to her lips to blow on it but never actually taking a bite. This was the way she always behaved at meals, so the undiscerning would think she was eating although no food actually passed her lips.

The second footman swept away their soup bowls, and another footman came in with the salad course and then the main course. Because Allyn had instructed the kitchen staff that Aveline was to be on a strict diet, the footman brought her a special plate, with wild rice, a thin chicken breast, and steamed broccoli, while the rest of the family enjoyed red meat and mashed potatoes.

To Aveline's left, Allyn scarcely touched her meal, taking a single bite of steak and washing it down with red wine. The first footman appeared to refill her glass. Aveline knew her mother's routine: she drank coffee throughout the day to stay awake, pills in the afternoon when her energy began to flag, and alcohol at night to wind down. Sometimes, if she had to give a speech in the evening, she would skip the alcohol and continue drinking coffee or taking pills.

"Monnag." Alfred set down his glass of wine. "What news from the Ministry of Civic Enlightenment?"

Allyn smiled. "Why don't you ask Yrgess first?"

Simon looked displeased at having been called by his sigil name, the lesser dragon, pronounced "*Air*-gess." But he cleared his throat and said, "Father, we arrested an enemy of the State today at the wall."

Alfred raised an eyebrow. "Is that so?"

Simon nodded. "A youth named Sandor Hayes published an article against the Party in a small underground newspaper, and the Stam caught him attempting to flee the Federal District. He is now detained at the Lawministry awaiting trial."

Short for Secret Tactical Arm of the Ministry, the Stam was the country's secret police under Simon's purview at the Ministry of Law and Peace. The Stam was assumed always to be lurking somewhere in the background, watching or listening.

Alfred, who had been swirling his wine in his glass, stopped abruptly and glared at his son. "When you say 'against the Party,' what exactly do you mean?"

"Well." Simon cleared his throat. "It's rather a lengthy screed, but in essence, he accuses us of corruption. He even goes so far as to name names."

"You?" Allyn smirked.

"Very funny."

"How many people have seen it?" said Alfred.

"We don't know yet. But we've confiscated every copy we could find."

"And have you arrested the printer, the publisher,

and whoever funded this…newspaper?"

"We're still looking for them, Father. But don't worry. We will find them and bring them to justice."

"What do you feel is an appropriate punishment?"

"Why, death, of course."

Aveline shuddered and looked down at her plate.

"And you, Monnag?" Alfred turned his gaze to his daughter. "Do you feel that death is appropriate?"

"Absolutely not."

"What?" Simon leaned forward. "Why not?"

Allyn paused before answering. "I agree that we must eliminate the Resistance, root, stem, and bud. However." She lifted a finger. "The goal of the Stam is protection, not punishment. Mr. Hayes quite obviously has a moral compass. If he hadn't known he'd committed treason, he wouldn't have tried to flee. The best way to handle such a person is to make an example of him. To reform him, not punish him. He is a Party member, so a course of reeducation in the Party ideals should be sufficient. At the end, he will publicly reaffirm the Sacred Oath."

"No." Simon pounded his fist on the table so that the wineglasses clattered, making the children jump. "We're talking high treason here, Father. Now is not the time to be lenient. If you let someone like Hayes off easy, he will do it again. And others will follow."

Alfred shook his head. "Your sister is right. True power comes from having the ability to punish but choosing to forgive instead." He turned to Allyn. "And how does the Lightministry propose to handle this?"

"We intend to portray him as a young man gone astray, one who admits his wrongdoing and sees the light. A timeless story arc. Then we shall refocus the public's attention. What we need is a gesture of goodwill on the part of the Ministry. A personal gesture. By me."

"What we need is a firing squad," said Simon.

"Enough," said Alfred. "No more of this talk in front of the children. Come, we'll continue this discussion in my study."

Allyn stood and kissed Aveline on the top of her head. "Be good, my darling. I have to return to the Ministry tonight, so don't wait up for me."

"Yes, Mother."

She watched as her grandfather, mother, and uncle disappeared into Alfred's study to drink brandy and talk politics.

****

In bed that night, Aveline closed her eyes but could not sleep because of the strong moonlight through her window, bathing the comforter in white. She clasped her hands and prayed to the God of the Sacred Order of the Monnag, a State God who presided over political affairs and blessed the country's leaders.

Please keep Grandfather and Mother and Uncle Simon safe, she prayed. Then she added, as she did every night, *Please bring Mother a husband and me a father*.

She hardly remembered her own father, a colonel in the Air Command who'd died in battle when she was only two years old. His name was Christopher Llewellyn III. Because he had the same name as his father and grandfather, everyone had called him Kit. Upon his marriage he had taken the Fleur name, as was customary for those marrying into the ruling family, whether male or female.

A black-and-white photograph of him in uniform hung above the mantel in the Great Room. Aveline's resemblance to him was striking; she had inherited his round face and broad nose and blond hair. She'd heard stories about his bravery and loyalty from her grandfather, but her mother never spoke of him, as though he'd never existed. Without her father, Aveline felt that she was missing out on half of who she was. Perhaps, had he lived, she wouldn't have turned out as such a cowardly person; she might have been someone who could stand up to the bullies at school.

Thank you for listening, God.

Her prayers finished, she closed her eyes and drifted off to sleep in the light of the moon.

Chapter 2

The trial of Sandor Hayes, the alleged traitor, was all anyone was talking about. It was in the papers and on television. Witnesses from across the Federal District—the part of the province where the capital city of Calador was located—were summoned to testify about his character.

One day before riding lessons, Aveline stood in the foyer of the carriage house with Jem watching Channel 1, which was dedicated to State news and the Daily Veneration of the Leader, a program that aired between twelve and one o'clock every afternoon, and was required viewing for all citizens of Alterra. Although the noon hour had passed, and Aveline and Jem were no longer obligated to watch Channel 1, their eyes were glued to the screen as Sandor's older sister cried on the witness stand, describing her brother as a pious boy, committed to God and country.

"Do you think the High Court will find him innocent?" asked Aveline.

"I sure hope so." Jem touched the Aspirant ribbon pinned to his shirt.

While they were riding, Aveline spoke a bit more freely. "My mother and uncle talk as if Mr. Hayes actually did publish that article. So the High Court would have to find him guilty, right?"

"If that's true, Miss Aveline, they'd have to find

him guilty. But they need to give him a chance to prove he's innocent. Everybody's supposed to get a fair trial, right?"

"But what if he can't prove it, though? What would his punishment be, do you think?"

"I don't know, but I don't think the High Court should go too hard on him."

"That's exactly what my mother said! She thinks he should get a course of reeducation in the Party ideals. What does reeducation mean, Jem?"

"Look." He stopped riding and pointed toward the sloping stone path leading to the stables on which a slender, black-clad figure was walking in their direction.

Aveline's stomach dropped. Was she in trouble? Was it possible that the Stam had planted bugs in the meadow and alerted her family to what she and Jem had been talking about? She didn't think she'd said anything seditious, and she knew there were no bugs out in the open like that. Nevertheless, her palms began to sweat, making it difficult to hold Paintbrush's reins.

Aveline and Jem rode back and met Allyn at the entrance to the carriage house. Her Monnag pin gleamed on her lapel in the late afternoon sun.

Jem dismounted his horse and placed a hand over his heart. "Madam Lightminister, please allow me to introduce myself. I'm—"

"Jem Caslon."

"H-how did you know that?"

"I make it a point to know every soul on my Estate." She smiled.

"It's an honor to meet you, Madam Lightminister."

They shook hands.

"Please, call me Allyn."

Aveline was shocked; she never allowed anyone to call her by her name, let alone a servant.

The two were a study in contrasts. He was tall and radiated a ruddy good health suggestive of the outdoors, of the woods and the heaths. She, on the other hand, was tiny and pale, a creature of the indoors, of airless rooms and fluorescent lighting. Had he wanted to, he could have easily thrown her over his shoulder.

She reached up and touched his Aspirant ribbon, causing him to flinch.

"You needn't be afraid of me, Jem. We both serve the same Leader." Then, after a pause: "Why aren't you a member of the Party?"

"That is my dream, but..."

"You can't find a Sponsor?"

He looked down. "No, I'm afraid not."

"Perhaps I can be of some assistance in that department."

He looked up, hopeful. "You...you would find me a Sponsor?"

"Oh, Jem, I can do better than that."

"I'm sorry?"

"*I* could be your Sponsor—if that is agreeable to you."

Aveline was stunned. She had not breathed a word to her mother about being Jem's Sponsor.

"Agreeable to me? It's more than agreeable, it's—" He fumbled for the words.

She raised an eyebrow. "I take that as a yes?"

"Yes, a thousand times yes. Thank you, Madam Lightminister—Allyn." He said her name as though handling a rare, breakable object.

"Well, then. Can I count on you to attend my speech tomorrow evening?"

"Oh, yes. I will be there."

Aveline did not know why she had asked, as attendance at such speeches was compulsory.

"I'll have a car sent for you." Allyn turned to her daughter. "Come, my darling. We're having dinner early tonight. Your grandfather and uncle and I have some important business to attend to."

****

The next day at school, Cynthia and Quintana were on Aveline's tail again. This time, however, they had brought Cynthia's older sister, Victoria. Fifteen-year-old Victoria stood about five-foot-seven and weighed twice what Aveline did. As Aveline tried to run, Victoria blocked her path and grabbed her, throwing her over her shoulder with a grunt.

"Let me go!"

She tried kicking Victoria, but she barely made an impact on the older girl's solid body. The three bullies laughed.

Victoria carried her down the servants' corridor to the trash bins.

"Put me down!" cried Aveline.

"All right," said Victoria, and hoisted her into a dumpster, where she crashed down on the remains of the day's lunch and all other manner of trash that stunk to the high heavens.

"Let me out! Let me out!"

"Crybaby!" said Cynthia. "Why don't you eat some trash while you're at it? I hear the slops are your favorite!"

In her misery, Aveline realized that the less fuss

she made, the more the other girls would become confused. She laid her head on a cardboard box and curled her knees into her chest and bit her lip to keep the girls from hearing her crying.

"You die in there or what?" said Victoria.

"Woohoo, the fatso's dead," sang Quintana. "Let's get out of here."

Aveline waited until she heard the girls' footsteps on the tile floor of the hallway. Holding her breath, she waited another few minutes, then released her breath, trying not to gag. Slowly, brushing herself off, she climbed out of the dumpster and sneaked out the back doors of the trash room into the courtyard.

Blinking in the harsh sunlight, she looked down and saw that her uniform was streaked with a smelly brown substance—probably the beans from lunch. A wave of nausea broke over her.

Bruno, who had been waiting for her at their usual meetup spot, put down his books and came running to her side. "What happened to you?"

Aveline started to cry.

"Those—" He swore and slammed his right fist into his left hand. "Why, I could—"

"Please, Bruno. It's all right. I don't want you getting in trouble."

Once he'd calmed down, he picked up his books. "Come on, let's go to my house. You can take a bath there."

She followed her friend off the school grounds and out the tall wrought-iron gate and onto the street, where they caught the public bus. Packed with schoolchildren and shift workers, the bus trundled over a bridge across the River Antoleme, which ran through the heart of

Calador. From the bus stop, they walked a short distance to Bruno's apartment building.

In Alterra, the Party held all the property and divided it up among the citizenry. Working-class citizens in Calador all lived in buildings identical to this one. They were cheaply made and not very nice. Some were infested with mice and cockroaches.

"Oh, they're not too bad," Bruno had said once about the roaches. "You just have to stay on top of them, with bleach and stuff, so they don't take over your house." Aveline had shuddered.

The friends rode the elevator up to the twenty-second floor. When Bruno knocked at the door of his apartment, his mother answered and ushered the children inside. Edwena Page was young and slender and wore her ginger hair cut to her chin as the Party required of married women. While they were neither Party members nor Aspirants, Bruno's parents—and Edwena in particular—were fiercely loyal to the Leader. They displayed official portraits of the Leader, Lawminister, and Lightminister in their home, as required by law, but Aveline knew that they would have displayed the portraits regardless. It was a little disconcerting, however, to look up at Bruno's wall and see her relatives staring back, as though they were keeping a close watch on her.

Through the living-room window Aveline could see the shimmering river and the skyscrapers of Calador, and beyond, the enormous gray stone wall that separated the Federal District from the rest of Illyria-Novo Templar, or Illyria for short, one of the seven provinces of Alterra. She had never been outside the Federal District, let alone Illyria. The only time she'd seen the other provinces was in news reports on Channel 1, the lush green fields and smiling farmers and factory workers. She often wondered whether these people were as curious about her province as she was about theirs, but travel between the provinces was forbidden without the Party's permission. Even Jem had had to get a special permit to travel up from his small farming village in the Province of Lystra to begin his job on the Fleur Estate.

"You poor thing," said Edwena to Aveline when she noticed her soiled clothes. She handed Aveline her bathrobe and a faded pink towel that was coarse from years of washing. "Just bring me your uniform and I'll run it down to the wash."

Aveline was grateful that Edwena didn't ask how her clothes had come to be so dirty. In the bathroom, she changed into the too-large robe and then emerged and sheepishly handed Edwena her balled-up uniform. When she finished bathing, she dried off and slipped on the robe again.

After braiding her wet hair and securing the end with her crimson loyalty ribbon, she joined Bruno in the living room, where he was sitting cross-legged on the carpet before the television set, watching a movie on Channel 2. Besides Channel 1, which was devoted to State news, there were only two other channels, both controlled by the Party. The Ministry of Civic Enlightenment operated the big movie studio in the City Center that produced all the programs on television.

The movie Bruno was watching was not a particularly happy one. Called *The Attack*, it was about a young man from the Province of Galatia who is sentenced to one year in prison for stealing a hundred ducats from his elderly aunt. On the day he gets out, he returns home and brutally murders his aunt for her chest of diamond jewelry. The purpose of the film was to drum up support for a law that imposed mandatory twenty-year sentences for theft.

Aveline had seen *The Attack* many times, and she knew Bruno had, too, so she didn't mind when he got up and turned the dial to Channel 3, which was showing the familiar lineup of after-school soap operas for young people. A commercial came on that featured a little girl with long brown pigtails, each secured with a loyalty ribbon. The girl spread margarine on a piece of white bread and closed her eyes, taking a bite and grinning as if it were the most delicious thing she'd ever tasted.

During the next commercial, Aveline's attention wandered to the wall behind the television set, to the Pages' family photos in plastic frames, and below, to the right of the TV, a bundle of gray-and-yellow wires protruding through a crack. She moved a bit closer to look at them, figuring that they somehow must have broken off the TV.

"Bruno—"

She was about to point out the wires when Edwena came out of the kitchen carrying two plates with grilled cheese sandwiches. Aveline tried to gulp hers down without tasting the synthetic Party cheese, which, thankfully (like the Party margarine) she did not have to eat back at the Estate. Her family's cheese came from real cow's milk.

"I'll be right back," said Edwena. "I'm just going to put the clothes in the dryer."

Several minutes later, there was a heavy knock at

the door. The children startled.

Bruno hopped to his feet. "Did you lock yourself out, Mom?"

When he opened the door, however, it was not Edwena but Allyn Fleur and her bodyguard, Colonel Zabel of the Stam. Zabel was dressed in his black uniform, and Allyn was in her black overcoat and stiletto heels. Her makeup was more pronounced than usual, her eyes rimmed with kohl, her lips bright red in contrast to her porcelain skin.

Aveline joined Bruno at the door. "Mother, what are you doing here?"

"Did you forget about the rally this afternoon?"

Aveline looked down at her feet. Her mother was right. After her tussle with the bullies, she'd forgotten all about it.

"Madam Lightminister." Edwena appeared, a bit out of breath, setting down her laundry basket and making the loyalty salute. "It's an honor. To what do we owe the pleasure of your visit?"

"I've come to collect my daughter." She looked at Aveline. "Why on earth are you wearing that…thing?"

Aveline gulped, looking at the yellowed bathrobe whose sleeves hung down over her hands. "I just spilled something, that's all. Mrs. Page was kind enough to wash my uniform for me."

Allyn nodded at Edwena. "Thank you for taking care of my Aveline."

"Oh, it was nothing, Madam Lightminister."

"May we come in?" Allyn spoke for herself and Zabel, a cold man who rarely said a word.

Edwena froze. "Uh…it's a bit untidy at the moment. But of course you may come in."

Allyn and Zabel stepped into the modest apartment.

"You have a lovely home." Allyn looked around, eyes drawn to the portraits of herself, Alfred, and Simon on the wall.

"Thank you, Madam Lightminister," said Edwena. "Why don't you come into the kitchen and have a seat at the table?"

"No, thank you. We'd prefer to sit here." She gestured to the sofa across from the television.

"Of course, of course! Sit wherever you like."

Allyn sat first, lifting her overcoat, and Zabel sat next to her, though at a respectful distance.

"May I take your coat, Madam Lightminister?" said Edwena.

"No, thank you, Mrs. Page. As I said, we won't be staying long."

Edwena nodded. "I'll go put the kettle on."

She returned to the living room carrying two cups of tea for her guests. Aveline could see from the teabags that they were plain black Party tea; some people liked to joke that it was half tea and half pencil shavings.

"Do you take cream or sugar, Madam Lightminister?"

"Neither, thank you." Allyn always took her tea black, as cream and sugar had too many calories. She lifted the cup to her lips and blew on it. "And how are you getting on? Have you enough to eat?"

"Yes, we have plenty, Madam Lightminister. We are grateful for everything the Party does for our family."

Allyn set the cup down on the coffee table and rose

from the sofa and walked over to the crack in the wall where the cables were sticking out. She crouched beside the wall and held the multicolored cables in her hand. "What's this?"

Edwena flushed. "Oh, Madam Lightminister, I'm sorry. Had I known you were coming, I'd have covered it up. It's unsightly, I know. My husband must have accidentally pulled out the wires when he was moving the TV."

"Quite all right." She straightened up. "Colonel, see to it that one of your men comes to fix this tomorrow morning."

Aveline wondered why her mother had directed the Stam to fix it, when it was clearly a problem for the Ministry of Energy because it had to do with the electricity. By law, the Stam was not allowed to bug private homes. But Allyn knew best, so Aveline didn't think any more of it.

She could tell that Bruno's mother was embarrassed by the hole in the wall. Red-faced, Edwena asked to be excused for a moment to the laundry room down the hall. When she returned with the dry uniform, Aveline changed quickly in the bathroom.

"Can we give you and Bruno a ride to the rally, Mrs. Page?" said Allyn.

"Oh, it's all right, we can just walk; it isn't far. I wouldn't want to trouble you."

"It's no trouble at all. I've got a car waiting downstairs."

After Edwena had picked up the still-full teacups and set them on the kitchen counter, they all got into the elevator and rode it down to the lobby. Once Edwena spotted the black limousine in front of the building, she looked as though she might faint. Aveline often forgot that the things she took for granted were unimaginably glamorous to ordinary people.

They rode in awkward silence over the bridge and to Armand Fleur Park—named for Aveline's great-grandfather—just north of the City Center in the heart of Calador. Elton, the driver, dropped off Bruno and his mother at the public entrance. He took the rest of the passengers to the private entrance about half a mile away, with a gravel road that led right up to a gigantic stage. Zabel ushered Allyn and Aveline through a door and up a narrow flight of stairs to join the other members of the Fleur family backstage.

Allyn removed her overcoat and handed it to one of her assistants. Like her father and brother and the Colonel, she wore her Party uniform. The effect of all these black uniforms was stunning. Especially her grandfather's, which bore a collection of gold medals with ribbons of various colors, for his victory over King Reuel IV and over the neighboring country of Ebria in the last war. Aveline couldn't wait until she turned sixteen and took the Sacred Oath to join the Party and be fitted for a uniform of her own. (Of course, she hoped to be much thinner by then.)

Allyn's stilettos clattered on the wooden floor as she walked over to Simon and straightened his tie. "Remember, nothing about the firing squad. We don't want to frighten the public now, do we?"

"As you wish, Madam Lightminister." He rolled his eyes. "I'll stick to the script."

Beyond the curtain, Aveline could hear the noise of the gathering crowd and the band warming up. She felt the surge of energy that always accompanied such public events.

She closed her eyes and opened them just as the curtain rose.

Chapter 3

From all four cardinal directions, the Armed Forces marched into the square at Armand Fleur Park with an energetic goosestep, lifting their legs straight out as if their bodies were made of iron. The soldiers at the front of each line held high the crimson banners emblazoned with Monnag's head and the fleur-de-lis. In the pit below the stage, the band played "My Heart Longs for the Homeland." The crowd sang along, then cheered as the Leader stepped onstage, the sole figure, illuminated by klieg lights, hand over his heart in the loyalty salute.

This was Allyn Fleur's finest work. She was the director. The auteur.

It was hard for Aveline to believe that, just a few years ago, Simon had been in this very role. Alfred had appointed him Lightminister, believing that he was the better fit because he had a creative bent and liked to play the *enfant terrible*. And that Allyn, the more intellectual of the two, and a former barrister in the Civil Division, was better suited to the role of Lawminister, overseeing the justice system and the Stam. Allyn had done her job superlatively well but had been bored and uninspired. Simon, on the other hand, had been a complete failure as Lightminister. He'd had no idea what the public needed or wanted. His rallies were dull, the soldiers marching in a single straight line, the band playing the same hackneyed tunes, the speeches lasting over an hour apiece.

But when Alfred reversed their roles, Allyn shined as Lightminister. It was her idea to use complex marching, for the soldiers to carry the banners, for the band to play popular music. She limited the number of speakers and cut their speeches to only fifteen minutes apiece. Rallies became exciting—the sort of thing people actually looked forward to, even though attendance was mandatory for all residents of Calador.

Allyn was careful not to overexpose her star, the Leader, so she had him appear only at the beginning of a rally and then for a brief speech. She and Simon and the other ministers, when necessary, did most of the speaking. But now that she, too, was a popular figure, she had started to limit her own exposure. Tonight, for instance, she planned to stay backstage until the last fifteen minutes of the rally.

When it was her time to step up to the podium, everyone cheered before she even began speaking. The applause lasted for what felt like several minutes, wave after wave of it.

She lifted her hands, and everyone in the park fell silent. Then she began speaking, her voice in sharp contrast to her physical frailty. Rich and resonant, it could have been heard even without a microphone. People often wondered how such a big voice could come from so small a woman.

"I'm not going to speak to you of loyalty and patriotism, of love and obedience. I'm going to speak to you of sedition. Of treason."

Aveline gasped along with the crowd.

"What is the purpose of sedition? Why do people commit treason?"

Allyn stepped from behind the podium, something politicians rarely did; they didn't like to expose themselves so completely in case anyone in the crowd had a weapon. But Allyn was not afraid.

"Consider Mr. Hayes. Imagine that you are young, twenty-three years old, frustrated with your government's policies. You don't feel that your voice is being heard. What would you do? Might you put your thoughts to paper, write an article? Hmm? Might you publish that article in an underground newspaper, hoping to vent your feelings to like-minded citizens? Certainly you might. *I* might."

Again, the crowd gasped and began murmuring. Our *Lightminister might do such a thing?* She held up her hands to quiet them.

"Mr. Hayes took the risk and published his thoughts. And why? Ask yourself that question. Why? Out of malice? A desire to harm the Party? No, I submit to you, it is the exact opposite. What he wants is to be heard. He wants change. He wants to feel that his ideas are valued. And you know what? We are listening. We want to hear from you, about what we are doing well and about what we could do better. Because, at the end of the day, we are *your* servants. My brother and I, and of course our father, your Leader."

She concluded her speech with the customary slogan, *Long Live Alterra!* The crowd answered back, *Long Live the Fleurs!* and then erupted in cheers and applause. Aveline knew that they wanted Allyn to say more, to linger another few moments, giving them light and hope.

But the curtain closed, and Allyn turned to her family and several ministers who had gathered backstage.

"Bravo, Madam Lightminister." Simon's voice dripped with sarcasm. "You've made sedition fashionable."

She shushed him with a flick of her hand.

Usually after a rally, Alfred held a cabinet meeting, but tonight he was feeling tired and decided to return early to the Estate. Simon, Lilia, and their children went with him, while Allyn remained absorbed in conversation with the Minister of Culture.

Beside her, Colonel Zabel was speaking into a walkie-talkie, and then he disappeared down the back stairs, returning a couple of minutes later with Jem. Aveline gasped. How handsome he looked! Allyn, perhaps afraid he'd show up in his stable garb, must have sent a tailor to fit him for the black three-piece suit he was wearing. And he was carrying a bouquet of crimson roses tied with a large loyalty ribbon.

"Hi, Jem!" said Aveline. "Those are beautiful. Are they for my mother?"

"Yes, Miss Aveline."

"Your Aspirant, Madam Lightminister." Zabel pushed Jem forward, as though releasing him into Allyn's custody.

Jem pushed a lock of hair behind his ears and smiled timidly, showing his dimples. He seemed to have no idea how good-looking he was.

"I—these are for you, Madam Lightminister," he said, handing her the bouquet. "Your speech—it was wonderful."

"Why, thank you. They're lovely." She inhaled from the bouquet. "Are you courting me, Jeremiah Caslon?"

The Minister of Culture stifled a laugh.

Jem's eyes went wide. "Oh, no, no, Madam Lightminister. I only got them for you to say thank you for being my Sponsor."

"Such a gesture is highly inappropriate, you know."

"I-I'm so sorry—"

"But not entirely unwelcome." She smiled, her eyes meeting his over the tops of the flowers.

"Oh." He exhaled, then laughed softly.

"Come. We're headed back to the Estate. Let us give you a ride home."

After bidding the Minister goodnight, Allyn gestured for Jem to come with her. Aveline and Zabel followed close behind. Immediately upon exiting the back doors of the stage, they were assaulted by the flash of cameras. Jem put up his hand, shielding his eyes.

"You'll learn." Allyn snapped on her little round sunglasses and smiled and waved to the cameras. The paparazzi were all employees of the Lightministry, and tomorrow she would decide which of the photographs were to be printed in the newspaper and shown on television.

The four climbed into the backseat of the waiting limousine. Jem seemed to be trying to keep a respectful distance from Allyn but kept looking in her direction. Beyond pleasantries, conversation was not really possible because Zabel, a Stam officer, was in the car.

As they crossed the bridge over the River Antoleme, the car hit a slight bump and Jem gripped the handhold above the window so he would not accidentally brush against her. Aveline could feel the electricity pass between them, even though they weren't touching.

"May we have a moment?" said Allyn to Zabel when the car had pulled up to the entrance of the Great House.

"As you wish, Madam Lightminister."

After the Colonel stepped out of the car, Jem began gushing about Allyn's speech, particularly the part where she had solicited feedback from the citizens of Alterra.

"Have you any suggestions for me?" said Allyn.

He nodded eagerly. "Please don't go too hard on Mr. Hayes."

"You know where I stand on that, Jem. If he is guilty of treason, he ought to be reformed, not punished. But ultimately that is not in my hands. It's in the hands of the High Court. We have to trust them to make the right decision."

"Is there anything I can do? I want to do something, but I just feel so…helpless."

"You can pray. Pray for Mr. Hayes, pray for the Justices of the High Court. Pray that God guides them in the right direction."

"Oh, I will. I pray all the time. I pray for you, too."

"And I hear your prayers." She put her hand to her heart. "I hear every single one. And they help me immensely. I don't know how I would do my job if not for everyone's prayers."

Elton came around and opened the door for his passengers. The driver extended a hand to Allyn, and then to Aveline.

"Doin' better, Miss Aveline?" said Elton. "Those troublemakers, are they keepin' away from you now?"

"Oh, yes," she fibbed. She didn't dare tell him that

the bullies had thrown her into a dumpster just that afternoon. Not only because she didn't want him to worry about her, but also because her mother and Jem were only a couple of feet away.

Aveline joined them on the grand driveway with its hand-laid stones. The autumn moon was in its waxing phase, shining bright and silvery-blue at the top of the sky.

"When can I see you again, Madam Lightminister?" asked Jem.

"Allyn. You are always welcome to call me by my name in private. Come to the House tomorrow night for supper. I'd like you to meet my father and brother."

"You mean the Leader and the Lawminister?"

She laughed. "Yes, of course. Perhaps it's different in your province, but here in Illyria, when a man is courting a woman, he ordinarily meets her family."

Jem looked at her; Aveline could guess what he was thinking. *But yours is no ordinary family. And I'm not just courting any woman; I'm courting the Lightminister herself.*

Allyn seemed to respond to that unspoken thought. "There is nothing special you need to do. Just be yourself. Come here tomorrow evening at six. We'll be expecting you."

"And I will look forward to it," he said.

Chapter 4

"I hear that my daughter has offered to act as your Sponsor." Alfred Fleur swirled the red wine in his glass, creating a small vortex.

Jem had joined the family for dinner, wearing the same black three-piece suit as last night, the only one he owned. Aveline could tell how nervous he was, sweat beading his hairline. She watched as he politely cut his meat into little cubes, though instead of switching the fork to his right hand, he just ate with his left, somewhat awkwardly, never having learned the delicate fork-and-knife method of the upper class.

Jem swallowed a bite of steak. "Yes, my Leader. I am very grateful for her sponsorship."

"So, Caslon," said Alfred, addressing him like a servant, "how do you suppose you'll find the time for Party activities while training horses all day?" He leaned back, one arm slung over the back of his chair.

Aveline knew that newly minted Party members were expected to join various social committees organized by the Ministries of Culture and Civic Enlightenment, to help the Party spread its message. She often saw men of Jem's age and younger up on cranes, hanging huge banners from the sides of buildings in the City Center. *Peace, Prosperity, Power. Order and Obedience. Silence, Intensity, Determination.* Slogans that had been drilled into people's heads since childhood.

"I will find the time, my Leader," said Jem. "It has been my lifelong dream to join the Party, but I promise not to shirk my duties on your Estate."

Nervously, he fingered the Aspirant ribbon on his lapel. He looked over to Allyn for encouragement. She smiled back at him.

"And what are your intentions for my daughter?" said Alfred.

Jem coughed, obviously startled by the question. "Well, I…I am wondering if I may…and I know this may be far beyond what I'm…"

"Don't mumble, Caslon. Out with it."

"Well, I am wondering, my Leader," said Jem, "if I may have your permission to court her."

Aveline's little cousins, Lily and S.J., started giggling. Simon shot them a look, and they stopped immediately, looking down at their plates. But Aveline could tell by the way his shoulders were shaking that her uncle was suppressing a laugh as well.

To everyone's surprise, Alfred also laughed. "Come now. Allyn is a grown woman and doesn't need my permission. But I do appreciate your asking."

"This conversation is ridiculous." Allyn scoffed and downed the rest of her wine. A footman instantly appeared to refill it.

"Yes, it is, because Allyn doesn't date," said Simon. "She's married to the Lightministry. Sorry to break it to you, Caslon."

Allyn smirked. "If only we could say the same about you and the Lawministry."

"Touché, sister." He chuckled and raised his glass.

Alfred downed the last of his wine and sucked the

excess meat from his front teeth. Aveline noticed that lately he had been looking older, putting on weight around the middle, slowing down. When he rose from the table, everyone else did the same out of respect. It was now time for brandy and political talk in Alfred's study.

"Are you coming, Monnag?" he said. "Caslon, you are welcome, too."

"Not tonight, Father. I am going to give Mr. Caslon a tour of the House."

Once Alfred and Simon had retreated to the study, and Lilia had taken the children upstairs, Allyn asked Jem what he thought of meeting the family.

"I'm worried that your father doesn't like me," he said, eyes downcast. "I'm not sure what I said or what I did—"

"Oh, don't worry, Jem. He's like that with everyone." Allyn placed a hand on his arm. "Especially with men who come to court me. He may seem harsh, but he's only trying to look out for my best interests. To protect me."

"I can't imagine why any man would ever want to hurt you."

"Not hurt me. *Use* me. You see, Jem, after Kit died in the war, I had many suitors. Men from some of the best families in Alterra. Men who hold important positions in the Party. Even the Underminister of Transportation and Public Works, if you can believe it."

Aveline made a face. The Underminister was an obese middle-aged man who sweated profusely and ate with his fingers.

Allyn continued, "They didn't want to be with me because they loved me or even particularly liked me. It wasn't about me at all. What they wanted was to gain something from me. Money, prestige, a better title. Perhaps to bend the ear of my father. So, Jem, maybe now you can understand my father's concerns a little better."

"I do. But I hope you can see—and I hope your father can, too—that I'm not like those other men. I only want to get to know you, Madam Ligh—I mean, Allyn. I hope it's not too inappropriate to say this, but I like you. I like you very much."

"I know that, Jem. I know your intentions are pure. I wouldn't have invited you here if I didn't." She looped her arm through his. "Come, let me give you the grand tour."

Aveline followed the pair through the den and the trophy room and the Great Room and the library, watching Jem's eyes grow wider and wider. She knew he must have been comparing these rooms with the ones he knew back in Ede's River, the farming village in Lystra where he was from. Tiny rooms with shabby furniture and too many people and poor ventilation.

"This is like being in a dream," he said. "I can't believe that only this afternoon I was in the stables feeding carrots to the horses, and tonight I'm here at the Leader's house."

Allyn pinched his upper arm.

Reflexively, he jumped back. "What was that for?"

"To prove that you're not dreaming."

"I still don't believe it."

"Shall I pinch you again?"

He grinned. "I wouldn't mind that."

She led him upstairs, where guests were normally forbidden, and showed him each wing of the house—

hers and Aveline's, Simon and Lilia's, even Alfred's. He was especially impressed by Allyn's room with its canopy bed and French doors that opened onto a porch overlooking the 5,000 acres of the Fleur Estate.

"If I lived here," he said, "I don't know how I could be unhappy even a single day of my life."

"Well, you know, if our courtship works out…"

"Oh! I wouldn't expect to live here."

"Excuse me, Mr. Caslon, I will *not* be living in the stables with you." She poked her finger against his chest.

"I happen to think the stables are rather nice, Miss Fleur. I'm a bit insulted that you don't."

Aveline giggled, enjoying their playful banter. "I'll live in the stables with you! On a pile of hay!"

"She would," said Allyn. "She'll sleep anywhere. Just put her up with the horses and you'll save money on a bed."

"Mother!"

"I'm only teasing."

Allyn led them back downstairs to the Great Room, where they played a game of cribbage and drank the hot cocoa that a housemaid brought them on a silver tray. Across the board, her mother's and Jem's hands accidentally brushed, hers translucently pale and smooth, his brown from the sun and rough from his work with the horses. Aveline felt the electricity pass between them as she had last night in the car. For a moment, the polished onyx in her mother's sigil ring glowed green.

As if magnetically drawn to the ring, he touched it, something she never allowed anyone to do. But she didn't stop him.

"I didn't realize your middle name was Monnag." His finger pressing on the onyx turned it almost neon. "I thought you were sometimes called that because it's the symbol of our country."

"It's not my middle name. It's my sigil name. You see, each member of my family has a sigil name that corresponds to a member of the clan of dragons from which we were descended. Well, mythologically speaking. Aveline's sigil name is Cyndess, which means 'Daughter of the West Wind,' and my brother's is Yrgess, 'Son of the Air.' "

"I wish I had a sigil name," he said.

"How about Mondren?"

"Is that a real dragon name?"

"No, I just made it up. The suffix 'dren' means 'companion' in Old Alterran. So, 'Mondren' literally means 'Companion of Monnag.' "

"I love it."

"Wonderful. We'll enter it in the Register of Names." She winked at him, then turned to Aveline and gently lifted the mug from her hands. "I think you've had enough cocoa, my darling. Why don't you go on upstairs and get ready for bed, hmm?"

Ordinarily, Aveline would have been hurt by her mother brushing her off, but tonight she knew that Allyn wanted to be alone with Jem. She hugged Jem and said goodnight to them both and went up to her room. Instead of ringing for Jossie, she took off her clothes and hung them neatly in her armoire, then slipped into the lavender-scented sheets, feeling warm and happy and complete, knowing that just downstairs her mother was falling in love.

Chapter 5

"He's picked an awfully inconvenient time for a courtship," Allyn said to Jossie one afternoon as the maid brought her a cup of tea in her study. Allyn's legs were double-crossed at the knee and ankle, in that peculiar way that only the thinnest of women could manage.

The trial of Sandor Hayes was gaining momentum, the State's prosecutor and Sandor's court-appointed barrister both making impassioned arguments. All across the country, people were glued to their television sets.

Although the trial seemed to be going in the State's favor, Simon often complained that the Stam had not yet made any other arrests in connection with Sandor's article.

"Have you tried talking to Sandor?" asked Allyn.

He looked at her as if she were stupid. "Of course we've tried that. We've also tried more, shall we say…coercive methods."

"And how's that working out for you?"

Simon gritted his teeth. "You've never interrogated anybody. You couldn't possibly know how hard it is."

"You're right, I haven't. But common sense tells me that tying somebody to a chair or hanging them upside-down is not going to get them to sell out their associates."

"So, what would you recommend? Offering him a cup of tea and a petit four?" He mimicked a high-pitched tone. " 'Gee, Sandor, would you mind telling me who helped you publish your article?' "

"You're the Lawminister. I'm not going to tell you how to do your job," she said. "But I will tell you this: when you can't go through, go around."

Aveline wasn't exactly sure what her mother meant, but she agreed that torturing Sandor was absolutely the wrong thing to do. Sitting on the window seat in her mother's study, doing her homework, she watched as Jossie handed Allyn the steaming cup of tea.

"It's always the right time to fall in love, Madam Lightminister. That's just what I think."

"That is very wise, Jossie."

After the maid left, Allyn picked up her pen and resumed writing. Aveline was intensely curious about whether her mother was writing to Jem or just doing ministerial paperwork, but she didn't dare ask.

When Allyn left her desk to dress for supper, Aveline peered into the wastebasket and picked up a crumpled note on the heavy, cream-colored bond paper that she used for personal correspondence. There was no salutation or closing. It read, in Allyn's flawless, right-leaning cursive:

You are weak where I am strong, and you are strong where I am weak. One touch, your fingertips against my wrist, is enough to consume me, to make me break. Sometimes I feel you are the only one who understands me, who speaks my language. Words, events, colors, fall through me. All day I walk in the suburbs of civic attention, existing only in the moments when I think of you. You are my shape and color. You are my eyes and voice. I give you this power over me, I give it freely...

Aveline blushed as she read it. She could feel her mother's passion emanating from these words, from her body itself, like waves of heat. Why hadn't she chosen to send it to Jem? He would have loved it.

She crushed the letter in her hand and tossed it back into the wastebasket so Allyn wouldn't know she'd read it. Then she scurried upstairs to her room.

Once she'd changed into a suitable dark-colored dress for family dinner, she walked down the hall to her mother's room but found it empty; Allyn must have already been downstairs talking with Alfred. It was rare for Aveline to be left alone among her mother's private things, so she took advantage of it. She crept into the walk-in closet, touching the expensive silk and cashmere, row upon row of dresses and skirts and blouses so small that no other grown woman in Alterra could wear them. She spritzed Allyn's gardenia perfume onto her wrists and held up a black silk dress before her in the mirror and twirled, imagining what it was like to be grown-up and in love.

****

"Time to wake up, my darling," whispered Allyn. "We have an exciting day ahead of us."

Aveline opened her eyes. It was the day they were to meet Jem at the stables to take a ride around the Estate.

She scrambled out of bed and dashed to the window where the day was dawning gold and crisp, still a bit warm for so late in autumn. She often thought of this window as a keeper of celestial bodies, trapping the sun and moon and stars that spun across the skies of

Alterra and displaying them especially for her the way actors made appearances onstage in a private theater.

Resting her palms on the sill, she blinked in the strong morning light and looked down at the pool, where an elderly servant was skimming particolored leaves from the surface. He looked up and waved, and she waved back.

As Aveline looked past the pool to the gardens and the meadows and the softly rolling hills and the green tops of trees in the forest beyond, she smiled to herself, knowing that someday all this land would belong to her mother, and then to her. She still had trouble believing that one day she would be Leader. But she supposed that when it was her turn she would be ready and know what to do.

It was times like these that she wished she had a father to guide her. She often wondered about Christopher Llewellyn Fleur. Because Allyn didn't like to talk about him, she knew very little, only that he had come from an upper-class family. That his father had served beside Alfred in the Revolution to overthrow the king and destroy the feudal system, bringing the country under centralized control. And that he had been a decorated member of the Air Command who'd died in a plane crash in the Ebrian War. A man like Kit was the perfect match for Allyn: a wealthy, cultured, accomplished airman. A loyal Party member, proudly displaying the Monnag pin on his gray uniform.

But Jem was none of these things. He was a simple horse trainer from a southern province with barely a ducat to his name. Although Alfred had said that Allyn was an adult and didn't need his approval for her courtship, Aveline knew that, deep down, her grandfather disapproved of the match. In his mind, Jem had little, if anything, to offer his daughter. But Aveline was hopeful. She saw the way Jem and Allyn looked at one another, the spark that passed between them whenever their hands brushed. They were in love. Wasn't love supposed to conquer all? She had seen enough films produced by the Lightministry to understand love's transformative power.

Realizing she had dawdled too long, and that soon Jossie would come to summon her downstairs, she rushed to her closet and changed into a fresh set of riding clothes.

After breakfast, she and Allyn walked down the stone path to the stables where Jem greeted them. The sun illuminated the gold streaks in his hair.

He greeted them warmly, and Allyn gave him a kiss on either cheek.

"Ready to ride?" he said.

"You'll have to be patient with me," said Allyn. "I haven't ridden in years."

"But I thought you were a dressage champion."

" 'Champion' is a bit of an overstatement. I earned a couple of blue ribbons in my day."

"You are very modest, Allyn."

She grinned. "Modesty is not something of which I'm often accused."

He helped her up onto Pacer, her black Oldenberg, and off they went in the direction of Wildweir, the glade where the Fleurs had played as children. Wildweir held Aveline's most cherished memories. Playing in the wooden playhouse with her dolls. Pretending to hide from the big, bad wolf. Swinging across a small creek on a rope tied to a tree and letting go and plunging into the crystal-clear, ice-cold water. The taste of that water—purer than any in Alterra, almost sweet, able to quench thirst with a single sip— would never leave her as long as she lived.

"When I was pregnant with you," Allyn had once told her, "I would wander through Wildweir in the afternoons, my hand on my belly, telling you the names of the trees, of the flowers, their beautiful names in Old Alterran. *Parsithius maricorum, delictatrus philistarborn*. I couldn't wait to show you the world."

The three riders stopped in the middle of Wildweir so that Allyn could show Jem the cottage where the groundskeeper lived with his family. The House with Too Many Lamps, Aveline and her mother called it, because every room had at least four or five lamps— floor lamps and green accountant's lamps and stained-glass lamps with bases that resembled tree trunks and dainty bedside lamps with pink lace shades and a fringe of beads. She and her mother could wander for hours in Wildweir, just making up stories—mostly Allyn making up stories and Aveline listening, then peppering her with outlandish questions.

In a sudden gust of wind, Aveline's hair slipped from its braid and flew into her face. She looked down and realized that her loyalty ribbon had fallen to the ground. Quickly, Jem hopped off his horse and picked it up and handed it back to her. Aveline smiled, blushing.

Allyn took the lead and guided them out of Wildweir and through a stand of oak trees until they reached Aveline's grandmother Marie's hamlet. The hamlet consisted of a cottage, an orchard thick with apple and lemon and quince trees, a hedge maze with forty-two possible solutions and one null set, and small pond ringed by weeping willows whose hair hung down into still water broken only by a solitary mallard. Allyn never showed the hamlet to anyone. This was a very good sign.

On the other side of the hamlet was a meadow. Allyn brought her horse to a stop and put her hand to her forehead.

"What's wrong?" Jem hopped down off his saddle.

"I'm feeling a little lightheaded. I apologize."

He reached up and helped her off Pacer, his long fingers nearly meeting around her waist. Sometimes Aveline wondered how all her internal organs could fit in so small a space.

As soon as her feet touched the ground, she swayed, and he caught her just before she fell. She laughed. "I don't know what's wrong with me."

"You're hungry, Allyn. It's all right," he said. Still holding her around the waist, he began to unzip his horse's saddlebags. "I've brought lunch."

"Oh, Jem, that wasn't necessary."

He reached into the saddlebag and took out a plastic-capped crystal bowl with a salad, and a tall glass bottle of water, and handed them both to Allyn.

She shook her head in disbelief. "What have I done to deserve such kindness?"

"Well, you take such good care of our country. Now you should have someone to take care of you."

Allyn looked as though she might cry, but she turned her head. When she gazed back at him, her eyes were dry. He took a blanket from the saddlebag and spread it across the grass and extended his hand, inviting her and Aveline to sit down. Then he removed several other bowls of food and utensils from the saddlebag and set them on the blanket. Together, they began to eat. When they had finished their meal, they leaned back on their elbows with a collective sigh of satisfaction and looked up at the clouds.

"When I was a girl," said Allyn, "I used to think I could see God's face in the clouds."

"I used to think I could see dragons," said Jem.

"Did you see Monnag?" asked Aveline. "Or Cyndess?"

"Yes, I think I did."

Allyn moved her body closer to Jem's and laid her head on his shoulder, and he put his arm around her as they both looked up at the clouds.

"Look at that one," said Jem, pointing up. But Allyn didn't respond; her eyes were closed. "Allyn?"

Both Jem and Aveline smiled at each other, realizing she was asleep. He placed a gentle kiss on her forehead, and she stirred, her arm across his chest. Aveline didn't dare speak a word, for she was so happy that her mother was finally sleeping that she didn't want to disturb her.

When Allyn awakened fifteen or so minutes later, she lifted her head, disoriented.

"It's okay, Allyn. You were only having a little nap."

She smiled at Jem as though having just emerged from a pleasant dream. "I never nap." She yawned.

"Don't worry. I won't tell anyone."

He smoothed her hair and pulled her to him again and she promptly fell back to sleep. Aveline slept, too, curled up next to her. It was a deep, dreamless sleep, broken only by the distant sounds of horse hooves and shotguns, probably Alfred and Simon out on their usual Saturday afternoon fox hunt.

When they awakened, the sun was no longer directly overhead. Aveline knew it was past noon. It had grown colder, and she shivered. She looked over at her mother, whose cheeks had a bit of color in them now, from the good food and sleep.

Jem extended his hand, and Allyn took it, rising to her feet. As she stood, the sigil ring on her other hand slipped right off her finger and into the grass. He bent down to pick it up and held it in his hand, the onyx glowing green.

Please, Mother, give him your ring, Aveline thought.

It was a tradition in the Fleur family to give one's sigil ring to your beloved, the person you planned to spend the rest of your life with. Alfred had given his ring to his wife Marie, who had worn it around her neck as was customary. When she died, he unclasped it from her neck and wore it again on the fourth finger of his left hand. Allyn did the same after Kit died. And Lilia wore Simon's ring around her neck on a delicate gold chain, her most prized possession. When Aveline turned sixteen, she would receive her very own sigil ring to give to her future husband one day.

Please, Mother, Aveline begged silently.

But Allyn held out her palm, and he gently placed the ring in it, seeming to understand that she'd chosen not to give it to him.

"Thank you," she said, slipping the ring back onto her finger.

****

After her last class, Aveline entered the school

chapel. She was alone. She looked around the small, octagonal room at the faded royal blue kneelers, the wooden floor heavily scuffed by two generations of schoolchildren. Walking to the front of the chapel, she stood before a white marble statue of Marie Fleur, Mother of Alterra, her hands clasped in prayer, eyes downcast. How beautiful she had been as a young woman, like Allyn.

Aveline turned and dipped into the first pew. Letting down the kneeler gently so it wouldn't squeak, she knelt on the soft velvet covering and threaded her onyx prayer beads through her hands. Closing her eyes, she tried to hear God's voice, although it always wound up sounding exactly like her own, just a wiser version of herself.

It was said that God favored the Fleurs. She hoped he would favor her now as she prayed for her mother and Jem to marry.

That evening, after dinner, she sat in the Great Room with her aunt Lilia listening to her little cousins practicing the piano with their instructor. Lily was playing very badly, but Lilia clapped enthusiastically at the end of each song and said, "Good job! Good job!"

As the children took turns at the piano, a young housemaid brought their tea on a silver tray: black tea made from the rind of bergamot orange, the Fleurs' favorite. Even though she had drunk it throughout her childhood, Aveline had never been especially fond of bergamot. She thought it was too strong, too perfumy, even with milk in it.

Kicking off her shoes and drawing her legs up beneath her on the sofa, she confided in Lilia about how Allyn's sigil ring had fallen off her finger in the meadow last Saturday and how she had decided not to give it to Jem. How Aveline had prayed in the school chapel that her mother would ask Jem to be her husband. She even told Lilia about Jem's love letter that she had seen in her mother's study:

I know I am poor and there is nothing I can offer you beyond what you already have. But I can offer you my love, which will never grow old and die the way my body will. Please write me soon and tell me when and where I can meet you. I can't bear any more of this being apart from you.

Lilia set her teacup in her saucer and placed them gently on an end table. She shook her head. "Goodness, Aveline, they've known each other only a few weeks. Their courtship has just begun."

"How long did it take Uncle Simon to give you his ring?"

"Almost a year." She lifted it from her chest, zipping it along the gold chain and pressing it to her lips. "He hemmed and hawed for ages, walking through the garden at night, talking to Alfred and Marie, talking to the family priest, even going to an astrologer."

"What's an astrologer?"

"A person who tells fortunes by looking at the positions of the stars. It's heretical, of course, but Simon simply *had* to have his fortune told before proposing, to make sure he wasn't making a mistake."

Aveline was intrigued by this heretical person who could predict futures by the stars. Nowadays, even priests weren't allowed to look into someone's future. Only God himself could do that. "What did the astrologer say?"

"He told him that we were meant to be together.

Naturally. I told Simon he could've saved a lot of money just by listening to me." Lilia smiled and patted Aveline's hand. "Don't be in such a rush, all right? Choosing a husband is a big decision for your mother. You have to trust that she will make it in good time."

****

"All students, report to the auditorium at once!" the headmistress, Mother Josephine, announced over the loudspeaker.

It was a little before eight o'clock, and Aveline had been gathering her books from her locker, thinking of what her aunt Lilia had told her the night before about the astrologer. Wondering how she might find one and ask him what was to become of Allyn and Jem's courtship.

But when she heard Mother Josephine's announcement, she slammed her locker shut and joined the crush of students headed for the auditorium. What on earth was so important that required an assembly at this hour of the morning? The last time they'd had one this early it had been to make an example of Hippolyta Klay, a scholarship student like Bruno, who'd written formulas on her hand to pass a mathematics test. Brutal old Mother Creagach, the former headmistress, had made the girl stand before a chalkboard and write *I am a cheater* over and over, filling the board and then erasing and starting anew until poor Hippolyta collapsed from exhaustion.

Now all six hundred students of Belfort Academy, ages five to seventeen, gathered in the old auditorium that resembled an opera hall, with vaulted ceilings and a crimson velvet curtain across the stage. They murmured among themselves, wondering why they had been summoned there.

The curtain rose onstage and Mother Josephine appeared at the podium in her severe black habit, shushing the students and directing them to take their seats. Behind her, a huge television set descended from the ceiling. Aveline gasped as the seven justices of the High Court of Alterra appeared onscreen in their black robes, seated at a dais.

The camera panned to Sandor Hayes, sitting beside his court-appointed barrister, wearing a navy-blue suit, as blue was the prisoners' color. He looked exhausted yet absolutely terrified. As the lens angled in on his face, Chief Justice Bertram Magnus announced, "Ladies and gentlemen, we have reached a verdict."

Chapter 6

Aveline watched incredulously as two black-clad marshals gripped each of Sandor's arms and hauled him before the dais. His whole body trembled. Chief Justice Magnus, a portly man whose goatee was as white as his powdered wig, stared down at the accused and began to speak. His deep, resonant voice echoed from the courtroom's vaulted ceilings.

"We the Justices of the High Court, having heard all the evidence in *State of Alterra versus Sandor Percival Hayes*, and having heard all testimony given for and against him, find the defendant guilty of the crime of high treason against our Supreme Leader, Alfred Monnag Fleur, and against the National Democratic Party."

Aveline gasped along with all the students in the auditorium.

Magnus continued, "We hereby sentence you to six months of reeducation at the Rjellsfall Institute for Mental Hygiene in the Province of Frelimar."

Aveline's fear melted into relief. Praise God! Praise the High Court! This was the lightest sentence anyone could have hoped for.

But Sandor began to panic. His legs collapsed beneath him, and the marshals lifted him back into a standing position and gripped his arms even tighter to keep him on his feet.

"No!" he cried. "Please, Your Honors, anything but that! Sentence me to death instead! Please, I beg you!"

The Justices looked at each other quizzically, as did Aveline and her fellow students. One of the Associate Justices actually suppressed a laugh. Magnus looked down at Sandor, smiling in a condescending, paternal way.

"Young man, did you not hear what we said? We have given you a second chance. Upon your release from Rjellsfall, you will affirm the Sacred Oath and return to Calador. Why, I've even spoken to the Minister of Culture, and he is willing to let you resume your position as a clerk in the Research Department. It doesn't get much better than that, son."

"I heard you, Your Honor. But what you have offered me is not a second chance. What you have done is condemn me to hell!"

Again, the children of Belfort Academy gasped. Because this was live television, the Lightministry had had no time to censor the swear word.

"The boy is mad." Magnus shook his head. "Marshals, escort him back to the prison."

The marshals gave the loyalty salute to the Chief Justice and slapped a pair of handcuffs on Sandor. They proceeded to drag him out of the courtroom and through a set of oaken doors as he screamed at the Justices, "Please, just give me the firing squad! Please!"

With that, Mother Josephine ascended the stage and switched off the television. The assembly over, the students returned to class, but Aveline could scarcely concentrate. All she could think of was poor Sandor Hayes, white as a sheet and yelling like a madman, unable to comprehend that the High Court had spared his life.

****

"Six months of reeducation! If it weren't so pathetic, I'd have to laugh," said Simon that night at family dinner. He speared a piece of steak with his fork and shoved it into his mouth. "I hope you're proud of yourself, Monnag." He eyed his sister across the table.

Allyn hadn't touched a single piece of food on her plate. Her cheeks were flushed from the two flutes of celebratory champagne she'd had. "I had nothing whatever to do with the High Court's decision. But I can't say that I'm not elated at the news."

Simon rolled his eyes. "Isn't it ironic that, out of everyone in that courtroom, only the boy knew what was best for him? That he begged to be sentenced to death?"

"That's not what troubles me," said Alfred. "Rather, I'm confused as to why the Lightministry chose not to cut away when the boy started raving like a lunatic." He looked straight at Allyn.

She fidgeted ever so slightly in her chair. "I beg your pardon, Father?"

"I thought it was a particularly…curious choice. To keep the camera focused on him. Not to cut to commercial. Or, rather, the decision to air the verdict on live television instead of to run an edited version a little later."

"I'm afraid I don't follow. This was breaking news."

"My concern," said Alfred, slowly and deliberately, "is that now the public is left to assume that reeducation is something terrible—something worse than death—by the way Hayes reacted to the sentence."

The high color drained from her cheeks. "Certainly they would understand that Hayes was terrified at the prospect of even six months at the Institute. He is a child of Calador, from a prestigious house. A promising civil servant. He has never been in trouble in his entire life. It was only natural that he would react that way, even though he has absolutely nothing to fear."

"Monnag, surely you can appreciate the way this must have looked to the average uneducated citizen of Alterra."

She bowed her head. "Yes, Father."

Simon folded his arms and leaned back in his chair, looking from one to the other, smirking.

After a long silence, Alfred said, "It had to be Leboeuf." Franz Leboeuf was the Underlightminister who headed up the Broadcasting Department.

Allyn looked up. "I'm sorry?"

"The one who made the decision to keep the camera on Hayes."

"Yes, of course it was," she said.

Simon's smug expression transformed into a frown. "Oh, come on. *She's* the one in charge. She's the Lightminister, for God's sake."

Alfred released a long sigh. "No matter. All I ask is that it doesn't happen again."

"Understood, Father," said Allyn.

****

After dinner, Aveline followed her mother down the hall to her study. There, she picked up Allyn's golden Monnag pin and held it in her hand, turning it so that it gleamed in the light of the desk lamp. She had never seen her grandfather chastise her mother before, and it upset her. She wanted to comfort her but didn't know how. Instead, she asked, "Mother? What is Sandor Hayes so afraid of?"

Allyn set her full flute of champagne on a side table and took her daughter's shoulders in her hands. "We are all afraid of the unknown." Her voice was calm, chastened.

"Even you?"

She smiled gently. "Even me."

"They're not going to hurt him up at Rjellsfall, are they?"

"Of course not. They're going to teach him. He's gone astray, but not so far that a little reeducation can't bring him back to center. Up at the Institute he'll be well-fed and well-cared-for. He'll even have a furnished room all to himself." Allyn tucked a strand of blonde hair behind Aveline's ear. "Don't you worry, my darling. Sandor will be back in no time, and better than ever."

****

No one was more delighted by the news of Sandor's sentence than Edwena Page. The next afternoon, Bruno invited Aveline over to their apartment to celebrate. Edwena had made a shrine on a small table below the Fleur family's portraits, replete with candles and musky incense that made Aveline feel as if she were in the school chapel for morning services. Edwena had the television tuned to Channel 1, which was broadcasting clips from the trial and the reading of the verdict—with Sandor's pleas for the death sentence edited out, of course.

"If only I had a portrait of Chief Justice Magnus, I would hang it here, too," she said, sighing. She also praised Allyn. "I know the Lightminister can't tell the High Court how to decide, but they all listen to her because she's merciful and always speaks the truth. Reeducation is exactly what Mr. Hayes needs."

While Edwena was putting the kettle on, Aveline glanced out the window. "Bruno! Look! It's snowing."

Her friend rushed up behind her and began jumping up and down like a five-year-old. "Mom, can we go downstairs and see the snow?"

Edwena padded out of the kitchen and looked over the children's shoulders at the white flurries descending on the River Antoleme and the City Center. "It's awfully cold out, hon. Why don't you two just drink some hot tea and sit by the window?"

"Aww, come on, Ma! Pretty please?"

After some light begging on their part, Edwena relented, on the condition that they wear their coats and hats and gloves. Throwing on their winter clothing as quickly as they could, Aveline and Bruno dashed out of the apartment and down the stairs to the eleventh-floor terrace.

As they pushed open the glass doors, the frigid air struck them in the face. Aveline wished she'd worn a scarf. Looking around the terrace, furnished with only a few rusted lounge chairs, Aveline spotted three younger children from their school whom she didn't know very well. They were standing by the railing, looking out over the city, joking and laughing with one another. But they stopped when they saw her and greeted her respectfully as "Miss Aveline." She blushed and glanced down at her feet.

It wasn't long, however, before the formalities melted away and the children all danced around and stuck out their tongues, hoping for a taste of the first snowflakes of the year.

Chapter 7

That winter, Bruno spent a lot of time at the Fleur Estate with Aveline. Jem took them sledding on the foothills and ice-skating on the frozen pond near Marie's hamlet. He gleefully threw snowballs with them and helped them make a snowman from the fresh powder that fell on the meadow. Aveline stuck a black Stetson hat on the snowman's head and tied a crimson scarf around his neck and gave him a thin, smirking mouth with three small pieces of coal.

"Look, it's Uncle Simon!" she joked.

Jem cringed and swiveled around as if at any moment the Stam would charge across the meadow on their black horses to arrest him.

"It's okay, Jem," said Aveline. "We're safe out here."

She and Bruno laughed and whooped and made snow angels, while Jem kept an eye out for spies that never materialized.

When they'd had enough of the cold, they returned to the carriage house to warm up. They enjoyed hot cocoa and petit fours, and cookies whose milk-chocolate chips melted in their mouths, and rainbow-colored marzipan in the shape of dragons imported from the neighboring country of Clunia. Bruno teased Aveline that she looked like a squirrel with her cheeks stuffed with marzipan, but she just couldn't get enough.

S. J. Carson

As she sat before her vanity mirror brushing her hair that night, Allyn walked up behind her, still dressed in her sleek Party uniform. Aveline lowered the silver horsehair brush and smiled, meeting her mother's eyes in the mirror, excited to tell her about the funny snowman they made.

"You've put on weight," said Allyn.

Aveline's heart sank. "I'm sorry, Mother." She didn't really know what she was apologizing for. Letting her down, she supposed. Embarrassing her by being the fat daughter. The one people laughed at when they saw her on Channel 1 at some public function, standing beside all her petite family members.

Allyn leaned over and smoothed her hair and whispered in her ear, "We've got to get you back on that diet. No more sweeties for you."

"Yes, Mother."

Allyn turned and walked out of the room, high heels clacking on the hardwood floor. Once she was gone, Aveline stared at her reflection and lifted her hand to continue brushing her hair. But she lacked the strength. She let the brush fall to the rug and doubled over and began to cry.

****

Nobody was talking about the Hayes Affair anymore. Allyn made sure of that. There was a new crisis now in the form of the Forbidden Books and Records. The Stam swept the country, confiscating books and music banned by the Party—works that were "degenerate" or "profane," or would "inflame the passions of the Alterran people." Anyone who possessed them or traded them on the black market was arrested and thrown in jail to await trial by the High

Court.

At school, all the students were talking about the Stam's arrests. One afternoon at recess, Aveline was playing a pickup game of football with Bruno and a few of the other scholarship students, but they were actually just kicking the ball around and trading gossip. She liked that her friends didn't treat her any differently because of who she was.

The central part of the country had recently experienced a warm spell, heavy rain melting all the snow, and the field was now patchy with mud. When Kira kicked the ball to Aveline, she darted away so as not to get mud on her new black ballerina flats, lest she upset her mother.

Milton intercepted the ball. "What do you think is in those books?"

Before Aveline could answer truthfully that she had no idea, as her mother wouldn't let her read them, Kira interjected, "Really bad things."

"Like what?"

Kira glanced over her shoulder, and Aveline knew she was looking either for Stam officers or old Brother Elias, the recess supervisor. When she saw neither, she continued, "Like that the Party shouldn't own all the land, and that the people should be able to buy and sell it and divide it up however they want."

Milton stopped the ball and rested his foot on top of it. "That just seems wrong."

"*Wrong?*" said Kira. "Don't you think it's wrong that we have to live in rat-infested apartments while the rich get to live in huge mansions?"

The other students turned instinctively to look at Aveline. She felt the heat creep into her face, despite the cold weather.

"Sorry," said Kira. "I didn't mean you, Avie."

"It's okay."

Aveline knew they were right about the land. The unfair way that the Party doled out property had always bothered her, like a splinter in her mind, but she had never known how to put it into words. Until now.

Soberly, they continued passing the ball back and forth until the bell rang and Brother Elias toddled out of the faculty lounge and onto the edge of the field, his little schnauzer in tow. He smoothed his black cassock and yawned as if he'd just awakened from a nap.

While the other students hustled back to the school entrance, Bruno grabbed Aveline's arm and pulled her aside.

"What is it?" she said. She noticed he'd been awfully quiet during recess.

"You'll never guess what I heard this morning."

"What?"

"When the Stam arrested a man in the District of Whitecross, they knocked him to the ground, and do you know what flew out of his coat pocket? I mean, other than one of the Forbidden Books?" Aveline shook her head. "Sandor Hayes's article!"

"You're kidding!" She clapped a hand over her mouth.

"Remember when you told me your uncle had said that the article named names? Well, it turns out he was right. It named your uncle and your mother specifically."

"What did it say about them?"

"Here." From his pocket he produced a folded-up piece of paper. "I got this from a girl in my building, who got it from her older brother, who got it from somebody at work. Don't read it until you get home. Then burn it in the fireplace. You can't tell anyone you've seen it or that I gave it to you. Promise?"

Her heart hammered in her chest as she shoved the paper deep into the pocket of her skirt. "I promise."

****

Alone in her room after school, with trembling hands, Aveline reached into her pocket for the paper Bruno had given her. It was a scrap from the underground newspaper, folded and refolded so many times that it was now soft and limp. Carefully, she unfolded it and began to read.

Fifty years have passed since Alfred Fleur and his Six Hundred stormed Castle Rovamina and beheaded King Reuel IV. Fleur promised to liberate us from the bonds of monarchy. From a tyrannical king and a feudal system where the noblemen held all the power. He promised us a democracy. He promised to eliminate all distinctions between the rich and the poor, to provide the same educational and career opportunities for everyone, to create a government in which all citizens had a voice. But he hasn't delivered. Not even close.

Aveline couldn't believe what she was reading. She had never heard anyone speak so ill of her grandfather. Didn't Sandor know his history? Couldn't he understand that Alterra had been trapped in the dark ages for centuries until Alfred Fleur came along?

The changes he made to our society are in name only. Instead of the King, we have the Leader. Instead of the Cavalry, we have the Armed Forces. Instead of the Inquisition, we have the Stam. And instead of the suzerain, the feudal overlords, we have the ministers. At least in Reuel's day, the lords were bound by an ethical duty to protect and provide for their serfs. But our ministers—specifically the two highest-profile ministers (unsurprisingly, Fleur's son and daughter)—are interested only in protecting and providing for themselves.

He's talking about Mother and Simon! she thought. She kept reading.

The Fleurs are sociopaths, demonstrating a callous disregard for people's basic human rights. Just last spring, there was a blight in Lystra that killed the potato crops and caused a famine unlike any that our nation has ever seen. Thousands of people, including infants and children, starved to death, without any aid from the Party. But did we hear about that on Channel 1? Of course not. All we heard about were the lush green fields and the "Promise of Alterra"—whatever that is. Who is to blame for the great coverup down south? None other than Allyn Fleur. Hearing her argue that all news and public life of the State should be subordinated to the Ministry of Civic Enlightenment, one cannot help but wonder whether she has a soul at all.

She stood there in disbelief, breathing heavily, insides shaking. Everything she had just read was a lie. It had to be. Allyn was not the person that Sandor had described. Couldn't he see that she loved and nurtured Alterra like her own child? And the famine in Lystra? There was no such thing. Jem was from Lystra. Surely, if there were a famine, he would have said something about it by now.

"Are you feeling all right, Miss Aveline?" asked

Jossie, who had entered her room with afternoon tea. "You look awfully pale."

Quickly, she crumpled the paper and shoved it into her pocket, then looked up at the maid. "Oh, I'm fine." She forced a smile. "I was out playing football at recess, and I think I must have caught a little chill." It was true; she was freezing cold. Even though the Fleurs had central heating—a luxury—the enormous House could get quite drafty in the winter. "Would you mind making a fire, Jossie?"

"Of course not."

After setting the tea tray on an end table, Jossie ducked out of the room. She returned with several old editions of the official Party newspaper, *The Egregor*, which she crumpled and placed between two pieces of wood in the fireplace. She then lit a match to the paper and added another couple of logs, stirring them with an iron poker. Pulling the screen closed, she said, "There! Now you'll stay nice and warm, Miss Aveline."

Once the maid had left, Aveline closed the door to her room. She ran back to the fireplace and opened the screen and tossed in the little piece of paper with its terrifying ideas. Taunted it with the poker until it vanished into the pages of *The Egregor*.

Watching the fire, she thought of Sandor's words. *He promised us democracy...But he hasn't delivered. Not even close.* Perhaps Chief Justice Magnus was right when he called Sandor a madman. Surely this article was the work of someone hateful and twisted. But she couldn't ignore the little nagging voice in her head: *What if it's true?*

Either way, Aveline had to tell her mother. She remembered Simon saying that the Stam had confiscated all the copies they could find. But, obviously, they had missed at least one. Who knew how many people had read the article by now? The number was probably increasing by the day. If they didn't do something quickly, the effect could be devastating. Not just to the Party but to their family. Aveline wouldn't tell Allyn that she'd actually seen the article, or that Bruno had given it to her, only that she'd heard about it through the rumor mill at school.

She stopped by her mother's study that evening, but Allyn wasn't there. She didn't come to family dinner, either. For the last few weeks, she'd been spending nearly all her time at the Lightministry planning the Cultural Purification Ceremony, a great book-burning rally that all citizens of Calador were required to attend. Whenever she had a free moment, she was with Jem. He knew how precious her time was, so he was willing to meet her anywhere, at any hour. Aveline would often see him at the breakfast table and know that he had stayed the night. She'd smile at him over her egg whites on wheat toast, her newest diet food. She loved how close Allyn and Jem were becoming, how speedily their courtship was progressing. Allyn seemed happy, so Aveline was happy for her. But her happiness had a coldness to it, a hard edge, like a raw diamond.

On the day of the ceremony, Aveline and Jem, dressed in their finest garb, arrived at Armand Fleur Park in a Party car. They joined the rest of the Fleur family and a few favored ministers onstage. Allyn took Jem's hand. He stood silently by her side as she spoke with the Minister of Culture. Jem nodded in agreement with everything she said.

Allyn's pin and sigil ring gleamed as she stepped up to the podium to give her opening remarks. She spoke of how the citizens of Alterra "must remain pure in spirit and intellect" and "clear away the refuse of the past" in order to move forward. She even talked about her dream of rewriting some of the Forbidden Books, of editing out the "anti-Alterran sentiments."

Simon stood a few feet behind the podium, arms crossed, watching his sister. Aveline was close enough to see his Mark of Yrgess, his pinky ring, turn puce with disgust. When Alfred walked by, he spun the ring around so that the stone faced inward, toward his palm.

Aveline looked beyond the stage to the enormous bonfire at the center of the square, encircled by Stam officers in their black uniforms. The band played "Eternal Reign of the Fleurs." Low-level employees of the Lightministry handed box after box of Forbidden Books and Records to the officers, who dumped them onto the fire. Never in her life had she seen a fire so enormous. The flames leaped high into the air, and the crowd cheered, waving tiny Alterran flags like a thousand tongues of Monnag.

Over everyone and everything, on the exterior of a building across the street, loomed a billboard of the little dark-haired girl from the commercials on Channel 3. Except that in this advertisement, instead of eating Party margarine on white bread, the girl held an oversized pointer finger to her lips. *Silence.*

Shivering, Aveline walked up to her mother, who had just ceded the podium to Alfred.

"Mother…" began Aveline.

She was about to tell her about Sandor's article, but she stopped herself. Bringing it up at a public event was not a good idea, she reasoned. Besides, she was afraid of getting in trouble for even *knowing* what the article said. And she was doubly afraid of getting Bruno and the girl from his building in trouble. She was not a good liar, and she was sure that Allyn would somehow pry the truth out of her.

She looked over at her mother, who was gazing intently at the bonfire, the flames leaping and dancing in her eyes. Aveline knew that she had read every single one of the Forbidden Books, had listened to all the Forbidden Records. It made Aveline just the tiniest bit envious that her mother had access to all this knowledge while she wasn't allowed so much as a peek under the cover of one of those books.

But, for some reason, Allyn did allow her to listen to one of the Forbidden Records, a collection of string quartets by Milo Fresenius. On a Sunday afternoon weeks earlier, Allyn put on the record and they lay on Allyn's enormous canopy bed and listened with their eyes closed for two whole hours. The music reminded Aveline of the first rays of morning sun breaking over the pond...of tall columns of glass...of galloping horses, the wind whipping their blond manes to seafoam.

At one point, Aveline opened her eyes and looked over at her mother. Tears were streaming down Allyn's cheeks from under her closed eyelids. Aveline was surprised. But as soon as the music ended, Allyn jumped up from the bed and wiped her eyes and yanked the record off the turntable.

"This must be burned," she said.

How? Aveline wondered. How could anyone burn music so beautiful? Music that opened its doors on infinity, that freed you from your own body?

But Allyn never brought herself to turn over the record to the Lightministry for the bonfire. Sometimes, from down the hall late at night, Aveline could hear the whisper of Maestro Fresenius's violins, and she smiled at her mother's little act of sedition. A year ago, the young composer had been sent away to the enemy country of Ebria. Aveline knew that he'd written those quartets in exile. She wanted to believe that he'd written them for Allyn, knowing that somehow they would find their way back to Alterra, to her ear, into her heart.

Chapter 8

"Aveline! Hurry up!" said Bruno.

She ran down the school corridor, huffing and puffing under the weight of her backpack. The students were on their way to an assembly to watch the mandatory Daily Veneration on Channel 1 from noon to one o'clock. But it was no ordinary day. It was spring, the sun's first warmth touching the land. Crocuses rose from the dirt, and cherry trees glowed with pink blossoms. It was also the day that Sandor Hayes would publicly affirm the Sacred Oath.

"I can't believe he's back!" said Bruno when Aveline had caught up to him.

"I know," said Aveline, still trying to catch her breath. "I feel like he's only been gone a few weeks."

The two friends followed the other children into the auditorium and took their seats as close to the front as possible. Usually they tried to sit as close to the back as they could manage, to avoid the bullies' spitballs, but that day they wanted to watch every detail unfold onscreen since they couldn't be there in person.

Aveline let her backpack fall with a *plunk* to the floor at her feet. At the front of the room, she watched the television slowly lower from the ceiling.

Before she could reflect on how quickly the last six months had passed, Mother Josephine cut the lights and plunged the auditorium into darkness. But the darkness lasted only a moment before an image of Alfred Fleur and Sandor Hayes appeared on the screen. The two stood facing each other at the head of the plenary room at the People's Assembly. Both men wore their black Party uniforms. Sandor seemed relaxed, yet focused, his blond hair swept back neatly from his forehead in the modern style.

"Repeat after me," said Alfred, raising his right hand. Sandor mirrored the gesture. "I hereby swear this Sacred Oath: That I shall bear true faith and unconditional allegiance to Alfred Fleur, Favored Son of Monnag, Father and Supreme Leader of the State of Alterra; that I shall be willing at any moment to lay down my life for him and for my country; and that I shall support and defend the Constitution and laws of the State of Alterra against all enemies foreign and domestic, so help me God."

After Sandor repeated the Oath, Alfred fastened a gold Monnag pin to his left lapel. "Welcome back to the National Democratic Party, Mr. Hayes."

"It is an honor, my Leader."

The camera panned to the legislators, who leaped to their feet and applauded. From somewhere offstage, Allyn appeared, smiling. Her dark hair was plaited and draped over her left shoulder and secured at the end with a crimson loyalty ribbon. Sandor smiled back at her and placed a hand over his heart. She returned the salute and put a hand on his arm and mouthed her congratulations.

Aveline shook her head in disbelief. The man before her looked like Sandor Hayes. He spoke in Sandor's voice; he displayed all the same mannerisms. But he was not Sandor Hayes. This man sincerely believed in the oath he had just recited. He admired, even loved, the Supreme Leader. He believed in Alfred's vision for the country—the "Promise of Alterra." He even allowed Allyn to rest her hand on his arm. The Sandor Hayes that Aveline remembered would have recoiled from her touch as if from a live snake. Recoiled from this woman whom he blamed for covering up the famine in Lystra. This woman who, according to him, had the blood of innocents on her hands. But now he leaned toward her, even crouching a little so she could whisper something in his ear. And when she was finished, he smiled a genuine smile, one that touched his eyes. He waved proudly at the audience like a war hero who'd just returned home.

Aveline looked over at Bruno. When he looked back at her with the same bewildered expression, she knew they had the same thought: *What on earth is wrong with Sandor Hayes?*

She glanced back at the screen and saw Sandor shaking hands with her uncle. Because Sandor's hands were bigger, his thumb covered Simon's Mark of Yrgess. Simon hated when other people touched his ring, but now he seemed only too happy to extend the privilege to this near-total stranger. This former traitor of the State.

When Mother Josephine raised the lights to signal the end of the Daily Veneration and released the children to eat lunch and play in the schoolyard, Aveline found herself unable to move.

"Hey!" said the older boy in the seat next to her. His face was rough with the first bloom of acne. "Did you put down roots or what?"

On shaky legs, Aveline rose to her feet and hoisted

her backpack onto her shoulder and followed Bruno out of the auditorium and to the cafeteria. Although she was relieved that Sandor Hayes had returned from Rjellsfall safe and sound, and perfectly functional, she could scarcely take a bite of her turkey sandwich. She had a cold, sinking feeling in the pit of her stomach that she just couldn't shake.

****

Toward the end of spring, just after Aveline had celebrated her fourteenth birthday, she had a very odd encounter at school. After the last bell had rung, she entered the first-floor girls' bathroom and heard someone whimpering. Peering under the doors of the stalls, she spotted a pair of legs with white ruffled ankle socks and black leather T-strap shoes. It was one of the bullies, Quintana.

"Quintana, are you okay?"

There was the honk of a nose being blown. "Get out of here, Fatsoline."

Aveline stepped back and started to turn. "Sorry to bother you." She turned to leave and go use the upstairs bathroom when she heard the toilet flush. Quintana came out of the stall, wiping her nose on a hunk of tissue paper, her eyes red from crying.

"What's wrong?" said Aveline.

Quintana shook her head. "You probably couldn't help me."

"Help you? With what?" Surely this must have been the prelude to another mean prank.

"My father is missing."

"Missing? What do you mean?"

The other girl blew her nose again and handed the wadded-up tissue to Aveline, who looked at it, covered in snot, and threw it into the wastebasket. Her hand felt sticky and she felt a tickle in the back of her throat that meant she was about to start gagging, but she didn't dare wash her hand for fear of offending the bully.

Quintana pushed back a few strands of hair that had come loose from her thick brown braid. "What don't you understand about the word 'missing'? He went to work yesterday and never came home. My mother and brothers have been looking everywhere—his office, the tavern, his friends' houses—but he still hasn't turned up. It's not like him just to leave and never come home. He *always* comes home. I don't know where he would have gone."

A dark thought crossed Aveline's mind. "Do you think it's possible that he did something against the Party?"

"Ha! Are you kidding? He's a *member* of the Party who works at the Ministry of Energy. He's a nuclear engineer. He's never done anything against the Party, not even spoken a single bad word."

The girl began blubbering again.

"Maybe a little cold water on your face would feel good," said Aveline. When Aveline used to cry as a child, Allyn would take her into the bathroom and hold her hair and splash water on her face; it always made her feel better. "I'll hold your braid."

To Aveline's surprise, Quintana nodded and did not protest. She leaned over the sink and splashed her face as Aveline held her braid out of the way, noticing that the hair was a little rough, as though Quintana had simply braided it without brushing it first.

When Quintana had dried her face, Aveline said timidly, "I can try to help you…if you want."

The girl hiccupped. "Will you ask your uncle if he could find my dad?"

"My uncle?"

"He's the Lawminister, isn't he?"

"Yes."

Aveline didn't know if Simon would be willing to expend the Stam's precious resources on this girl's dad, but she promised Quintana that she would ask him.

****

After dinner that evening, Aveline knocked quietly on the door of Simon's study.

"Come in," he said brusquely.

She pushed open the heavy oak door and entered. It wasn't often that she went into Simon's study. When she gazed around, she saw piles of papers and full ashtrays and newspapers strewn across the leather couches; it was no wonder that he didn't usually allow visitors. On the wall above his head was a portrait of Yrgess, his namesake dragon, fierce-looking, with yellow-gold scales. (On her study wall Allyn had similar portrait of Monnag, twice the size of Yrgess, with red-gold scales.)

"Sit down," he commanded.

She sat in the high-backed leather chair on the other side of his desk.

He leaned back and lifted his feet up on the desktop. Aveline was struck by his resemblance to Allyn, the high cheekbones and straight nose and thin lips, but the corners of his mouth were always turned up, as though he were perpetually amused by an inside joke. From his shirt pocket he took a pack of cigarettes and put one in his mouth and lit it with his silver lighter, then blew a large smoke ring into the air. The act of lighting the cigarette had caused his Mark of Yrgess to glow yellow for a moment.

"Let's make this brief, shall we, Aveline? I'm awfully busy."

"Okay."

He didn't seem awfully busy, judging by his languid gestures and the smoke rings he was blowing, which traveled upward, one through the other, sticking to the stained-glass windows. The glass was supposed to be clear, but over the years it had taken on a yellowish, almost amber appearance from the smoke.

Aveline took a deep breath before she spoke. "This girl at school, Quintana Bailey, told me her father went missing. I promised her I'd ask if you could help. Is there anything you can do, Uncle Simon?"

He lifted his feet from the desk and lowered them to the floor with a thud. He flicked the ash from his cigarette into a gold ashtray. She could see by the way his ring was glowing that he was annoyed by her, this interruption in his nightly routine.

He cleared his throat. "He probably abandoned the family. Nothing unusual, I'm afraid."

"That's the thing," said Aveline, sitting up straight and trying to double-cross her legs the way her mother always did. "Quintana said he comes home every night. He's a Party member who works in the Ministry of Energy."

"What's his name? I didn't catch it."

"Leopold Bailey."

"Leopold Bailey," he repeated. "Doesn't sound familiar. I suppose he isn't very high up."

"I don't know."

"He abandoned the family," repeated Simon, but

with more conviction now. "Probably keeps a mistress in the city and decided to run off with her."

Aveline shook her head. "I don't think so."

"Listen, I'm not going to get involved in the family drama of one of your school friends—"

"She's not my friend. She's…kind of mean, actually."

"She must have gotten that from the mother. No wonder he left."

Aveline didn't know what to say to get through to him. She stood and placed her hands on his desk, leaning forward and begging, "Please, Uncle Simon, isn't there anything you can do?"

He flicked her hands away. "Calm down, Aveline. This is most unbecoming."

"Sorry."

She took her seat, watching the moisture from her palms evaporating from the mahogany surface of the desk. She didn't see what the big deal was about her hands on his desk; it was so dusty and cluttered anyway. Surreptitiously, she wiped her hands on the sides of her skirt.

Her uncle sighed. "All right. I'll mention it to Cade the next time I see him." General Belarius Cade was the head of the Stam, who reported directly to Simon. "This isn't something you need to trouble yourself about."

She could tell by his tone that the conversation was over. Clearly, he wasn't taking this very seriously, but she was determined to get to the bottom of it. Not because she had any particularly warm feelings for Quintana, but because something wasn't right. She could feel it in her gut.

Rising from her chair, she thanked him for his time

and turned to leave.

"Oh, and Aveline," he called, "please close the door behind you."

****

Aveline had just stepped out of the school chapel and into the commons when she ran into Quintana and her sidekick, Cynthia, standing together with their arms crossed. A human wall. Even though Quintana was not her favorite person, she'd still been praying for the safe return of her father.

"Well?" said Quintana. "What did he say?"

Aveline avoided her eyes. "Nothing yet. Uncle Simon is still working on it."

"My dad's been gone for three days! Three whole days! My family is a wreck! How much longer do we have to wait?"

"I-I'm not sure. He said he'd mention it to General Cade and—"

"What did Cade say?"

Aveline kept her eyes on her feet. "I don't know."

The girl released a long sigh. "I guess it's fine. You tried your best. It's not your fault that you have a moron for an uncle."

Aveline couldn't believe she'd been bold enough to call Simon a moron in the commons where the Sisters could easily overhear her. But what surprised Aveline the most was how easily Quintana seemed to be letting her off the hook. Was this a joke?

The bullies exchanged glances. Then Cynthia said, "Want to come play cricket with us in the yard?"

"Really?"

"Why not? We're getting a bit tired of this cat-and-mouse game, aren't you? You know, where you're the mouse?"

"I-I guess so."

"I thought we should try to bury the hatchet. Let's go."

Aveline hesitated. "Hatchet" sounded ominous. She was sure they were up to something, but what options did she have? She could run away, in which case they would chase her down, or she could go with them and give them a chance. What if they really did just want to play cricket? Besides, the schoolyard was right under the second-floor office of Mother Josephine, who stayed until five o'clock every evening to watch over after-school activities.

Putting aside her doubts, Aveline followed them down to the gymnasium. When they arrived at the large closet where Brother Elias kept the sporting equipment, Cynthia unzipped the front pocket of her backpack and produced a large skeleton key with which she unlocked the door.

"Why don't you go in and get the bats, Aveline?" said Quintana.

"Um, why can't we all go in?" she squeaked.

"They're behind a whole bunch of stuff and I'm too exhausted from worrying about my dad."

"And we got the key from Brother Elias," Cynthia chimed in. She flicked on the light switch. "So now you have to do your part."

From the threshold of the door Aveline looked inside for the big wooden barrels that held the cricket bats. Quintana was right—they weren't immediately visible.

"I…I don't think I want to go in," she said quietly.

"Why not? Is the widdle baby sca-a-ared?"

Before she knew what was happening, one of the girls shoved her hard from behind and she fell on her knees onto the hardwood floor inside the closet. She heard the door slam shut. Then Cynthia and Quintana were on top of her, attempting to tie her wrists with a rope. She screamed, but Quintana clamped a hand over her mouth. She kicked and tried to bite at Quintana's hand, but she managed only to lick her palm, leaving the unpleasant taste of salt in her mouth.

As hard as she struggled, they still got the rope around her hands and another around her feet. They also put a bandana in her mouth, tying it tightly around the back of her head, under her braid, so she wouldn't cry out. As they lifted her onto an old wooden chair, she looked with horror as Quintana pulled a shiny pair of scissors from her backpack. She tried to scream again but succeeded in making only muffled squeals. Cynthia and Quintana imitated the noises, laughing and high-fiving one another.

"Don't worry," said Quintana, "we're not going to kill you. Just give you a little trim."

Aveline shook her head vehemently, hot tears flowing down her cheeks. Not her hair. Please, God, not her hair!

It was an old tradition in Alterra for a girl to wear her hair long until marriage. On her wedding day, a Cutter would snip off her braid at the nape of her neck to symbolize her new position in society as a wife. For a girl to cut off her own braid—or to have someone else cut it off—before marriage was considered a sin.

But it didn't matter to Quintana. The girl yanked at the end of Aveline's loyalty ribbon, letting it fall to the floor. She bent down and picked it up and held it up to

Aveline's face, snipping it in two.

"I bet you never even asked your uncle to look for my father." Quintana stepped behind her with the scissors. "He's useless, just like you."

"No! No! No!" she cried into the bandana.

But it was too late. With one quick motion, Quintana snipped off her braid at the nape of her neck and hurled it across the room. She then handed the scissors to Cynthia, who began making maniacal little snips at the remaining hair, on the tops and on the sides.

"Give her spikes! Make her look like a dragon!" said Quintana.

"Give her some bald spots," said Cynthia, passing the scissors to her friend. "Cut down as low as you can."

At one point, Quintana cut a bit too low and nicked Aveline's scalp with the blade. She winced and felt a trickle of blood flowing down the side of her head, pooling in her ear.

"Voila!" Laughing, Quintana tossed the scissors to Cynthia. "Let's bury these. Just like the hatchet."

"Her braid, too?"

"No, she can keep that. A little souvenir."

Cynthia's face had turned pale. "Quin, what if someone finds out it was us?"

"How will they find out unless this one squeals?" She pointed at Aveline. "You're not going to squeal, are you?"

Aveline shook her head no. She was too afraid.

"Good. Because if you do…" Quintana traced a line along her throat. "Right, Cyn?"

Cynthia nodded.

"If I take the gag out of your mouth, you're not

going to scream, are you?" asked Quintana.

Aveline shook her head vehemently.

"Swear to God?"

Again, Aveline shook her head. She was not one for swearing to God, but she would have taken any oath right about now.

Quintana untied the bandana and Aveline began sucking in as much air as her lungs would hold, which made her cough. She felt as if she were choking, drowning in air. Then the girls untied the rope around her wrists and ankles. When she held up her hands she saw that her wrists were red and raw from struggling against the ligatures. Her ankles above her socks looked the same.

"Enjoy your new haircut, Fatsoline!"

"More like *Bald*oline!"

The girls laughed, slamming the door behind them. Aveline waited a few minutes before moving, just to make sure they were gone. When she no longer heard the clatter of their shoes on the hardwood floor or their rankling voices, she tried to stand up from the chair, but her knees were so shaky that her legs collapsed and she plummeted to the floor. She lay there for some time, crying, running her hands over her sheared head.

On her hands and knees, she scoured the floor for her braid, which she found behind a wrestling mat. It was surreal to be holding her own hair in her hands.

Shakily, she stood. After steadying herself, she crept out of the equipment closet to the gymnasium entrance. When the coast was clear, she darted to the girls' bathroom down the hall, where she dumped her braid in the trash and covered it up with the crumpled paper towels already in the bin.

Only then did she dare look at herself in the mirror—and jumped back in horror. She looked like the haunted doll in one of the Lightministry's early films, cursed by a wicked dollmaker and made to come alive and attack children at night.

Mother is going to kill me.

Unable to continue looking at her reflection, she wet a fresh paper towel and used it to clean up the side of her face where blood had dripped from her scalp.

To keep her mind off of her mother's inevitable reaction, she tried to focus on practical things. Putting one foot in front of the other, remembering the combination to her locker, taking out the correct books for her homework, keeping an eye out for anyone in the hallway who might see her. On the second shelf, she noticed the big sunhat her mother forced her to keep there to protect her fair skin from the sun. She would have been mortified to wear it under normal circumstances, but now she put it on gratefully.

On the way home, Elton caught her eye in the rearview mirror and remarked, "That's some mighty fine millinery you've chosen today, Miss Aveline!"

"Thanks, Elton," she said sheepishly. Fortunately, he didn't ask her *why* she'd chosen to wear it, when she'd never voluntarily worn a hat before.

Back at the Estate, she ran up the spiral staircase and to her room. After shutting the door, she flung herself onto her bed and began to weep.

Chapter 9

Aveline wept so hard she got the hiccups. Whenever she heard footsteps in the hallway, her stomach clenched until they passed by her door. But it was only the maids running back and forth, cleaning and picking up laundry.

She flipped onto her back and watched the sun fade from the walls and the shadows grow longer. Closing her eyes, she tried to pretend that the whole day had never happened. But she was startled by a knock at the door. Nervous butterflies filled her stomach.

"Mother?"

"No, it's only Jossie. May I come in?"

She leaped up and hurried to the door. She opened it slowly, staying behind it as Jossie entered the room.

"Miss Aveline?" Jossie looked around. "Are you hiding?"

"Yes," she whispered. Then she hiccupped loudly. Embarrassed, she clapped a hand over her mouth.

"What's the matter?"

Jossie looked behind the door and saw her hair and gasped. Aveline had been worried she'd react this way. Quickly, Jossie shut the door. Aveline wished she could lock it, but unfortunately, it locked only from the outside.

"Who did this to you?"

"Those mean girls at school. What am I going to

do, Jossie? How am I going to explain this to my mother?"

The maid pulled her into a hug. "I don't know, Miss Aveline. First, let's go into the bathroom, and I'll try to even it out, okay?"

"Have you ever cut hair before?"

"I used to trim my younger sister's hair."

Aveline felt relieved, knowing she was in good hands. She followed Jossie into the adjoining bathroom and sat on the stool before the vanity. Jossie switched on the vanity lights, which always made Aveline feel a little like a starlet backstage at the Lightministry's film studio. Only this time she cried upon seeing her reflection.

"I'm so ugly."

Jossie stood behind her, hands on her shoulders. "No, sweetie, you're beautiful. With or without your braid."

From a top drawer Jossie took a pair of scissors and began snipping at the longer strands to bring them in line with the shorter ones. It didn't take very long, since the bullies hadn't left her with much to work with. When Jossie was finished, it did look a little better, almost as if she'd intended to cut it that way.

"I'm so scared of what Mother will say when she sees me," said Aveline. "I wish I could wear a hat for the rest of my life. Or at least until my hair grows out."

Jossie's cornflower-blue eyes met hers in the mirror. "Don't worry, I'll tell your mother so you don't have to."

Aveline turned around. "Would you really do that for me, Jossie?"

"Of course. When I came upstairs, your mother had

S. J. Carson

just come in from the Ministry. She's downstairs in the Great Room with Mr. Caslon. I'll go down and ask to have a word with her privately."

"No, no, don't do that. Tell her in front of Jem. She'll be less likely to be cross when he's around."

Jossie nodded. "Of course, Miss Aveline. I'll be right back."

Aveline sat at the vanity and prayed that all would go well downstairs. It wasn't long before she heard the *clack clack clack* of her mother's stilettos flying up the staircase. She braced herself for what was to come.

The door to her room flew open and she heard her mother's voice calling her name. Timidly, she stepped out of the bathroom and saw Allyn and Jem. Allyn was dressed elegantly for dinner in her black slacks and cream-colored silk shirt, dark braid draped over her shoulder.

Aveline sobbed. "It's not my fault, Mother!"

"Of course not, my sweet girl."

Before, Allyn would have dropped to her knees to be at eye level with Aveline, but that wasn't necessary because they were now almost the same height. Allyn ran her hands through what was left of her daughter's hair and embraced her.

Jem also hugged her, and she cried all over his suit jacket as she had cried all over Allyn's silk blouse. She apologized profusely.

Jossie quietly stepped out into the hallway, closing the door behind her. The three sat on the floor together, on the soft pastel rug. Allyn kicked off her shoes and drew Aveline close. Aveline closed her eyes and inhaled her mother's gardenia perfume.

When she had finished crying, she lifted her head

and dried her eyes. Allyn's shirt was open at the collar, displaying her strand of pearls. As a young child, Aveline had touched those pearls as though they were prayer beads, warm from her mother's body and glossy with the light they had absorbed.

"Don't worry, my darling," said Allyn. "I will make this right. Those wretched girls will regret the day they dared to do this to my Aveline."

Aveline sniffled. "W-what are you going to do?"

"I don't know yet. But, believe me, they will be punished."

"Please don't go too hard on them, Mother." Despite what they'd done to her, Aveline still felt bad about what had happened to Quintana's father.

Allyn smiled. "Of course not, sweetheart. I'll see to it that this is a—how shall we say—a *teachable* moment for Miss Quintana and her little friend."

"You know, I was bullied when I was about your age," said Jem.

"Really?" Aveline couldn't imagine someone as good-looking and strong as Jem being a target for bullies.

He nodded. "Oh, yes. They were some older, tougher boys from the neighboring farm back in Ede's River. They threatened to whip me if I didn't muck out the stalls of their horses."

"Yuck." Aveline wrinkled her nose.

Allyn stroked the side of his face. "Poor Jem. If only I'd known you then, I'd have taken care of them for you."

"How?"

"Oh, I don't know. Maybe with some strongly-worded admonishments from the Scripture." She chuckled.

"That would've scared them right off."

She playfully punched his arm. In response, he put his arm around her and kissed her, and she caressed her sigil ring that hung from a gold chain around his neck. A symbol of their engagement.

Around the time that Sandor Hayes had returned and reaffirmed the Sacred Oath, Jem had taken the Oath for the first time and become a full member of the Party in a public ceremony. Allyn had unfastened the crimson Aspirant ribbon from his lapel and crushed it underfoot, as was customary, and replaced it with a gleaming gold Monnag pin.

"Welcome to the National Democratic Party, Mr. Caslon," she had said.

Then, to everyone's surprise—Aveline's, too—Allyn had also given him her sigil ring. Slipped it onto a chain and fastened it around his neck as he bent down graciously, wordlessly.

Watching Allyn play with the ring, Aveline felt a surge of envy. Her mother's life was going so well. The reeducation of Sandor Hayes and the Cultural Purification Ceremony had both been successful. So successful, in fact, that Alfred was again singing her praises. And she was getting married the following weekend.

Aveline began to panic and touched her sheared scalp. "What am I going to do about my hair at the wedding?"

Allyn turned to her with a smile. "Not to worry. We'll have a wig made for you. The finest wig money can buy. It will be made from natural hair the same color as yours so no one will ever even know the difference."

****

On Sunday morning, Aveline stood before the full-length mirror in her bedroom. She wore a pink taffeta dress with an empire waist and pink roses sewn around the waistline, which the village seamstress had made especially for her. It was a beautiful dress, but she didn't feel beautiful at all. In fact, she felt more hideous than ever in her blonde wig. Although it was nearly the same color as her hair, perhaps half a shade lighter, and braided over her shoulder according to custom, she was sure that everyone would know it was a wig. And, to make matters worse, it was itchy. She dreaded having to wear it the entire day.

Mid-morning, Jem's family arrived at the Estate to meet the Fleurs, their soon-to-be in-laws. Aveline curtsied before Dora and Artyr Caslon, Jem's parents, and Jem's sister and four brothers, and his brothers' wives and all their children.

The Caslons were a sprawling, rowdy bunch, with heavy Lystra accents that Aveline found difficult at times to understand. They were as effusive as the Fleurs were restrained. It was their first time in Calador, and of course their first time to the Estate, so they wandered around the hallways looking at the paintings with their mouths hanging open like codfish. The children tittered and whispered among themselves; some even jumped around.

When Alfred entered the Great Room in his uniform and regalia, the Caslons fell to their knees. Dora and Artyr took turns kissing his sigil ring.

They also tried to kiss Allyn's hand, but she told them to rise, that she was not royalty and such displays were not necessary.

Marinda, Jem's younger sister, came up to her and blurted, "You're so much smaller than you look on television!"

Dora bowed her head. "Please forgive her, Madam Lightminister. She's only sixteen and doesn't think before she speaks."

"It's all right. She is far from the first to say it." Allyn laughed easily and pulled Marinda into a warm embrace.

Simon seemed to be enjoying the spectacle, letting the Caslons fawn all over him. At luncheon, when he and Allyn stood off to the side talking, Aveline heard him call the family "a bunch of country bumpkins" as he rolled his eyes.

"Keep doing that and your eyeballs will get stuck back there," said Allyn.

"Oh, ha, ha," he replied, lighting a cigarette. "You're thinking the same thing, Sister Dear, but you're too much of a priss to admit it."

Aveline stroked the end of her fake braid and watched the little kids. There were over twenty, each of Jem's brothers with five or six each, heaping their plates with food from the buffet table: lobster tails, shrimp, steak, prosciutto, pate, caviar. All the kids were skinny and knobby-kneed, with dark eyes too big for their heads. With slender, greedy fingers, they shoveled the delicacies into their mouths as if at any moment the Stam was going to march in and snatch all their food away.

"Stop! Stop!" scolded Dora when one boy, about six or seven, doubled over with stomach cramps and looked like he was about to vomit. "You've had enough!"

Aveline wasn't sure whether the grandmother was more concerned for his health or embarrassed at his uncouth behavior. But she was certain of one thing: Sandor wasn't lying when he wrote about the famine in Lystra.

****

The Church of the Monnag stood in the City Center beside the River Antoleme. Formerly King Reuel's cathedral, the Church had been badly damaged during the Revolution fifty years earlier. When the Fleurs came to power, they repaired its choir and nave, its central spire and ancient façade, and the gutters upon which fierce-looking stone gargoyles sat, looking down over Calador.

Although it was the holiest place in Alterra, the Church now teemed with television cameras and journalists from *The Egregor*. The Lightministry was broadcasting the wedding live on Channel 1. Standing to one side of the altar, Aveline felt the cameras angling in on her face, her every expression of discomfort. She scratched at her braided blonde wig, which had become itchier and itchier as the day wore on. All she wanted to do was tear it off her head and hurl it across the room, cropped hair be darned. But she knew that her mother's wedding was the event of the decade, if not the century, and that she had better behave herself.

She forced a smile for the cameras as the choir began to sing "We Two Shall Be Reunited," slow and solemn, but punctuated by bright notes of mirth. The traditional wedding song, it was about a girl marrying her sweetheart who had just returned from war.

Turning to the wide-open doors of the Church,

Aveline watched her mother, in a halo of afternoon sun, walk down the aisle on Alfred's arm. Aveline drew a breath; she'd never seen her mother look more beautiful. Allyn wore a wedding gown of ivory silk, a veil of fine gauze over her face. Her dark hair was done up in elaborate twists and braids, decorated with tiny white flowers and pearls.

Traditionally, a bride wore her hair in a long braid, which a Cutter would snip just below the nape of her neck after she'd taken her marriage vows. Aveline had seen photographs of Allyn from her wedding to Kit Llewellyn: with a braid as she walked down the aisle, and afterwards, at the reception, with chin-length hair. But this time, she had chosen not to have a Cutter at her ceremony.

Simon had disapproved. "I suppose you're going to go around looking like an unmarried woman?"

"This is my second marriage," she'd replied. "I can do as I please."

This gave Aveline hope that when her own wedding day arrived, she would not have to have her own hair cut. But that was a long way away, and her hair under the wig was still only half an inch long.

She looked over at Jem standing on the other side of the altar. He wore a black tuxedo with his Monnag pin on his lapel and Allyn's sigil ring resting just below his bowtie. He must have been nervous in front of all these cameras. She tried to catch his eye, to let him know that everything was going to be okay, but he didn't look in her direction; he was too focused on his bride.

The pianist played a few solemn notes, signaling to the guests, who had been standing for the arrival of the bride, to take their seats. The Fleurs sat to the right of the altar and the Caslons to the left, their large family filling nearly all the pews. Aveline took the ring box from her pocket, which the seamstress had thoughtfully sewn into her dress for this purpose.

When Allyn and Alfred reached the altar, he lifted her veil from her face, as was customary for the father of the bride. The priest then solemnly recited the marriage rites. Aveline saw that there was not a single dry eye on the Caslon side. Even she herself had begun to cry. She wanted always to remember her mother like this, ebullient, seeming to float a few inches off the ground.

At the appointed time, Aveline walked over to the couple and stood before them. She opened the box to reveal the rings. She handed the larger one to her mother and the smaller to Jem, who slid them onto one another's fingers. While exchanging the rings, they promised to love and honor and obey one another until death do them part.

"By the power vested in me by the Province of Illyria-Novo Templar, by the State of Alterra, and by our Lord God of the Monnag, I now pronounce you husband and wife," said the priest. "You may kiss."

Jem leaned in to kiss her softly and chastely. She returned the kiss with a passion that seemed to surprise them both. Aveline saw that it was a tongue kiss and felt her face flush. Both sides of the family rose to their feet amid claps and cheers.

Aveline's cousin Lily leaped up and followed the couple down the aisle, scattering tulip and rose petals from a pink wicker basket. Lily's brother S.J. reached into the black velvet pouch he was carrying and began throwing rice, not understanding that it was too soon; he was supposed to wait until the couple had left the Church. Lilia, mortified, jumped into the aisle and snatched up the little boy.

But Allyn laughed, telling her nephew to throw as much rice as he wanted. Jem then lifted Allyn into his arms, gathering up her beaded train, which weighed more than she did, and carried her out of the Church and into the bright spring sun.

Chapter 10

Nothing was different after the wedding, and yet everything was.

That summer, Jem officially moved into the Great House, carrying with him only a couple of small boxes of belongings that he unpacked with care in Allyn's room. Allyn was shocked to see how few clothes he had, and how shabby they were. She had the village tailor take his measurements so that a new set of garments could be made for him of the finest fabrics. The cobbler also came to fit him for new shoes to be made of the softest leather, and the jeweler came to design him a watch of gold and diamonds.

Aveline often saw him in his fancy new suits walking aimlessly through the halls of the House, gaping at the paintings and statues and furniture, just like his little nieces and nephews on the day of the wedding. As if someone would pinch him and tell him it was all a dream and he'd have to go back to his family's farm in Ede's River.

It took him some time to adjust to the rhythm of life at the House, the formalities and the servants forever coming and going, bringing meals, running baths, cleaning, collecting laundry. He resisted being waited on hand and foot, trying to do as much as he could for himself. And when he did allow the maids and butlers to bring him tea or take his clothes to be laundered, he thanked them incessantly. Allyn broke him of that habit.

"Why can't you still work with the horses?" said Aveline.

He sighed. "I wish I could, Miss Aveline, but I don't think your mother or grandfather would approve."

"Why not?"

"I think it wouldn't really be proper for me to still be acting like a servant on your family's Estate."

"This is your Estate now, too," said Aveline, "and you should be able to do as you please. You love horses, Jem. You can't give them up."

But he just shrugged in reply. Now that he was no longer at the stables, there was little for him to do besides go to district Party meetings. Aveline observed him, in his vast swathes of free time, sitting in Allyn's study sipping her brandy and thumbing through her old history books, looking for the pictures.

Eventually, he grew bored of her library and instead began watching television in the parlor. Lying on the sofa, he indulged himself in all his favorite foods; Aveline once saw him eat half a chocolate cake in one sitting. She began to grow concerned with how unhappy and despondent he seemed.

One autumn afternoon, weary from a long day at school, she decided to join him in the parlor. His eyes were glassy, affixed to the news highlights on Channel 1. She sat next to him on the sofa and ripped her itchy wig off her head and tossed it onto the floor. She liked that she could be completely herself around him and he wouldn't judge her.

"Can I have some?" she said, gesturing to the bowl of popcorn beside him.

"Sure." He slid the bowl across the sofa to her.

Greedily, she reached in and scooped up a handful of buttery popcorn and shoved it into her mouth. She looked up at the television, which showed a clip of Air Command planes taking off into a clear sky, leaving cottony contrails in their wake.

"Can you believe we're at war?" she said.

Jem shook his head. War had recently broken out between the countries of Brixia to the west and Uria to the north. No one knew exactly why they had gone to war, only that Alterra was supporting Brixia, sending troops and supplies. Which meant that, on the home front, Alterra had to tighten its purse strings.

While rations were reduced for the lower class, nothing changed for the Fleurs and their wealthy peers. Worried for Bruno and his parents, Aveline tried to give him cartons of good food—cow's milk and real butter and fresh vegetables—to take home. But he kept refusing, too proud to take her handouts.

When Allyn came home that evening from the Lightministry, she found her husband and daughter glued to the television. With an exasperated sigh, she marched over to the window and threw open the drapes. Aveline and Jem held up their hands to shield their eyes from the sudden blinding light of the setting sun.

"Really, Jem?" Allyn glared at him. She snapped up her left wrist and looked at her watch. "A quarter to six in the evening and you're still not dressed? What sort of example are you setting for my daughter?"

Aveline noticed that she said *my*, not *our*.

"I'm sorry." He looked down at his black silk pajamas that bore the Fleur sigil on the left pocket. "I just feel so…useless lately."

"Then why don't you apply for a job? You're a member of the Party now. You'd be eligible for virtually any job in the civil service."

"Like what?"

She stood with her hands on her hips. "I could get you a job at the Lightministry. Reviewing film studio contracts. Answering correspondence."

He ran his hands through his disheveled hair. "I don't know. I'd rather not sit in an office doing paperwork all day. I want to help people. Like the people in Brixia. It's awful what they're going through with the war and all."

Allyn let her arms fall to her sides and went to sit beside him on the sofa, taking his hands in hers. "Have you considered joining the Armed Forces?"

He blinked. "Me? I've never shot a gun before. Goodness, I've never even *held* a gun before. I would have no idea what to do in a war."

"Well, that's all right, my love." She chuckled softly. "No man comes out of the womb knowing these things. They'll teach you."

"I don't know if I'm brave enough."

"Kit didn't think he was brave enough, either. He was just like you, Jem. He didn't know how to shoot a gun or fly a plane when he joined the Air Command. But when the last war started, he knew he couldn't just sit by idly and wait for the Ebrians to ransack Alterra and slit the throats of his fellow citizens. So he did what he knew was right and took up arms for the country he loved. It was because of men like Kit that we won the Ebrian War. That we can enjoy peace and freedom. That we can sleep at night without worrying about the barbarians at the gate."

Aveline frowned. It sounded like she was giving a speech at a rally, or before the People's Assembly.

What about us? Aveline wanted to say. *My dad may have died a hero, but was it worth it to leave us behind? To leave you without a husband and me without a father?*

"I'm not sure, Allyn," he said. "I'll have to think about it. I know you're right, though. I can't sit here all day long and watch women and children die on Channel 1. I have to do something. I took the Sacred Oath when I joined the Party, right? I promised that I would be willing at any moment to lay down my life for the Supreme Leader, for the State of Alterra, and for my God."

Don't do it, Jem, Aveline wanted to tell him. *I've already lost one father. I can't bear to lose another.*

****

Aveline was surprised that nothing had happened to Cynthia and Quintana yet. Months ago, before the wedding, her mother had promised to punish them for cutting off her braid—well, perhaps not quite *punish*, but at least teach them a lesson. Still, they continued walking freely through the halls of Belfort Academy, harassing Aveline about her "dragon spikes" that she kept hidden under her blonde wig. She was frustrated with how slowly her hair seemed to be growing; it barely even covered the tops of her ears.

Then, one day, the bullies failed to show up for school. Aveline didn't see them anywhere. They were not in class or in the cafeteria or in the schoolyard, where they usually stood off to the side with the other popular girls, ranking the boys according to their football skills.

Maybe they got expelled.

It would serve them right for what they'd done to her. She had a twisted little fantasy that Quintana's dad suddenly returned from wherever he'd been all these months, and learned that his precious baby had been expelled, and was so upset that he sent her to boarding school in the faraway Province of Corinthia. Aveline felt guilty at the thought, but it made her chuckle a little to herself. She couldn't wait to tell Bruno.

But she never got the chance. When she passed him in the hallway, he wore a look of absolute terror as he pressed a small, folded note into her palm.

"Bruno—"

"Can't talk now," he said, and continued walking.

Her stomach plummeted as it had on the day he'd given her the scrap of Sandor Hayes's article. Quickly, before her next class, she ducked into the girls' bathroom and locked herself in a stall and read the note:

Help! Something awful happened! Meet me in the usual spot after school.

As soon as she read it, she tore it up and flushed it down the toilet. Was he in trouble with Mother Josephine? She couldn't imagine what he'd done wrong; he was one of the best students in their grade. It must have been something else. With a shudder, she wondered if it had something to do with Sandor's article. Did the Stam know he'd seen it? And if they did, they knew that *she* had seen it, too.

She couldn't focus on anything else the rest of the day. All she could do was think of the danger he might be in—and that she might be in, as well. Whenever she tried to turn her attention to something else, like the great oak at the center of the schoolyard that she could see through the classroom window, Bruno's words inevitably resurfaced in her mind.

After school, she met him in the courtyard by the statue of the Leader. She started to ask him what was wrong when he interrupted her. "Can we talk back at your house?"

"Okay."

Elton picked them up in a limousine, and they made awkward small talk as they rode back to the Estate. She knew she was talking too fast and too excitedly about their latest lesson in Alterran History. From time to time, she glanced nervously at the driver, hoping he wasn't picking up on the fact that something was amiss.

But she could never hide anything from her old friend Elton. "Everything okay back there, kids?" he asked.

She faked a laugh, which came out almost like a whinny. "Everything's great!"

"If it's those troublemakers again, I'll—"

"Don't worry, Elton. It's not them."

Not this time, at least. I don't even know where they are!

As soon as the car pulled up in front of the House, the two friends were careful not to run up the steps; that would have been suspicious.

"Let's go out back," whispered Bruno.

Leaving their backpacks in the parlor, they exited onto the pool deck and walked down the marble steps and onto the lawn. From there, Bruno took off running across the meadow.

"Come on!" he said.

"Where are we going?"

"Wildweir."

Wildweir. The glade that held so many of Aveline's happy childhood memories.

"Bruno, slow down!" She held her wig so it wouldn't fly off as she ran. Her lungs burned, and she felt a stitch forming in her left side. "I know…you have something important to say… but…why did we have to come all the way out here?"

"It's the only place that's safe!"

He kept running and she did her best to keep up. Once they were well into the glade, he stopped and sat down by the creek. She was so winded that she practically collapsed on the bank. After she'd taken off her itchy wig and caught her breath, she looked around. They were all alone. The only sound was the rush of water over rocks and the occasional birdcall through the trees.

"The Stam arrested my mom," he said.

Her heart jolted. "What?"

"They pounded on the door in middle of the night, and my dad answered it and asked them what they wanted. They said they had an arrest warrant for my mom. My dad tried to stop them from coming in, but they pushed him away and went into the bedroom and grabbed my mom out of bed and put her in handcuffs and dragged her out of the house." His voice quavered as tears began to fall down his cheeks.

"Oh, Bruno…" She reached out to him, didn't quite touch his arm. "Why did they arrest her?"

"I have no idea!"

"They can't just arrest someone for no reason."

Edwena Page was the most loyal person Aveline knew. She went to all the rallies and never missed a single Daily Veneration. Nobody loved the Leader more than she did. It just didn't make sense.

"They must've had something on her," he said.

"Like what?"

"They must've caught her doing something that they thought was against the Party. I didn't tell you this before because I didn't want to scare you, but the Stam has been spying on us this whole time."

"What do you mean, *spying* on you?"

"Remember that hole in the wall by the TV in my living room?"

"Yeah." It had been a long time, but she still remembered that hole with multicolored wires sticking out of it.

"And remember how your mom told Colonel Zabel to send over one of his men to fix it?"

"Uh-huh."

"Well, I kept thinking how weird that was. Like, isn't that something for the Ministry of Energy?"

"I thought so, too. Did the Stam ever come to fix it?"

"Yeah. When I came home from school the next day, it was all fixed up, with a new plate and everything." He brushed a lock of honey-brown hair from his eyes. "A couple days later, there was a bunch of guys doing work around the building. They had tall ladders and these funny-looking poles with metal rings on the end of them. They told us they were replacing electrical wires that the mice had chewed through. But that sounded like a lie. Those guys were sent by the Stam. Everybody knows the Stam's in charge of surveillance. I realized that the whole building was bugged. Every apartment. Even ours. They've been spying on us through that outlet!"

Aveline could hardly believe what she was hearing. "But…but it's against the law for the Stam to bug people's homes."

"Ha! The Stam doesn't obey the law. If they did, they wouldn't be taking innocent people like my mom. I think they took Quintana's dad, too."

"Really?" she squeaked.

"How else do you explain that he just vanished into thin air?"

"I don't know."

"I've been hearing things, Avie. Bad things." His eyes reflected her own fear back at her. "The uncle of a guy in my building got taken last week, and he lives in Galatia. So they're not just taking people in Illyria but from other provinces, too. They're even taking kids now. You know Milton from school?"

"*Milton* got taken? But I just saw him—"

"No, not Milton. His cousin a couple districts away, in Shem Sherrion. He was thirteen. Nobody knew what he did to make the Party mad."

A dark thought occurred to her. "Do you think they took Cynthia and Quintana, too?" While she wanted to see the bullies squirm, she certainly didn't want them arrested by the Stam.

"I thought of that when they didn't show up at school today," he said.

"Where do you think they're taking them?"

"The same place they took Sandor Hayes—"

"Rjellsfall," she said at the same moment he said it. *The Rjellsfall Institute for Mental Hygiene*. "I knew something wasn't right with Sandor when I saw him on TV," she continued. "He seemed…off. It was the look in his eyes. Like there was nothing *there* anymore. You think they tortured him?"

"Maybe. They definitely did something to him." He tugged at the grass on the creek bank, pulling up some dirt with it. "I think they also took this guy my dad works with at the factory in Whitecross and sent him up where Sandor was. I knew the guy a little bit. He was a real animal lover. The type of person who'd see a sick cat in the street and take it home with him and nurse it back to health."

"What happened to him?"

"Well, one day, he just disappeared. Didn't show up to work. Nobody knew where he went. A few weeks later, he was back. My dad and I were getting our rations in the City Center when we saw him talking to a lady outside the tavern. As we were walking by, a bird came flying out of nowhere and smacked into the front window of the tavern and fell on the sidewalk. It was so sad. This little bird kept trying to get back up, but I think one of its wings was broken. Anyway, the guy just looked at it for half a second and walked away."

The hairs on the back of her neck stood on end.

"Aveline," he said, "I don't think you're safe here anymore."

She turned to him. "Why not?"

"Because your mom is involved in this. And your uncle. If they find out that you know what's going on, you could be in danger."

Her chest tightened. "Why do you think my mom's involved? Because she talked a lot about reeducation on TV during Sandor's trial?"

"Yeah."

"Well, maybe she doesn't know what it really is, or

107

how bad it is."

His eyes went wide. "Wake up, Aveline! Your mom definitely knows what reeducation is. She's probably the one who thought it up in the first place."

"No—"

"She and your uncle are using the Stam to arrest people and send them up to Rjellsfall. I know they're your family, but what they're doing is just plain evil."

His words cut deeply. But she couldn't deny that there was some truth to them. She remembered Sandor's article. *The Fleurs are sociopaths, demonstrating a callous disregard for people's basic human rights.*

"I don't know what to do." Her throat was tight with the effort of holding back tears. "Maybe I ought to say something to Grandfather."

"No way!" said Bruno. "You can't breathe a word of this to him. What if he's in on it?"

She couldn't fathom the idea that her grandfather— the Leader of Alterra—was in on it. But it terrified her nonetheless.

"W-what about Jem?" she said.

"What about him? I thought he already left."

It was true. About a week ago, he'd enlisted in the Army and was sent to a base in an undisclosed location. She knew that after completing basic training, he'd be given a rifle and sent to the front lines in Brixia.

"I just thought there might be something he could do," she said lifelessly.

"Like what? Ask the general of the Army to make the Stam stop arresting people?"

She took a deep breath. He was right. There was absolutely nothing Jem could do to help them. He couldn't even stand up to Allyn and tell her that he didn't want to go off to war.

"My dad and I are leaving Calador tomorrow," said Bruno.

She looked at him, aghast. "Where are you going?"

"To the Great Central Forest. My dad heard there's a Resistance camp there, and they're building an army to take down Rjellsfall and free everybody in it. My dad and I are going to join them. I want you to come with us."

"Me? You want *me* to join the Resistance with you?" He nodded. "But I'm the Lightminister's daughter." If the situation weren't so dire, she might have laughed. "How are we even going to get past the Sentries at the district wall?"

Bruno began speaking excitedly. "Meet me tomorrow at sunrise in front of my building. Tell Elton you have an early school thing, but first you have to pick up a book you forgot at my place. He'll drop you off and then we'll sneak on the bus with my dad and go to the factory in Whitecross. The bus driver is good friends with my dad and will let us hide under the seats. The bus will go over the bridge and pass through the checkpoint at the wall. That's how we get out of the Federal District."

"I don't know, Bruno." Like him, she began nervously plucking at the grass, digging into the dirt with her fingernails. "This is all happening so quickly. So many things could go wrong."

"I know. But, listen, we have to do something fast or my mom'll end up like Sandor."

"Bruno, I really want to help you, but I just don't know if I can do what you're asking me."

"What do you mean?"

"Run away. Leave everything behind. What about my family? I mean, what will my mother and everyone think when I go off to school tomorrow and never come home? Don't you think it would be kind of suspicious that the Lightminister's daughter has just disappeared?"

"Don't you think it would be worse for you if you stayed?"

"How?"

"You know too much now. You'll be a target for Simon or the Stam. Or both."

"You don't think he would actually…" She couldn't bring herself to say it out loud.

His eyes started to fill with tears again. "Turn you into a robot? In a second. That's the kind of person he is. Don't you see it yet?" She hung her head. "Please, Aveline. You have to come with us. I don't want to lose my best friend."

"Don't cry, Bruno." Then, gathering all the strength she could muster, she whispered, "Okay. I'll be there tomorrow morning."

Chapter 11

As she put her wig back on, Aveline looked out at the creek, at the clear water tracing delicate sine curves around the rocks. She glanced up at the long, fraying rope tied to a tree limb. Just this past summer, she and Bruno had swung from this rope and shrieked with delight as they plummeted into the deepest part of the creek. She remembered the sensation of water closing over her head. Of plunging down through striations of warm, then cool, then cold, like glassy bands on igneous rock, until she hit the bottom. Velvety mud under the soles of her feet.

What if this is the last time I see Wildweir?

Silently, the friends walked out of the glade and across the meadow and back to the House. Bruno climbed into one of the family's limousines to return home.

"See you tomorrow," he said as casually as if they were just going to meet in the school courtyard by the statue of Alfred Fleur.

She nodded and waved goodbye, her throat thick with tears that she wouldn't allow to fall.

After he left, she went to the pool deck and looked across her family's vast property. Crystalline music wafted from the piano in the Great Room; her aunt Lilia must have been playing. The smell of honeysuckle was heavy on the air. Hawk moths clustered at the blossoms, their wings flitting as rapidly as hummingbirds'.

Aveline had thought she'd spend her whole life here. Even when it came time for her to marry, her husband would have to move to the Estate because she, as a Fleur, would be of higher rank. She could scarcely believe that tomorrow morning she would have to leave. Leave *forever*. Each thing she saw—the honeysuckle, the hawk moths, the pool—suddenly took on new significance because it was the last time she would see it. From now on, all her childhood memories would be sealed off like a ship in a bottle.

She still struggled to process what Bruno had told her about the Stam arresting his mother, and the fact that they'd bugged his entire building.

What could they have on Mrs. Page? What could she possibly have done that was disloyal to the Party?

Because she couldn't fathom an answer to that question, she began to wonder how she and Bruno and his father were actually going to escape the Province of Illyria. Sure, they could get past the district wall on a bus, but how would they get out of the District of Whitecross where Mr. Page worked? Take another bus? A train? Would they have to walk?

She had seen the Great Central Forest on a map, and it looked far from Calador. Hundreds of miles. Thousands, maybe. Was it even possible to make the journey on foot? She had heard legends about monsters in the Forest. Monsters that snacked on human bodies, cracked bones with their teeth. Of course, she knew these were only stories designed to scare little kids, but she also knew that every horror story had a kernel of truth to it. There had to be some kind of danger awaiting them in the Forest—but what kind of danger, she couldn't imagine. And what if the Resistance didn't have a camp there? What if it was just a rumor? How could a single adult and two kids take down Rjellsfall all by themselves? She prayed that Mr. Page had a plan. A good one.

When she heard the Monnag clock in the parlor chime six, Aveline went back inside to join her family at the table. It was warm in the dining room, yet she found herself shivering, the sweat under the arms of her uniform shirt having turned ice-cold.

Pulling her sleeves down over her hands, she realized that she had been so absorbed in thought on the pool deck that she hadn't even gone upstairs to change into formal attire for dinner. Her grandfather gave her a sidelong glance but didn't say anything; for that, she was grateful.

Aveline took a seat to her mother's right, sat up as straight as possible. Usually, she ate everything the footmen served her, leaving not so much as a crumb on her plate. But tonight, she scarcely touched her chicken breast and rice, her diet dinner. Her hands trembled so much that she didn't even trust herself to reach for her water glass. She wished Jem were there. Just one look from him, from his kind dark eyes, would have calmed her.

Instead, she looked to her mother for a gesture of comfort—a smile, a nod, anything. But Allyn wasn't paying attention to her. She was talking to Alfred about their troops' advances in the Brixian War, her gestures expansive, almost cavalier. She leaned back in her chair, holding a glass of red wine. Aveline noticed she hadn't touched her steak, having since dropped the charade of pretending to eat at dinner. And yet she appeared to be thriving. She was a cactus while the rest of them were ferns and impatiens that needed water and nutrients to grow.

Aveline looked to her uncle, still in his Party uniform with medals of valor pinned all over it, and finally to her grandfather at the head of the table. She did not want to believe that her family was responsible for sending her best friend's mother to Rjellsfall. Did not want to believe that they could invent reasons to send innocent people to be tortured. To be turned into human robots like Sandor Hayes.

As soon as dinner was over and she was making her way to the staircase to go up to her room, she felt a hand on her shoulder. Simon's. She tried to shrug it off but found that she couldn't; he had her in an iron grip. For a small man, he had very strong hands.

"Let's talk in my study, shall we." A command, not a question.

"Yes, Uncle Simon."

Again, she found herself in his handsome yet cluttered office. He closed the door behind them.

"Sit," he said, as if to a dog.

Trembling, she lowered herself into one of the leather chairs in front of his desk. Her uncle had the air of a man alone. A man with all the time in the world. She watched him stride across the room to his liquor cart, where he used a pair of silver tongs to lift a few ice cubes from a small chest and drop them into a crystal tumbler. The ice crackled as he poured amber-colored grain-spirit over it. She caught a whiff, smoky as a forest fire.

Settling into his chair, Simon lifted his feet up onto

the desk. His black boots looked new, spit-shined by his valet, the bottoms so clean they must have been wiped. He took a sip of his drink. The more casual he acted, the more afraid she became.

What is he thinking? What does he know? Her palms prickled with sweat.

"So," he said finally, "your little friend thinks your mother and I are spiriting people away." His tone was more amused than angry.

She swallowed over a dry throat. "I…I don't know what you're talking about."

"Oh, I think you do."

He lifted his feet and set them down on the floor, then pressed play on the reel-to-reel portable tape recorder on a corner of his desk. She heard her own voice. Then Bruno's. The conversation they'd had just a couple of hours earlier in the glade.

"How—" she began.

In her shock, she couldn't finish the question. She could hear the wind blowing and the rustling of leaves on the tape, meaning that the Stam had hidden listening devices in the trees. Bruno was wrong; they were not safe in Wildweir. They were not safe anywhere. The Stam had every nook and cranny of Calador bugged, even the Fleurs' own property.

Simon stopped the tape, lit a cigarette with his silver lighter. Dark clouds swirled in the Mark of Yrgess ring he wore on his pinky.

After she'd been silent a few moments, he said, "Well, Aveline? What do you have to say for yourself?"

She slid to the edge of her chair, clasping her hands, pleading with him. As if she were no longer in control of her body. "Please, Uncle Simon, tell me it's not true."

He tilted up his chin and exhaled a smoke ring into the air above them. "What's not true?"

"You don't believe in reeducation, do you? I once heard you say that traitors ought to be shot...right?"

He smiled. "I used to believe that, yes. But your mother has made a convert of me. I saw how beautifully the treatment worked on Sandor Hayes. Allyn proved to me that instead of killing a traitor, it's possible to reform him from the inside out. To make a new man out of him, as it were."

"But what about Bruno's mom? And—and Quintana's dad? They're not traitors. They're innocent people!"

"What gives you the impression that they're innocent? Both Leopold Bailey and Edwena Page were involved with the publication of Hayes's article."

She gasped.

"While the rest of the country has long moved past the Hayes Affair, I have not. I may not be a man of sundry talents, but I do have a long memory. Recall how your grandfather asked me whether I had arrested the printer, the publisher, and so forth? And how I promised him that I would track down every last one and bring them to justice? Well, a Fleur never breaks a promise. I have brought them to justice—using Sandor Hayes himself! My God, it was brilliant! The poor fool led us right to Bailey. He was the one who put up the money to publish the paper."

Stunned into silence, Aveline shrank back in her chair.

He continued, "As for the Page woman, she was an editor of the paper. We weren't on to her yet, but

Hayes's arrest appears to have triggered her paranoia. And with good reason—every unit in that building is bugged. When she discovered the listening device in the outlet in the living room, she tore the box out of the wall and mangled the wires. Clever little minx."

That hole by the TV, thought Aveline. *That was Mrs. Page.*

"As soon as we stopped picking up audio from her living room," he said, "we knew she had found the device. It was no coincidence that your mother visited the Pages' apartment. Naturally, Allyn went under the guise of picking you up for the rally. But she wanted to see the damage for herself."

Aveline remembered that day last autumn. Allyn and Colonel Zabel had stopped by the apartment looking for her. Edwena had not wanted them to come in and see the outlet, but when Allyn did, Edwena lied and said that her husband must have broken it while moving the television set.

Simon tapped the end of his cigarette against the ashtray. "Well, we fixed that right up. Then we started making some improvements to our listening devices around the building. We hoped it would serve as a warning. Not for her, apparently. We used Hayes to sniff her out like a bloodhound. He led us to the basement of the Veil and Dagger where she was meeting with her Resistance pals. How apropos."

"But she was so loyal—"

"Everyone's loyal until they're not. I have to say, though, her shrine to the Leader was really a nice touch." He chuckled, smoke coming out of his mouth in small bursts.

Aveline didn't know where she found the courage,

but she looked him in the eye and said, "Uncle Simon, where is she?"

"On her way to the Institute," he said as he stubbed out his cigarette in the overfull ashtray. He held up his left wrist in a show of looking at his watch. "Well, what do you know? She ought to be arriving right about now."

Aveline nearly jumped to her feet. "But she's entitled to a fair trial! That's the law!"

"What makes you so certain she didn't have a fair trial?"

"Because…trials take a long time. Like weeks. And she just got sent up there yesterday or today. So she mustn't have had a trial at all."

"Tell me, Miss Aveline, Esquire." He smirked. "Where in the law is it written that a trial must last for weeks?"

She wracked her brain. *Didn't we learn this in Alterran History? Isn't it somewhere in the Constitution? Which Article?*

"By all means, take your time," he said dryly.

"I-I'm not sure."

"There is no such requirement. A trial need not be a three-month-long public spectacle like Sandor Hayes's. After her arrest, the Page woman was brought before a district magistrate who heard the case and found her guilty and sentenced her all in the same day."

"That's not fair! If the magistrate did it all so fast, Mrs. Page couldn't have had a chance to prove her innocence."

"Sure she did. And your little friend—what's his name again?—will have the same opportunity."

"Bruno?"

"Ah, yes." He stretched out his fingers before him, his Mark of Yrgess so dark it was nearly black, with only flecks of yellow visible within the stone. "How could I have forgotten that name? One of my men has a little chow he calls Bruno."

She brushed off the insult. "W-what do you mean Bruno will have the same opportunity? To do what?"

"To prove his innocence, of course. Let's hope he's better at it than the mother. Stam officers are headed to his apartment as we speak."

At those words, she burst into tears. "Please, Uncle Simon, don't hurt him! Bruno didn't do anything wrong!"

"Oh, really? Conspiring to join the Resistance doesn't qualify as doing something wrong?"

"He…" She paused, catching her breath. "He's scared about what might happen to Mrs. Page. That's why he's leaving for Rjellsfall. He just needs to see her and make sure she's okay."

"I remember it a bit differently." He tapped the recorder. "Shall I play back the tape to refresh your recollection?"

"Please, Uncle Simon." She was blubbering now, and she knew it and couldn't stop herself. "You're a good person. I know you are. You have the power to stop the Stam. You have the power to let Mrs. Page out of Rjellsfall. I know you wouldn't want to see anyone suffer."

"No one is suffering, Aveline. These people are being *reformed*. We are acting in their best interest." He tapped the badges pinned to his uniform jacket, making them clatter. "The Stam is simply doing its job by bringing traitors to justice. The law is the law. It must be applied fairly and evenly to all."

"Nothing about this is fair or even. The *Stam* doesn't even follow the law!"

"So high and mighty, are we? You speak like someone who believes herself beyond reproach."

She shook her head. "I did nothing wrong."

"Is that so?" Again, he tapped the recorder. Harder this time. "I have proof right here that you also conspired to join the Resistance." He added, as though dropping a footnote, "And I know you read Hayes's article. As I'm sure you are aware, given your superlative knowledge of the law, possessing contraband is high treason."

"How could you possibly know that?"

"Our eyes and ears are everywhere." His thin lips curled into a smile.

He has spies at school! Who could it have been? One of the other kids playing football in the yard? Brother Elias? Or was it someone closer to home, like Jossie?

"I didn't believe a word of that article, I swear," she said. "It was all rubbish, so I burned it in the fireplace."

"Don't get cute with me. Playing dumb is not going to work anymore. You're fourteen, Aveline; you're no longer a child." He threw back the rest of his drink, cracking an ice cube with his molars. "Now get out of my sight. I will think on what to do with you."

Chapter 12

Aveline lay in bed watching the shadows play across the ceiling. There was no way she was going to fall asleep after everything that had happened that day. But she forced herself to close her eyes and try to rest; she had no idea what the morning would bring. Faintly, from Allyn's room down the hall, she could hear the strains of Milo Fresenius's string quartets. That beautiful music with the power to transport her to a different world.

Mother is up late.

More than anything, she wanted to knock on her mother's door, sit on the end of the bed, pour her heart out the way she used to when she was a little girl. But she couldn't. Allyn had invented reeducation. It was she who had changed Simon's mind about how traitors should be handled. And it was she who had gone to the Pages' apartment after Edwena had destroyed the listening device. Allyn and Simon were, without a doubt, working together.

Aveline's mind spun. She felt as though she were trapped in her grandmother Marie's hedge maze, a dead end in every direction. She couldn't talk to her mother or grandfather. She couldn't talk to any of the household staff, either. No one could be trusted. Not even Jossie.

The music faded away. She opened her eyes and

sat up, hugging her knees to her chest.

Why did Uncle Simon tell me all of that tonight? she wondered. *Why would he reveal all his secrets to me? State secrets?*

There could be only two reasons why he would have spoken to her so openly. The first was that he knew she had nobody to tell, so he could be as candid as he wanted.

The second reason was much darker, and much more likely, knowing Simon—he was planning to send her to Rjellsfall. Once she was tortured or brainwashed, or whatever they did to people up there, it wouldn't matter what Simon had told her. She would be silenced forever. She shivered at the thought.

And there was a possible third reason. By letting her in on the secret, he was making her complicit. As a Fleur, she might be expected to help kidnap and "reeducate" people. A diabolical family business of sorts.

She wracked her brain trying to think of an escape, a way out of the hedge maze. Now that the Stam was going to arrest Bruno, and maybe also his father, Aveline no longer had a means of getting past the district wall. No way of even getting out of Calador. She could try to run away from school, but she knew that Simon would have the place surrounded by Stam officers on high alert.

The only way out—and it wasn't a great idea by any means—was to align herself with Quintana. She'd tell the bully that she was interested in helping find her father. Maybe they could sneak out of the district with Quintana's mother and brothers, hide on one of the Party's buses, get past the Sentries at the wall. From there, they would find their way to the Great Central Forest, to the Resistance camp.

But, with a sinking heart, she realized that Quintana was unlikely to come back to school anytime soon. There was no doubt that Quintana had been taken by the Stam and was either at Rjellsfall or on her way there. Cynthia, too.

It's just me. I'm all alone now.

****

When Jossie entered her room to wake her for school, Aveline was already up and dressed, applying a bit of rouge to her cheeks to make herself look more alive. She had not slept a wink.

"What's the matter, Miss Aveline?" The maid's brow was furrowed with concern.

Aveline shook her head. "It's nothing, Jossie. I'm just worried about my Language Arts exam today."

How had she learned to lie so fluently?

Jossie ruffled Aveline's short hair. "You're going to get an 'A,' Miss Aveline. I know how hard you studied."

"Thanks, Jossie." She lifted the blonde wig from the mannequin on her bureau and fitted her hair under it.

She hadn't actually studied at all. Then she caught herself—there wasn't any exam. Her next assignment in Language Arts was an essay on the plays of Florentine Elgar, the darling of Alterran theater, due at the beginning of next week.

If I make it to next week.

****

In the car on the way to school, Aveline's mind was still racing. How would she get all the way to the

Forest on her own? Bruno and his father would soon be gone. The bullies were gone, too. She considered hiding deep in the school basement, or even at the bottom of one of those dreaded dumpsters, until the final bell rang. Then she'd make a break for it.

But what if the Stam found her first? If she wasn't in class, one of the Sisters would call Allyn or Simon. It would be only a matter of time before the Stam located her hiding place. Those black-clad officers would turn over heaven and earth at Simon's command.

If I'm cornered by the Stam, maybe I can jump out a window. Once I'm in the schoolyard, I can take off running, hop the fence. The River Antoleme's not terribly far away. Maybe a boat will pick me up and I can hide in the cabin and get all the way to Whitecross.

She shook her head. She was not a cat. There was little chance that she could jump out a window and land on her feet without breaking a leg—or two. But perhaps it was better to end up at the City Hospital than at Rjellsfall.

Think, think. Come on.

As the car hit a bump in the road, Aveline felt queasy, her breakfast turning into a noxious stew in the pit of her stomach. Just thinking of the bowl of oatmeal she'd forced herself to eat made her gag.

She leaned her head against the cold window and watched the familiar scenery pass by. The Victory Bridge, built to commemorate the day when Alfred Fleur and his Six Hundred defeated King Reuel at Castle Rovamina. The enormous marble statues of her grandfather and great-grandfather, hands outstretched to one another, at the entrance to Armand Fleur Park. The tall buildings of the City Center that housed the ministries, windows alight with morning sun.

Along the entire side of one building was an advertisement featuring a young, sandy-haired soldier in gray Air Command uniform, Monnag insignia on his left breast, hand over his heart in the loyalty salute. The caption below read *I AM ALTERRA*.

Aveline couldn't help but think of Jem. She remembered how proud he'd been at his induction ceremony as he'd taken the Sacred Oath and Allyn had replaced his Aspirant ribbon with a Monnag pin and crushed the ribbon underfoot. But before he'd had time to enjoy his status as a new Party member, he'd enlisted in the Army and gone off to the front lines in Brixia. She missed him every day. Wondered if he was homesick and if he missed her, too. Prayed that he was safe and would come home soon.

With a sigh, she turned her attention to the sights beyond the window. Something was wrong. Instead of turning right on Heritage Way, the driver instead continued straight on the Avenue of the Acacias, which did not pass by Belfort Academy.

"Um, Elton?" she called. "I think we missed our turn."

She expected the driver to wink at her in the rearview mirror, as he always did, and tell her that his morning cup of coffee hadn't kicked in yet.

But he was silent.

"Elton, you've got to turn around! I'm going to be late for school! If my mother finds out, she'll have my head on a platter!"

In response, however, he pressed a button that drew a blackout shade across the glass partition between them.

"Hey! What are you doing?"

But that was not all. The safety locks clicked shut. She tugged at the handle of the door closest to her seat but couldn't open it. She slid to the other door. Exactly the same.

She scurried to the front of the passenger compartment, where she knelt on the seat and knocked on the partition.

"Elton!"

No answer. As she turned to the window to see where they were, and where they were headed, she found that she could not. All the windows, which were tinted to begin with, quickly turned opaque. How was that even possible from the press of a button?

Her stomach plummeted like an elevator in freefall. It was now so dark inside the compartment that she couldn't even see her own hand in front of her face. She felt around the door for the power window controls, but when she found the correct buttons and pressed them, the windows wouldn't budge.

With both fists, she banged again on the partition. "Elton, can you hear me? Please…stop the car! Let me out!"

When he didn't reply, she began to panic. Like a trapped animal, she pounded on the windows and doors, groped frantically around the compartment for something she could use to break the glass. From her backpack she dug out a heavy textbook and threw it against one of the windows, but it merely bounced off and tumbled to the floor.

Of course the glass won't break. These windows are bulletproof.

She even tried pulling down the backseat, hoping

she could crawl into the trunk and escape from there. But the heavy leather seat wouldn't budge. Her breathing quickened, and cold sweat dripped from under her arms and down her sides.

This is the punishment Uncle Simon was going to "think on" last night.

Surely Simon had bribed the driver. Or…maybe Elton was working for the Stam. Kindly old Elton, who would have punched the bullies in the nose if she'd asked him to. She never would have suspected him of being in the Stam's pocket. Then again, she wouldn't have suspected her uncle or her mother of disappearing people either.

Everyone's loyal until they're not. She had thought Simon was being melodramatic when he'd said that last night, but now his statement had a ring of truth to it.

She pressed her hand to the cold, black window. Without being able to see where they were going, she could only guess. To the Lawministry for her trial before the magistrate? But they had passed the ministries in the City Center fifteen or twenty minutes ago.

She wrapped her arms around her waist and began to sob. She was truly alone now.

Elton drove on. She could tell when the terrain changed by the sound of the tires and the vibrations through the chassis. Mostly, they were on roads, the great symmetrical avenues of Calador, but she knew they were passing over a bridge when she could hear the rush of water beneath them. Which bridge, she couldn't tell, as there were many that spanned the mighty Antoleme.

Once on the other side of the bridge, the car

traveled a little farther and came to a stop at the checkpoint at the wall, the engine idling. Her stomach lurched.

Please, please, open the door, she silently begged the Sentries. *Demand to perform an inspection.*

She didn't know what she'd do if they did. Try to run? Beg them to send her home? Demand to speak to her uncle immediately?

But no one checked the back of the limo. After all, this was a Party car—a Fleur family vehicle, no less—and she was sure that Elton would have some good reason for leaving the district that he would relay to the Sentries. Or Simon may already have phoned ahead to the checkpoint. Whatever the case, she couldn't hear Elton's conversation with the Sentries up front, if he was even having one at all. The glass partition, now covered by the blackout shade, may have been soundproof.

She decided to test her theory by banging on the partition and crying, "Help! Help!" to see if the Sentries could hear her. Then she banged on the windows. Even if the partition was soundproof, the windows and the rest of the cabin were not because she could hear noises through them—the tires over the road, the water under the bridge. She even kicked at the doors.

They've got to be able to hear that!

But it was futile. The Sentries ignored her. Elton kept driving.

She realized with a jolt of horror and fascination that she was about to leave the Federal District for the first time in her entire life. Since she was a little girl, she'd always wanted to see what lay outside the district wall.

Now that I got my wish, I can't see a thing outside the window. And I'm a prisoner in my own family's car!

All she wanted, irrationally, was her mother. She closed her eyes, and a memory came back to her of when she was five years old, playing a game of hide-and-seek with nine-year-old identical twin girls, daughters of one of the servants at the Estate. The twins told her to hide in a large black trunk that looked like a piece of luggage one might have brought aboard a steamship. As soon as she climbed inside, they slammed the lid shut and locked it. Feeling as though she'd been buried alive, Aveline screamed and banged on the lid until she fell unconscious. The next thing she knew, the trunk was open, and a pair of slender alabaster hands were lifting her from the cramped space. Her mother's hands.

But her mother wasn't going to save her now. In fact, Simon had probably told Allyn what he'd done, and Allyn was not going to make any move to stop him, to force Elton to turn the car around and bring her daughter back home. Allyn and Simon were on the same team.

She could sense by the sound of the tires, and the way the car had begun to bounce and lurch, that they were now on a rutted country road in the District of Whitecross. When she tried to picture a map of Alterra, she drew a blank; she could not recall the name of the district after Whitecross. Was it Unshin? Shem Sherrion? She wished she'd paid more attention in her geography class. She'd had no idea that one day this information could save her life.

The road transitioned from bumpy to smooth to bumpy again. She wondered why, in a country as rich as Alterra, all the roads would not be as well-maintained as those in Calador.

She began to grow cold and thirsty from all her crying and trembling, and a little bit hungry, too. There seemed to be no end to this drive. She desperately wanted to look out the window to see where they were, and what time of day it was, but not a single ray of sunlight passed through the blackened glass.

Removing her wig, she lay helplessly on the passenger seat, hiccupping from crying so hard. She did not know how much time passed, but it felt like hours.

Finally, the tires crunched over a gravelly surface. She bolted upright. Were they coming to a stop?

The crunching sound subsided as the car pulled into a drive. Or maybe it was a garage, because Aveline could hear the electric whine of a door closing, similar to the sound the garage doors made back home.

She shook her head, clearing her senses. While she couldn't recall the exact location of Frelimar on the map, she did remember one of her teachers, Sister Imelda, saying that it was a twelve-hour journey by car from Illyria to the country's northernmost province. So, she reasoned, they could not possibly be at Rjellsfall.

If we're not at Rjellsfall, where the heck are we?

She gasped as the car's safety locks clicked and released, and someone yanked open the back door. She screamed and slid as far back into the passenger compartment as she could when she saw, in dim greenish light, the face of a young woman staring back at her.

"Welcome, Miss Aveline," said the woman in dulcet tones. Aveline recognized the accent and speech pattern of Calador. This woman was upper-class. She wore a white Party uniform—Aveline had never seen one in that color—and a loyalty ribbon tied to the end of her long red braid.

"W-who are you?"

"Manánn Morrigan. I'm in charge of the Care Team. It's a pleasure to finally meet you." She extended her hand. "We've been waiting for you."

"I want to talk to my uncle! Now!"

Manánn signaled to someone outside Aveline's field of view. A heavily muscled man in his twenties, also in a white Party uniform, lunged into the car. Aveline dashed to the opposite end of the compartment—not that there was anywhere to go, but she wanted to get as far away from this brute as possible.

With lightning reflexes, he seized her by the ankles and dragged her out of the backseat. She kicked and screamed, trying to free herself. "I'm the Lightminister's daughter! You can't do this to me!"

But no one responded. As if they didn't hear her at all.

She was now lying on cold cement, the muscular man holding her arms above her head, and another white-uniformed Party officer holding her legs. Manánn crouched beside her, smiling. Behind the woman's head she could see Elton looking on with curiosity, wearing a smirk. That traitor. Aveline hated him.

From an inner pocket in her jacket Manánn produced a small plastic container about the size of a pencil box. Flipping open the cover, she lifted a syringe filled with a milky liquid.

"Get away from me!" Aveline spat up into the woman's face.

She expected Manánn to slap her across the cheek or even to punch her. But the young Party officer continued smiling, wiping the spittle away with the back of her free hand.

"You've come a long way from Calador, my dear," she said. "This will relax you."

Before Aveline could react, Manánn jabbed the needle into Aveline's upper right arm.

Almost immediately, she felt her muscles slacken. Her mind was still racing, but she found that she could no longer control her speech, the movements of her body. As her vision blurred, the faces around her—the red-haired woman, Elton, the moon-faced officer who held her feet—warped and blended together.

"Please—"

Her eyelids grew heavy, and she could no longer resist the overwhelming pull of sleep.

And then the world went black.

Chapter 13

Slowly, Aveline opened her eyes. A breeze, slightly cool and tasting of salt, brushed across her face. Pale bands of sunlight stretched across the ceiling. It must have been early in the morning. Dawn. In the distance, she could hear the hush of waves. Seagulls. So different from the twittering of budgies she was used to.

Turning her head to the right, she saw the source of the breeze: two high windows with white curtains billowing in. Below, an old-fashioned stone fireplace, much older than the ones at the Fleur Estate, with charred remains of logs inside.

As she blinked, other objects came into focus: a battered oak table, two large white wicker chairs, a rocking chair with peeling sky-blue paint. Bookshelves at the opposite end of the room extending to the ceiling, filled with old leather-bound books.

The breeze from the open windows was slightly chill, but she was warm under a white down comforter. She lay in a huge four-poster bed, much larger than the one in her own bedroom. Her head was propped up on pillows.

Turning to the left, she saw the door. It had an oblong brass doorknob that was lower than the ones at the Fleur Estate, a relic from a time when people weren't as tall as they were now. This room had an ancient feel to it. Of crumbling elegance.

Where am I?

She had to be somewhere near the sea. The cry of gulls, the hiss of surf beyond. The briny taste of the wind.

But where? There were only two provinces that bordered the Shinar Sea: Lystra, where Jem was from, and Belmarin.

Then she remembered.

The traitor Elton locking her in the limousine's passenger compartment. The long, terrifying ride in the dark. The white-clad officers holding her down on the cement floor of a garage.

Now, she had only one thought. *I've got to get out of here!*

Wherever "here" was.

Throwing back the comforter, she discovered that she no longer wore her school uniform. Someone had taken off her clothes and replaced them with a pair of white silk pajamas. What had they done with her shoes?

But no matter. She scanned the room for an exit. The door was probably locked, so she'd have to find another way out. Maybe there was a bathroom that led somewhere else. Maybe she could jump out of a window if this room wasn't too high up.

The thought intensified. *I've got to get out of here! Now!*

As she leaped out of bed, however, her vision went black and she collapsed on the hardwood floor. When she came to moments later and tried to lift her head, a sharp pain burst through her skull and stars appeared before her eyes. The sunlight streaming in the windows only made the pain worse. Her limbs felt so heavy that she could barely lift them. As if she'd lain in the wrong position all night and they'd fallen asleep.

Get up, Aveline, she chided herself.

But she couldn't move. She was stuck.

Just then, she heard a key turn in the lock. The creak of the old door opening. Her stomach clenched.

A young, red-haired woman in a white uniform entered the room and knelt beside her. For a moment, Aveline thought she might be Sister Soraya, her Mathematics teacher. Everyone always said that Soraya resembled an elf princess in the legends, with hair the color of wild strawberries.

But this was no Sister of Monnag. This was Manánn Morrigan, the Party official who'd stabbed her in the arm with a syringe last night.

"Misbehaving again, are we?" That tart upper-class accent.

"Stay away from me!"

The utterance caused Aveline's head to throb and her vision to blur.

"Get back into bed."

Aveline wanted to resist, to spit in this woman's face again and run away, but she lacked the strength. And Manánn's tone suggested grave consequences if she did not comply. Her uncle used the same tone when he was angry with her, and it always drove a stake of fear deep into her heart.

With great effort, Aveline peeled herself off the floor, holding her aching head. Manánn grasped her arm and helped her back into bed and pulled the comforter up to her chin. Tucking her in like she was a young child and not a girl of fourteen.

"Now, that's better," said Manánn.

The woman hoisted herself up and sat on the

mattress, so close that their legs were touching. Instinctively, Aveline jerked hers away just a fraction of an inch.

Now that she was lying down, her vision became a little clearer, and she looked up to the windows. These were not the leaded-glass casement windows she was used to from back home, on hinges that opened outward. Rather, these windows appeared to be the kind that slid back and forth on a track. Each stood open just a few inches. She would have to investigate whether they opened farther, and what was below, and whether she could jump out without breaking a leg.

With a single cold finger under her chin, Manánn turned Aveline's head to face her.

"I've been told you're a dreamer."

Is that a bad thing? And who would have told you that, anyway?

Smiling, the woman leaned in and passed her fingers over Aveline's forehead, brushing away a lock of frizzy blonde hair. Aveline was sure Manánn meant the touch to be maternal, but instead it felt menacing.

She studied Manánn's high cheekbones, slender nose, and thin lips—all markers of high-born ancestry. Allyn and Simon's faces bore those markers, as well. So did Aveline's, even if her features weren't quite as refined as theirs. Though no one from the upper class wanted to admit it, they were all descendants of the noblemen who'd ruled Alterra before the Revolution, the coup that had ousted the king.

"Where am I?" Aveline managed to choke out.

"Gilsevain Landing."

"Where's that?"

"Belmarin."

She had been right; she *was* in one of the seaside provinces. At least this wasn't Rjellsfall.

"Why am I here?"

"On orders from your uncle."

Aveline's heart skipped a beat. Maybe this wasn't Rjellsfall, but it had to be another institute for mental hygiene. How many were there? Was the Party building them all over the country?

She tried to sit up, but the pain in her skull forced her back into a prone position.

"I don't want to be reeducated!" she cried with all the energy she could muster. A wave of nausea broke over her.

"Don't be silly." Manánn chuckled. "This is a care home. We don't reeducate anyone here. You're going to receive treatment for your illness. Then, in a few weeks once you've recuperated, you'll be on your way back to Calador. It's as simple as that."

"Illness? But I'm not sick."

She shook her head. "Why, Miss Aveline, you have Frugheili's Syndrome."

"What is *that*?" It sounded made-up.

"It's a psychological disorder characterized by persistent, worsening delusions even when the patient is confronted with reality. It was named for the late Dr. Helmut Frugheili who discovered it. He also happens to be the founder of this care home."

"What do you mean, 'delusions'?"

"You seem to believe that your family is involved in a conspiracy to arrest Alterran citizens and send them to a faraway prison to brainwash them."

"That's not a delusion. It's true! Uncle Simon told me himself the other night that's what he's doing!"

With a singular, rapid motion—the type a magician might make when performing a sleight of hand—Manánn produced from her inner jacket pocket a handheld tape recorder. Aveline's stomach trembled. She had learned to be wary of tape recorders. The last time someone had used one, she'd ended up here.

The woman pressed play.

Please, Uncle Simon, tell me it's not true.

Aveline drew a breath. That was her own voice.

What's not true? said Simon.

You don't believe in reeducation, do you?

These people are being reformed, he said. *We are acting in their best interest.*

Uncle Simon, where is she?

On her way to the Institute. The Stam is simply doing its job by bringing traitors to justice. The law is the law. It must be applied fairly and evenly to all.

Please, Uncle Simon. You're a good person, I know you are. You have the power to stop the Stam. You have the power to let Mrs. Page out of Rjellsfall. I know you wouldn't want to see anyone suffer.

No one is suffering, Aveline.

Manánn stopped the tape recorder.

Aveline was stunned. The Stam had altered the tape, cut bits and pieces of the conversation and stitched them back together in the wrong order. To form the story that *they* wanted to tell. Conveniently, they'd omitted what Simon had said about reeducation working beautifully, that a traitor could be remade from the inside out without having to kill him. And about using Sandor Hayes to track down every last individual who'd played a role in the publication of his article in the underground newspaper. *The poor fool*, Simon had called him.

But this version of the tape made Simon seem like a reasonable man just trying to maintain law and order.

Manánn replaced the tape recorder in her pocket, patted it. She smiled slowly, showing a row of even, white teeth. She was as lovely as a fairy princess, but there was something twisted about her. Twisted like Simon. As if he'd schooled her in his interrogation techniques.

"The tape goes on for more than an hour," she said.

That's a lie, thought Aveline. *Simon and I talked for fifteen minutes, tops, before he sent me away so he could think on my punishment.*

"You insisted that he and your mother and the Stam are involved in an evil plot to turn people into robots. And that the Stam is using those robots as spies."

That's what he told me…well, sort of.

Manánn continued, "Clearly, there is no evil plot. We don't have the science or technology to turn a human being into a robot, even if we wanted to. What you are observing are the normal workings of the Alterran justice system. When the Stam has enough evidence that someone has committed a crime, they will arrest that individual in a peaceful manner. After a fair trial, if he is found guilty, he is sent to be reformed, not punished. Reeducation in Party ideals is one such way to reform a wrongdoer. But it's not by any means the only method. The Lawminister tried to explain that to you."

He said exactly none of that to me.

She went on, "But you wouldn't listen. You called him many foul names, which I shall not repeat. During this temper tantrum, you picked up a vase of flowers from his desk and threw it at his head. He ducked just in time, and it shattered against the wall."

Aveline almost wanted to laugh. *I don't use foul language. And there wasn't any vase of flowers in Simon's study. No living thing could survive in all that cigarette smoke!*

"Two members of the household staff escorted you out of the Lawminister's study and gave you a sleeping tablet and put you to bed. After you went to sleep, your uncle reached out to us because he didn't know how else to help you, to get you the treatment that you need to recover from this terrible syndrome. He told me that he is afraid of you…but, more than that, he is afraid *for* you."

Simon playing the victim. That's so like him to turn things around and point the finger at someone else. Me.

"No, that's not how it happened," said Aveline. "He said—"

Manánn interrupted, "This is part of your condition, that you don't listen to reason. You are absolutely resistant to it. But not to worry. We have the cure."

"Let me out of here!" Aveline's voice was little more than a croak.

A look of concern passed over the woman's face like a shadow. "You're tired. And very, very thirsty." She gestured to a full glass of water on the bedside table to Aveline's left.

As soon as she spied the glass, Aveline could think of nothing else except how to get that water into her body. That cold, clear, clean water. Like the kind from the creek in Wildweir.

Manánn lifted the glass to Aveline's lips and she took a sip. Swallowed. The water had an odd metallic aftertaste, as though an iodine tablet had been dissolved in it. But because she was so thirsty, she ignored the taste and downed the rest of the water, wishing she could have more.

Almost immediately, she began to feel sleepy. More than sleepy—exhausted. A weariness came over her entire body, all her muscles, the way she felt after running a dozen consecutive loops around the track at school. Her vision grew fuzzy around the edges.

Manánn brushed Aveline's cheek with the tips of her fingers. Aveline recoiled a bit from the coldness of that hand.

"Rest now, love," she said. "I'll check in on you later."

Chapter 14

At first, Aveline didn't know if she was dreaming. She was walking through Wildweir on a summer day. She held out her arms, the shadows of leaves dappling her pale skin.

This has to be a dream. I'm asleep in a bed in a strange place called Gilsevain Landing. With a creepy elf princess/Stam officer beside me.

As a child, Aveline had had lucid dreams. Not many, but enough that she would recognize another one when she had it. In those dreams she was able to do anything she wished—fly, turn somersaults in the air, travel back and forth through time.

Except now. While she knew she was dreaming, she had no sense of urgency. She could not simply turn around and walk out of Wildweir. Instead, she kept moving forward, through the trees. She could hear the babbling of the creek nearby, the call of blackbirds. It was as if she were watching herself, observing the scene, from somewhere just outside her body.

Soon, though, she lost all sense of the "watcher" and became one with her body, as in waking life. Walking a little farther, she came upon the caretaker's cottage, the House with Too Many Lamps as she and her mother used to call it. She walked up the two slate steps, stood on tiptoe, and peered through the window in the door. All dark. Not a single lamp burning now.

The sofa, the chair, the card table—all covered with sheets.

How curious. The same caretaker, Felix Grimaldi, had lived there for as long as she could remember. Where had he gone?

She tried the door and found it unlocked. Inside, she walked around the living room, ran her hand over the mantel, the green glass shade of a lamp. Lifting her fingers, she saw that they were thickly coated in dust as if the cottage had been abandoned for years.

"Felix?" she called.

No answer.

"Brigitte?" That was his wife.

Silence.

Wandering into the kitchen, she saw two people sitting at the table. Her mother and a large blond man in a gray Air Command uniform. With a chill, she recognized her father, Christopher Llewellyn Fleur.

That can't be. He's dead.

"Kit, this is your daughter, Aveline." Allyn gestured to her.

Kit looked no older than in his portrait on the wall in the Great Room. Her own features were reflected in his—the light-blue eyes, unlike the Fleurs' gray. The nose wide at the bridge. The flaxen hair.

Her mother looked the way she did in old photographs, when she was fresh out of university, a first-year law student in a black brocade coat and high black boots. Thin, but not emaciated the way she'd become in recent years.

Kit extended his hand. Aveline took it, unable to believe that she was seeing and touching her father. She marveled at how much bigger his hand was than hers—

and smooth, the way an upper-class person's was supposed to be. A symbol that he was exempt from a life of manual labor. Kit's father had been one of Alfred Fleur's Six Hundred, after all.

"Father?" said Aveline. "W-where have you been all these years?"

But he didn't answer. He just kept talking to her mother as if she weren't there. She could feel the tension, the urgency, between them. She realized that they were speaking Ebrian with Alterran accents. She didn't speak Ebrian herself, but she had learned just enough at school to recognize some basic words.

Kirja. Signal.

Uknatù. Rock.

Shebon. Boat.

All words that a soldier might use. But the Ebrian War—the war in which Kit had died—was long over, the enemy defeated.

"Father?" she said again.

This time, he turned to her. His handsome face began to stretch and lengthen as if the flesh were made of putty. His mouth became a gaping hole. His pale-blue eyes turned solid black, not a spot of white left in them.

She screamed.

When she awakened, she was in her bed at the care home, her silk pajamas soaked with cold sweat. Morning light streamed in the windows. The surf crashed against rocks in the distance. It might have been an hour after she had fallen asleep, or it might even have been the next morning. There was no clock in this room. And even if there were, it could not tell her what day it was. With her eyes closed, she could still see her father sitting there at the kitchen table, her mother across from him in the House with Too Many Lamps. She felt that strange sense of urgency, of foreboding.

When she opened her eyes, she saw Manánn sitting on a chair beside the bed, smiling down at her. Just as she had in her dream, Aveline shrieked.

The Party official clapped a hand over Aveline's mouth. Aveline tried to push her hand away, but her grip was like that of a vise. Astonishing for such a small, slender woman. But Aveline was also still very weak.

"You want the needle again?" Manánn hissed. "Fight me, and you shall have it."

Aveline shook her head. *No! Not again!*

When Manánn lifted her hand, Aveline cried, "You drugged me! You put something in my water!"

"Nonsense. The only drug we gave you was a distillate of *Rubicoris rubicorum* when you arrived. The effects should have worn off by now."

Rubicoris rubicorum. Common dram thistle. Mothers often mixed an elixir of dram thistle, a mild sedative, in bottles of milk to calm colicky babies. There must have been an extraordinary amount of dram thistle in that syringe to make Aveline fall out of bed and lose control of her body.

Manánn turned and lifted a white wicker tray from the bedside table. "Sit up," she commanded. Aveline obeyed, but with some difficulty. Her muscles were still somewhat numb, and those that weren't were beginning to feel sore.

Manánn placed the tray in Aveline's lap. She studied it: a small bowl of oatmeal with a swirl of saffron syrup; a plate with scrambled brightwing eggs, a piece of buttered toast, and two slices of green melon, still in their rinds; and a plastic cup of elderflower juice. To her relief, there was no glass of water. But the sedative could very well have been mixed in with the juice.

Her stomach growled. As hungry as she was, she knew she still needed to be cautious.

"Eat," commanded Manánn.

Aveline picked up a fork and speared a tiny bit of egg and lifted it to her nose. It smelled like eggs from the common brightwing. Manánn eyed her, goading her to place it into her mouth. She complied. Waited. It tasted normal and did not cause her limbs to go numb again.

She took another bite, and then another, until the eggs were gone.

Ten or fifteen minutes passed. No numbness. No other weird symptoms.

With more confidence now, she finished her breakfast and juice. When she was finished, she leaned back, satisfied, against the pillow. Perhaps she felt this way because she hadn't eaten in so long. Or maybe because the food was so good, so fresh, the way it was back home. A sense of ease permeated every cell of her body.

"Good girl. I'm glad to see your appetite is back. And that our food was to your liking." Manánn lifted the tray and set it back on the nightstand. She smiled down at Aveline. "What did you dream?"

Aveline blinked. *Does she know what I dreamed? Is she testing me?* It was as if the woman were peering into her mind. Despite being fully clothed, she suddenly felt naked.

"I dreamed…about my father."

The moment she said it, she regretted it. But the dream's immediacy, her sense of fright, had already worn off.

"It's not uncommon to dream of the dead," said Manánn.

"What does it mean?"

Aveline couldn't believe that she was actually engaging this woman in conversation, but she wanted to see whether Manánn had an answer. The part of her mind that should have been fighting, questioning, had been tamped down, like a lamp turned low at bedtime.

"A dream doesn't mean just one thing." The woman's voice was soft, soothing, like creek water over rocks in Wildweir. "That's the beauty of dreams, that they are open to interpretation. Perhaps your father had a message for you."

Aveline shook her head. What message? The Ebrian battle language? She understood the words, but they didn't mean anything to her. They just might have been some of the last words he heard before he died.

Manánn placed her palms flat against her thighs, as if to stand. Breezily, she changed the subject. "Well, Miss Aveline. How would you like to see the grounds today?" A command, not a question. So much like Simon.

"I'm not going anywhere with you." The sentence was not as harsh and forceful as Aveline had meant it to be. Instead, it sounded almost peevish, like a child refusing to obey a parent.

The corners of Manánn's mouth turned up. "Oh, I think you'll like it."

Aveline knew she had no choice. But she realized that the tour was an opportunity to case the place for possible exits—doors, stairs, windows—and begin planning her escape. She'd also be able to see who else was in the care home, whether any of them could band together to overpower the staff.

But even the thought of escape made her weary. Although she could now flex her fingers and wiggle her toes and lift her legs, her mind was still muddled.

Mother, when are you coming for me?

She watched as Manánn turned down the white comforter to let her out of bed, and she briefly closed her eyes, praying to God. The God of the Monnag, who was supposed to favor the Fleurs. She asked him whether Allyn had forgotten about her. By now, her mother had to have known that she was gone. More than a day had passed since she'd left for school and never returned.

Is Mother so deep in Simon's web of lies that I don't even matter to her anymore?

She couldn't help but feel that she was a burden to be rid of, like the unwanted babies that occasionally turned up in baskets on the doorsteps of the great estates.

Help me, God. What should I do?

She opened her eyes, trying to avoid looking into Manánn's ice-blue ones.

Patience is a virtue, came the answer in her own voice.

****

Manánn had been kind enough to allow her to use the bathroom before the tour of the grounds. But, to prevent her prisoner from escaping, she had stationed a tall, burly orderly in a white Party uniform right outside the door. As Aveline washed her face and under her arms, she looked around for an exit. There were no windows, but maybe there was some kind of hatch, a trapdoor.

Nothing.

And yet, curiously, she didn't panic. The feeling of satiety she'd had after breakfast was growing stronger. Calmness suffused her body and mind.

When she came out of the bathroom, Manánn smiled as she handed Aveline her wig. Aveline nodded in thanks and tucked her short strands up under it, wondering when her real hair would be long enough that she could finally discard the itchy thing.

While she secured the wig on her head, the orderly rolled an old, high-backed wooden wheelchair toward her.

"What's that for?" she said.

"For you, of course," said Manánn. "For your safety on our little outing. We don't want to risk a fall now, do we?"

"I can walk, you know." Aveline clenched her jaw.

"*Sit.*"

By now, she knew better than to disobey this woman. Simon may have trained Manánn, but it was clear that she was running the show down here in Belmarin, hundreds of miles south of Calador.

Hesitantly, Aveline turned around and gripped the arms of the chair and lowered herself into the seat. As soon as she did, the orderly secured a metal restraint over her right wrist.

"What the—"

As hard as she could with her left hand, she tried to

push him off, but the orderly was a mass of muscle. She would have had about as much luck breaking through a wall of solid rock.

The force of the exertion caused stars to flash before her eyes. A wave of dizziness passed over her, so strong that she lost consciousness for a moment. Her limbs were almost completely numb. The same way they'd felt on her first morning—or was it the second?—when she'd tried to leap out of bed but had tumbled to the floor, unable to get up.

In her mind, she was kicking and screaming against the tight restraints on both of her wrists, and now on her ankles. But her body wouldn't cooperate. Her limbs didn't move. Her screams echoed only within her head.

It must have been the breakfast, she thought. The Party must have developed some tasteless, odorless chemical that they'd baked into the food. Maybe they'd also stirred it into the juice, which didn't have the telltale metallic taste of the water she'd drunk before falling asleep and dreaming of her father.

They've given me no choice—I can eat and be drugged, or choose not to eat and starve.

The orderly opened the heavy wooden door to the room, while Manánn wheeled her out into the hallway. The hall was silent. On either side were rooms with identical doors, widely spaced. She could hear nothing from within. Not a scream, not a single voice.

They want us separated. They're afraid of all of us ganging up on them and making a break for it.

The antique metal wheels creaked over the floorboards as Manánn wheeled the chair down the hall to an old elevator with a brass gate. The orderly pulled back the gate and pressed the Down button. Aveline looked up, watching the dial sweep slowly across a brass half-moon as the lift ascended.

Despite barely being able to move her body, she felt her heart hammering in her chest. The sense of calm she felt earlier was all but gone.

When the dial stopped at "4," the lift dinged.

A thought registered dimly in her mind. *I'm on the fourth floor. Too high to jump out the window without breaking my legs. Naturally, they'd put me all the way up here.*

The elevator car was small and cramped, and musty with disuse. The orderly pressed a button, and the lift shuddered as it descended. When it reached the ground floor, the doors sprang open onto a windowless, fluorescent-lit hallway. Along each side of the hall was a series of mahogany doors with old brass knobs.

This hall reminded Aveline of the basement of the Lightministry, where they kept the Forbidden Books. Aveline knew that her mother would go down there and read for hours, emerging at dawn like a diver from a deep-sea expedition, glowing with secret knowledge.

The Lightministry basement smelled as one might have expected, of the leather and parchment and vellum of old books, but the care home's basement smelled of chemicals. Aveline recognized the pungent odor of formaldehyde from the biology lab at school where she and her classmates had been forced to dissect frogs and fetal pigs. She had wanted to be excused, but the Sisters of Monnag had made no exception for a child of the Fleurs. Bruno, like most of the boys, had enjoyed dissection, but it disgusted her. The stench was so overwhelming that she'd had to excuse herself to the girls' room to dry-heave.

That is exactly what it smelled like down here. The Party officials who ran this place must have used these rooms to cook up the chemicals they put in the food—or injected directly into people's bodies. Feeling her breakfast churn in her stomach, she wished she hadn't eaten everything on her tray. But then she caught a whiff of lavender laundry detergent—the same scent that the servants used back at the Estate—and her stomach settled a little.

At the end of the hallway was a door that looked like an emergency exit. As the orderly gripped the metal bar and pushed it open, Aveline instinctively squeezed her eyes shut and held her breath. What horrors awaited her in the next room, the next hallway?

To her surprise, a damp salt breeze struck her face. She opened her eyes. They were outside on a concrete ramp that led away from the care home. As Manánn wheeled the chair down the ramp, Aveline took in as much of the scenery as possible. She couldn't turn around to see the house, but there was a large slate patio before her. Beyond, an emerald lawn, and farther out, the sea.

We're up on a cliff!

Her spirits sank. Even if she could somehow escape the house without having to jump out the fourth-floor window, she'd have to scramble down that cliff. Assuming she made it without plummeting headlong to her death, she'd have to swim to dry land, or to an island. But, from this vantage point, she couldn't see any islands, only inky water stretching all the way to the horizon. She remembered from a map of Erodith, the continent they lived on, that across the Shinar Sea, to the south, lay the country of Ebria. Enemy territory.

It was so far that she couldn't even see it from here.

Now I know why they took me on this tour. To show me that there is no escape.

As if to prove this point, at that very moment, two black-clad Stam officers crossed in front of Aveline, pistols gleaming at their hips, and headed toward a small forested area. Through the trees, she could just make out the dark shape of a squat building, a hut. The Stam's headquarters.

Wearing only her silk pajamas, she shivered. The wind had died down from earlier that morning, when it had whipped her curtains to seafoam, but still it blew chilly and humid from off the sea. Out on the lawn there was a flagpole where a black-and-crimson Alterran flag socked lightly in the breeze, never quite revealing the full face of Monnag.

They crossed the slate patio, the rickety wheels of the chair catching on the gaps between the huge slabs from which weeds had sprouted. The sort of patio where a wedding reception might have taken place in olden times.

They passed a cracked fountain basin at whose center was a sculpture of Eradril, ancient god of the sea, posed with a conch shell to his lips. Aveline could imagine the basin full, children releasing paper lanterns at dusk onto the water as they had back home after Allyn and Jem's wedding. All those delicate floating, twinkling lights. Music of lutes and violins. Laughter. A time when she was so happy she might have left her body and ascended into the Beyond. It felt so long ago.

At the end of the patio, the yard sloped gently down, and they followed a stone path across the lawn. From above, the lawn looked empty, but now she saw several people. Two women, one old and one young, with a towheaded boy about five years old chasing a hoop with a stick. Other small groups of people, both adults and children, sitting on battered wicker furniture or milling around peacefully. Their white uniforms resembled those of the staff, though slightly looser-fitting. The scene was like something out of a Lightministry nostalgia film.

These must have been the "good" prisoners. The well-behaved ones. Aveline perceived the subtlety of the lesson: *You must be like them.* To her surprise and relief, they didn't seem brainwashed. The closer she got to them, the more she could see the light in their eyes. They didn't seem like Sandor Hayes, a fully functioning human being but without the spark of life.

It was possible, just maybe, that Simon had brought her here to scare her. When he thought she'd learned her lesson—*Thou shalt not disobey your elders*—he'd send a car for her, and she'd be back at the Estate in half a day's time.

The orderly parked Aveline's wheelchair at the center of the lawn, allowing her to see beyond the edge of the cliff. Crystalline light dazzled the horizon, and she could just make out the coast of Ebria. Two black-clad Stam officers patrolled the cliff's edge, presumably to stop anyone who even contemplated climbing down to the sea below. As if they could survive the journey anyway.

Aveline turned her head to the left. Farther down the cliff's edge, there was a lighthouse, its sweeping beam cutting through a thin layer of fog and spray.

To her right, about ten feet away, were two boys about her age sitting on a wicker bench before an older teacher perched on a high-backed chair. The teacher, with her creased face, reminded Aveline a bit of Mother Josephine, the headmistress.

As the teacher read aloud from a thick book of Scripture, Aveline couldn't help but notice the boys' completely bald heads.

Sensing that she was staring at them from behind, they turned in unison. Aveline froze. She recognized them immediately—they weren't boys; they were *girls*. Cynthia and Quintana. The bullies.

Their once-ruddy complexions were now sallow, almost gray. They no longer wore mischievous grins but rather expressions of fear. They stared at Aveline with wide eyes, as if to say, *Please help us!* until the teacher snapped her fingers and they turned around obediently.

Manánn commanded the orderly to wheel Aveline back into the house. Apparently, she had seen enough.

But Aveline couldn't stop thinking of the girls. Their shaved heads. How embarrassed and exposed they must have felt.

She remembered what Allyn had said on the day they cut off her braid: *Don't worry, my darling. I will make this right. Those wretched girls will regret the day they dared to do this to my Aveline.*

Now, she felt cold all over. *Mother has had her revenge.*

Chapter 15

It was the middle of the night when Aveline awakened to a man in a black mask standing over her bed. She was about to scream when he clapped a gloved hand over her mouth. In the dim moonlight, she could just make out the stocky, wedge-like shape of his body. The gleam of his eyes through two cutouts in the mask.

An assassin. Uncle Simon is trying to have me killed!

She tried to fight him off, to push away his hand, kick at his torso. But her strength was no match for his, especially in her weakened state. The hand clasped firmly over her mouth was enough to keep her pinned to the bed.

He raised a finger to his lips, warning her to remain silent.

Then he lowered his finger and began tearing something sticky from her forehead. Suction cups? She had no recollection of anyone putting anything on her head before she fell asleep that night. Had Manánn drugged her again? Was this all a dream?

But it was too real to be a dream; she could feel every sensation acutely. Pain seared her forehead as the masked man ripped the strange objects off her skin. She glanced to her right and saw that she was hooked up to some kind of machine, half-obscured in darkness, with blinking green lights. The suction cups might have been electrodes attached to long wires.

He's not trying to kill me, she realized. *He's trying to* save *me.*

At that moment, she stopped resisting. Did not make a sound.

Once she was free of the electrodes, the masked man whisked her from the bed with a singular motion and carried her out of the room as if she weighed no more than a toddler. She clung to him tightly, gripping his black ribbed sweater. She didn't know who he was, nor did she care. All that mattered was that he was getting her out of this awful place.

Down the darkened hallway, by the lift, she spotted a second black-clad, masked man. Her eyes were drawn to a person crumpled at his feet, face-down. It looked to be a member of the care home staff, in white Party uniform. The legs were inside the lift's car, the torso and arms extended over the gap between the car and the hallway floor. The old brass gate was partway open, jammed up against the body.

In the yellow light rising from the shaft, Aveline could see a cascade of red hair fanned over a spreading pool of blood. Next to the body was an overturned plastic basket, syringes scattered all over the floor.

Manánn Morrigan.

Aveline glimpsed a pistol with a long barrel in the second man's hand. She looked from the pistol back down to Manánn's body and realized with a jolt that he had shot her. A scream lodged in Aveline's throat. While she had never wished to see this woman dead, she was glad that Manánn could never hurt anyone ever again.

The second man gestured farther down the hall to a

narrow door that Aveline hadn't noticed before. A third man stood just outside the door, holding two young children, one in each enormous arm. She recognized the little towheaded boy who'd been playing in the yard, chasing a wooden hoop with a stick. The boy looked at her, wide-eyed. Held a finger to his lips. He already understood that these men were good guys. Rescuers.

When the third man opened the door, a musty smell assaulted Aveline's nose. The smell of close quarters and unwashed bodies. These were the utility stairs, which the staff must have used to travel between floors with laundry and medicine and meals. *Poisoned meals*. She also caught a whiff of formaldehyde wafting up from the basement below. The stench turned her stomach.

Not only did the stairway smell bad, but it was also pitch black. She thought one of the three rescuers would turn on a flashlight, but none did. Still carrying the children, they descended the stairs swiftly, silently, on cat feet. She realized they must have cased the place before sneaking in tonight. Perhaps this was how they'd entered the house, from the basement, padding up these very stairs.

When they reached the third-floor landing, a door identical to the one upstairs opened to reveal another black-clad rescuer holding two more children. The men must have been trying to evacuate as many kids as possible. Aveline recognized one of them, her head as bald as the darning egg that Jossie used to mend socks back home.

"Quintana!" she cried.

"Aveline!"

"Shush!" said two of the rescuers at the same time.

Before Aveline could process what was happening, they were all racing down the stairs again, picking up two more rescuers and several children on the lower floors. At the bottom of the stairs, the rescuers stopped abruptly. One shined a dim red beam onto a body that lay face-down in a pool of blood. A Stam officer. Aveline recognized him by his black uniform. She suppressed a gasp. Had the rescuers shot him while sneaking into the house?

"I'm going to put you down for a second," Aveline's rescuer whispered in her ear. It was the first time he'd spoken—that any of them had spoken, except to shush the kids. She observed that he had a foreign accent. Light, but noticeable. What was it? Brixian? Ebrian?

"Don't leave me," she said. "Please."

"I won't. We're right here. You are safe with us."

As he gently lowered her to the ground, she leaped when her feet hit the cold cement floor. She'd forgotten that she was barefoot, and that she hadn't had time to grab her wig either. She didn't even know where it was. Someone must have taken it off of her before sticking those electrodes—or whatever they were—all over her head while she was sleeping. She was grateful now that she didn't have to worry about the wig. Its itchiness. Strands always slipping loose from her braid and whipping into her eyes and mouth.

She watched as her rescuer grabbed the dead Stam officer's ankles and dragged him back into a narrow hallway that disappeared into darkness. A hallway that probably led to the basement where Manánn had wheeled Aveline the other day. But she wasn't sure. In all this mayhem, she'd completely lost her bearings.

She felt a bit like the boy in the legend who got lost in a labyrinth while hunting the Minotaur.

She looked down at where the body had been. The beam of red light shining on the floor made the streaks of blood appear black. She tried not to gag. She'd seen more blood tonight than ever before in her life. The sight of it—her own and others'—had always made her squeamish. This was another reason why she could never dissect animals in the school laboratory, besides the noxious odor of formaldehyde.

One of the other rescuers had put Quintana down next to Aveline so he could draw his gun. Aveline's heart raced. She knew danger could come from any direction. The bully grasped her arm. Aveline had never seen her so terrified. The sweat from Quintana's palm soaked through the sleeve of Aveline's thin silk pajama top.

Good, a part of her thought. *Now you know how I felt when you guys threw me into the dumpster. And when you trapped me in the gym closet and chopped off my hair!*

But pity overwhelmed her. She couldn't possibly hate this girl who was now in the same predicament as she. And whose head had been sadistically shaved. Having one's head shaved was worse than having one's maiden braid cut off. At least Aveline still had some hair left, while Quintana had none.

Aveline grabbed the girl and held her tightly. "It's going to be okay," she whispered, although she had no idea whether it would.

She wished she could talk to the rescuers. She would have asked, *Where are you taking us? Don't you know the Stam has this place surrounded?*

But she kept her mouth shut. Besides, there was no time to ask questions. They had to act. Now that her rescuer had dragged the dead officer out of the way, he opened a door that the body had been blocking. Immediately, they were hit with a wall of steam and the scent of lavender. The laundry room. White-clad men and women screamed when they saw the rescuers and children enter. Some made a break for it, knocking over baskets of sheets and towels. In the commotion, someone spilled an open bottle of detergent. Bright blue liquid lacquered the floor.

A black-uniformed Stam officer rushed in from the other end of the room, cutting through the stream of white bodies and narrowly avoiding the pool of detergent. The second he drew his gun, a rescuer standing behind Aveline shot him with his pistol. She heard a *thwpt thwpt*, and the officer gasped and clutched his chest and fell backward. Aveline realized that the long barrel on the pistol was a silencer. She'd noticed these same silencers on the Stam's pistols back home, though she had never actually seen any of the officers shoot anyone.

Another Stam officer rushed through a side door into the laundry room, only to meet the same fate. He crumpled to the ground, his blood mixing with the blue detergent in awful purplish rivulets.

"Now!" Aveline's rescuer commanded.

The rescuer who'd shot the two Stam officers pressed something he held in his left hand. An ear-splitting *BOOM!* issued from somewhere close to the laundry room but outside the house. At that moment, the room's windows flared bright orange.

"Go! Go! Go!" the rescuers shouted.

As alarms began blaring, the group of escapees rushed out the side door where the officers had charged in just seconds earlier. Aveline covered her ears. The deafening sound reminded her of one of the many drills they'd had at school, in the event that an invading army dropped bombs on Calador. Except this time, it was real. *Too* real.

Now outside, Aveline saw that one of the house's garages was on fire. And probably also the small filling station beside it. Flames shot up what seemed like hundreds of feet into the air.

The place was in chaos. The entire house was lit up now, the alarm sounding through every window. White-clad bodies ran in all directions, screaming. It was impossible to tell which were the house staff and which were the inmates.

"Run!"

At the rescuers' cue, Aveline grabbed Quintana's hand, and together the girls dashed toward the large slate patio where Manánn had pushed Aveline in the antique wheelchair. As fast as their legs would carry them, they sprinted past the dry fountain with its cracked statue of Eradril and down onto the lawn, slick with dew. Two rescuers flanked them, turning back occasionally to shoot at the pursuing Stam officers. Aveline heard the *thwpt thwpt* of the silenced guns, and then a scream or a groan, and the heavy thud of a body falling.

"Keep going! Don't look back!"

But she disobeyed the rescuers and glanced back over her shoulder. The lawn, once a peaceful green expanse, was now a battlefield full of black- and white-clad bodies. Closer to the house, she could see other white-attired bodies falling as they ran, and she realized that Stam officers were shooting them from the widow's walk on the roof.

Beside her, Quintana shrieked and dropped to the ground, nearly taking Aveline down with her since they were still holding hands.

Oh no! Has she been hit, too?

"My foot!"

Aveline looked down and saw a stream of blood darkening the grass, flowing from Quintana's left foot. Had she stepped on glass? Shrapnel?

Before they could figure out what it was, a rescuer lifted a shrieking Quintana into his arms and slung her over his shoulder like a sack of flour.

It wasn't long before they reached the edge of the cliff. Aveline stopped abruptly, feeling queasy.

"W-where are we going?" she said.

"Down the rock," barked one of the rescuers.

Rock. Why did that word trigger something in her mind?

Then she remembered. That dream she'd had of her father the other night, the one where he'd been speaking Ebrian battle language. *Signal. Rock. Boat.* The signal must have been the alarm that went off when the rescuer detonated the bomb in the garage. The rock was the cliff. And, down below, there must have been a waiting boat.

Manánn was right. Father did send me a message after all!

But Kit's message was little comfort when she learned she'd have to climb hundreds of feet down the rock face. The rescuers had staked a thick, knotted rope to the cliff's edge. One of them—the one who'd surprised her in her room and carried her down the stairs—went first.

"I will be behind you every step of the way." His tone was raucous, not soothing in the least. "Don't turn around. And whatever you do—don't let go of the rope."

Aveline looked over at the rescuer who held Quintana. He'd taken a white cloth or handkerchief and tied it around her foot to stanch the bleeding.

"Is she going to be able to climb?" Aveline asked Quintana's rescuer.

"Don't worry about her. Do as he says."

Heart in her throat, Aveline turned around and got down on her knees and grasped the top of the rope. Going over the cliff was the hardest part because she felt that at any moment she might lose her balance or her grip and tumble into the sea. The cliff must have been as tall as the Lightministry building in the City Center. The crashing waves below were no match for a fourteen-year-old girl who'd learned to swim in the shallow creek at Wildweir.

As soon as she was over the edge, she felt the rescuer's solid body right behind her. That gave her the smallest bit of comfort. She knew he wouldn't let her fall into the sea.

God, if you still favor the Fleurs, she prayed, *please keep me safe. Keep all of us safe.*

Above her, she saw several other white-pajamaed children looking over the cliff's edge. She didn't know how many there had been originally, but there seemed to be fewer now than in the utility stairs. Some children must have fallen victim to the Stam officers shooting from the roof. But there was no time to mourn them now. The remaining escapees had to keep going.

On the battlefield-lawn, Aveline could see officers tussling with prisoners in white, the figures advancing toward where the rescuers stood with the children. An officer materialized from the darkness to lunge at one of the rescuers from behind.

"Go! Now!" shouted Aveline's rescuer below.

Gripping the rope tightly, she began to clamber down. The rocks were frigid and rough on her bare feet, and slippery, too, having been continuously blasted with salt spray. She shivered in her thin pajamas, the wind whipping through her cropped hair and chilling her scalp. She struggled to maintain a firm grasp on the rope, which was almost as wet and slippery as the rocks. Below, she could hear waves crashing against boulders.

She could no longer see anything above her, as another rescuer's stocky body blocked her view. She understood how the rescuers were working together to protect the children—one rescuer behind each child to break their fall in case they lost their grip. Except that there were several more children than rescuers, so some kids would have to go down two or maybe three at a time, with only one rescuer behind them.

"Faster!" commanded the rescuer below.

Aveline tried to pick up the pace. She knew she was the one who was holding up the line of people above her. But she was scared. Terrified, actually. As terrified as she'd been the day Elton had locked her in the limousine and darkened the windows. There was no way out of this situation, no way to escape the Stam and the care home and whatever brainwashing they had in store for her—except down.

A cloud passed over the face of the moon, leaving them in near-total darkness. The only light came from the illuminated house and the burning garage a few hundred feet away. And the lighthouse down the shore whose beam swept several miles out over the water.

Now that she could no longer see what was going on above, she relied on her sense of hearing. She heard grunting, then the *thwpt thwpt* of a silenced gun. She couldn't tell who had shot at whom—the Stam officer or the rescuer—or whether both had shot at one another at the same time. To her left, a black-clad body sailed over the cliff and just grazed her elbow as it fell. She screamed.

"Shut up!"

The crash of water against rocks was so loud that she could not hear the splash of the body as it fell into the sea. Was it the rescuer? The Stam officer? There was no way to know.

The scream remained trapped in her throat. It was impossible to tell who were the good guys and who were the bad. She just had to blindly trust that the men above her and below her had her best interests at heart and were not taking the children to some remote island to brainwash them. She had to trust that these men were not working for Simon. It wouldn't have made sense for the Stam—in the guise of rescuers—to be fighting other Stam officers whose job it was to guard the care home. But Aveline wouldn't have put anything past Simon, orchestrating new ways to scare her from the comfort of his smoke-filled office. He enjoyed watching people suffer. Sandor Hayes. Quintana's father. All the other people he'd disappeared and sent to the Institutes for Mental Hygiene, or care homes, or whatever the Party was calling them.

Her hands trembled so much that for a moment she lost her grip on the rope. But she scarcely moved, owing to the rescuer's solid body that kept her own pressed to the rock. She remembered that he was wearing gloves that allowed him a firm grasp on the rope.

Calm down, she admonished herself. *He's got you.*

After what felt like hours of climbing—and of hearing the shrieks and cries of the kids above her— they made it all the way down the cliff face to a narrow strip of rocky beach. Aveline was so grateful that she could have kissed the cold sand under her feet.

All was dark except for the lights at the end of the large powerboat awaiting them offshore. While the boat wasn't at a great distance, she realized they would have to swim there. But there was no time to slowly get adjusted to the water temperature. Rather, the rescuers pushed the children into the black water, so cold it burned. Several of the kids started crying again, but the rescuers shushed them.

Aveline walked until the water was so high that she was forced to swim. Quintana was right beside her.

"Your foot—" began Aveline.

"It's okay." The girl's voice was shaky, her teeth chattering. "I can't even feel it anymore."

Aveline didn't know if that was a good or bad sign. She could scarcely feel her own body, numb with cold. Looking behind her, she saw the last rescuer pulling the rope from the cliff so the Stam couldn't follow them.

When they reached the boat, Aveline spotted the silhouettes of a man and woman on deck. In her delirious state, she half-expected them to be her mother and father. But, even in the wan moonlight, she could see that they were not.

One of the rescuers climbed up a rope ladder off the side of the boat and onto the deck. Two other rescuers, the ones not carrying small children, followed his lead. One held down the ladder and the other began pulling the older children up to safety. Aveline collapsed onto the deck, panting, shivering, soaked. The silhouetted woman emerged, a kerchief over her hair. She threw a woolen blanket onto Aveline and started rubbing her shoulders and back vigorously before moving on to the other kids.

Aveline kept her eye on the woman's companion, whom she presumed to be the boat's captain. Even in the partial darkness, she could see that he was tall, lean, moving quickly, competently. He pulled the ladder up from the water and folded it and set it aside on the deck. He spoke in a low, even tone to the rescuers, suggesting that he was in charge. Aveline could tell by his lack of an accent that he was Alterran, and she detected in his voice the speech pattern of Calador.

We're from the same place. That spark of recognition brought her a small modicum of comfort.

"Only forty-six minutes until high tide," he was saying. "We've got to go. Now!"

Chapter 16

Aveline watched the captain leap to the helm of the powerboat. The kerchiefed woman and the rescuers remained on deck with the children.

"Where's Paolo?" the woman asked one of the rescuers. She spoke with the same slight but noticeable foreign accent as Aveline's rescuer.

The man shook his head solemnly. The woman gasped, clapping a hand over her mouth.

Aveline understood that Paolo was the rescuer who'd fallen over the side of the cliff after his standoff with the Stam officer. The poor man. He'd lost his life to help Aveline and the other kids to safety. She wanted to cry for him, though she hardly knew him. He must have been a friend of the kerchiefed woman, or maybe a relative.

Looking around the small deck, she counted five rescuers—Paolo must have been the sixth—and nine children, including herself. She was relieved that the little towheaded boy, whose name she learned was Leo, had made it. But she wondered what had happened to Cynthia. She hadn't seen Quintana's lieutenant at all that night, not in the hallway or in the utility stairs. Had the rescuers forgotten about her? Perhaps they'd only had a limited number of kids they could rescue, and she wasn't among the lucky ones.

Aveline no longer hated the bullies. What had

transpired between them back at Belfort Academy felt like it had happened a hundred years ago. The only thing that mattered now was that she and Quintana banded together to stay alive.

With a jolt, the motors revved up, and the powerboat started moving. The captain turned the boat around in the small inlet at the base of the cliff and headed down shore, in the direction of the lighthouse.

Meanwhile, the kerchiefed woman opened a hatch, which resembled a kind of trapdoor, and ushered the children down to the cabin below deck. Aveline nearly tripped down the narrow wooden stairs, except that she was able to grasp the railing at the last second to steady herself.

Once all the kids were inside, packed into the cramped space like sardines, she heard the hatch slam shut behind them. Her stomach dropped. They were in almost total darkness. The only light—weak light, at that—came from two small portholes on either side of the cabin. Someone cried for their mother. Another let out a high-pitched wail.

Then Aveline heard someone calling her name. It was Quintana.

In the dark, she and the other girl found each other. She gave silent thanks to God that they were both safe.

The cabin was musty and damp, like the groundskeeper's shed back home. It smelled somewhat earthy, like dry soil after a spring rain. *Petrichor*, Allyn called it. Allyn always knew the word for everything. The dominant odor was not of petrichor, however, but of motor oil and grease. As Aveline tried to move a little to her right, her bare foot bumped into a metal object. She looked down, but it was too dark to see what it was. It could have been an oar or a spade or even the barrel of a rifle.

Her feet ached, having been cut up by the rocks on the cliff face. But she said nothing, knowing that the other girl's foot injury was probably even worse. Quintana whimpered, whether out of pain or fear Aveline didn't know.

"It's okay," Aveline found herself reassuring the girl again.

She could feel the boat racing now, the motors noisier than ever. Her stomach roiled. This was her first time on a boat, and she hadn't anticipated that its motion would make her feel so queasy. On either side of her, she heard kids retching. Even Quintana was hiccupping, on the verge of dry-heaving.

Through one of the small portholes she could just make out a line of faint moonlight glittering on the waves. Without dry land or the horizon line as a marker, she had no way to tell where they were headed, or even in what direction. East, maybe? She assumed that that was the direction of the lighthouse.

The boat lurched as it hit a wave, and Aveline stuck out her right hand to grasp the side of the cabin so she wouldn't fall, taking Quintana down with her. That was when she felt something unusual, like a carving on the cabin wall. When the boat steadied a little, she lifted her hand and examined the carving in the dim light. It wasn't so much a carving as a raised crest with the faded outline of a roaring tiger inside of it.

Roaring tiger. It had to be a sigil belonging to the ruling family of some other country. The Fleurs' sigil was the great dragon Monnag's head encircled by the fleur-de-lis. But whose was the tiger? She scoured the annals of her brain, mentally turning the pages of her history book.

That's when she remembered. *Ebria*. The roaring tiger was the sigil of the Virolannens, the ruling family of Ebria.

That accent she'd heard in the rescuer's and the kerchiefed woman's speech was Ebrian. The same language she'd heard her parents speaking in her dream. She had been able to recognize Ebrian spoken with an Alterran accent, but it had taken her much longer to recognize Alterran spoken with an Ebrian accent. Perhaps because Ebrians in Alterra were extremely rare, so she'd never actually heard one speak. Although the Ebrian War had ended more than twelve years ago, Alterra still considered the country across the Shinar Sea to be its enemy. Ebria was where the Party exiled its high-profile prisoners. Like Milo Fresenius, the heretic composer whose music Allyn secretly adored.

They're taking us to enemy territory!

In her panic, Aveline wanted to shake off Quintana's grasp and rush the hatch, breaking free onto the deck above. Then her rational mind kicked in. Three possibilities loomed before her. The first was that she'd emerge from the hatch only to be shot and killed—or thrown overboard—by the captain or the rescuers. If that happened, all their efforts to save Aveline and the other kids from the care home would have been for naught. Whoever orchestrated their rescue would be very disappointed. At the very least, Aveline had to have some political value. A commodity to be traded for favors or weapons or other valuable goods. It made sense to keep her alive.

The second possibility was that she could evade her captors on deck and jump into the sea and start swimming for shore—perhaps the same beach where their journey had started. But they were miles from that beach now, and Aveline knew she wasn't that strong of a swimmer. She'd tire and drown long before reaching that rocky shoreline.

And the third possibility was that she could do nothing and stay in this cabin clinging to Quintana and allow herself to be taken to Ebria. Upon arrival, she would ask for an audience with Kirtje Virolannen, the equivalent of Alterra's Leader, and beg for his mercy. She remembered from her history lessons that Kirtje had a beautiful young daughter named Torje. Maybe Torje would take pity on Aveline and her fellow escapees. Send them back to their families in Alterra.

Quintana broke Aveline's thoughts by whispering, "W-what do you think that man meant when he said it's only forty-six minutes until high tide?"

"I have no idea," she replied truthfully. Why would high tide matter when they were out on the open sea?

But maybe they weren't. If they'd been on the open sea, Aveline reasoned, the piercing beam of the lighthouse would have swept over them. They'd have seen it through the portholes. The fact that they hadn't seen the beam suggested that they were closer to the shore. Which made sense if one were trying to evade the Stam, who patrolled the cliff's edge and would be looking for a boat farther out at sea, not directly below them.

If that were true, and they were merely hugging the coast, they were not headed to Ebria. Instead, they were headed toward another part of Alterra. Somewhere either in the Province of Belmarin or Lystra, along the southern seaboard. But it would be impossible to confirm whether Aveline was right since they had such a limited view through the portholes, and the moon had once again slipped behind the clouds, relegating the cabin to total darkness. All they could do was hold fast to one another and pray that the journey would end soon. On dry land.

Aveline didn't know how much time had passed when she heard the sound of the engines change. It became louder, almost as if the boat had entered an enclosed structure. Maybe a cave.

Curiosity got the better of her. "I'm going up for a second," she whispered to Quintana.

"No! Don't leave me!"

"I'm not leaving you. I'll be right back."

With that, she pried herself from Quintana's sweaty grasp. Carefully, she navigated the wooden staircase and placed her hand flat against the hatch. To her surprise, it was not locked. It flew open when she pushed on it with a little force.

The first face she saw was the kerchiefed woman's.

"Miss Aveline!" said the woman.

How does she know my name?

The woman extended a hand to her and pulled her up on deck. Below her, at the bottom of the staircase, Aveline could hear the other children clamoring, but the woman shushed them. Then she closed the hatch again, casting them back into darkness.

It wasn't much lighter up on deck. Aveline's surroundings were illuminated only by the rescuers' red-covered flashlights and the brighter red light on the front end of the boat. But her eyes had adjusted to the dark from her time below deck, and she could make out the shapes of people and objects quite well. In the eerie light, she saw that the woman was young, about her mother's age, and had light-colored eyes and an aquiline nose.

Now that she was standing on deck, Aveline saw that they were indeed in some kind of enclosed space. It seemed to be a channel carved into a cliff. Tilting her head upward, she could see, high above, the night sky thick with stars in a narrow gap between two walls of rock. For a moment, she forgot to be afraid and stared up at it in awe. She felt so small in comparison to just this tiny swatch of universe.

The farther they went into the channel, the narrower and more enclosed it became until they were inside a bona fide cave. Stalactites hung down from the ceiling. These jutting mineral formations weren't low enough to brush against the top of the boat, but they dripped cold water onto Aveline's head.

She remembered how, when they were a few years younger, she and Bruno had lain on their stomachs in the Great House's library, reading to each other from the illustrated legends. Their favorite stories had featured sea caves just like these, glittering with stalactites and stalagmites. How badly they had wanted to be adventurers when they grew up! How they truly believed that they could make it happen, that Bruno wouldn't grow up to be a factory worker like his father and Aveline wouldn't grow up to be a Party official like her mother. Bruno would have been enchanted by this cave. He might even have pretended that they were pirates on the hunt for treasure buried deep within.

Will I ever see him again?

Her heart sank as she pictured him in a care home like the one at Gilsevain Landing, hooked up by electrodes to a brainwashing machine or whatever that blinking contraption was by her bed.

"This is Desperation Pass." The woman's voice cut through Aveline's thoughts. "A fitting name, yes?"

Aveline gulped.

The woman draped an arm around Aveline's shoulder and looked to the enclosed cockpit where the captain stood at the wheel. He turned, a gaunt-faced but handsome man about the same age as the woman, maybe a little older.

"It's going to be all right, isn't it, Benjamin?" she said.

He answered her dryly, "We entered the channel later than expected. The water is rising quickly."

Later than expected. Aveline now understood the captain's reference to having only forty-six minutes. A short window of time before high tide.

"Where are we going?" asked Aveline.

"There's a floating dock about half a mile away. Inside the channel." The woman gestured. "We'll stop there and climb a ladder up through a tunnel to the land above."

Aveline had so many questions, not least of which was, *What's on the land above?* but she asked only one. And the most important: "Will we make it in time?"

"Of course we will." Her uncertain tone suggested that she was trying to comfort herself as much as Aveline.

"What happens if we don't?"

The woman let her arm fall from Aveline's shoulder. Looked down at her feet.

"Then it's all over for us," said the captain. "Isn't it?"

Aveline disliked him at once.

"Benjamin, don't scare the girl!"

Shuddering, Aveline tried not to think of the imminent danger they were in. If the tide completely filled this cave, the boat might capsize, or water would flood the deck and pour into the cabin and they'd all drown. It wouldn't matter what was on the land above because they would never make it there.

In the distance, she could hear the sound of rushing water. She could hear it when she stepped up on deck, but the sound grew louder now. Gurgling, pulsating, echoing in the depths of the cave.

"I-is that the tide coming in?" she stammered.

"No," replied the woman. "That is the sound of a great river tumbling over a gorge into the channel. The waterfall is a few miles ahead of us still."

Benjamin added, "That's the danger of entering the channel too late—that it fills up from both the tide and the river."

"Benjamin, please—" She had to yell above the sound of the waterfall to be heard.

As much as she disliked the captain, Aveline had to admit that he was right. The water level was already rising, pushing the boat higher, inching it up toward the ceiling of the cave. Still not high enough to break off a stalactite, but a little too close for comfort.

The boat continued making its way deeper into the channel, Benjamin navigating by its red beam. Up ahead, the channel narrowed again, the roof even lower. It was if they were in an endless honeycomb, except that each hexagon was smaller than the last.

She tugged on the woman's sleeve. "Are we going to make it?"

"Benjamin!"

The boat just narrowly passed through the neck of the cave and into the chamber. But as soon as it entered, its top caught a bouquet of stalactites, raining sharp mineral fragments onto the deck. Aveline shrieked, and the woman pulled her into the covered cockpit. On deck she could hear the rescuers clamoring and yelling.

"Watch it, Captain!"

"Steer clear!"

"What would you have me do?" he bellowed. "You all spent too much time going down the cliff!"

It's not our fault, Aveline wanted to tell him. But her voice would have been lost in the sound of rushing water. Besides, it no longer mattered whose fault it was. The only thing that mattered now was making it to that floating dock. They couldn't have been very far.

In the midst of another rainstorm of stalactites, Quintana threw open the hatch and came rushing up from below deck. She yelped, dancing around the chunks of mineral that pulverized as they hit the wooden deck.

"Get back inside!" shouted a rescuer.

"I can't," she protested. "They're all screaming bloody murder down there. I can't take it anymore. I feel like I'm dying!"

"You ain't dying," he said. "Ain't nobody dying. Not on our watch!"

But the second the words were out of his mouth, the top of the boat scraped the roof of the cave and came to a stop. The captain revved the engines, spun the wheel.

"Benjamin!" shouted the woman again.

"I can't push it any harder, Catherine. It won't budge. We're going to have to swim."

Swim? Now?

The water was rising—from what direction Aveline could no longer tell—and filling the cave. It was even beginning to spill over the sides of the boat. She realized how dire their situation was. If they didn't leave right now, the cave would fill entirely and they would all drown. There was still a sizable gap between the water and the roof of the cave that would allow them to swim out, into the next honeycomb, and the next, until they reached the dock. Wherever it was.

Now that Quintana had opened the hatch, the other seven children came streaming up, crying and pushing against one another. As soon as the kids were on deck, Catherine ran down the staircase into the cabin.

One of the rescuers yelled something to her in Ebrian, which Aveline guessed to mean, *What on earth are you doing?*

She emerged moments later, her arms full of life vests. Instead of putting the first one around her own neck, she handed it to Aveline. Aveline slipped it on, then realized that there weren't enough vests for all the children. Without deliberation, she yanked hers off and gave it to Quintana.

"Put your vest on at once!" said Catherine.

"No. My friend doesn't have one. I know how to swim."

"It's okay," said Quintana. "I know how to swim, too."

"Miss Aveline." Catherine's voice was stern now. She meant business. "You are the one we were sent to rescue. You and only you. The Lightminister's daughter."

Aveline gasped. "Who sent you?"

But before she could answer—and before Catherine could rip the life vest from Quintana's neck and put it around Aveline's—Benjamin charged out of the cockpit, yelling at them to jump ship.

Aveline obeyed. Holding Quintana's hand, the two girls leaped off the side of the boat into the frigid water. Letting go of each other's hands, they started swimming around the trapped boat to the other end of the cave, following Benjamin and two rescuers.

She heard screaming behind her and turned her head to see that it was little Leo, whose life preserver had come loose and floated away. The poor child, unable to swim, flailed his arms above him in the water, his head bobbing like a cork. Fortunately, a rescuer scooped him up with a meaty arm.

Although a cramp was developing in her left side, Aveline pushed onward. This was no time to slow down. No time for weakness.

The group of swimmers reached the entrance to the next cave and swam through it, gasping for air in the increasingly small space between the rising water and the roof. She banged her head on a stalactite and yelped in pain as water rushed into her mouth.

She spat, struggling to keep her head above the surface. *Don't think about the pain. Just keep swimming.*

Everywhere, the beams of the rescuers' red flashlights shot through the dark and intersected, aimed up to the roof, across the kids' panicked faces. In these brief flashes of light, Aveline tried to dodge clusters of stalactites as she swam against the force of the water gushing into the cave from the gorge.

"Grab the dock!" called a male voice.

Despite the roving flashlight beams, the cave was so dark that she could barely see the floating dock. She swam a little farther until she felt a pair of solid arms pulling her up onto a slick wooden surface. She had made it.

Because the dock was quickly rising to the roof of the cave, she was only able to stand up partway. The rescuer whom she was following had to crouch on his hands and knees, crawling like a baby. She followed him to the other end of the dock. He shone his flashlight up on a ladder which appeared to be built into the cave wall. The water was high enough now that the lower rungs were in the water, hidden below the dock. She followed the red beam and saw that the ladder led upward into a gaping black expanse. This must have been the tunnel that Catherine had spoken of earlier. The tunnel that led to the land above, their next destination.

Aveline watched as the rescuer grasped the ladder's handrails and hauled himself up onto the first rung above the water line. He jammed his flashlight into his turtleneck so that it would point upward, into the darkness.

"Climb!" he barked to Aveline and the children below. "Don't let go of the ladder!"

Her mind was an echo chamber where his words reverberated. Obediently, she grabbed the handrail and began to climb up into the dark tunnel.

Chapter 17

Inside the tunnel, Aveline clung to the slippery metal ladder. The old claustrophobia was back. She had felt it as a little girl when the servant's twin daughters had locked her in an old steamer trunk. She had felt it when Elton had trapped her inside her family's limousine. And she felt it now, ascending this narrow, dark tunnel, faintly illuminated by the rescuers' red-covered flashlights.

The tunnel smelled of mildew and another foul odor she couldn't identify. Skunk, maybe. As she climbed, long strands of cobwebs stuck to her face. Shuddering, she tore them off, remembering a legend she'd heard once about a mountain where, every autumn, millions of tarantulas came out of hiding to seek mates. Some of these tarantulas were the size of dinner plates, or even bigger. Legend had it that some could even swallow kittens whole.

She shook her head to clear the images. Those were just made-up stories. No kitten-eating tarantulas lived inside this tunnel. Below, the younger kids' screams echoed upward through the tunnel, rattling Aveline's already addled nerves.

The more she climbed, the more she realized that she wasn't cut out to be an adventurer.

I'm sorry, Bruno.

"Faster! Faster!" shouted the rescuer above.

Although she couldn't turn around to see the danger, she heard it: a rumble and gurgle in the cave below. The water had gotten so high that it was starting to fill the tunnel as well. The floating dock must have been completely underwater by now.

She began climbing as fast as she could to keep pace with the rescuer. Someone below, perhaps one of the younger girls, was close on her heels. Aveline's heart was beating so hard she feared it might burst. All the climbers were backed up into one another, making a desperate bid to exit this tunnel. It was unnerving not to be able to see the top, to identify it by a circle of blue sky and sunlight. But it was still nighttime.

She kept climbing blindly until an enormous rush of water from down below propelled her, and the line of climbers behind her, up through the tunnel. It was as if a geyser had just burst forth from the earth. Aveline briefly blacked out. When she awakened, it was to someone standing over her, shining the red beam of a flashlight into her eyes. Then the figure passed, the red light gone. She sat up, coughing, blinking in the dark, trying to get her bearings. All around her, she could hear the cries of the other children. But her first thought was of Quintana. She screamed her name.

"Aveline! I'm here!"

But Aveline could not see where. Red beams of flashlights shot through the dark.

"Benjamin!" came Catherine's voice. "We're missing Reza and the boy...that little dark-haired boy."

Aveline's stomach sank. Reza was one of the rescuers. She'd heard Catherine address him on the boat. And the little dark-haired boy was a child of about nine or ten, slight of build, whose name she didn't know. Two more of their party lost.

But there was no time to mourn their fallen compatriots, just as there had been no time to mourn Paolo, the rescuer who'd fallen over the edge of the cliff.

She felt Quintana's hand on her arm.

"W-where are we?" asked Quintana.

"I don't know."

Aveline could hear the night noises of a forest: crickets, cicadas, the rustle of leaves high above in the trees. The air was warm and humid and close. They must have been somewhere down the coast from the care home. Probably in the far reaches of Belmarin, or even in Lystra.

"Follow me," growled a male voice, which she recognized as Benjamin's. "Stay together."

That was how they made their way through the forest, in single file, one adult for every two or three children. Only Benjamin carried a flashlight. Quintana followed close behind Aveline, hobbling on her injured foot. She jumped whenever she heard a strange sound, like the hoot of an owl or a scurrying in the underbrush.

"Do you think it's a wolf?" she whispered.

From earliest childhood they'd been warned of big, bad wolves in the forest. Aveline had been scared all her life until she realized that adults only said that to deter their kids from wandering off into unknown territory. Not that there was much chance of that in the Federal District, where there wasn't any true wilderness, only the glades and hamlets of the great estates. And the Federal District was separated from the rest of the country by an enormous stone wall. If there were any wolves, they roamed on the other side.

"Nah, it's just a squirrel," replied Aveline. She wasn't confident of that but didn't want to scare the girl even more.

As they walked, the forest seemed to grow denser and darker. Whereas at the mouth of the tunnel she could see the moon half-obscured by clouds, she could now not even see her hand in front of her face. Though the night was warm, she shivered from fright. Her wet silk pajamas stuck uncomfortably to her skin. She wanted to ask one of the adults where they were headed but was afraid to breach the silence.

They reached the edge of the forest at daybreak. The interminable night was over. Benjamin switched off his flashlight and paused for a moment. The others gathered around him. Aveline was grateful for the momentary rest. While the forest floor was mostly soft and springy, her bare feet ached terribly, the soles cut up from climbing down the rocky cliff at Gilsevain.

The land sloped down gently into a valley. Outstretched before them, in all directions, were empty fields with nothing but the occasional bale of hay. Farther in the distance, the burnt sienna color of the fields became a mossy green that glowed almost yellow in the early light.

"Welcome to Alterra," Benjamin pronounced solemnly.

****

As they followed a dirt trail down the slope and into the valley, Aveline pondered his words. *Welcome to Alterra.* Of course, she knew they hadn't left their home country, but she sensed a hint—maybe more than a hint—of irony in his voice. She was sure now that they were in Lystra. The heartland of Alterra. The breadbasket. At least, that's what they called it on Channel 1. It had always appeared so lush. Fat with crops and happy farmers tilling the soil.

In reality, it was the harvest season and the fields lay fallow. The mossy greenness gave the illusion of fertility, but up close, the moss was more like a weed. The sort of weed that would choke anything that tried to grow in the soil before it even had a chance to put down roots.

They continued walking until they reached a small village. The village was actually more of a shantytown, with clusters of dilapidated houses arranged along wide dirt roads that were slightly muddy, perhaps from an overnight rain shower. The sun was barely rising through the clouds, and the village was eerily silent. Not a person or an animal in sight. Aveline could hear the twittering of birds in the distance, although she saw no trees on which they could alight. Only some scraggly bushes and mounds of dirt in yards enclosed by wooden fences.

"Don't worry, the Stam doesn't patrol this far out," said Catherine, answering the children's unspoken question. "They don't even have electricity here. So, no televisions."

"No televisions?" one of the younger girls piped up. "How do they watch the Daily Veneration?"

Catherine smiled wearily. Aveline noticed that she'd lost her kerchief and her hair flowed over her shoulders in dark waves rather than in a braid whose end was tied with a loyalty ribbon. "The Party has other ways of exerting its control."

"Like how?"

"Well, there is a famine here, so there is very little

to eat. The people must rely on the Party to send rations."

Aveline could not believe what she was hearing. "The famine is *still* going on?"

Catherine nodded. "It wasn't always this way. The Party has made it so. They exploited the farmers. Left them to live in squalor on smaller and smaller farms where they could grow only potatoes, while the landlords back in Calador collected rent and got fat. The Party caused the blight. They show this place on television as a sort of paradise. The Promise of Alterra, ha! It is a wasteland. Now, they only send rations because the Lystrans threatened to revolt."

Aveline's face burned. She knew that when Catherine said "the Party" she meant the Fleurs. It was shameful what her family had done. The situation was even worse than what Sandor Hayes had described in his article. Not only had the Fleurs failed to respond to the famine, but they had created it themselves!

The group continued walking, avoiding pieces of rusted farm equipment abandoned in the road, until they approached a cluster of darkened houses. In one, she heard a baby cry. As they passed the front window, she saw a dark-haired woman sitting in a wooden chair, rocking a baby wrapped in a dirty white blanket. The woman looked up, startling Aveline, her dark eyes glittering in an emaciated face. This mother was probably only in her twenties but the privation of her life made her look much older, like a woman of forty. Two small, skinny children, a boy and girl, darted into the front room and stood on either side of their mother's chair. They pressed their faces to the dirty glass to study the strangers, big and small, walking past their home.

After they had passed the house, Aveline could not forget their eyes. The boy and girl reminded her of Jem's little nieces and nephews, stuffing their faces at the wedding buffet as if they'd never seen food before.

The dirt road ended in a burbling stream. Two young women in dark blue, sack-like dresses, hair plaited down their backs and secured at the ends with crimson ribbons, knelt at the stream, where the water rushed over rocks, scrubbing clothes on wooden boards. Aveline watched them incredulously. She thought that that method of washing had gone the way of the covered wagon. She also couldn't believe that they still wore their loyalty ribbons after the Party had robbed them of everything. Their land, their livelihoods, their food supply.

When they saw the group of strangers, the women stopped washing and looked up. Aveline averted her eyes, ashamed to have been staring at them. But she could feel their eyes on her as she walked past. As if they knew she was the Lightminister's daughter, even without her long blonde braid.

She and the others followed Benjamin downstream, across a wooden footbridge. As they crossed, she looked down into the water, the way it eddied and foamed around the rocks, tracing delicate sine curves. She was suddenly homesick for the creek in Wildweir.

Will I ever go home again?

Across a dry meadow stood a lone two-story farmhouse, larger than those in the village, with a front porch spanning its entire length. Aveline could see that the house had once been white, but the paint had all but worn away, revealing the weather-beaten wood beneath. Several of the upper windows were cracked or broken. She didn't like the look of this house at all. If she still believed in ghosts, she might have said it was haunted. It emanated a sort of dark, sinister energy.

As they approached the front steps, a young woman in a long dress and apron bolted out of the house, her curly dark hair slipping loose from its braid. She was carrying a small white plastic box.

"Dr. Cachtice!" she said, addressing Benjamin.

He's a doctor? Aveline had thought his occupation was boat captain. And his surname caught her attention. Cachtice was a prestigious house in Alterra, its members serving in important Party positions and in the People's Assembly.

"Come quick!" said the woman. "There's a lady upstairs who's far gone. She needs treatment right away, but we didn't know what to give her first."

The woman shoved the box into his hands. Opening the lid, he lifted out a packet of dry ice and a vial of colorless liquid. He removed several other vials and examined them closely.

Aveline looked past him, through the open front door. A sandy-haired boy about her age was bounding down the stairs.

Her breath caught in her throat when he stepped out onto the porch. It was Bruno.

"Aveline!" he cried when he saw her.

They nearly knocked each other over in their rush to embrace. She held him close, unable to believe it was really him. That he was still the boy she remembered, her best friend since they were six, and that he hadn't been turned into a human robot.

When they pulled away from one another, she

could see that he'd been crying. She realized that she'd been crying, too. She laughed and wiped her eyes, overcome with relief.

Bruno spotted Quintana behind her. It didn't seem to matter to him that she had been a bully, or that she was now as bald as a darning egg. He hugged her like they were old friends.

Then Aveline heard an ear-rending scream issue from the second story.

"It's my mom." Bruno tugged on Aveline's hand. "She's been brainwashed really bad!"

Aveline's heart picked up speed. This was exactly what she had feared for Bruno—and now it had happened to Edwena.

She followed Bruno into the house, the wooden floorboards rough on the soles of her bare feet. Quintana was fast on their heels, but Catherine held the girl back. Benjamin and the curly-haired woman darted upstairs behind the children.

The main bedroom was in chaos. A raven-haired young woman was attempting to pin a flailing Edwena Page, clad in dirty white silk pajamas of the kind Aveline wore, onto the bed. The bed was no more than a soiled mattress atop a four-poster oak frame. Besides a dresser and a couple of wooden chairs, the room was bare.

Edwena's ginger hair was in disarray, her eyes wild. "Don't touch me, you traitor scum," she spat at the woman. "I demand to be taken back to Calador this instant. I shall have an audience with the Leader, to tell him what you have done to me. What fool notions you are trying to plant in my head against the Party. Against the Leader himself. Wait until he hears about this. You will be arrested at once and face the High Court for your crimes!"

Aveline stood in the doorway trembling. She had always known Edwena as someone who was fiercely loyal to the Party and to the Fleurs. But Edwena now delivered her pronouncements at such a pitch, like a raving lunatic, that Aveline could draw the conclusion only that she had been brainwashed. The odd thing, though, was that Edwena did not behave like Sandor, who had returned from Rjellsfall meek and compliant. Edwena was combative, full of righteous fury.

Bruno's mother bolted from the young woman's arms and fell on her knees before Aveline, who froze in terror.

"Aveline! Aveline Fleur! The Lightminister has sent you. Thank God! Maybe you can talk some sense into these people!"

At that moment, Benjamin and the curly-haired woman and two rescuers rushed into the room. One of the rescuers easily picked up Edwena and threw her down on the mattress while Benjamin filled a syringe with clear liquid from one of the vials in the white box. Aveline flashed back to the care home, the burly man in white grabbing her out of the limo and stabbing her with a needle. She winced as Benjamin injected the syringe into Edwena's upper arm.

"Don't hurt my mom!" shouted Bruno.

Aveline and Bruno clung to each other, watching as Edwena's eyes closed and her body relaxed.

"She'll sleep for a while," said Benjamin to the others in the room. "I'll give her the next dose in three hours."

Chapter 18

Sigrid and Cora. Those were the names of the two young women who had looked after Edwena Page until help arrived. Sigrid, the one with curly brown hair, was the village healer. Cora, whose hair was as black as a raven's wing, was Sigrid's younger cousin and apprentice.

Once Edwena was asleep, the healers came downstairs and gave each of the children a towel and a tiny bar of soap imprinted with the Fleurs' sigil. Sigrid told them that rations were not regularly delivered from Calador, so their friends inside the Party had had to make a special delivery. Aveline held the soap in the palm of her hand, studying Monnag's head encircled by the fleur-de-lis. She had once been so proud of this symbol. Now it made her feel ashamed.

Cora then took the children across the meadow to the stream to bathe. The water was cold, but not nearly as cold as that of the Shinar Sea. Parched from almost two days without water, Aveline drank as much as she could until her stomach felt like it would burst.

After bathing, she put on the stiff, scratchy linen shirt and pants that Cora had given her. The pants were too loose, and she had to roll up the sleeves of the shirt. But she was grateful for the linen, which kept her much warmer than the thin silk of her pajamas. And she now had a pair of sturdy rubber-soled shoes. They gapped a little at the back, but it was much more comfortable to walk in shoes that were too big than too small.

The healers gave each of the children two pieces of bread and margarine, and a few strips of dried beef, from their store of rations. The children nibbled at their food, trying to make it last, as they sat beside a roaring fire that one of the rescuers, Balthazar, had made in the fireplace in the house's chilly living room.

Aveline looked around the room, wondering who had lived here and where they had gone. *Maybe they died of hunger*, she thought with a shudder.

On the wall above the fireplace hung the legally required portraits of Alfred, Allyn, and Simon. Except that the portraits showed them as they had looked many years ago. She guessed that Allyn's photograph had been taken when she was still in law school, or as a new barrister in the Lawministry's Civil Division. Alfred still had dark hair in his photo; now it was completely white. And Simon's face, though rounder with baby fat, still bore that familiar, indelible smirk.

She wondered if these were the same portraits that had hung in Jem's family's house in Ede's River. Perhaps he had prayed to them every night before going to sleep. Had dreamed of one day training horses on their estate. Did he ever think that he would fall in love with Allyn, who'd send him off to war? If he'd known his fate, would he still have gone to the capital city?

But, had he stayed in Ede's River, he might have died from the famine. Or at least suffered terribly along with his family.

Aveline wanted badly to talk to Bruno, but he was upstairs keeping watch over his mother. Instead, she sat on a tattered sofa next to Sigrid, who was treating

Quintana's injured foot with a poultice. Sigrid packed the soft, damp plant material into Quintana's open wound, then wrapped her foot with a clean linen bandage.

"How are you feeling, love?" Catherine walked by and stooped to kiss Quintana's bald head, which was just beginning to shadow with new hair growth.

"I'm okay," the girl replied a bit lifelessly.

"In no time, you will have a healed foot…and a long, beautiful braid again."

Quintana smiled faintly.

Aveline couldn't help but be drawn to this foreign woman. To her quiet strength in a time of crisis. In this way, she was like Allyn. Aveline sat beside her on the floor by the fire, talking as they warmed their hands.

"Mrs. Page…she's brainwashed, isn't she?" asked Aveline.

Catherine sighed. "Yes."

"Where did they take her?"

"A place called Stellenkirk, north of here. Your friend was there, too." She pointed upstairs.

Aveline sat up a little straighter. "What about Bruno's dad?"

"I'm afraid he did not survive."

"Didn't survive? You mean he died at Stellenkirk?"

"No. When the Stam came to arrest him, he resisted. They killed him."

Aveline's hand flew to her mouth. She sat there in silence for a few moments, trying to process the news. Then she asked, "How did Bruno and his mom escape from the care home?"

"Same as you. The Dagkorodh came for them."

The "r" rolled off her tongue.

"The *what*?"

"The Dagkorodh. An Ebrian word. It means 'Stealth Force.' "

"Oh, the rescuers!"

Catherine nodded.

"How did they know where to find us?"

"We all work for the same organization. Manatha Dé. It means 'Tribe of the Gods' in the language of the ancestors. You might know us better as the Resistance."

Aveline gasped. That the Resistance had come to her aid was not a total surprise to her, but she never thought she would have direct contact with this band of outlaws. Honestly, she'd always been a little frightened of them.

"We were sent on a mission to rescue you, Aveline, and as many children as possible, from the Gilsevain care home."

"Who sent you? Was it my family? My mother?" she asked hopefully.

Catherine shook her head. "We don't know their identities. You see, Manatha Dé is made up of many clans, and many factions within those clans, and they don't reveal everything they know to one another. One person, one clan, cannot have all the intelligence. It's too dangerous if we were to be caught by the Stam. We do know that the order for your rescue came from someone who works for us inside the Party. Inside the Exchequer."

Aveline's heart sank. The Exchequer was the old name for the Ministry of Finance. If Allyn had issued the rescue order, it would have come from the Lightministry or even from the Ministry of Culture, which often worked closely with the Lightministry on events like the Cultural Purification Ceremony. Allyn had nothing to do with the country's finances.

"So, this person in the Ministry of Finance told you where I was and to come get me?" asked Aveline.

"Not directly. The order came to us through other channels. Think of Manatha Dé as a big web with many threads." She traced a circle in the air with her fingertip, simulating the weave of a spiderweb. "These threads branch out from the center to the middle, and so on, to the edges of the web. Not all the individual threads connect to one another. But, if you trace them back far enough, you will see they all lead back to the center. To the spider."

Who is the spider? thought Aveline.

"The order came from the Exchequer, at the center. Through different threads it reached the Dagkorodh, who were sent to Gilsevain."

"Are you part of the Dagkorodh?"

"No, but my husband and I are members of a clan that works closely with them. We call ourselves the Tigerborn. We borrowed a boat from my Ebrian friends and picked up the Dagkorodh and dropped them off at the cove below the cliff. They staked the rope and sneaked into the care home through the steam tunnels under the house."

So that's how they got in. Aveline stopped rubbing her hands together. Another thought occurred to her. "Benjamin is your husband?"

The woman eyed her strangely. "Yes. Does that surprise you?"

"Oh!" She felt herself blush. "I'm sorry. It's just that you don't seem…" She wanted to say *close* or *loving* but didn't want to risk offending her new friend. "I just wouldn't have guessed you were husband and wife."

"I know how Benjamin might seem to others. Cold, distant. But it's not his fault. It was the war, you see. The war changed him."

Aveline pulled her knees to her chest. "The Ebrian War?"

Catherine nodded. "He was a medic in the Alterran Army. Although Alterra invaded my country, he never thought of my people as the enemy. In fact, he even saved my father's life from a gunshot wound. It was then that I fell in love with him. My father gave Benjamin his blessing to take me back to Alterra and marry me. When we came here, I changed my name from Katje to Catherine."

Aveline could picture a war-torn Ebria. Soldiers charging across battlefields, rifles in hand. Innocent civilians shot to the ground as they tried to flee. Exploding bombs so bright they turned night into day. A young woman, dark hair held back from her face with a kerchief, reaching her arms up around the neck of a handsome Army doctor in uniform.

Catherine continued, "I was used to fighting. The Virolannens, our ruling family, were always at war with the countries to the south. I saw things that no child should see. Men ripped apart by bombs. Children missing limbs. Women raped and beaten. My own sister—" She paused, taking a deep breath.

While Aveline wanted to ask what had happened to her sister, she didn't dare. It sounded too horrible.

"But Benjamin had never seen war before," said Catherine. "He had known only peace and happiness in

Alterra. He's from a wealthy family, you know."

Aveline nodded. "His father was one of my grandfather's Six Hundred during the Revolution."

"Yes. Old Harald Cachtice did not think fondly that his only son had chosen an enemy bride. So, we moved from Calador to a little village to the south. That's where we got involved with Manatha Dé. Benjamin saw what the war had done to his country. The war had no victors. The barbarians were not defeated. There was only bloodshed on both sides. To the Party, the war was just a distraction so no one would see what they were really doing. Robbing their own people to build up their coffers. Stealing resources from the other provinces to feed Illyria. Benjamin wanted to stop them. To end the reign of the Fleurs. And as his wife, I promised to support him."

My family. He wants to overthrow my family.

"I'm not like them." Aveline swallowed over a lump in her throat.

"I know you're not, love."

The woman gestured for her to come closer, pulling her into an embrace. Aveline could smell sweat and salt water emanating from her dress, and just the faintest hint of lilac.

She lifted her head from Catherine's shoulder. "My father was in the Ebrian War, too."

"Yes?"

"His plane went down. He died."

"I know, Miss Aveline. I am so sorry. But, you know, you carry him with you here." She gently tapped Aveline's chest above her heart. "Your father lives on in you."

A tear slipped down her cheek, and the woman

brushed it away with her thumb.

"Catherine, I dreamed of him."

She smiled. "Where I come from, dreams have power. You must always pay attention to your dreams."

"The craziest part was that he was speaking Ebrian in the dream. He said three words: *signal, rock, boat*. That was exactly how I escaped from the care home!"

"I'm not surprised that he led you to us. You see? He's looking out for you from the afterlife."

"Do you think I would've been brainwashed at the care home if you didn't come for me?"

She nodded solemnly. "They already had you hooked up to the deep-brain stimulation machine."

"The *what*?"

"Do you know how reeducation works, Miss Aveline?"

She shook her head no.

"Think of the way a building is built. Most of the time, you're building not on empty land but on the site of a building that already exists. You have to knock down the old building before making a new one from scratch. That is the way the Party treats the human mind. They put drugs in your food and water to break down the person you were before, so a new person can be built in its place."

"I *knew* they put something in my water." Her stomach felt queasy, remembering it. "And when I ate brightwing eggs—well, they didn't taste weird or anything, but they made me feel sort of lightheaded and giddy."

"Oh, yes. That was the first step. They were priming your mind for their teachings. With the drugs and the machine. The next step was to drill the Party propaganda into you for ten or twelve hours a day. And your mind was ready for it. It would drink up that poison the way a traveler in the desert drinks water from an oasis. At the end, you would be a completely different person. A person who lives only to serve the Party and the Leader."

Aveline found herself shivering again. "How long does it take?"

"The whole process? About three weeks."

She remembered what Bruno had told her about the man in his neighborhood who had mysteriously disappeared for a few weeks, then returned. This man who had loved animals suddenly didn't care about a poor bird injuring itself by flying into a window. She knew Catherine was telling the truth, but something didn't make sense to her.

"If it only takes three weeks, why did the High Court sentence Sandor to six months at Rjellsfall?" she asked.

"The Party had to make it seem like a punishment. Three weeks is not a punishment."

They must have held him prisoner for the rest of the time, she thought. *Maybe tortured him. Poor Sandor.*

"Can it be reversed?" she said. "The brainwashing?"

"Yes. But it must be done before the process is complete. Once that happens, there is no turning back. The structure of the brain is forever changed."

"How is it done? Reversing it, I mean?"

"With new drugs developed by our friends at the Ministry of Health. That is what we are giving to Bruno's mother."

"The drugs from that little white box?"

"Yes. Delivered by *dzizi*."

"What's a *gee-gee*?" Aveline tried to pronounce it the way she did and failed.

"A small, radio-controlled flying device. Sigrid collected it in the forest before we arrived."

"Has it worked before?" said Aveline.

"The treatment is still experimental. Very harsh on the body. But we have had success. A few of the people we treated now work in the Stam as double agents."

"Double agents?"

"They pretend to still be brainwashed so the Stam won't suspect anything. But they feed us top-secret information through our web of connections. We get some of our best intelligence that way."

Aveline's mind spun. She pictured Manatha Dé's spies acting exactly like Sandor Hayes while making secret drops of information in the middle of the night. Hiding files under bridges. Sending encrypted messages through the radio waves. It was all very exciting, and she wanted to know more about how these "double agents" operated. And what they knew about the Stam's plans.

But she did not have that chance. From the second story, she heard an earsplitting cry from Edwena. The scream seemed to go on and on, echoing through the house.

Then silence.

Benjamin came downstairs with Bruno in tow. Her friend looked as if he'd seen a ghost.

Catherine leapt up. "How is she?"

"Holding steady," said Benjamin flatly.

After the couple had stepped outside on the porch

to talk, Aveline asked Bruno how she *really* was.

"Not good." His eyes were red from crying. "When Dr. Ben gave her the second shot, she started puking and having a fit like she was possessed by a demon. The guy from the Dag-whatever-it's-called could barely hold her down. Then she started screaming."

"But she's sleeping now?"

He nodded. "Avie, I'm scared she's not going to make it."

Chapter 19

That night, Aveline and Bruno huddled together on a twin mattress in one of the upstairs bedrooms, wrapped in a scratchy Army blanket. While the days were mild in Lystra, the nights were cold. Aveline drifted off to sleep, thankful for her friend's body heat.

Almost immediately, she had a dream. It was not a lucid dream. In fact, it was the exact opposite. She had no agency, no ability to move around or fly or change the ending. Rather, she was not even present. It was as if she were watching a film.

Before her was a battlefield in Ebria. A large green tent in which Army medics were tending to wounded soldiers. Inside the tent she saw Benjamin Cachtice, his white coat no longer white because it was drenched in blood. He sat on a wooden stool beside a cot where an injured soldier rested. The soldier's arms were attached to IV drips. One bag contained a clear fluid, the other what looked to be blood. All around the tent the soldiers cried and groaned in agony. Two ragged-looking nurses attended to them.

A single lantern burned on a battered iron table beside the cot where Benjamin sat. Aveline wondered whether he knew the man, his face wrapped in bloody gauze. Benjamin appeared drained, his cheeks and forehead striped with blood, dark circles under his eyes made darker by the dim light and shadows inside the tent. He rested his elbows on his thighs. Lowered his head. Ran his hands through his hair.

As the flap of the tent opened, he raised his head. At once, Aveline recognized the soldier who entered. It was her father in his gray Air Command uniform.

"Kit?" said Benjamin incredulously. "What brings you here?"

"Well, hello to you, too, old chum."

"Old chum"? They know each other?

Benjamin rose from the stool, extended his hand to his old friend. Kit laughed, brushing away the gesture. Benjamin examined his hands and laughed, too, realizing they were covered in dried blood.

"Who've you got there?" said Kit, stepping over to the cot to examine the gauze-wrapped figure.

"It's Willem."

"Oh, God." Kit's eyes went wide. "Willem Ewing?"

Benjamin nodded. "Not likely to make it, I'm afraid."

"Who's going to tell his poor mother?"

"A messenger will have to do it. When we're back, I'll pay a visit to her personally."

"Come," said Kit, clapping his friend on the arm. "You could use a break. Let's have a drink."

The men stepped outside the tent. Above them, the early-morning sky was gunmetal gray. Aveline could hear the faint twitter of birds. The movement of heavy Army vehicles in the distance.

Kit and Benjamin ducked into the mess tent and sat at the end of the table, away from a group of Army men in their camouflage fatigues. From an inner pocket in his jacket, Kit produced a silver flask, which he offered to Benjamin. Aveline recognized the style of the flask; it had been made in Illyria. The doctor took a long pull from the flask.

"Any word from home?" he asked.

Kit reached inside his jacket again and handed the doctor a small color photograph. Aveline could see that it was a portrait of herself as a two-year-old, in a pink dress with a frilly white collar.

"She's growing up fast." Benjamin handed the photograph back.

Kit stared at the photo. Caressed Aveline's face with his thumb. "I miss her so much."

I miss you, too, Father. If only you knew how much, she thought.

"And Allyn? How is she faring?"

Kit took a gulp from the flask and set it down on the table. "Sometimes I think she's glad that I'm gone. I know she loves me, but…"

"But what?"

He sighed deeply. "I think she's really not the marrying kind. She's very content with her work. You know, her trials at the Lawministry. I often feel as if she doesn't miss me. That she doesn't need me at all."

Benjamin shook his head. "That's the war speaking, my friend. The distance. Once you return, it will be as if you never left."

Reaching below his collar, Kit lifted Allyn's sigil ring which he wore on a gold chain. Briefly, he lifted it to his lips.

"I'd keep that hidden away if I were you," said the doctor. "If they knew you were married to the Leader's daughter—"

With a sigh, Kit tucked the necklace back into his

collar, buttoned the top button of his gray wool jacket. "Look, Ben, I didn't really come here to visit. I came here to warn you. After we wiped out a couple of their villages in the south, the Tigers rallied. They're making their way up the coast to the northern waste. They'll be here by nightfall. You need to leave now if you're going to stay ahead of them."

Benjamin startled. "But the wounded—"

"Cyril and I can take six each in our planes."

"There are more than a hundred."

"We'll take your sickest and come back for more as soon as we can."

In the distance, Aveline heard the quick *rat-a-tat-tat* of gunfire. And then she hit the ground.

"Father! Benjamin!"

She opened her eyes. The dream was over. She lay on the cold, rough wooden floor of one of the upstairs bedrooms of the abandoned farmhouse.

"Avie?"

Shaking her head, she realized it was Bruno calling to her.

"Avie, you fell out of bed. Are you okay?"

"I had the craziest dream. I need to tell Catherine."

"Why?"

Before she could explain, she darted out of the room and downstairs to where Catherine slept on one of the sofas cradling Leo, the littlest boy. It was still a few hours until dawn, and the fire had burned down to embers. A small oil lamp, turned low, sat on the floor beside the sofa.

Gently, she shook Catherine's shoulder until the woman awakened.

"What is it, Miss Aveline?"

"I had a dream."

Gently, Catherine lifted the sleeping child and laid him down on the sofa. He stirred, and she covered him with a blanket and kissed his forehead. Then she picked up the lamp and turned the flame a little higher.

"Come, let's go to the kitchen and you can tell me about your dream."

Aveline followed her across the living room and through the swinging door to the kitchen. A moment later, Bruno came in, and the three stood in the corona of Catherine's lamp as Aveline told them everything she had dreamed. She could still hear the groan of Army vehicles crawling over the northern waste. Could smell the rotting flesh and vomit in the hospital tent, enough to make her gag.

Catherine's eyes widened. "We must tell Benjamin at once."

Quickly but quietly, the three exited the kitchen and climbed the stairs. Catherine slowly pushed open the door to the main bedroom where Edwena lay recovering from the brainwashing. The scene reminded Aveline of a painting that hung in a drawing room back at the Estate. It was of a young woman in a flowing white gown lying on a chaise longue, ringed by demons in lamplight. Except that those at Edwena's bedside were not demons; they were Benjamin and the rescuer Tjelmund. Sigrid bent over her, dabbing her forehead with a cloth. Edwena moaned.

"Benjamin, the Stam is coming," whispered Catherine.

The doctor looked from her to the two children who had followed her into the room. "Have you received a *dzizi*?"

"No. Aveline had a dream."

Even in the lamplight, Aveline could make out a smirk on his face. "Come now, Catherine."

"The child has prophetic dreams," she insisted.

He sighed. In Alterra, dreams were viewed as just that—dreams. The mind's nightly flights of fancy. She wondered how often he indulged his wife's strange Ebrian beliefs.

Taking up his own lamp from the floor, Benjamin gestured for Catherine and the children to follow him. To Sigrid, he said, "She's ready for the next dose."

"Yes, Dr. Cachtice."

Back downstairs, in the kitchen, Benjamin set his lamp on the huge oak table and took a map of Alterra from his breast pocket and unfolded it before him. He tapped the southern part of the Province of Lystra to indicate their location. When he lifted his finger, Aveline saw that the name of the village was Caelmorden. And that the next one over was Ede's River, Jem's hometown. The stream where they had bathed the day before must have been the Ede's River for which that village was named.

"What makes you so sure the Stam is headed here, Aveline?" said Benjamin.

She didn't like his tone, or the fact that he'd deliberately left off the honorific "Miss." Although he was from a prominent house, hers was the most prominent of all, and she felt that he should pay her some respect.

Aveline straightened her back. "I dreamed about you and my father during the Ebrian War. My father told you the Tigers rallied after the Alterran Army had destroyed their villages in the south, and that they'd be in the northern waste by nightfall."

"Your father?"

"Christopher Llewellyn Fleur."

"Yes, I know who your father was, child." His voice was cold, stern. "Tell me what else you saw."

Aveline recounted the entire dream, beginning with the hospital tent.

He scoffed. "How could you possibly have known about Willem Ewing? Who told you about him?"

"Nobody." She stiffened. "Who was he?"

"He was the son of the head housekeeper at my family's estate. He was a good friend of mine."

"You see?" interjected Catherine. "Her father is speaking to her through her dreams. She couldn't possibly have known about Willem otherwise. And the Tigers—he means to warn her about the Stam. Tell him, Miss Aveline, about the dream you had at Gilsevain. About the Ebrian code."

Aveline described it for him.

"Well." The doctor did not seem convinced. "If the Stam knew where we were, they'd waste no time in flying a plane from Calador and landing in one of the adjacent fields and storming the house. But if they were tracking us from Gilsevain, they'd have to make the journey by foot. This is rough terrain. You can't see it on the map, but it's much too rough for trucks or tanks. And certainly too rough to land a plane." He traced a line with his finger on the map from Gilsevain Landing to Caelmorden. "Assuming they will be here by nightfall, we must leave immediately to stay well ahead of them."

She shuddered. Although she knew they were in danger, she wasn't ready to leave so soon. The soles of

S. J. Carson

her feet ached. Her whole body was weary and cried out for rest.

"What about my mother?" said Bruno.

"She's not yet ready to travel, but she will have to be. I wanted to give her another two to three days for the antidote to work its way through her system, but I'm afraid we don't have the luxury of time."

"Can she walk?"

"Yes. It's not her mobility I'm concerned with. It's her mind." He tapped his temple. "Her understanding that we are not the enemy."

"So, you're saying she won't go with us willingly?" said Bruno.

"She may resist us, yes. But the Dagkorodh will be there to protect her from herself. To carry her, if necessary."

"Where are we going?" Aveline cut in, articulating the question she knew was also on Bruno's mind.

Benjamin traced his finger due north from Caelmorden over what appeared to be vacant land. "The original plan was to head to the Great Central Forest, about a four-day journey from here by foot. Just beyond the Forest, over the border in the Province of Frelimar, is Terrabaia, where Mount Segog sits. The land was sacred to our ancestors who colonized the continent of Erodith thousands of years ago. Deep within the mountain is Manatha Dé's stronghold. We will be safe there for the time being."

"So, what's the plan now?" said Aveline.

"The same. Only now, to evade the Stam, we'll need to head northeast. It's a shorter distance to the Forest, but the way is more treacherous. Much more treacherous." He showed them on the map. She couldn't see what was so treacherous. But, by the way the Forest curved around and down, she understood that they would indeed hit its outer edges faster by going northeast.

"Why would we do that?" said Bruno. "You want to get us killed?" In the lamplight, Aveline could see her friend's stubborn look. The same expression he had used on the bullies at school.

Benjamin smirked. He was not the sort of man who was used to being questioned. "Do you have a better idea, Page?"

Bruno's expression tightened at being addressed like a servant.

"If we take the straight northern route," continued Benjamin, "we make it easier for the Stam to pursue us on foot. And easier for them to call in reinforcements. The land is perfectly flat. They can send in their vehicles, even land a plane." He gestured on the map to the more treacherous path. "But the northeastern route is extremely difficult to cross even by foot. The land may look flat from a distance, but it's riven. Full of sharp slopes and fissures and crevasses. Many traps for the unwary."

"There's no other way?" Bruno clenched his jaw.

"No, there isn't. Fortunately for you, I've had extensive training in the Army on how to cross terrain just like this. I've crossed it many times in the northern waste in Ebria."

"That makes me feel *so* much better," said Bruno peevishly.

"No one is forcing you to come with us. What you do is your business. You are welcome to stay here and wait for the Stam to take you back to Stellenkirk."

S. J. Carson

"Oh, Benjamin, don't be cruel." Catherine placed a hand on his arm.

But he shrugged her off. Folded the map and replaced it in the breast pocket of his jacket.

"What a jerk," whispered Bruno to Aveline after the doctor had stalked out of the kitchen, with Catherine following close behind. "What's his problem?"

"Catherine said the war changed him. Made him a different person." She lowered her voice. "He wants to overthrow my family."

"Well, I don't like him much, but maybe that's not such a bad idea."

Aveline frowned. "What's that supposed to mean?"

"Your mom and uncle—they started this whole thing. They're the reason why my dad is dead, and why my mom and I were thrown into the Stellenkirk prison. The reason why my mom's upstairs on her deathbed, practically."

She still had trouble admitting it to herself, but she knew he was right. That her family was behind all this. She wished they could just be peacefully removed from power. But she had a feeling that Manatha Dé was not exactly a peaceful organization. They were out for blood. She didn't care much about what happened to Simon; she just didn't want to see Allyn killed. She had already lost her father, and then her stepfather, and she did not want to lose her mother, too. Even if Allyn had done some pretty evil things.

"I'm sorry." Nervously, she played with the ends of her too-long sleeves. "I can't help what my family is doing. I wish I could make them stop…but I can't."

"I know it's not your fault. It's just hard, you know?" He sniffled. "Losing my dad. Seeing my mom

212

like this. I don't know how she'll make it through those badlands."

"Bruno, what if my dream was wrong? What if the Stam isn't coming for us after all and we're just making a big fuss over nothing?"

"Aveline." His voice was steely. For a moment, he sounded like a grown man. "I never wanted to say it back at school, but I think the bullies liked to mess with you because you were always so unsure of yourself. You're the Lightminister's daughter, but you acted like a servant girl."

His words cut deeply, and inwardly she winced. *Like a servant girl.* It was an odd thing for a boy of the lower class to say, because it was also insulting to him. But he was right. Because she had always felt like an outsider, and doubly so when she started putting on weight, she had acted cowardly. Tried to make herself as small as possible.

"Your dreams are trying to tell you something," he continued. "And the grownups are listening."

Well, Catherine is listening. Benjamin...not so much.

Just then, Cora burst through the swinging door into the kitchen, black braid flying behind her. The apprentice healer began opening drawers and cupboards, dumping rations into knapsacks.

"Let me help you," said Aveline.

As they packed the knapsacks, some of the other children filtered into the kitchen, rubbing sleep from their eyes. It was barely morning and the whole house was aflutter with activity. Catherine and Benjamin must have spread the word of their imminent departure.

After the bags were packed and Bruno was upstairs

helping Sigrid get his mother ready for the journey, Aveline stepped out onto the porch to catch her breath. When she spotted Benjamin standing in a far corner, looking out over the land with a pair of binoculars, she froze.

He must have sensed her presence because he turned. "Want to have a look?"

"Um…sure."

Hesitantly, she walked over to him and accepted the binoculars, which were heavier than they looked. Peering through the eyepieces, she swept her gaze out over the land. The fields looked burnt, as if someone—or the sun—had passed over them with a torch. Imperceptibly, the roan color turned to green, then deeper green. This was the faux-vegetation that was really just a kind of mossy weed. From this vantage point, Aveline couldn't see any difference between the northern and northeastern routes to the Great Central Forest. Benjamin had been right; the land looked almost entirely flat, with the exception of rolling hills in the distance.

"The natives call it Greenglen," he said, "which makes one think of emerald pastures and ripe vegetables. Indeed, this land was once worthy of its name."

She heard the unspoken implication: …*until your family destroyed it*.

"It's still beautiful." She handed the binoculars back to him.

After a pause, he said, "You know, what you saw in your dream was not a fantasy."

"Really?" She raised her eyebrows. Looked up at him. "You and my father, that meeting, it actually happened?"

He nodded. "Kit took six of our most critically injured men in his plane. That was his last flight. No one ever saw him again."

Wordlessly, he turned and walked back into the house, the screen door creaking and swinging shut behind him.

Aveline looked out at the lightening land, which seemed to glow from within. Benjamin may have spoken the truth—but how cruel he was just to drop that piece of information on her and leave.

Again, she thought of her dream. Kit's photograph of her as a baby. The sigil ring he wore around his neck. The love that filled his heart for his wife and daughter.

Gone. Gone forever.

She felt the wound of his death as if it were fresh. As if his plane had been shot down only yesterday.

Wrapping her arms around her waist, Aveline braced herself in the raw dawn wind.

Chapter 20

As they walked across the fields heading northeast, a mist rolled down from the far hills. It was the strangest mist that Aveline had ever seen. It didn't appear to touch anything, even the ground. Instead, it hovered like a ghost a few feet in front of them, so that they never quite walked *through* it, and it never seemed to end.

By noon it had burned off entirely, evaporating in an instant as if it hadn't been there at all. While the morning had been chilly, the afternoon was warm, even hot. The sun beat down on the top of Aveline's head, making it throb.

"Here, love, drink some water." Catherine handed her a plastic bottle from the small pack she was carrying. The Dagkorodh bore the heavier loads of rations and blanket rolls and other supplies for their journey.

As Aveline drank, she noticed that Catherine's face was shiny with perspiration, and her thick, dark hair was knotted at the nape of her neck.

Aveline handed the bottle back to her. "Did you ever wear the loyalty ribbon?"

"Never." Catherine sipped from the bottle, then tucked it away in the side pocket of her pack. "Oh, but that angered Benjamin's mother!" They were far enough away that he couldn't overhear them. "She

216

would tell me, 'If you're going to be an Alterran citizen, you must adopt our customs.' Naturally, I would adopt your customs, speak your language. But there was one thing I would not do, and that was to pledge allegiance to your Party. In Ebria, we were allowed to choose between one party and another. Both had their faults, but at least we had a choice. Here in Alterra, there is no choice."

Aveline hadn't considered that before. In Alterra, there were no parties, only *the* Party. And the Party, essentially, was the Fleurs. She wondered whether she would ever join it now. Whether she would ever stand onstage on her sixteenth birthday in her black uniform in front of all the citizens of Calador and recite the Sacred Oath. Receive her sigil ring from her grandfather. A part of her still longed for this future that she had imagined for herself. But another part of her knew that that future no longer existed. So much had changed in the span of just a few days.

The group continued slogging through fields so green with weeds they were nearly chartreuse in the late morning sun. At certain places, they skirted fissures in the ground as if the earth's skin had opened up and then healed poorly, leaving behind jagged scars. Benjamin kept them far enough away from these fissures so that nobody would trip and fall in, but they still made her weak with fear.

"Huge glaciers passed through this valley many thousands of years ago," said Benjamin. "This is their legacy."

Aveline was grateful to be wearing sturdy shoes instead of going barefoot on this terrain. And she was glad that the healers' poultice had worked for Quintana, who walked beside her on two strong feet.

The girls talked of goings-on at school, and about their teachers, the Sisters of Monnag, to make things feel more normal. Even though nothing about this situation was normal.

Finally, Aveline worked up the courage to ask, "Why were you and Cynthia always so mean to me? Was it because I never spoke up for myself?"

Quintana gulped. "Well…you did make kind of an easy mark. But…" She looked down at her feet. "We were actually jealous of you."

"*Jealous?* Of *me*?"

"Yeah."

"But why?"

She looked at Aveline incredulously. "You're a Fleur."

"But you're from an upper-class family, too. Your parents are members of the Party. Your dad—" Aveline stopped herself from saying too much about Quintana's father, who was still missing. "I guess I just don't understand."

The girl sighed. "There's a big difference between being from an upper-class family and being a Fleur. I mean, your family *runs* Alterra. You live on the biggest, most beautiful estate in the entire country. It's hard not to be just a *little* jealous."

Aveline tried to take all this in. "But if you were jealous, why didn't you try to be my friend? Like, if we were friends, I would've invited you over to my house and you could ride horses and swim in the pool and—"

"We didn't want to be your friend. We wanted to make you suffer."

Aveline stopped in her tracks, Quintana's words

like a bullet to the chest. Quintana stopped, too. Lightly touched her arm.

"It was terrible of us. We should have just left you alone. Do you know that every day I cry because of how bad I feel for what we did to you?" She ran her hand over the stubble on her head. "Now I know what it feels like to lose your maiden braid. To lose *all* of your hair."

Balthazar wolf-whistled, and the girls started walking again, side by side. Aveline was still at a loss for words. She touched her own hair, which was beginning to curl over the tops of her ears.

"I didn't mean for that to happen to you," she told Quintana. "I'm sorry."

"I know. Me, too. I'm sorry for everything. And I know if Cynthia was here, she'd say the same."

Aveline looked at Quintana. "What happened to her?"

"I don't know. When you saw us sitting together on the lawn with Mrs. Gregorius, that old teacher woman, that was the last I saw her. They took us back inside and locked us in our separate rooms and I never saw her again. The next thing I knew, I was waking up to a strange man standing over me with his hand over my mouth."

"That's exactly what happened to me, too!"

The girls laughed, though not exactly with mirth. It was simply a relief to release all that tension that had built up between them over the years.

"I wish we could turn back the clock," said Quintana. "Go back to school and start all over again and be friends. Don't you?"

Nodding, Aveline said, "Maybe we can start being

friends right now."

"I'd like that."

"I'll tell you something I've never told anyone before." She dropped her voice. "It's not easy being a Fleur. I know you're probably thinking, 'Yeah, right.' But it's so lonely. People treat you differently. That's why it's always been so hard for me to make friends. And my mother is never around when I need her. She's always at the Lightministry doing important business."

Aveline told Quintana that her mother would attend family dinner, talk briefly with Alfred and Simon, and then return to the Ministry where she would stay until all hours of the night. She never helped Aveline with her homework, yet always demanded perfect grades. She also demanded perfection in the way Aveline looked.

"She had me on this strict diet," said Aveline. "I was only allowed a small breakfast and dinner, nothing more. At school, I used to be able to eat whatever I wanted, but when she found out that I was eating chocolate muffins and stuff like that, she told Mother Josephine to let me have only a sandwich or a salad for lunch. People think I'm so rich that I sit around eating cake and ice cream all the time, but if I ever tried to sneak into the kitchen to get a snack when I was at home, the cook would rat me out to Mother and I'd be in deep trouble."

"Gosh! I had no idea. I'm sorry she did that to you."

"I feel like I'm never going to be good enough for her. I always thought if I tried harder to be perfect, she would love me more—" Her voice broke.

"It's okay." Quintana looped her arm through

Aveline's. "Out here, you don't have to be anybody anymore. We're all equals."

****

As the morning wore on, and then the afternoon, the group's energy began to flag—not that they'd had much to begin with. They had begun their journey with only a few pieces of bread and some dried beef, but now that their paltry meal had worn off, Aveline's stomach began to growl. Though she hadn't been away from home for very long, she could already feel herself losing weight. As she tightened the drawstring that held up her linen pants, she scoffed, thinking of how pleased her mother would be.

All around her she could hear the other children's stomachs growling as well, like an off-key chorus of bullfrogs. Hungry and tired, they neither talked nor sang as they had in the morning. Now, they walked in silence.

The silence gave Aveline a lot of time to think about last night's dream. The Ebrian battlefield, the mess tent. She mulled over her father's words. *I know she loves me, but I think she's really not the marrying kind. She's very content with her work. You know, her trials at the Lawministry. I often feel as if she doesn't miss me. That she doesn't need me at all.*

What if her mother hadn't loved her father as much as he had loved her? Aveline had always thought that Allyn never spoke of Kit because she was devastated by his loss. If anyone mentioned his name, she'd immediately change the subject. Even when Jem had asked her, naturally wanting to know about the man who had come before him, she had put him off. Told him that certain things were better left in the past.

Maybe she never really loved my father at all. Maybe her true love was her work.

The thought was too much to bear. Aveline shook her head to clear it. She did not want to have thoughts like these. Thoughts like giant birds of prey hovering over her head. Flocking in and out of her chest. If this was what it meant to grow up, then she wanted to stay a child forever.

A cry from Edwena Page breached the heavy silence. It was loud enough to startle Aveline from her thoughts. Edwena walked slightly ahead, the rescuers Anax and Tjelmund on either side of her, holding her arms. The other two rescuers, Balthazar—who was carrying little Leo—and Pitre, walked closely with Aveline and the other children. Aveline liked to think of Balthazar as *her* rescuer, the one who'd saved her from the care home. She was thankful that he hadn't been lost like Paolo and Reza. When Aveline had asked about them, Catherine had said, "We do not speak their names anymore."

"Where are the other Dagkorodh?" Aveline asked Catherine now, skipping steps to catch up to her. "The ones who rescued Bruno and his mom?" She had never even met them. They hadn't been at the farmhouse in Caelmorden.

"They are on their way to Mag Ramach in Galatia. Another 'Institute for Mental Hygiene' that the Party made out of an old fortress. They received orders to rescue more people there."

Aveline wanted to ask where their orders had come from—the Exchequer again?—but she was interrupted by another cry from Edwena. It was hard to tell whether Bruno's mother was speaking some ancestral language like Old Alterran or just gibberish. Whichever it was, it was certainly better than her raving about how much she loved the Leader. Benjamin had given her the final dose of the antidote about an hour ago. When would she finally snap out of the brainwashing and again become the woman that Aveline remembered? The woman who made tea and sandwiches for her and Bruno after school. Who danced with them around the living room to popular music.

When Benjamin brought the group to a halt, Aveline saw that Edwena hadn't been crying for no reason. Up ahead, the land was broken in half, as if by a glacier or an earthquake. In the gorge below was a river that ran so swiftly that the water was white. Spanning the gorge, linking the cliff on this side to its twin across the river, was the scariest, most rickety-looking footbridge that she had ever seen. The slats of the bridge were closely spaced, but she noticed that some were broken or missing, as if unlucky travelers before them had fallen through. And the sides, which she supposed had once been tightly woven with rope, were frayed or slackened, or had gaping holes.

No way am I setting foot on that bridge.

She looked to the left and to the right, but this fissure in the land seemed to extend infinitely in either direction.

"There's got to be another way," said Bruno, articulating what they were all thinking.

"There is," said Benjamin. "If you'd like to walk three or four hours east, we can climb down the cliff and cross the river at its shallowest point, then climb back up the cliff on the other side. Your choice."

Bruno scowled.

Edwena began whimpering, speaking gibberish again. She lifted her hands to her mouth, nibbling on the ends of her fingers as if she meant to gnaw them off.

"It's okay, Ma. It's okay." Bruno stroked her hair. Took her hands as if she were a small, frightened child.

Balthazar, the bravest of them all, the first rescuer to descend the Gilsevain cliff, handed Leo off to Pitre and walked over to test the bridge. He gripped the sides and tried to rock it with all his might. It lurched nauseatingly back and forth. As Aveline's stomach roiled, beads of sweat broke out on her forehead.

Quintana clung to her like a lifebuoy in a storm. "I think I'm going to be sick," she said.

"Can it bear the weight of all of us?" Benjamin asked Balthazar.

"I think it can." Then he added, in his careful, precise way, "We must walk single-file and not clump together. Putting too much weight on any one of the slats will cause it to give out."

Balthazar stepped up onto the bridge, gripping the sides. Pushing her fear down into the dark place where she stored all her unpleasant feelings, Aveline broke free from Quintana's iron grasp and stepped forward. She wanted to set an example for the others, but mainly for Bruno and his mother. Wanted to show them that it was safe to cross—even if she wasn't entirely sure of that herself.

"I'm coming, Balthazar."

He grinned at her. "You are brave, Miss Aveline."

She beamed. No one had ever called her "brave" before.

Following his lead, she gripped the fraying rope on

either side of the bridge and stepped onto the first slat. It held. Then another. She exhaled a huge sigh of relief.

"I'm right behind you, Aveline," said Quintana. And then she shrieked.

Aveline turned to make sure she was all right.

"Don't look down!" shouted Balthazar.

That was exactly what Quintana was doing, and now Aveline couldn't help but do the same. Bile rose in her throat as she glimpsed the swiftly-moving river twenty or so feet below them. White water crashed and eddied against rocks downstream. Behind her, she could hear Edwena screeching, the younger children crying out for their mothers.

But she kept going, placing one foot in front of the other. Trying to swallow over the lump in her throat. Her vision narrowed to the next step, and the next. She had never felt so alert in her entire life. Living from moment to moment.

They were about halfway across when Quintana cried out sharply again.

"Are you okay?" said Aveline without turning around.

"My foot! It's killing me."

"What's wrong with it? The poultice didn't work?"

"I don't know. I just have this awful sort of cramp. It hurts like the devil! Like I'm being stabbed with a thousand knives."

Aveline gulped. "It's only a little farther. You can make it, Quintana. I know you can." She wanted to lighten the mood by joking that the Party had banned the devil long ago, but she thought better of it.

Her friend began crying hysterically. "Oh, it hurts. It hurts so bad!"

Quintana lost her footing and lurched forward, clutching at Aveline's shirt. The weight of the two girls was too much for the fragile old wooden slat, and it broke in half, causing them to plunge into the river below.

Aveline screamed and paddled as hard as she could to keep her head above the surface, but every time she did, a rush of freezing-cold water filled her mouth. Although she spat it out, she could barely get enough air into her lungs.

"Quintana!" she gasped. "Quintana! Where are you?"

Then a wave hit the side of her head and she went under again.

Please, God, if you can hear me, don't let me drown!

As she struggled against the force of the current, which held her underwater, she heard a voice.

God, is that you?

But it was not God's voice. It was her own.

Stay calm. Don't resist. Float on your back. Point your feet downstream.

She obeyed and stopped resisting. Felt her body rise to the surface. Took a deep breath. Let the waves rush over her, ferrying her past rocks and debris that brushed against her arms.

Don't resist. Let the water carry you.

The less she resisted, the easier it was to breathe. All her muscles slackened, and she became nothing more than a hollowed-out log. Without a mind of her own. Drifting, drifting.

After some time had passed—she didn't know how much—she sensed that the current had slowed. The sound of rapids no longer rang in her ears, drowning out her thoughts. Water no longer rushed over her nose and mouth. She was floating now in a wider, shallower part of the river. A pool perhaps.

Finally, she stopped moving. She sat up, coughing, opening her eyes. Indeed, she was in a bend in the river, a pool that was only about a couple of feet deep. It was very quiet. All around her, on either bank, were deciduous trees, afternoon light filtering down through their leaves. Dappling her arms. She was in a forest.

She looked down at her feet. Miraculously, she still had both shoes on.

Next to her, she heard coughing and sputtering. To her great relief, it was Quintana. The girl was on her knees, trying to catch her breath, water streaming off her back.

When the two realized that they had both survived the plunge into the river, they hugged each other tightly.

"Is your foot okay?" said Aveline. "Can you walk?"

Quintana lifted it, rolled her ankle. "Yeah. It was so weird the way it cramped up like that on the bridge. It feels a lot better now."

Out of the corner of her eye, Aveline noticed a small body floating face-down.

It can't be. Not little Leo. How on earth did he get here?

She raced over to him and lifted his body from the water and turned him over. He wasn't breathing. His face was starting to turn blue. Without a further thought, she carried him to the riverbank and laid him on his back and starting pumping on his chest with her palms. She'd seen this maneuver performed in safety films at school, but she never thought she'd have to do it on anybody in real life, let alone a small child.

No luck. The maneuver didn't work. The boy just lay there, turning bluer still. Even his little lips were a bluish-white.

I'm not going to lose you.

Aveline was about to redouble her efforts when Leo suddenly sat up, spewing a stream of vomit-laced water from his mouth into her face. As gross as it was, she didn't care. He was alive!

Immediately, he began crying, and she held him against her body. The boy was shivering violently, but she had nothing warm and dry to wrap him in, only her arms.

When he calmed down a little and stopped shivering, he looked up at her with large blue eyes and said, "Are you going to be my big sister?"

There was nothing she could say in that moment except "yes." She had always wanted to be a big sister, and had been so excited when her little cousins, Lily and S.J., were born. Many times, her aunt Lilia had asked her to babysit them, but they'd treated her like the bullies at school, ordering her to bring them toys and sweeties. Then, when Allyn married Jem, she'd hoped they would have a child together. That was not to be. When Aveline looked at this little boy, her heart filled with love for him as it would have for her own sibling.

"Where are we, Big Sister?" he asked.

"Good question," said Quintana, eyes roving around their new environment. "Do you think we should stay here or try to walk back upstream to find the others?"

Aveline couldn't believe that Quintana was asking *her* that question. As if she was their leader. For the first time in her life, she felt a sense of pride. A belief in her own capabilities.

"We'd better stay here. I'm sure they'll come for us soon. If we start wandering around, we might get lost and make it harder for them to find us."

"How are they going to find us? What if they're already on the other side?"

"Quintana, they're not going to leave us behind," she said with more confidence than she felt. "They'll have to figure out a way to come down here and look for us. Benjamin and Catherine and the Dagkorodh are really smart. I know they can do it."

"How far downstream do you think we are?"

"I have no idea."

At Aveline's direction, they sat on broad, flat stones on the riverbank and waited. And waited. The dappled light began to fade and the shadows lengthened. It was evening, and there was still no sign of the others.

"I'm hungry," whined Leo.

"Me, too," said Quintana.

"You know what?" said Aveline. "Waiting here was a bad idea. I think we should start walking upstream again before the sun sets. We can't get lost if we follow the river. Maybe we'll run into them along the way."

What a great job I'm doing as their leader, she chided herself.

Their clothes halfway dry by now, they stood, shivering in the wind that blew through the trees.

Behind them, in the distance, Aveline heard what sounded like hoofbeats.

"Do you hear that?" she said.

Quintana nodded. "You think someone's coming on horseback?"

The girls looked at each other, frozen in terror. Together, they said, "Stam."

The sound of the hoofbeats intensified. They were coming closer now, galloping from downstream.

"Run!" shouted Aveline.

Scooping up the boy, she discovered that he was light when holding him but heavy when trying to run with him.

As the girls began sprinting up the riverbank as fast as they could, three men on black horses overtook them from behind, circling around to block their way. Aveline turned back only to find three other men on horseback. There was nowhere to run. They were surrounded.

She looked up at the men in front of her. Each wore a black cloak and had a wide strip of dark hair along the center of an otherwise bald head. At their sides she could see the black tops of swords. And holsters with handguns. An odd mix of medieval and modern weaponry.

Aveline began to sweat. Had she not been with Leo, she would have grabbed Quintana's hand and tried to dodge them. Outrun them. Even jump back into the river. Anything to get away.

But she was frozen there, in a circle of menacing riders. They clearly weren't Stam. Who were they, and what did they want?

The man at the center of the original three

dismounted his horse. He began walking toward them, his hand on the hilt of his sword.

Chapter 21

Leaves crunched under the man's boots as he approached the children. Aveline clutched Leo tightly to her, and she and Quintana inched backward.

"Aren't you a bit young to be traveling Gholon's Pass all alone?" The man spoke with the *clain*, the harsh, guttural accent of the nobility prior to the Revolution.

"W-who are you?" she asked.

"*I* ask the questions. Not you." In the fading light, she could see his smile. Two rows of even, white teeth. With a quick, singular motion, he unsheathed his sword and pointed it at her. "Now, what brings you here?"

She trembled all over, never having been on the sharp end of anyone's sword before. Her instinct was to tell him the story he wanted to hear, but she didn't know who he was or what story would please him. What magic words would make him let her and her friends go.

"W-we were coming from Lystra," she began. "On our way to the Great Central Forest. We crossed a bridge up there—" She pointed. "—but it was a very old bridge, and one of the slats broke and we fell into the river. That's how we got here." She knew she was starting to ramble, but she was so nervous that she couldn't help it. "We didn't mean to trespass on your land…if this is your land. I-I'm very sorry about that. If you could just show us the way out of here, we'll—"

"What business have you in the Great Central Forest?"

Quintana piped up, "We were just going to be passing through the Forest, sir. You see, we're on a journey to Terrabaia. To…to pay our respects to the land of the ancestors."

Aveline was impressed with her friend's quick thinking, using what Benjamin had told them about the land on which Mount Segog sat.

That didn't seem to fool the man. "No one makes the pilgrimage to Terrabaia anymore," he said. "No one believes in the wisdom of the ancestors. Only in the Party."

Aveline's stomach knotted. The derisiveness in his tone when he mentioned the Party suggested that he was an enemy of the State. Maybe he belonged to Manatha Dé. In that case, he was a friend, but she couldn't be sure. She didn't know whom she could trust out here in the wilderness.

"What is your name, child?" Again, he pointed the sword at her.

She didn't want to tell him but couldn't think of a fake name fast enough, so she told the truth. "Aveline Fleur."

His eyes widened, as did his smile. But it was a cold smile. "Aveline Fleur. Descendant of Alfred Fleur, usurper of King Reuel IV."

She swallowed. "I-I didn't have anything to do with that."

"And you." He pointed the tip of his sword at Quintana. "Are you her sister?"

"No. I'm her friend. Her *best* friend."

She locked eyes with Aveline. If the situation hadn't been so dire, Aveline would have smiled.

"Name?" said the man.

"Quintana Bailey."

"And the boy?" He pointed his sword at the child.

"His name's Leo," said Aveline. "I don't know his surname. He's of no relation to us."

"She's my big sister!" said Leo.

Aveline wanted to clap a hand over the boy's mouth. "I can explain. I rescued him from drowning in the river. He calls me 'Big Sister' now."

If this strange man was going to kill her for being a Fleur, she at least wanted him to spare her friends.

The man's eyes widened. By this point, his five compatriots had dismounted their horses and joined him, closing in on the children.

He clucked his tongue. "I'm sure Alfred Fleur would be very upset to see his grandchildren lost and alone out here in the woods, wouldn't he?"

Adrenaline surged through Aveline's body. She called upon that voice, that inner strength she had summoned during her plunge into the river. "If you don't let us go, my grandfather will have you shot by the firing squad!"

Rather than terrifying him, as she had intended, she only made him laugh. He looked around the circle at his friends, and the six men erupted with raucous laughter. Then their leader held up his hand and they all fell silent.

"Alfred's puny firing squad is no match for the Bhorowan. We wear the aegis of our King. We cannot be killed."

This sounded like some kind of ritualized saying.

The man sheathed his sword and bent down on one knee and looked Aveline in the eye. "I know you don't really mean us any harm. Poor, lost little girl. Your grandfather must be worried sick." He rose and gestured to his cronies. "Don't worry. We'll keep you safe."

Aveline was about to pick up Leo and try to run again, but one of the men—huge, all muscle—grabbed her and clapped a hand over her mouth. Silencing her scream.

As she struggled against his superior strength, he suddenly loosened his grip and fell. She looked up and saw Balthazar holding a gun with a long barrel. He had shot her attacker in the back.

Before she could comprehend what was happening, Balthazar scooped her up and darted behind the thick trunk of a tree. There was no time to ask questions. He held her around the waist with his left hand, and with his right he shot at the enemy. All around her she could hear the *thwpt thwpt* of the Dagkorodh's silenced guns and the sharp *bang* of the Bhorowan's pistols. Men's shouts and groans. The whinnying of horses. The heavy thud of a body falling to the forest floor.

Please, God, may it not be one of the rescuers.

Balthazar lifted her and sprinted deeper into the forest, pausing behind the great trunks to stop and shoot. As he ran, she caught glimpses in the failing light of the Dagkorodh and Bhorowan in hand-to-hand combat. She saw the flash of a knife in Catherine's hand. Saw her sink the blade into a Bhorowan's chest. She'd had no idea that the Ebrian woman could fight like that—or even that she'd been carrying a knife in the first place.

One of the rescuers—Anax, maybe—passed in front of her field of view, carrying Leo in one arm and Quintana over his shoulder. A Bhorowan lunged at Anax with a sword, and he ducked, hitting the forest floor. Aveline did not see where her friends went. She only heard them scream. She wanted to cry out to them, but thought better of it, not wanting to give away her location in the growing darkness.

It was like being in a nightmare. At any moment, she hoped to tumble out of bed onto the floor of the farmhouse in Caelmorden, Bruno grasping her shoulder and telling her that it was all just a terrible dream.

More cries and gunshots. More neighing of horses and galloping hooves.

Then silence. The forest was so silent now that she could hear the hum of cicadas. Could hear Balthazar's labored breathing beside her. One side of her face was smashed into the dirt. She could taste its earthiness, its grittiness.

Balthazar helped her sit up. She spat the dirt from her mouth and wiped her lips on the back of her hand. Wrapped her arms around herself.

"A-are they gone?" she whispered.

"I think so."

She was shaking all over as he helped her to her feet. Nearby, she heard crying and followed the sound to where Quintana was sitting on the forest floor with Leo. Anax had his arm protectively around the two of them.

When Quintana saw Aveline, she leaped up. "I was so scared I'd lost you."

"Me, too."

"I hope you didn't mind me telling those guys you

were my best friend. Because it's true. You are. The best friend I've ever had."

Aveline brushed tears from her eyes and laughed unexpectedly, then pulled the girl into an embrace. Now she had two best friends, Bruno and Quintana. For the first time, she truly felt like the luckiest girl in Alterra.

Off to their left, she could hear a horse neighing and snorting. A very agitated horse. Tjelmund ran his hand along its muzzle to calm it down. The gesture reminded her of Jem, and she felt a pang of longing. At Tjelmund's feet was the rider of the horse, face-down in the dirt, his black cape billowing around him like a funeral shroud.

"Are they all dead?" she asked.

"Two of 'em rode off," said Tjelmund. "The rest are with the ancestors."

"Where are the others? And Mrs. Page?"

"Upriver with Pitre."

"Where did Benjamin and Catherine go?" she asked. "I saw them fighting."

"I don't know," answered Tjelmund.

The group began heading upriver to find the others. It was nightfall now, the forest almost entirely dark but for the waning moon shedding silvery light through the trees.

They hadn't been walking long before they encountered their two leaders. To Aveline's shock, Benjamin was lying on the riverbank, Catherine crouching over him, hands on his chest trying to stanch the bleeding.

He's been shot in the heart.

"Please, Benjamin," Catherine was saying. "It is not your time yet to go with the ancestors. Stay with me. Please."

Wordlessly, Balthazar bent down to the doctor. Catherine fell back, sobbing, saying something to the rescuer in her native language.

Aveline watched as Balthazar passed his hands over Benjamin's chest, as if feeling for the bullet. She wondered whether he was going to pull it out. She remembered from her Health and Safety class at school that sometimes it's better just to leave the bullet in and wait for a surgeon to operate. Otherwise, the victim could die from blood loss.

She did not see Balthazar pull anything out of his chest, however. "He was not shot," the rescuer told Catherine. "They stabbed him. The wound runs deep."

Catherine stood pacing on the riverbank, then stopped, her hand to her mouth. Even in the moonlight Aveline could see that it was covered in blood.

"Will he survive?"

"That I don't know, Katje. We will take turns watching him through the night."

"But we can't stay here."

"Katje, your husband is not fit to travel."

Catherine sank to her knees beside Benjamin. Aveline wished she could take away the woman's pain, but all she could do was keep Catherine company, touch her shoulder. She and Quintana and Balthazar stayed with their leaders as the other two rescuers continued upriver to meet the rest of their group. Aveline wrapped her arms around a trembling Leo, kissing the top of his head and calling him "Little Brother."

Later in the evening, the others joined them at this spot on the riverbank. The rescuers carried the heavy bags of supplies that they had left behind when they charged ahead to rescue Aveline and her friends. Aveline was happy to see that the other children—and Edwena—had arrived more or less unscathed. Only hungry and exhausted.

The Dagkorodh thought it too dangerous to make a fire, so they ate bread and strips of dried beef in the dark. Aveline, who had been ravenous earlier, now found herself without appetite. She forced herself to finish her meager meal and lay on a thin blanket beside Quintana and Bruno, thankful to be reunited with her two best friends.

But she couldn't relax, worried about whether Benjamin would make it through the night. Her first impression of him had been of a taciturn man, embittered by the war. Protecting the children was incidental to his real agenda, which was to stage a coup against the Fleurs. He had only rescued them from the care home because he was ordered to do so by Manatha Dé.

She saw now how wrong she had been. Benjamin Cachtice was a good man. A man willing to risk his own life to save the lives of others. He had taken a sword wound to the chest for her and her friends. And for that, she was deeply grateful.

The Bhorowan were also on her mind. The ones who got away—where did they go? Were they rousing their cronies right now? How many of them were there?

Unable to sleep, she got up and tiptoed over to where Balthazar was crouched, keeping watch over the campsite. The lone horse stood slightly downriver, its reins hitched to a boulder.

"Everything okay, Miss Aveline?"

"Can I ask you something, Balthazar?"

"Anything."

"Who are the Bhorowan?"

"The King's Guard. Sworn to protect and defend King Reuel. Now that he's dead, they've vowed to avenge their fallen king. Their sons and grandsons have taken the vow, too."

"What did they want with us?"

"To take you prisoner, Miss Aveline. Demand that your grandfather pay ransom for your safe return."

"So all they wanted was money?"

He nodded. "First money. Then power. To take back their kingdom from the Fleurs."

A chill went down Aveline's spine as she imagined legions of Bhorowan marching on Calador.

"What if they come back?" she asked.

Balthazar replied, "Then we will be prepared for them."

****

But the Bhorowan did not come back.

They stayed for two more days in Gholon's Pass. While they had plenty of water from the river to drink, they were beginning to run low on rations. Pitre had caught a couple of squirrels and cooked them over a small fire, but the meat was oddly sour-tasting and practically inedible. Worried that the children would starve, Catherine tried to forgo her own rations so that they could have more. But Balthazar insisted that she eat to keep up her strength and be able to tend to Benjamin.

The first night, he barely clung to life. Catherine had stayed awake to watch over him. But once the dawn came and she saw that he was still breathing, she became more confident that he would recover. Out here in the woods there were no healers, no herbs to make a poultice, only a few bandages and medical tape from Sigrid and Cora's store of rations. Fastidiously, she cleaned and dressed the wound; Aveline could see that the sword had narrowly missed his heart. His face was a death mask, but by the second day he could nibble on a bit of breadcrust and drink a little water, and the color began to return to his cheeks.

Out of habit, Aveline thanked God. Although, after her stint in the river, where God had spoken to her in her own voice, she was starting to doubt that it was God who was making these miracles happen.

By the end of the second day, Benjamin could sit up, albeit painfully. He insisted that they start moving. Every day they spent here in Gholon's Pass was another that the Stam was gaining on them. They still had to cross the Great Central Forest to get to Mt. Segog, to safety. It would be an arduous journey, he warned them.

This is all my fault, thought Aveline. *I got us into this whole mess with my dream. What if the Stam's not actually chasing us and we could've just taken the easy route to the Forest?*

"You are still weak, Benjamin," protested Catherine.

"But I can ride." He gestured to the Bhorowan horse, still tethered to the boulder.

It was a black Oldenburg, which reminded Aveline of her mother's horse, Pacer, whom Allyn used to ride in dressage competitions. Aveline mentioned this to Catherine, as well as the fact that she herself used to own a Dutch Warmblood called Paintbrush. She closed her eyes briefly, remembering those days back at the stables with Jem, taking her riding lessons. Remembering her mother coming down the path from the Great House to collect her for dinner. Allyn's fingertips brushing the ends of Jem's Aspirant ribbon. Those days felt so long ago they may as well have belonged to another lifetime.

She watched Anax and Pitre help Benjamin up into the Oldenburg's saddle. Catherine climbed up into the saddle in front of him and instructed him to hold on to her around the waist. Aveline hadn't noticed until now that her skirt was split for riding. The expert way she took the horse's reins and spoke to him in a low voice, a melodic blend of Alterran and Ebrian, suggested that she had ridden in her native country, and perhaps in their country, too, in the southern Illyrian village where she and Benjamin had lived. Aveline was continually surprised by this woman. By her strength, her skills with a knife, the way she calmly and competently cared for her ailing husband. In a way, she reminded Aveline of her mother. Except that the Ebrian woman seemed to have no penchant for, or attraction to, darkness of any kind.

While the couple rode, the rest of the group traveled on foot. They crossed the pool where Aveline and Quintana had landed after their terrifying ride downriver. A little way through the forest, Aveline looked up. She was astounded at the length and depth of this crevasse, running like a long, jagged scar across the earth. It was not on the maps that hung on the classroom walls at Belfort Academy. Day after day, she had studied those maps. She would have remembered this enormous rift valley, this Gholon's Pass.

When they reached the cliff on the opposite side of

the gorge, Aveline drew in a sharp breath. Although there was a trail up the side of the cliff, it was steep, with many switchbacks. Bravely, Catherine led the horse up first, with the Dagkorodh and older children following. The rescuers carried the smaller children in their arms and the supplies on their backs. Aveline admired how indefatigable they were and wondered what kind of military training they had undergone back in Ebria.

Her heart pounded as she walked uphill. There were no guardrails or staked rope on this trail—not that she expected there to be any—but the idea that one misstep could send any one of them careening off the side of the cliff, like the rescuer Paolo, filled her with terror. She was also on guard for the Bhorowan. She figured they must have come down a trail just like this one into Gholon's Pass, and they could appear at any time on their black steeds, like phantoms.

"Where do the Bhorowan come from?" she asked Balthazar.

"Rakan Fo," he answered.

"Where's that?"

"In Galatia. They call it the Iron City."

She hadn't heard of it before. How odd that the map of Alterra in the classrooms back at Belfort Academy did not display it. Maybe because the Party had wanted to erase all traces of what had once been Reuel's kingdom.

"Is the city really made of iron?" she asked.

"Not the whole city, just the main gate," said Balthazar. "It's known as the Iron City because of the inhabitants' iron will. During the Revolution, when your grandfather's troops attacked, they barricaded themselves inside. Their iron gate and enormous wall were impenetrable. No troops were ever able to break through and take them prisoner. The people of Rakan Fo and their descendants still live there today and remain loyal to their dead king."

"So they never come out?"

"Some do. The Bhorowan venture beyond the city wall. But the rest stay inside, too afraid to leave."

"But what happens when there are too many people to fit in the city? Won't they have to go someplace else?"

Balthazar shrugged. "I don't know. Maybe they've decided to keep their population small. What happens inside Rakan Fo is a mystery."

****

Once they had safely arrived at the top of the cliff, and again were on flat land, Aveline bent over, hands on her knees, panting from the exertion. Her shoes were covered in dusky sand from the trail. When she stood, she shielded her eyes from the harsh sun and saw a stretch of flat, mossy land before them—or at least it looked flat from this vantage point.

And it was, to her relief. As the day wore on, with only a few pieces of bread and fake Party cheese to tide them over, her initial relief faded to weariness. Hunger pangs gnawed at her stomach. She and Bruno and Quintana grumbled their discomfort to one another. Occasionally, she glanced over at Edwena. The Dagkorodh still held her arms, but she walked quietly, without complaint. It was impossible to tell whether the antidote had worked. Aveline hoped that her silence was not a sign that she had slipped back into the brainwashing.

They had started walking early in the morning, a little after daybreak, and it was now mid-afternoon. Aveline could tell they were nearing the Great Central Forest because the landscape was changing. Trees began to appear in the fields. A few pine and deciduous, then more and more until it became apparent that they were within the ambit of the Forest.

The children stopped and looked upward, into the canopy so thick the sunlight barely broke through. Curiously, all the leaves and pine needles were a deep rust-red color. And there were no sounds—no birds, squirrels, raccoons, or any animals at all. Only the sound of the wind rustling the leaves.

"This place is scary," said Aveline, drawing closer to Bruno.

"Yeah," he agreed. "They should call it the Dead Forest."

They continued walking, deeper into the Forest, their despair matched by the growing darkness. The only thing she could see in the gloom was an occasional pair of yellow or green eyes gleaming through the foliage for just a moment. Was she hallucinating?

"D-did you see that?" Quintana brushed up against her, making her jump.

"The eyes?"

"Yeah."

Aveline nodded, glad she hadn't been the only one to see them. "What do you think they were?"

"Wolves."

"No, I don't think so." Surely, if there weren't any other animals, there weren't any wolves living in this Forest.

"This place is haunted," said Bruno.

Aveline's heart leaped into her throat. It had been a long time since she believed in ghosts, but now she was starting to think that maybe Bruno was right. Still, she would rather be pursued by ghosts than the Bhorowan or the Stam.

Thankfully, there was no sign of either. She wondered if the Stam had come upon the farmhouse at Caelmorden and found it empty except for the two healers, assuming they had stayed behind. She prayed that the cousins wouldn't be taken prisoner and tortured—or worse, brainwashed—for aiding the Resistance.

As they walked, it kept getting darker and darker until the Forest was pitch black—so black you couldn't even see your hand before you, like what Aveline imagined blindness to be. Catherine brought the horse to a halt and called for the group to stop walking.

"We will camp here for the night," she said, leaping off the Oldenburg with a red-covered flashlight in her hand. "There's no sense in continuing in total darkness. We mustn't lose our way."

As the Dagkorodh built a small fire, Aveline thought for sure it would attract insects the way the campfire did back in Gholon's Pass. But none came. There were no night noises. And no footfalls, either, much to Aveline's relief.

She looked into the frightened faces of the other children around the fire. In her lap Quintana held Leo, who had begun to cry. Aveline figured he'd seen the glowing eyes in the brush, just as they had.

The rescuers began to pass around the last of the rations from their packs. By now, Aveline's stomach was so empty that it had given up the will to growl, and instead felt as heavy as a rock. She bit into a thin slice of Party cheese, not fond of the sour taste but trying to make it last. On their walk today, she and her friends had tried to imagine the delicious food that awaited them in Terrabaia—beef stew, shepherd's bread, flagons of real milk—but they'd had to stop because the game was making them too hungry.

"Why is there nothing alive out here?" Bruno asked Catherine. "Do you think this place is haunted?"

It was Benjamin who answered. "Many years ago, when he first came to power, Alfred Fleur ordered a test site for nuclear weapons, called Cascadia, to be built in northern Lystra. It was the radiation that killed the wildlife. And the trees."

In his weakened state, those few words cost him dearly, and he lay back on the blanket that one of the rescuers had unrolled on the ground for him. Catherine smoothed his hair. Told him to close his eyes and rest.

Aveline felt a chill, though not from the cold breeze that whipped through the dead leaves and branches above her. *Grandfather never told me anything about Cascadia. No one else in my family ever mentioned it, either. All these secrets and lies...*

From the shocked look on Quintana's face, she could tell that her friend's father—a nuclear engineer at the Ministry of Energy—must not have told her about it either.

"Are we going to die from the radiation?" said Bruno, drawing his knees to his chest.

Catherine replied, "It has been almost thirty years since the last explosive test at Cascadia. But there is still a risk of illness, of cancer, yes."

"What are we doing here?"

Aveline turned. It wasn't Bruno who was speaking; it was Edwena. Her voice was little more than a hoarse whisper, but Aveline could see the firelight reflected in her eyes. Edwena Page was still in there. She hadn't been lost like Sandor Hayes. The antidote had worked.

Bruno leaped up from where he had been sitting next to Aveline and ran over to hug his mother. As he smoothed her hair and tucked loose strands behind her ears, he explained that they had been rescued by a stealth force from Ebria, and they were on their way to safety at Mt. Segog. Catherine pulled a bottle of water from her pack and offered it to Edwena, who drank nearly all of it in one gulp.

She was quiet a long time before she spoke again. "I don't remember any of that. The last thing I remember is the magistrate sentencing me to six months at the Stellenkirk Institute for Mental Hygiene. The rest was…how can I describe it? Like one long dream, I guess." She rubbed her head as if she'd fallen down and hit it.

"What did you dream?" said Catherine.

"I…" Edwena closed her eyes, remembering. "I was a girl again, in the slums of Lupine Falls, the village where I grew up. My sister and I were catching rats. Rats for our family to eat, that's how poor we were. Then I was grown up, the same age as I am now. I was a scullery maid for a strange woman dressed all in black. It was some kind of religious order, I think. Something to do with a prophet they called Elignon…The woman made me scrub the pots in the kitchen, scrub the floors on my hands and knees. Hours and hours and hours every day until my hands started to peel from the chemicals." She held them up before her, examining imaginary wounds. "It was awful. Was that at Stellenkirk? I have no idea."

"Elignon calls himself a prophet, but he's not," said Catherine. "He's nothing more than a dictator in religious garb."

"He's a real person?"

She nodded. "Oh, yes. He is the ruler of Abaddon, in the Tormen Badlands in the far east."

"The Tormen Badlands?" Edwena scoffed. "But...but I've never been out of Illyria in all my life. Well, except for now. I was never brave enough to leave, let alone go all the way to the Badlands." After a long pause, she said, "Do you think maybe I was dreaming of a past life?"

Aveline cringed. Back in Calador, that was a heretical thing to say. Before you were born, you didn't exist except as a part of God's body. There were no past lives.

"Maybe," said Catherine. "There are many things we know so little about. Past lives, glimpses of other realms, that come to us in dreams. The human brain is very small in comparison to the size of the universe."

When the fire had burned to embers and it was time to bed down for the night, Aveline huddled with Bruno and Quintana. She couldn't sleep, listening to the grownups talk in hushed voices. She heard Edwena say to someone, maybe Catherine, "We'll force the Leader to kneel on his driveway on creaking knees and turn over every last stone with Monnag's face on it...As for Allyn and Simon, we'll do the same thing to them that they tried to do to us."

Aveline swallowed uneasily. If there was any doubt in her mind that Edwena Page was a member of

Manatha Dé, and that she had helped Sandor Hayes publish his article, it had now been erased.

She fell into an uneasy sleep. Right away, she was transported to a tiny garret in a high tower. On a straw pallet, lying on his side facing away from her, was a man in tattered clothing, with a shaved head. He stirred, seeming to sense her presence, and turned over on the pallet. In the wan moonlight passing between the bars of a high window, she saw his face. It was Jem Caslon.

She awakened with a start. Her poor stepfather. The Urians, whom the Alterrans and Brixians were fighting in the war, must have captured him. How could Allyn have allowed this to happen to Jem? This was the man she supposedly loved. She knew the consequences when she encouraged him—*pressured* him—to join the Army.

The grownups were still sitting around the remains of the campfire, talking, laying plans. After rising from the hard ground, Aveline tugged on Catherine's sleeve. "I had another weird dream."

"Tell us about it, Miss Aveline."

After she had relayed the dream, she added, in a cynical tone she almost didn't recognize, "Why did Mother even marry him in the first place?"

"The Lystrans were threatening to revolt because of the famine," said Edwena. "She needed a way to build goodwill between the Party and the people down in Lystra. So she decided to marry a poor farmer's son. One who'd look good in front of the cameras, of course. She sent her associates to search for such a man, and when they found him they brought him up from Ede's River. There was no other way that someone like Jem could have ended up in Calador, working on her estate."

Aveline shook her head. The courtship, those love letters, the wedding—they were all a sham. Jem was nothing more than a tool for Allyn's political gain. And when he was no longer useful, she simply got rid of him.

"Oh, I shouldn't have said that, Miss Aveline." Edwena reached out to her in the darkness. "I didn't mean you any harm. I only wanted to tell you the truth."

"It's okay."

But it wasn't okay. Nothing would ever be okay again.

****

They packed up their campsite at daybreak, although it was hard to tell the difference between night and day in the Great Central Forest. Thin beams of grayish light broke through the dead leaves of the trees, so weak they didn't even reach the ground.

The group stayed close together, absolutely silent but for the crunching of leaves beneath their feet, listening for approaching footsteps. Once in a while, the Dagkorodh heard something the children didn't, and they snapped up their long-barreled guns at an invisible target.

As she walked, Aveline tried to forget the pain in her feet. Yesterday, she'd begun developing blisters which had since popped, leaving her skin red and raw. Each step she took felt like someone was stabbing her with a knife. She now understood Quintana's pain that day on the rickety footbridge when her foot cramped.

"Chop-chop." Quintana tugged at her elbow. "Don't fall behind."

She groaned, feeling a bit like they were back at school, with one of her friends pushing her to keep up while running around the track. She wanted to ask how much longer until they were out of the Forest, but she was careful not to annoy Catherine, and especially Benjamin, who was still recovering from the sword wound, and had to ride in the saddle behind his wife.

In the brush ahead, Aveline jumped when she saw a pair of glowing yellow eyes, narrow and menacing. When she blinked, they were gone. Again, she reminded herself that there were no wolves in these woods, that it was only a scary legend, but she couldn't shake the feeling of being watched.

Quickening her pace to keep up with the others, she felt something sharp strike her left ankle. At first, she thought it was just a briar, but when she looked down she saw that a small dart had punctured her skin through the fabric of her pants.

"Ouch!" She stopped and pulled out the dart and held it up to examine it.

Before she could, an enormous gray wolf sprang from the brush, snapping its jaws, knocking her backward onto the ground. She screamed.

"It's the Fleur child," hissed the wolf, which was so close to her that she could smell its sour breath. Could feel its claws at her throat.

"Help! Balthazar!" Her voice echoed as though she were inside a tunnel. Surely she must have been dreaming if there was a talking wolf.

"At ease, Claudius," said a baritone voice she didn't recognize.

She heard Catherine call, "Miss Aveline!"

The whinnying of the Bhorowan horse. The

stamping of hooves. Then shouting and the *thwpt thwpt* of silenced guns. Her vision began to break apart, like those collages she had made in childhood which crackled when brushed with lacquer.

With a low growl, the wolf leaped off of her, and the man who had spoken to the wolf lifted her into his strong arms. She was so sleepy all of a sudden; she wanted nothing more than to be carried.

All she could see, before she fell asleep, was the black collar of a uniform and a gleaming Monnag pin.

Chapter 22

Aveline opened her eyes. Blinked several times in the dim light. Her head ached and her vision was fuzzy the way it had been at the Gilsevain care home, after Manánn had fed her the drug-laced food.

When at last she came to her senses and her vision cleared, she saw that her wrists were bound to the chair on which she sat. They weren't bound with metal restraints like when she was strapped to the wheelchair at the care home. Instead, her wrists were held firmly in place with nylon zip ties. The zip ties were fastened so tightly that one would not even have been able to slide a pencil under them.

At her feet was Claudius, the wolf that had attacked her. Snarling, growling up at her, saliva foaming at his black-rimmed jaws. Now she saw that Claudius was not really a wolf but a wolf-like dog whose gray fur was dappled white along his back. Though he was a fearsome creature, she realized he was only an animal and could not possibly have spoken to her.

"Where am I?" she said. Or perhaps she just thought it. Her lips were as dry as sandpaper, her tongue swollen in her mouth.

To her left was a small, round window. A porthole of sorts, covered with a putty-colored shade.

Am I back on the Ebrian powerboat?

That was not possible. Down in the boat's cabin, she had heard the sound of waves outside. Had felt the boat moving and vibrating. But here, wherever she was, there was no motion.

She turned her head to the right. Sitting in an identical chair across a narrow aisle was a Stam officer.

I'm on an airplane.

It must have been one of her grandfather's private planes, or perhaps one belonging to the Lightministry, in which her mother had traveled to different parts of the country. Through the officer's window she caught a glimpse of clouds, of green fields below.

It all flooded back to her: the trek through the pitch-black Forest, the dart in her ankle, Catherine's shouting, the stamping of hooves. Panic gripped her, although her heart didn't beat any faster and her breathing didn't quicken. She was so weak, so tired, from whatever sedative they had put in that dart.

"Where are you taking me?" she managed to croak, although before the officer said anything she already knew the answer.

"To Calador." He didn't turn to face her, but his tone implied an eye roll.

"I want to see my mother."

He said nothing, only smirked faintly.

What's funny? she wanted to ask.

Instead, she said, "Take these handcuffs off me. They're hurting me."

"Shut up."

She wanted to scream at him, but she knew it would do no good. She'd scream her throat raw and he would keep her tied to this seat. Better to conserve her strength for whatever awaited her back home.

When the sun began to set in the officer's window, the plane touched down at the airport just beyond the Calador city limits. The officer unbuckled his seatbelt and stood. Claudius leaped from where he was lying at Aveline's feet and snapped to attention at his master's side, emitting a low growl. From a *saya* on his belt, the officer slid out a knife and slashed Aveline's wrist restraints.

Before she could rub her raw, aching wrists, he yanked her out of her seat and held her upper arm in an iron grip. Emerging from the cockpit, the pilot opened the door and pressed a button to lower the stairs to the tarmac below. Then the officer escorted her down the stairs and pushed her into the backseat of a waiting limousine. Another Stam officer, whom she hadn't seen on the plane, followed his partner into the backseat and sat opposite Aveline. The last time she'd been in one of her family's limousines, she'd been alone, but now she was trapped between two giant, steel-faced men. She thanked God that Claudius had not come with them.

As the door locks clicked, she startled. She could not understand why the driver would lock the doors when two Stam officers were there to guard her, only a few inches away, with pistols and knives at their hips. What were they afraid of—that she'd try to jump out?

Yes, she thought, *that's exactly what they're afraid of. That I'll take my own life before Uncle Simon can take it from me.*

But she had no intention of taking her own life. She did not know what the future held, but she knew that she had to remain strong. Remain alive.

Fortunately, the windows did not black out, and this time she could see where they were headed. After they left the airport and entered the capital, she watched buses on either side of them lumbering down the wide avenues. On the sidewalks, ordinary people were walking home from work; kids were walking home from school. All were wearing modern, machine-made clothing. She felt as if she'd been plucked from the country's medieval past and dropped into the future.

For the last week or so, her eyes had been trained on long distances, fields, and forest. After the old farmhouse in Caelmorden, the tall buildings were a jarring sight.

The car crossed the Victory Bridge and entered the City Center. From the time Elton had kidnapped her, to the Stam's attack in the Great Central Forest, she had prayed to return home to Calador. Ironically, now that she was back, she wanted nothing more than to return to the Forest with Ben and Catherine, with Bruno and Quintana and Balthazar and little Leo.

As the drug from the dart wore off, she became more and more lucid. She licked her lips, which only made them drier when her saliva evaporated. Shaking with fear, cold sweat trickling from under her arms, she tried to make herself as small as possible. To shrink away from the officer beside her, who smelled of hair oil and the dank interior of Stam headquarters inside the Ministry of Law and Peace.

Surreptitiously, she tried to sniff her clothing. She stank of sweat and horse manure. *What will Grandfather say when I walk into the parlor?* Those days seemed so long ago, when she would wander past the old Monnag clock on her way to the dining room, worried that she smelled of the stables.

A part of her still held on to a small shred of hope

that her life would go back to exactly what it had been before she left. That she would return to school and take riding lessons and attend family dinners and do her homework in the Great Room under the portrait of her father and run through Wildweir on days when the weather was fine.

But her rational mind knew that such was not possible. Too much had changed. No one she loved was there anymore. Not Jem. Not Bruno. Even the bullies were gone. She couldn't trust Jossie, who might have been the one to rat her out to Simon for having read Sandor's article. And she especially couldn't trust her mother. Her entire world had shrunk to just one person—herself.

Overcome by sadness, she began to cry silently. Had either one of the officers looked at her, they would have seen only her clenched jaw, her shoulders shaking. She wished Catherine were beside her. The Ebrian woman was as calm as the eye of a storm. But she was all alone.

The car pulled up to the back entrance of the Ministry of Civic Enlightenment. At 600 feet, with a glass façade, it was one of the tallest and most imposing buildings in the City Center.

As the car entered the underground parking garage, she stopped crying. *So they* are *taking me to Mother after all.*

What would she say to Allyn when she saw her?

Mother, you knew what Simon did to me. You had to know. Yet you did nothing to help me, your own daughter. Manatha Dé had to send the Dagkorodh all the way from Ebria to come save me.

Had the rescuers not come, she still would have

been at the Gilsevain care home, deep in the throes of brainwashing by now. She shuddered at the thought.

****

Aveline stood before the large oak-paneled doors of her mother's office on the fiftieth floor of the Lightministry building. One Stam officer stood on either side of her, holding each of her arms in a viselike grip. As if she had the strength or courage to try to run away. As if there were anywhere she could actually run.

She could hardly believe that she was here, just a few feet away from the place where Allyn spent so many of her waking hours. While some kids at school had been to their parents' workplaces and knew exactly what they did during the day, Aveline had been to her mother's office only a handful of times, and each time for just a few minutes. Allyn was very private about her work, and rarely if ever spoke of it to Aveline. What she did at the Lightministry was a complete mystery.

The officer on Aveline's right leaned forward to rap on the door. Nervous butterflies filled her stomach. In just moments, she would be face-to-face with her mother.

"Come in," said a female voice. It belonged to Miss Dagyan, Allyn's elderly secretary.

The officer opened the right-hand door and led Aveline into the room. She drew in a breath. The office was exactly the same as she remembered it from the last time she was here, years ago, but its size and elegance never ceased to amaze her.

Twice the length of the dining room at the Estate, the office boasted a fireplace with a crackling fire, an ornate carpet spread before it, and two leather club chairs on either side of a coffee table. Above the fireplace hung a painting of Monnag, his red-gold wings spread wide, fangs bared, spiked tail coiled upward. On the other side of the room were a long meeting table and chairs and floor-to-ceiling bookshelves. At the center of the office was a huge mahogany desk the size of two or three ordinary ones put together, with an electric typewriter and several stacks of heavyweight file folders. The black leather chair was turned to face the window so that Aveline couldn't see Allyn's slender figure in it.

When the chair swiveled around, she was startled to face her uncle rather than her mother.

"Leave us," said Simon to Miss Dagyan and the Stam officers.

Before exiting, the officer holding her right arm dropped her, with some force, into one of the high-backed chairs before Allyn's desk. As they walked out, the officers' heavy boots made the wooden floorboards creak. Then she heard the door close behind them. She wanted to run but knew the two black-clad ogres would be standing right outside.

As she fumbled for her words, Simon smiled at her, his Mark of Yrgess gleaming on his right pinky. He was dressed in his black Party uniform as if he had just come from some important State function.

"What is this stunning ensemble you're wearing?" he began. "Wait, wait, don't tell me." He paused, always so good at controlling the silences. "Caelmorden Couture?"

"What do you want with me?" she demanded. "Where is my mother?"

He raised a stubby finger. "Objection. Compound question, as the barristers say."

Heat crept into her face. She could tell how much he was enjoying this by the way the firelight played in his gray eyes.

"What do I want with you? Well. I couldn't have the country wondering where the Lightminister's daughter had gone, now, could I? Thinking she'd disappeared off the face of the earth?"

Aveline glared at him.

"Truthfully, I couldn't have cared a whit for what happened to you out there in the hinterland. Let the wolves of the Forest eat you alive and all your little friends. Alas, poor Aveline!"

As he placed his hand dramatically over his heart, his medals jangled.

How vain he is, she thought. *He's never fought in any war. Earned no medals of valor.*

"How did you find me?" she asked.

"Please, Aveline. Did you really think you could slip away from me that easily? I've had my men tracking you and your Ebrian entourage since they broke you out of the care home."

She looked at him, aghast.

He chuckled. "Come now, did you really think me that much of a fool? That I didn't know about the Resistance stronghold at Mt. Segog? Or that you were on your way there when my men intercepted you?"

She gulped. They'd been so careful to take the northeastern route, through the riven land, where the Stam couldn't follow. How had Simon found them in the Forest? His men must have come from some other direction. The north, maybe.

And how did he know about the stronghold at Mt. Segog? With a sour feeling in her stomach, she realized that he might have learned of it through his double agents, those newly un-brainwashed people that Manatha Dé had sent back to infiltrate the Stam. Maybe one of those agents had flipped on Manatha Dé, or perhaps was not quite as un-brainwashed as they had thought.

Her head spun. "I want to see my mother."

"I'm afraid that's impossible. We arrested her yesterday." Simon folded his hands before him on the desk.

Aveline gasped. "Arrested her? For what?"

"High treason."

"What did she do?"

The shadow of a smile played across his lips. "She had the audacity to cross me."

"What did she do, Uncle Simon?"

Casually, he said, "The charges will be read soon enough at her trial. Until then, I am Lightminister." He lifted his hands and gestured around the room. "This office once belonged to me, you know. I like what she's done with the place. Made it all cozy for me. I'm sure she knew I'd be back to claim it eventually."

Aveline was in no mood for his idle ruminations. "Take me to Grandfather. *Now.*"

"My, my. Demanding, aren't we?" Simon exhaled a dramatic sigh. "Unfortunately, he's indisposed at the moment. Taken ill, sadly."

"Ill with what?" Her stomach dropped.

"Pneumonia. Very serious case, it seems. But he's an old man now, susceptible to any virus that comes along. Not much to be done except offer our prayers."

She could see clearly the game her uncle was playing. *First, he tried to brainwash me. Then he trumped up charges against Mother. And now he wants to kill Grandfather. He's trying to steal the Leadership.*

"Grandfather was just fine when I left!" cried Aveline. "He doesn't have pneumonia. You did something to him. You made him ill!"

Simon snapped upright in his chair. Pointed a finger at her. "Watch your tongue, young lady. What you are accusing me of is high treason. Not only am I your Lightminister while Allyn awaits her trial, but I am also your Leader. I demand the proper respect."

Respect. Ha! Simon was not, and never would be, fit to lead Alterra. He was too weak, too selfish.

How was it possible that he had outsmarted Allyn? If there were ever a battle for succession, Aveline thought that her mother would certainly win. She was much smarter, much craftier, than her brother. But now he had her locked up in a cage, like an animal, in the bowels of the Lawministry. Aveline couldn't help but think of all the terrible things that Simon had probably ordered his men to do to her. As angry as she was with her mother for not coming to her rescue, she did not want to see Allyn suffer.

Although she felt the urge to cry, she summoned all her strength and did not let a single tear fall. She would not allow Simon the satisfaction of seeing that he had made her upset. That he had made her lose control of herself. Clenching her jaw, she said, "Where are Benjamin and Catherine and Dagkorodh?"

"Someplace where they will learn never to disobey again."

He must mean Rjellsfall. Or Stellenkirk or one of the institutes.

Without any thought for her own safety, she said,

"Take me to them."

Again, he folded his hands atop the desk. His lips thinned as he concealed a smile. "My dear niece, you are never leaving Calador ever again. You will be under the supervision of a minder at all times. I have hired the strictest, most iron-willed Sister of Monnag in all of Alterra. I am confident that you and she will get along famously." He allowed himself a smirk.

Aveline immediately thought of Sister Janus, one of the hall monitors at Belfort Academy. This hatchet-faced old Sister would box the ears of any student who roamed the hallways between classes, even if he or she were only going to the bathroom. Sometimes, if she was in an especially foul mood, she would make the younger kids bend over and proceed to spank them with a thick wooden paddle. Fortunately, to the relief of the entire student body, Sister Janus had retired last year. Aveline would not have been surprised if Simon had tempted her out of retirement with a fat bundle of ducats.

"Your care and keeping, your education, and your travel—limited as it might be—are in your minder's hands," he continued. "When you do leave the Estate, it will be only to show your face at public events. Because, unfortunately, you are a Fleur and we must keep up appearances."

With that, Simon wolf-whistled, and the two Stam officers barged into the room through the heavy doors and took Aveline into their custody.

Chapter 23

Aveline stepped out of the limousine onto the grand driveway of the Fleur Estate with its hand-laid stones imprinted with Monnag's head. Edwena Page had said that, one day, Alfred would kneel on creaking knees and turn over these stones one by one.

That was not going to happen now. Alfred's downfall was not going to be Manatha Dé but rather his own son. Simon had the entire Party, the Stam, and all three branches of the Armed Forces behind him. He may not have been a strong man himself, but he didn't have to be with tens of thousands of people doing his bidding for him. If Manatha Dé ever tried to free the care homes or march on the capital city, Simon would squash them like bugs.

As the two officers led her up the front steps, Aveline shivered in a chill breeze. It was nearing the end of autumn. Besides spring, this used to be her favorite time of year. When candles were lit and the smell of cinnamon and pumpkin filled all the rooms of the House. When Calador would celebrate the harvest with feast days and parades down Heritage Way.

There never was any harvest, she thought bitterly. *At least, not since the famine struck Lystra the spring before last.* The food must have come from farms in other parts of Alterra, maybe even from neighboring countries. The "abundance" of Alterra's breadbasket region was nothing more than a lie that Allyn had told through the Lightministry.

A new butler whom Aveline didn't recognize opened the front doors to let her and the two Stam ogres inside. He eyed her suspiciously. Had Simon replaced the household staff, too? What about Jossie? Not that Jossie could be trusted anymore, but Aveline did not want to see anything bad happen to her.

In the entryway, instead of the head housekeeper, Mrs. Pelletier, stood a figure in the black habit of the Sisters of Monnag, though without a veil. To Aveline's relief, it was not Sister Janus. This Sister was tall for a woman, perhaps five-foot-eight or nine, and about Allyn's age. Her green eyes seemed like those of a much older woman who had lived through many ages and seen many things, but her skin was taut and youthful. She had high cheekbones and delicate features, and wore her black, waist-length hair in a braid tied with the loyalty ribbon. Aveline admired her beauty but distrusted her at once. Perhaps it was the cruel way she smiled.

"Welcome home, Miss Aveline," said the woman. "I am Sister Morfyd. Your uncle has hired me to take care of you and keep you safe."

The woman spoke with a highborn Caladorian accent, richly intoned, like Allyn's. But the odd emphasis she placed on certain syllables made Aveline think she might have been faking the accent. Why? Was this strange woman really a Sister of Monnag? She knew Simon hadn't hired Morfyd to keep her safe.

He only wants to keep me out of sight...until he needs to parade me around like a good little pet for the television cameras.

Morfyd inclined her head toward the two officers. "Thank you for taking such good care of my charge. May God hold your spirit in his hands." One of the many benedictions of the Sisters of Monnag.

The officers returned her nod and departed.

Now alone with Morfyd, Aveline shivered. The House looked the same, and even smelled of pumpkin and spice, but something in the air had changed. It reminded her of the dark energy emanating from the Caelmorden farmhouse. The sort of darkness that could seep into one's pores. She wanted to break free and run outside, but she sensed in Morfyd a certain agility, a tensile strength, the sort of woman who could crush bones with her slender fingers.

Morfyd's smile did not touch her eyes. "It's a pleasure to finally meet you, Miss Aveline. Your uncle has told me so much about you."

I'm sure he has. Has he also told you that he had me kidnapped to Belmarin to brainwash me? And that he failed?

Aveline did not smile back, or reply.

Morfyd leaned down to her and raised her chin with a single finger. Aveline had no choice but to look up into those eyes like green ice.

"You don't have to be coy with me, child. I already know all your secrets."

Aveline's heart raced. *What secrets? What does she know?*

Before she could speak, Morfyd grabbed her arm and began leading her upstairs. As they climbed, a massive ring of keys jangled at her hip. The ring reminded her of the one that the groundskeeper's wife Brigitte used to carry on her belt. But Brigitte was kindhearted and would allow Aveline and Bruno to admire the giant skeleton keys and pretend that they opened gates to other worlds.

When Aveline hesitated on the landing, Morfyd yanked her up the next flight of stairs. Even through the rough linen of her shirt, Aveline could feel the woman's sharp nails digging into her skin. With her sadistic streak, Morfyd wasn't much different than Sister Janus. Except that she had the advantage of youth and beauty.

Once upstairs, Morfyd led her down the hall to her bedroom. It looked exactly the same as she had left it. The bed was neatly made, her many silk-covered pillows stacked against the headboard. Her set of monogrammed silver brushes were lined up neatly on her bureau. A fire roared in the fireplace. She could feel its warmth on the exposed parts of her body: her neck, her hands, her ankles. Although she was a prisoner here, it was still good to be home, surrounded by her familiar things.

Morfyd released her arm, and Aveline rubbed it, knowing that a bruise would develop where the woman had gripped her so tightly.

"Sleep well, Miss Aveline."

Morfyd turned and exited the room, closing the door firmly behind her.

"Wait—"

Aveline was about to ask her if she could have something to eat and drink when she heard the key turning in the lock. As if it wasn't bad enough to be held prisoner at the Estate, the Sister was locking her into her own room!

She tried the knob to no avail, then banged on the door. "Sister Morfyd!" She screamed the woman's name over and over until her throat was raw.

In a panic, she raced to the nearest window and threw open the curtains. Instead of a pane of glass, she came face-to-face with solid wood. Someone had boarded up the window.

She ran to the next window, and the next, but all four had been made impenetrable by thick wooden boards. She began tearing at the sides of the boards, hoping to yank the nails out of the window frames, but they refused to budge. She tried throwing heavy books at the boards, but they were not heavy enough even to make a dent.

Frantically, she searched the room for some other kind of object that she could use to break the boards. To her chagrin, the pokers and other fireplace instruments had been removed. Even her two beloved white wicker chairs were gone. Everything else was either too light to do any damage to the boards or too heavy for her to lift.

Her legs gave way, and she collapsed on the rug, finally allowing herself to cry. But she was so dehydrated that only a few tears came.

Why imprison me here? Isn't it enough that I can't go anywhere without my minder?

Aveline knew that Simon didn't really want to starve or kill her. She was too valuable to him. Well, not exactly valuable as a person, but valuable to keeping up the appearance of a cohesive family unit. To show the public what a wonderful uncle he was, caring for his beloved niece while his sister was on trial for high treason. Or at least to keep them from speculating as to her whereabouts.

Sitting up, she brushed the scant tears from her cheeks. Sniffled. The last time Simon had trapped her, it had been in the family car, headed for Gilsevain Landing. Awaiting her at Gilsevain Landing was a strange, beautiful woman with a Caladorian accent. Brightwing eggs laced with drugs. And a deep-brain stimulation machine.

She understood now what was coming.

Uncle Simon is going to reeducate me.

Chapter 24

When Aveline awakened, it was not in her bed but on the floor where she had collapsed last night, in her soiled linen clothes, her worn-down shoes still on her feet. Sitting up, she swallowed over a bone-dry throat and looked around the room. Nothing had changed except that the fire had burned down to embers. She looked to the windows. Although she'd thrown open the curtains, she couldn't tell whether it was morning or night. The clock on her bedside table had been removed, the only instrument that provided any insight into the world beyond this room.

Peeling herself off the floor, she opened the door to the adjoining bathroom and staggered in and turned on the light. She glanced upward. The skylight was dark, rain spattering against it. With a chill, she realized that she must have slept through the entire day.

Standing before the mirror above the sink, she could scarcely recognize the face staring back at her. Her eyes were glassy and bloodshot, her forehead and cheeks smeared with dirt, her lips parched and caked with blood. And her hair was a fright, partially matted to her head and partially frizzed. She turned on the tap and scrubbed her face until all the dirt was gone. Gratefully, she filled her palms with water and drank until she was satiated and her stomach was full and sloshy.

As she was drying her face on a soft pink towel, she heard the key turn in the lock. She dropped the towel and her heart leaped. Maybe the wicked Sister Morfyd was finally bringing her something to eat.

But when the door opened, the person who entered was not Morfyd. It was Jossie, carrying a tray with plates covered by silver cloches.

"Jossie!"

Once the lady's maid had set the tray down on a table, Aveline ran to her and embraced her. She was so relieved to see a familiar face—this woman who'd taken care of her since she was a baby—that she temporarily forgot that she might not be able to trust her.

After their hug, Aveline studied Jossie. She still wore her black maid's uniform with the white apron. Still wore her hair in a long plait secured by the loyalty ribbon. But she had dark circles under her eyes, and her skin was sallow.

"Jossie, please tell me it's not true," said Aveline. "Tell me you didn't rat me out to Uncle Simon for reading Sandor's article."

The maid lifted a finger to lips, then slid a small notepad and pencil from her apron pocket. Turning to the first blank page, she wrote:

I would never betray you, Miss Aveline. Please be careful what you say. This room is bugged.

When the shock of this revelation wore off, Aveline thought, *Of course Uncle Simon bugged my room. How could I have been so stupid to believe that I had any privacy here when he's got the whole Estate bugged? And the city of Calador, too.*

She gestured for the pad and pencil, and Jossie

handed them to her. She pointed to the dinner tray and wrote, *Does that food have drugs in it?*

Jossie wrote, *No. M told B to put it in your food but she disobeyed.*

Aveline knew that "M" stood for Morfyd, and "B" stood for Mrs. Beauregard, the head cook. She breathed a sigh of relief, then looked into Jossie's kind blue eyes. Aveline understood that both the cook and the maid had risked their own lives so that she would not be brainwashed.

"Thank you," she mouthed. Then she wrote on the pad: *Why was my mother arrested?*

Jossie replied in writing, *I don't know. It's not on TV yet. No one tells us anything.*

"I'm so sorry, Miss Aveline," said Jossie aloud. "I saved something of hers for you."

From deep in her apron pocket, Jossie produced Allyn's sigil ring and handed it to Aveline. She gasped.

"This is all that's left," said Jossie.

Aveline accepted the ring and slipped it onto her pinky, the only finger on which the tiny ring would fit. This ring had survived two wars now, she realized. The first was the Ebrian War. She imagined that when Kit's plane went down, a fellow soldier had recovered it from the crash site and returned it to Allyn.

The second was the Brixian War. There was no possibility that Jem had given it back to Allyn when she sent him off to join the Army. Jem would not have done that; he loved her too much. The only way the ring could have returned to Allyn is if Jem had died at war. Just like Kit.

No. That can't be. Jem can't be dead.

Jossie put her arms around Aveline as she began to

cry.

"In my heart, I would have felt him die," she whispered. "But I didn't. I dreamed that he was imprisoned in a tower. Do you think he might still be alive?"

"I pray for his safety every day. Just as I prayed for yours. And look! Here you are."

Aveline hugged Jossie tighter. There were so many things she wanted to say but could not speak them aloud. And they were too complicated to put into writing. She'd need about a hundred notepads to tell Jossie the story of her journey from the care home to Caelmorden to Gholon's Pass to the Great Central Forest.

"Come," said Jossie. "You must be starving. Have your dinner while I add a few logs to the fire. Then I'll draw you a bath."

As Aveline sat at the table, shoveling food into her mouth, not even tasting it, she watched the flames in the fireplace grow higher. Watched Jossie tear the scraps of paper from her pad, crumple them up, and toss them into the fire, where they glowed briefly and blackened and turned to ash. Just like Sandor's article.

After her bath, dressed in her soft cotton pajamas, the sigil ring safely locked in a drawer in her vanity, Aveline climbed into bed. Just as Jossie was tucking her in, the way she used to when Aveline was a little girl, the door to the bedroom flew open and Sister Morfyd appeared. Aveline sat bolt upright. The woman wheeled a deep-brain stimulation machine into the room.

"Get that thing away from me!" cried Aveline.

"Please, Sister Morfyd," begged Jossie on her behalf. "It's too soon. The drugs haven't taken effect yet."

Morfyd yanked the maid up from where she was sitting on the edge of the bed, and practically dragged her across the floor and into the hallway. Aveline cowered. She had no idea where the Sister found the strength to drag another grown woman across a room.

Closing the door, Morfyd turned on her heels and commanded Aveline to lie down. She was about to protest when she realized that the machine couldn't hurt her—Jossie had given her food and water free from any drugs. There was no way that the machine could do anything to her mind. As Catherine had explained it, the machine and the drugs worked together to break down a person's identity so that the Party could rebuild it through their propaganda.

Aveline took a deep breath and closed her eyes and kept still as Morfyd rubbed ointment onto her forehead and secured the electrodes into place. She opened her eyes only for a moment to see the green light on the machine turn on. Except for a gentle whirring, she heard nothing. Felt nothing. Just a strange coldness on her head from the ointment.

Morfyd caressed her cheek with the back of her hand. "Sleep well, Miss Aveline."

****

Aveline awakened with a start. Sat up. Rubbed her head. Curiously, the electrodes had been removed, and her forehead was neither greasy nor sticky. She was no longer hooked up to the deep-brain stimulation machine.

But she wasn't in bed. Or wearing her pajamas. She was dressed in her "Caelmorden Couture," as Simon had called it, the rough linen shirt and pants and rubber-soled shoes. Instead of her mattress, she was sitting on a damp floor. All around her she could hear night noises—cicadas, frogs, the distant hoot of an owl. A warm breeze stirred her short hair.

Blinking hard, she glanced around and saw that she was in a forest. Moonlight dappled the green leaves silver. This was not the Great Central Forest whose leaves were rust-colored and dead. She was somewhere else. Wildweir? In the distance she thought she heard the rush of a stream, the sound of voices, the whickering of horses.

Suddenly, almost before she could blink again, she was surrounded by six men on horseback, carrying torches. She recognized them immediately from their black tunics and capes, and by the stripes of dark hair down otherwise bald heads. The Bhorowan.

This has to be a dream. When I fell asleep, I was at home. There's no way I could have traveled all the way back out here to Gholon's Pass.

She looked around at the men, who came closer and closer to her on their horses, forming a tight circle so she couldn't run. But one man looked different. He was of slighter build and wore a black hood so that she couldn't see his face. He did not carry a torch.

The man dismounted his horse and walked toward Aveline. As she cowered, she heard behind her the low growl of an animal. Without turning around, she knew it was a wolf.

Once he had thrown back his hood, Aveline saw that this rider was not a man at all. It was Sister Morfyd. She jumped back, and the wolf snarled.

"At ease, Claudius," said Morfyd, and the animal fell silent.

Claudius. The same wolf-like dog that belonged to the Stam officers. What on earth was he doing here?

She studied Morfyd in the torchlight. Shadows delineated her cheekbones, the fine, square structure of her jaw. Her thick black hair was no longer in a braid. Instead, she now wore it loose, cascading in long waves over her shoulders and down her back.

"Miss Aveline, we've missed you."

"W-who are you?" Aveline knew she was not a Sister of Monnag. "Or *what* are you?"

"You're asking wrong questions."

"What am I doing here?"

As Morfyd smiled, two small commas formed on either side of her mouth like the beginnings of dimples. "Again, the wrong question."

If these were the wrong questions, then what was the right one?

"Am I dreaming?"

The fire leaped and danced in the Sister's green eyes, giving them an almost manic appearance. Aveline had said something that affected her, but Morfyd didn't say whether that was the right question.

"Pinch yourself," commanded Morfyd.

She obeyed.

"Feel anything?"

She nodded. The pinch hurt, just like it would have in real life. Then she remembered that she had once fallen and scraped her knee during a lucid dream and didn't wake up. Now she pinched herself again, and again, and she felt it each time, unable to trust her own perceptions. Was it possible that the machine could work on the subconscious mind even without the drugs? Was this what Edwena meant when she said that she felt as if she'd been dreaming the whole time since being sentenced by the magistrate?

Aveline began to sweat. She wondered whether she might be going mad.

When she looked back at Morfyd, she saw Claudius at her side. The Sister reached down to scratch behind his ears, and he whimpered with pleasure, saliva dripping from his jaws onto the forest floor. "Good boy." Then Morfyd turned her attention to Aveline. "Is this dog able to speak?"

"I…I don't know."

Claudius barked.

"Is he speaking to you now?"

"No. He's barking."

"Barking as a dog is wont to do?"

Aveline nodded.

"Then you can draw your own conclusion."

And that conclusion was that she was not dreaming. But, if she were not dreaming, then nothing made sense. Being here in Gholon's Pass, surrounded by the King's Guard, was only explainable by dream-logic.

"B-but I've been here before," she stammered. "I left already. I walked up the cliff on the opposite side of the river. I…"

She trailed off, thinking. *The Dagkorodh killed these men. Or a few of them. And scared the rest off. I saw it. I saw it happen with my own eyes.*

As if she could read Aveline's mind, Morfyd said, "Surely there are more Bhorowan in Rakan Fo? Or do you really believe that the ones you met in this forest were the last of their kind?"

The men around her laughed.

"What do you want from me?" demanded Aveline.

Morfyd laughed along with them. "What do I want from you? I already have it. I told you that I know all your secrets."

"What secret? What do you have?" Aveline's voice was so high-pitched that it was almost a squeak.

"I know your greatest fear."

She's messing with your head, Aveline told herself. *She just met you. She knows nothing about you. Maybe she has Benjamin and Catherine in captivity and forced them to tell her about what happened last time with the Bhorowan.*

Aveline was convinced, now more than ever, that this was only a dream. She willed herself to wake up.

But, when she closed her eyes and opened them, she did not awaken back in her bed. She was still in the forest, surrounded by black-clad men on horseback. The one difference was that she and Morfyd were no longer alone in the circle. To her left, Quintana appeared, a gag in her mouth, bound to a tree that had sprung up before them out of the earth. Her friend locked eyes with her, straining against the coiled rope that bound her body. The gag muffled her screams.

"Quintana!"

As Aveline tried to run toward her, she collapsed to the ground. All her muscles slackened. She felt as weak as she had at Gilsevain after Manánn had dosed her with the drugs.

This is only sleep paralysis. You learned this in science class, remember? Loss of muscle control just after falling asleep. Wake up! Wake up!

All around her, the men roared with laughter.

Morfyd slid a slender arm around her. "You see,

your biggest fear is your own cowardice. You run and hide from danger. You want to run toward your friend, but you can't. You're not trapped by sleep paralysis, only by your own mind. Your own limitations. We could shoot her, or slit her throat, or simply leave her to die out here in the forest, in the dark, and let the maggots devour her carcass. Whichever way we choose, you cannot save her, Aveline. You never could save any of them. You may be a clever girl, but you're not brave."

Before she could reply, the scene vanished, and she and Morfyd stood by the riverbank, the exact spot where she and Quintana had come to a stop that day after their terrifying journey downriver. It was no longer night but mid-afternoon. Floating face-down in the pool was the body of little Leo.

"Leo!" she cried and splashed through the water to reach him. This time, she was not hampered by fear or sleep paralysis or the limitations of her mind. She was going to prove this evil woman wrong.

Picking Leo up, she carried him to the riverbank and turned him over on the sand. His face and lips were blue. Like before, she performed compressions on his chest. She had already saved him once, and she was going to save him again. At any moment, she expected him to spew vomit-laced water into her face. To take a deep breath. To call her "Big Sister."

But the boy remained still, lifeless. She continued to press on his chest to no avail.

This can't be.

"You acted too late," said Morfyd, crouching beside her. "He's already gone." With a singular swift motion, the woman yanked her up from the riverbank, pulled her away from the dead child. "But it doesn't have to be like this. There is a way to overcome your weakness. To acquire bravery so that you can stop hating yourself."

"How do you know that I hate myself?" Her voice was barely a whisper.

"Come now, Miss Aveline. It's written all over your face."

"How do I stop it?"

Don't trust her, warned the wiser voice inside her. *Don't tell her anything she can use against you.*

But, in her weakened state, she felt her internal resistance eroding. She missed her mother. Missed Jossie, wherever she was. All she wanted was someone to help her. To tell her that everything was going to be all right.

With a flick of her hand, Morfyd made Leo disappear. She sat beside Aveline on the riverbank, taking the girl into her arms, gently stroking her hair. "You must realize that, alone, you are nothing. With your family, you are everything. If you cooperate with your uncle, he will be your strength. He will give you everything you desire. Your freedom. Your friends. He is the only one who can."

She shook her head. "No, he wants to hurt me."

Morfyd stopped stroking her hair. "Hurt you? He loves you like his own children. He wants to save you. Just as he saved me."

"Saved you? From what?"

"You may find this hard to believe, but I was a member of Manatha Dé. People may criticize the Party for controlling them and making them conform, but the Resistance is no different. They want you to serve them. But when Simon found me, he showed me who they really are. From that day on, I would not serve."

"But you serve my uncle…Don't you?"

"I serve no one. I have no master. Simon and I are equals. We work together. I'm afraid you've misunderstood him, Aveline. As the second child of Alfred Fleur, Simon was always in his sister's shadow. Now he has broken free. He is free to pursue his own vision of Alterra. One where there is no hunger. No poverty. Where there are no Aspirants and no Sponsors. Where everyone is free to join the Party, and where the Party serves *them*, not the other way around. Won't you join us, Aveline?"

"I won't."

With that utterance, Morfyd stood and grabbed Aveline by the hair, also yanking her into a standing position. The woman was so strong that she almost lifted Aveline off the ground. With her other hand, Morfyd slapped her across the face. So hard that Aveline's eyes smarted with tears.

"You will break," said the Sister. "I have broken those much stronger than you."

In an instant, Aveline was miles back upriver, standing on the rickety wooden footbridge. It was noon, the sun directly overhead. She grasped the guardrails and looked down, saw the rapids foaming beneath her. Her heartbeat echoed in her ears.

Gingerly, she took a step forward, but the next slat vanished, and she tumbled down, down, into the rushing water.

Chapter 25

The next thing Aveline knew, she was waking up in her bed, coughing, gasping for breath, as someone tore electrodes off her head.

When she was finally able to breathe normally and realized that she was not drowning in the river, she opened her eyes and stared directly up into Morfyd's green eyes. She screamed.

"Quiet now, Miss Aveline," said the Sister sweetly. "What did you dream?"

Aveline cleared her throat. "I...I dreamed of you...except you said it wasn't a dream."

The woman smiled slowly. "Did I? How would I know?"

Aveline pinched her own arm and felt her nails digging into her skin. Was she still dreaming? Could she trust the sensations of her body? Her own thoughts?

"Speak, child."

Taking a deep breath, Aveline was about to scream for help when Jossie appeared, carrying a breakfast tray. As she set it on the table, Morfyd stood and walked over to her. "Give the child her breakfast, then dress her and send her down to me. Our lessons begin today."

Morfyd glanced over her shoulder at Aveline, throwing her a little smirk, and sauntered out the door, closing it noisily behind her.

Jossie rushed over to Aveline's bedside, pushing aside the wheeled machine, the electrodes dangling from it on long wires.

With a cool, damp washcloth, Jossie began cleaning the ointment off Aveline's head. "You're safe. You're safe now," she whispered. "It was only a dream. The machine can't do anything to you without the drugs. It was only a bad dream."

Aveline experienced only a momentary sense of comfort. "What lessons was she talking about?"

Jossie bent down and whispered into Aveline's ear, "Reeducation. But don't listen to it. Just remember, none of it is true."

Morfyd cannot be trusted, the inner voice added.

After she bathed and dressed in a white collared shirt and tartan skirt, Aveline followed Jossie downstairs and down the long hallway to Allyn's study. The room that used to be Allyn's study, anyway.

She gasped when she saw that the room was nearly bare. The books had all been removed from the floor-to-ceiling bookshelves even though, to Aveline's knowledge, none were Forbidden Books. The ornate rug and her mother's cozy leather club chairs were gone, too. Not to mention Allyn's desk—the whole thing had probably been confiscated after her arrest. The only vestige of her mother that remained was the huge painting of Monnag on the wall above where the desk used to be. But someone had thrown a black drop cloth over it.

Sister Morfyd emerged from the shadows in a corner of the room, wearing her black habit. Her hair was braided over one shoulder, the loyalty ribbon tied at the end in a perfect bow. Exactly how Allyn used to wear hers.

"Miss Aveline, how lovely you look this morning. Come. Have a seat." She gestured to a wooden throne-like chair toward the far end of the room, which Aveline had never seen before. It resembled the chairs in her grandfather's study; someone must have brought it from there.

"I will, but only if Jossie is allowed to stay."

Morfyd raised a thin eyebrow. "Jossie is a very busy woman. She has many chores to complete. Isn't that right, Jossie?"

The maid swallowed nervously and inclined her head. "Yes, Sister Morfyd."

Aveline couldn't believe that Jossie was just going to abandon her here with this awful woman. But she could sense Jossie's fear, and she understood, from her dream last night, just how powerful and manipulative this so-called Sister of Monnag could be.

"Then I'm not staying, either," said Aveline.

Morfyd glanced in the direction of the door. A burly Stam officer—one of the two ogres who'd kidnapped her from the Forest—lumbered into the room and grabbed her and deposited her in the chair, holding her arms down with both of his hands. Behind her, she could hear the voice of a second officer, and Jossie crying out. Then the slam of a door. Silence.

Please don't hurt her, she begged silently.

The only sound she heard now was the *clack-clack* of Morfyd's high-heeled boots on the wooden floor. Together, Morfyd and the Stam officer zip-tied Aveline's wrists to the arms of the chair. The Sister then forced a gag into Aveline's mouth, the fabric as bitter as under-ripe strawberries. She suppressed the

285

urge to dry-heave.

Morfyd stood over her, placing her large hands over Aveline's smaller ones, and looking directly into her eyes. They were not simply green but a mosaic of emerald and agate, the tiles of green getting deeper the closer they got to the iris. The strangest, most complex pair of eyes that Aveline had ever seen.

"I know how afraid you are to dream again," said Morfyd, "so, this time, I promise to keep you awake."

The Stam officer pressed a button on the remote control he was holding, and down came a projector screen from the ceiling. Aveline was astonished. She had never known her mother's study to have such a screen. Behind her, a projector turned on and filled the screen with images of Army soldiers in their dark green uniforms, in long rows across Armand Fleur Park, arm in arm, hopping in an energetic goosestep to a song called "Praise the People's Party."

The image of the soldiers soon dissolved, and her grandfather, as a much-younger man, took their place. In a grainy, black-and-white film reel, Alfred stood at a podium addressing thousands of people in the park, proclaiming his victory over King Reuel IV, promising peace and prosperity for all Alterrans. Freedom from tyranny and oppression. Equality between rich and poor...

Just remember, Jossie had said, *none of it is true*.

When Aveline looked away, just for a moment, she felt something strike her face. It was Morfyd with a small, tasseled leather switch in her hand, and a gleam in her eye that said, *Look away again and you shall have more than just the flick of this switch*.

The film continued—for hours and hours, it

seemed—progressing through the last fifty years of Alterran history. She watched soldiers march up and down Heritage Way, the Armed Forces invade Ebria, the happy farmers of Belmarin and Lystra tilling the soil, Aspirants taking the Sacred Oath. Then came a series of home videos of the Fleur family (her mother as a child, and then herself as a child, in her father's arms). A detailed documentary about the nuclear tests performed at Cascadia, how effective and beneficial they were to the development of weapons that kept the citizenry of Alterra safe.

And then the film began again, spliced with images of herself and her mother playing in Wildweir. Tears flowed down her cheeks when she saw herself as a two-year-old in a pink dress with a frilled collar. The same dress she wore in the photograph that Kit had showed to Benjamin in her dream.

Then an image of her standing on her father's feet and dancing. And another of her with her uncle, a chubby-cheeked young man barely out of his teens. She and Simon were playing a duet on the piano, his bigger hands over her tiny ones, guiding her through scales and arpeggios. Her heart swelled at the memory, how much fun they used to have together. How safe he used to make her feel.

Don't fall for it, she scolded herself. *They're trying to make you believe he's a good person.*

Hours passed. The same film played over and over. She ran through Wildweir with her parents; splashed in the creek; rode through the trees on Allyn's horse, Pacer, her mother behind her in the saddle.

Was this what it was like to be reeducated?

Eventually, she became so exhausted that her head

began to bob. But, each time it happened, Morfyd hit her across the face with the switch. She did this so often that Aveline's nose and cheeks were flayed raw. Blood dripped from her split lower lip onto her starched white shirt. After a while, she could no longer feel the pain. She also needed to use the bathroom very badly, and asked Sister Morfyd for permission.

"Soil yourself for all I care, child," answered the woman. "You'll have to stay in those clothes until I allow you to rise from that chair."

"When will you allow me to rise?"

"When I am satisfied that you belong to us."

"I will never belong to you."

"Then I suppose we will be here a very, very long time."

Again, she lashed Aveline across the face.

****

"What did you dream?"

Aveline jolted awake, feeling for electrodes on her forehead. Feeling for the slashes across her face, the deep cuts in her lip. The fresh blood.

But there were no electrodes. No wounds at all on her face. Her skin was smooth, unblemished, her lips soft.

"What did you dream, Miss Aveline?"

She realized that it was not Sister Morfyd who spoke but Jossie.

"W-where am I?"

"Asleep in bed. Well, you were until a few seconds ago."

"Where is she?"

"Who?"

"Morfyd."

"I haven't seen her yet this morning."

"Am I still dreaming?"

"I don't think so."

How could she possibly explain to Jossie the torment of not knowing whether she was asleep or awake? How many false awakenings had she had in the past twenty-four hours? Or however long it had been since she had first gone to sleep?

"Today is the first day of your mother's trial," said Jossie. "Sister Morfyd will be accompanying you."

Aveline sat up, rubbing her head. "How...how long have I been sleeping?"

Jossie looked at her strangely in the pale light seeping into the room from the bathroom skylight. "Since last night, Miss Aveline."

Had that all happened in one night? In one dream? Or one dream-within-a-dream? Her head throbbed and her mouth felt stuffed with cotton wool.

She motioned to Jossie for the notepad and pencil. The maid dug them out of her apron pocket and handed them to Aveline. She wrote, *Am I brainwashed?*

Jossie took the pad and pencil from her and replied, *Do you love the Party?*

Aveline thought for a moment, then shook her head no. She still despised the National Democratic Party, and probably always would.

Do you trust M?

She shook her head no again.

Do you trust S?

She shook her head no for a third time.

S wants to see you before you leave for court. You must pretend.

As Jossie crumpled the paper in preparation to burn

it in the fire, Aveline nodded. How was she supposed to pretend to be brainwashed for her uncle? Act like Sandor Hayes?

Not enough time had passed for her to be fully brainwashed—only one night. She rubbed her eyes. Had it really been only one night? She distinctly remembered going to sleep with the electrodes on her head, and waking up with them off, the deep-brain stimulation machine nowhere in sight. Perhaps two nights had passed, maybe more.

After she bathed and changed into a plain black woolen dress that was now a bit too big for her, Jossie presented her with a brand-new blonde wig that looked exactly like the one she'd left behind at the Gilsevain care home. She scrunched up her nose and asked whether she had to wear it.

"Your uncle insists," whispered the maid. "He says he wants you looking presentable for the cameras."

Aveline rolled her eyes, but nevertheless she donned the itchy wig, and followed Jossie downstairs to her uncle's study. She was startled to see through his windows a light dusting of snow over the meadow. She had returned home at the end of autumn, when the wind was only starting to acquire a chill. Now it had snowed. More time had passed than just a couple of nights.

With a sinking feeling in her stomach, she realized that a few weeks had probably gone by. Plenty of time to complete the entire reeducation process. A glance at Simon's desk calendar confirmed that the month was no longer Vintage but Frost.

"Aveline, my dear," said Simon. "Please, have a seat."

Jossie locked eyes with her and closed the door

behind them.

As she lowered herself onto a chair before her uncle's desk, Aveline's whole body prickled with sweat. *Pretend. Pretend you're Sandor Hayes. Make no expression, no sudden moves. Don't let him know what you're thinking.*

"It's good to see you, Uncle." Her voice sounded distant, mechanical, to her own ears.

Simon grinned. "I trust that Sister Morfyd has been treating you well?"

"More than well, Uncle Simon. She taught me everything I needed to know."

He sat at his desk, lifted his boots up onto the blotter. She could see the soles were caked with snow and mud from walking around outside.

"Oh, yes? And what was that?"

"The history of our family and of the Party."

"Delightful. Tell me about it."

Though she was trembling inwardly, Aveline described, calmly and precisely, the film she had watched over and over again. She even told him about the interspliced scenes from the Fleur's home movies, because she assumed that a brainwashed person like Sandor always told the whole truth. Sandor had spilled the beans on his former associates, Leopold Bailey and Edwena Page, without even a second thought for whether it was the right thing to do.

Lowering his feet back to the floor, Simon stood and walked around his desk to where Aveline sat. He stood over her, looking directly into her eyes.

"Hmm," he said. "Something indeed is different about you, niece. A positive change, overall. Quite an improvement from the day you arrived. I must admit that I'm pleased. Morfyd has performed her duties well. However." He lifted a finger. It took all her willpower not to let him see her tremble. "A newly reeducated individual must be tested."

"What kind of test must I be given, Uncle?"

"One that will allow me to know, beyond a shadow of a doubt, that the reeducation process has worked."

Her heart picked up speed, but she took a deep breath through her nose to remain calm. She strained to keep her expression neutral. "I would be happy to take any test you desire, Uncle. What will it be? And when? Please tell me so that I can be prepared."

Grinning, he replied, "Ah, my dear. It wouldn't be an effective test if you could prepare for it, now would it?"

Chapter 26

On the ride to the Lawministry building in the City Center, Aveline couldn't stop thinking about the test. She wished that Simon had just given it to her in his office. The anxiety of not knowing when and where it would take place—and what it would be—was worse than whatever horrors he might subject her to. Certainty was always superior to uncertainty. She was still not even confident of whether she was awake or asleep. After so many false awakenings, and because she could feel pain whenever she pinched herself, she could not trust her own sense of reality.

She pressed her face to the cold window of her family's car. Snow fell softly from a gunmetal sky, coating the streets and sidewalks and buildings, even the shoulders of the pedestrians' overcoats.

When she was a child, she loved to drink hot cocoa in the Great Room and watch the snow fill the meadow and dust the treetops of Wildweir. But watching the snow fall today was anything but peaceful; the entire world seemed tense, on edge, hurrying back to their television screens to watch the trial of their Lightminister.

Beside her, Sister Morfyd adjusted her skirt, pulled her loyalty ribbon a little tighter on the end of her braid. Aveline hated having to pretend to be brainwashed. That meant that she had to do everything Morfyd told her without complaint or even a little sass. When Sandor returned from Rjellsfall, he seemed to lack all personality or sense of humor. He had no wishes or desires, from what Aveline could tell, apart from the wishes and desires of the Party. She needed to draw inspiration from him.

When the car pulled into the underground parking garage and the gate slammed shut behind it, Aveline drew a breath. After the driver opened the back door, she followed Morfyd to the building's entrance, where they met two Stam officers who led them down a fluorescent-lit hallway to an elevator. Aveline had forgotten how large the Lawministry was, with most of the complex being underground: Stam headquarters; evidence rooms; a jail where they held accused individuals awaiting trial.

The elevator dinged when they reached the fourth floor. As soon as the doors opened, Aveline and Morfyd were assaulted by paparazzi from the Lightministry. Morfyd slid a large pair of sunglasses from her jacket pocket and snapped them on, then took Aveline's hand and followed the Stam officers into the courtroom.

Aveline was careful not to let her expression betray her shock or curiosity. She ignored the reporters who cried out to her, "Miss Aveline, do you believe your mother is guilty? How does it feel to see her accused of these terrible crimes? Do you think she should be sent up to Rjellsfall like Sandor Hayes?"

"Pay them no mind." Morfyd tucked her sunglasses away once they had entered the courtroom and the Stam had shut the heavy doors behind them.

"Yes, Sister."

She didn't yet know what "crimes" her mother was accused of, so she could not have offered a comment even if she had wanted to. She also wondered whether that was Simon's test—would she speak to the reporters? To the paparazzi that *he* had sent from the Lightministry? If so, she had passed with flying colors by keeping silent.

But she suspected that Simon still had other tricks up his sleeve. His test would not be quite so easy.

Morfyd still held her hand as they walked up the steps to the box reserved for the Fleur family. Aveline had never seen the courtroom in person, only on television, where it had looked much smaller. In real life, the room was enormous and luxurious, like an opera house. Except that instead of a stage there was a bench upon a dais where the seven justices of the High Court would sit.

In the box, which was more like a private suite, Aveline exchanged cheek kisses with her aunt Lilia, whom she had not seen since returning home a few weeks ago.

"We've all been praying for your safe return." Lilia caressed her wig.

She looked into her aunt's eyes and thanked her, hoping Lilia could see that she was still in there. That she hadn't been brainwashed out of existence. She wanted desperately to tell her aunt everything, but Lilia was married to Simon. She couldn't be trusted.

Aveline took a seat beside her aunt and her little cousins, with Morfyd on her other side. Lilia and Morfyd had acknowledged one another politely, but Aveline could tell that Lilia had no great affection for this Sister of Monnag. The two women could not have been more different. Lilia was the velvet to Morfyd's steel.

And the way Morfyd acted around Simon, when he arrived in his black Party uniform with its clanging medals, could be described only as flirtatious. Lilia eyed Morfyd suspiciously as she lifted one of Simon's medals and commented on how brave he must have been to earn it.

Sick of watching the two of them, Aveline turned her attention to the courtroom below. People were beginning to fill the rows of seats: members of the People's Assembly; ministers; underministers; and other Party officials and civil servants, including Sandor Hayes in black uniform, Monnag pin gleaming on his lapel. She was careful to avoid his eye. Cameras were stationed on tripods around the room to capture the drama from every angle. She knew their lenses would be hyper-focused on Allyn's every expression, however minute.

The courtroom looked exactly as it had during Sandor's trial except for one thing. In the left-hand corner, on a wooden platform that reminded Aveline of the prow of a ship, sat a clear glass booth. Was that the new witness stand?

A trumpet sounded, and everyone rose, placing their hands over their hearts in the loyalty salute as the seven justices marched out onto the dais and took their seats. Aveline looked at them from left to right, all black-robed and white-wigged and solemn-faced. They ranged in age from late thirties to late sixties. The eldest and most senior, Chief Justice Bertram Magnus, sat at the center. Magnus rapped his gavel, calling the Court to order.

Then, from the left-hand side of the dais, a door opened. Two Stam officers walked the defendant out into the glass booth and sat on two chairs behind her. Aveline gasped along with the audience. She scarcely recognized her own mother.

Allyn wore a cobalt pantsuit, as blue was the prisoners' color. Her dark hair had been hacked off at the chin like a married woman's. But the most noticeable change in her appearance was her weight. Over the past few weeks, her captors must have force-fed her, because she was no longer emaciated. Any other prisoner would have been starved, but in Allyn's case, they had probably offered her the finest foods in Alterra. Required her to eat breakfast, lunch, and dinner. She now looked to be a normal weight for her height, the suit delineating her new curves. Her skin glowed, and her cheeks were flushed with good health.

She had never looked more beautiful. Aveline knew that she must have been uncomfortable in her own skin, but whatever she was feeling, she did not show it. Her expression remained neutral, even serene.

From her seat in the bulletproof glass cage, Allyn looked up to the Fleurs' box. For a moment, she locked eyes with Aveline. Aveline's heart began to race. She wanted to give some indication that she still knew her own mother, but she could feel Simon's eyes on her. The eyes of everyone in the room, including those of the justices and Sandor Hayes and all the Stam officers. She did not react. Kept her expression as stoic as Allyn's.

Below the dais were two long tables, the one on the right for the prosecution, and the one on the left for the defense. Allyn's barrister was a State-appointed defender as Sandor's had been. A young man who looked nervous and ill-prepared for the task ahead of him, fiddling with a stack of papers. Aveline knew that Allyn had not had her choice of barristers, or she would have picked someone much more experienced.

Magnus asked the defendant to stand. He then read the charges that the State had laid against her: "Allyn Monnag Fleur, you are accused of high treason against the State of Alterra and its Supreme Leader by way of involvement with the Resistance organization known as Manatha Dé. You are accused of espionage and harboring spies against the State of Alterra, of obtaining and using classified information against national interest. You are accused of embezzlement of over thirty million ducats from the Ministry of Finance, and of diverting said funds to the Ministry of Health for the development of drugs to reverse the reeducation process. You are accused of failure to destroy approximately 800,000 Forbidden Books and Records…"

The list went on and on, and was made even longer by Magnus's reading of the corresponding criminal codes. Allyn smiled almost imperceptibly.

It took a moment for Aveline to process what she was hearing. Allyn Fleur, Minister of Civic Enlightenment, was a member of Manatha Dé? Had conducted secret activities within the Ministry of Finance? If that was true, then *she* was the spider at the center of the web that Catherine had described. The person giving orders to dispatch the Dagkorodh. Her mother had come to her rescue after all.

Aveline wanted to cry with gratitude and relief. But she could not let her mask slip, even for a second.

After the prosecutor gave a lengthy opening statement, Allyn's defender made no remarks except that his client was innocent of all charges. He even told the justices that he intended to call no witnesses.

Aveline knew that every defendant was entitled to prove his or her innocence. In fact, that was the whole purpose of a criminal trial. Why had Allyn decided not to put on a defense? Was she that defeated? Or did she realize that this was merely a show trial, like Sandor's, where the fate of the accused had already been decided?

Don't give up, Mother, begged Aveline silently. *You can't let Simon win.*

What followed was a parade of prosecution witnesses, some of whom cowered and trembled on the witness stand as if they had been coerced to testify against their Lightminister.

One witness in particular stood out to Aveline—the Lightministry's head librarian, Thorsten Fenschel. She had not seen him in years, but he looked exactly as she remembered him: stout and bald, with a bushy salt-and-pepper mustache. Thorsten told the Court that he had seen Allyn, luminous with intellectual passion, down in the library night after night reading the Forbidden Books. And how she had ordered no actual Forbidden materials to be burned at the Cultural Purification Ceremony. Instead, what had perished in the fire were actually Party-sanctioned books and records.

"She said nobody would even notice. She said nobody sees what they are not looking for," said Fenschel. "And she was right."

The audience gasped and began clamoring so loudly that Magnus had to bang his gavel and shout for order. The witness himself was then arrested on the stand for failure to turn in his boss as soon as he had learned of her disobedience.

By the end of the day, Aveline's nerves were frayed. She could hardly eat the meal that Jossie had brought her. Without even taking off her dress, she collapsed on her bed and instantly fell asleep.

****

Curiously, she did not dream. But she was awakened in the middle of the night by someone vigorously shaking her shoulder.

She opened her eyes, and in the light of the lamp on her bedside table, she saw her uncle Simon standing over her. She startled as he sat on the edge of her bed. He was still dressed in his Party uniform. There were tears in his eyes.

He stroked her hair. "My dear niece. I have come to relay the unfortunate news that my father, your grandfather, the Supreme Leader of Alterra, Alfred Fleur, has passed away."

Instinctively, she sat bolt upright, not knowing how a brainwashed person would have responded to such news. Was it better to cry or to remain stoic?

"I am your Leader now," said Simon. "Father gave me his blessing before his soul ascended to heaven. He told me that, despite being his second-born, I was always his favorite child. And that when he passed on, he intended to entrust the Leadership to me." With a monogrammed handkerchief, Simon wiped crocodile tears from his eyes.

That was the biggest load of malarkey that Aveline had ever heard. But, putting her feelings aside, she obediently lifted her hand to her heart and said solemnly, "Long live the Leader. Long live the Fleurs."

"Good girl," said her uncle.

"May I see Grandfather? I would like to say goodbye to him."

He shook his head. "It's not safe. He was very ill with pneumonia, you know. I don't want to risk the health of my favorite niece." He smiled down at her.

I'm your only *niece*, she thought. And then: *He didn't die of any contagious disease. You poisoned him.*

"But, not to worry," continued Simon. "You will be able to see him in his glass coffin tomorrow."

Chapter 27

Allyn's trial was postponed for three days, the official mourning period for a State leader who had passed away.

The day after he died, Alfred was embalmed and dressed in his black Party uniform and placed in a glass coffin. The coffin was driven in a hearse down Heritage Way, with a long motorcade behind it, to Armand Fleur Park, where the citizens of Alterra could come and pay their respects. Most of the mourners were from Calador, but thousands had made the pilgrimage from other parts of the country to say goodbye to their Leader. Ordinarily, people had to apply for travel permits if they wanted to leave their provinces, but the Party gave them special dispensation to travel to the capital city for this occasion.

In her white dress—the traditional color of mourning—Aveline stood over the coffin, looking down through the glass at her grandfather. His hair and beard were pure white, his face deeply creased but peaceful. His hands were folded over his chest, his sigil ring on the fourth finger of his left hand. Without its wearer alive to animate it, the onyx was dark. Though he had not been a very warm man, and her relationship with him had been distant at best, she hoped that Alfred had not suffered in his last days.

She regretted that she hadn't gotten to know him

better. Their interactions had consisted mainly of him giving unsolicited advice about her education and her deportment. He was forever quizzing her on things she had learned in school and telling her to stand up straight with her shoulders back. She wished she could've known what he was really thinking and feeling. Particularly about his son and daughter. He had always favored Allyn, and thought she was the better choice for Leader. Even if she had made the mistake of showing Sandor's reaction to his sentence on live television. But maybe it hadn't been such a mistake after all. Maybe she'd been trying to show the country how terrible reeducation really was, and that Sandor had recognized it as such.

A tear fell from Aveline's eye and splashed onto the glass lid of the coffin. She sniffled, wiping her nose on her sleeve. Now Allyn would never be Leader. Would never be able to prove to her father that she was the better choice—the *only* choice—to succeed him.

Stepping back from the coffin, she allowed others to move forward to view their departed Leader. A group of white-clad women holding bouquets of calla lilies rushed up from behind her, and practically threw themselves upon the coffin and began to weep. Other men and women wept openly while waiting their turns, mouths open, tears streaming down their faces. Children followed their parents' lead and wailed. Aveline couldn't tell whether they were genuinely upset over losing their Leader or whether they cried out of fear of punishment for not seeming adequately distraught.

Simon stood a few feet away from her, wearing the white Party uniform, watching the mourners with a combination of disdain and amusement. He had not yet announced his succession to the Leadership, nor had he had his swearing-in ceremony. That would have been premature, as his sister's trial had not yet concluded, her fate not yet sealed.

Sister Morfyd sidled up to him, rubbing her hands in the raw Frost-month wind. She was dressed in her usual black habit, as Sisters were not allowed to wear anything else, and this time she also wore the black veil over her hair. She and the Lawminister made quite an odd couple, as she stood several inches taller than he. Although Lilia was close by, Simon ignored her and spoke only to Morfyd in hushed tones. At one point, he said something to make her smile. But she quickly corrected herself and returned her expression to neutral in case the television cameras were watching.

Back at the Estate after the funeral, Simon hosted a reception for the ministers and other high-ranking Party officials. Conspicuously absent, of course, was Allyn.

Simon paraded Aveline around the Great Room like a trained monkey. Showing off how well the reeducation process had apparently worked on her, although the word "reeducation" was not spoken, not even once. She played the role of the perfect child: seen and not heard. Both Simon and Morfyd appeared convinced.

Morfyd, for her part, did not keep as close a watch on Aveline as she probably should have. Instead, she sipped from a flute of champagne and removed her veil to show off her freshly-cut hair. Although Sisters of Monnag were not allowed to marry, they were empowered by Scripture to cut their hair like married women when in mourning. With her chin-length hair slicked back from her forehead and green eyes lined with kohl, Morfyd looked like a glamorous assassin. Aveline remembered her in the dream: dressed in a black tunic and cape, pistol and dagger at her hip like the Bhorowan. Simon's eyes did not leave her all evening.

Aveline, meanwhile, sat alone on a chintz sofa. The air was permeated with the scent of white roses and calla lilies, the flowers of mourning. She stared up at the portrait of her father posed proudly in his Air Command uniform, silently begging him to give her strength.

****

Once the official mourning period for Alfred Fleur had ended, Allyn's trial resumed at the Lawministry. Aveline sat in the box with her family, disguising her tears for her mother as those for her dearly departed grandfather. Lilia rubbed her back lovingly. Her aunt seemed to know what was troubling her, and that simple gesture said more than Lilia's words ever could.

Simon was proving himself to be quite the showman, keeping the citizens of Alterra on the edges of their seats. Through the State's prosecutor, he brought forth witnesses from the Ministry of Finance, Party officials who had helped Allyn embezzle millions of ducats to fund the anti-brainwashing drugs. Testifying on the promise of prosecutorial immunity, these witnesses were stunned when the Stam arrested them as soon as they gave their evidence. This was Simon's way of showing the country—the world—that he could do whatever he wanted.

As the days went on, the prosecutor called more witnesses from all four corners of Alterra. Dredged people from the woodwork like at Sandor's trial. Even those who had known Allyn at university returned to speak ill of her character. One man, who described himself as her academic rival, stated that she had taken illegal stimulants to stay awake all night and study.

Aveline had a sneaking suspicion that Simon had paid all these character witnesses to testify against his sister. Each witness on his or her own did not provide any particularly illuminating information. But together, they were like death by a thousand papercuts. Aveline saw how much her uncle was enjoying the spectacle. He even ate candied popcorn from a silver dish, passing it to Morfyd, who pushed it back and smiled and said she didn't want to get her fingers sticky. One might have been forgiven in thinking that these two were at a colosseum watching a single gladiator fight a dozen tigers.

Except that Allyn did not fight back at all. Her barrister made not a single objection even when the testimony was clearly hearsay. And she declined to testify in her defense. She only read documents that the prosecutor passed to her up in the glass booth. Aveline wondered whether her passivity pleased or frustrated Simon.

On the last day of the trial, the prosecutor announced that the State would like to call its final witness: Aveline Cyndess Fleur.

The second she heard her name, she forgot how to breathe. As all eyes in the room turned to her, she felt as embarrassed if she had been naked. She looked down at her mother, whose eyes went wide—the first time she'd shown any reaction during the trial. Then Aveline looked over at her uncle, who said, very calmly,

"Come, niece. Colonel Zabel will escort you down to the witness stand."

On shaking legs, she rose from her chair, trying to keep her expression blank. Colonel Zabel, her mother's bodyguard whom she hadn't seen since before Simon had her kidnapped to the care home, met her at the door to the Fleurs' box. With a firm hand on her shoulder, he led her downstairs and across the back of the courtroom and up an aisle on the far right. When they reached the witness stand, Zabel inclined his head and turned his charge over to the prosecutor. The prosecutor opened the little wooden door and gestured for Aveline to step up and have a seat on the stand.

It was so bright down here, blindingly bright, like the stage at Armand Fleur Park. Her whole body trembled as she gazed up at the seven justices in their black robes and powdered wigs, and out at the audience, who stared at her expectantly. And at the television cameras aimed right at her face. She knew her fright was probably giving away her secret, but she couldn't control it.

"Please state your name for the record," said the prosecutor.

"A-aveline Cyndess Fleur," she stammered.

"Miss Fleur, please place your right hand on the Book of Scripture and repeat after me: 'The testimony I give today shall be the truth, the whole truth, and nothing but the truth, or so I shall be forsaken by God.' "

Haltingly, she repeated the oath.

"Miss Fleur, please state the name of each and every individual who assisted you in escaping from the Helmut Frugheili Institute for Mental Hygiene at

Gilsevain Landing in the Province of Belmarin."

With a chill, she realized that this was Simon's test. If she testified against her mother, and ratted out her associates, the way Sandor had ratted out his friends at the underground newspaper, Simon would be satisfied that she had been successfully reeducated. But if she did not, he would know that she had been faking the whole time.

"Miss Fleur, please answer the question."

Swallowing over a lump in her throat, she stood. "I will not. I will not testify against my mother."

The audience gasped, and everyone began talking at once. From up in the box, Simon stood and drew a line across his throat. The videographers switched off their cameras and stepped away from their equipment, holding up their hands.

"Arrest her!" said Simon.

Two Stam officers rushed up to the witness stand and grabbed her arms and slapped a pair of cold metal handcuffs on her wrists.

"Mother!" she cried, looking up to the booth.

Allyn stood and pressed her palm to the glass.

"Your mother can't help you now," boomed the Chief Justice's voice from the dais. "Marshals, remand the child to the custody of the Sheriff of Illyria-Novo Templar."

Chapter 28

"Do you know how I got into your dreams?"

Aveline opened her eyes to fluorescent lights overhead. She was curled up on a cold stone floor, shivering, barefoot. Instead of her black woolen dress, she wore a blue cotton jumpsuit. The prisoner's uniform.

As she sat up, blood dripped from her mouth onto the stone. She lifted her hand to her lip and found that it had been split open.

Where was she? And how had she injured herself?

The voice returned. "I asked you a question, Miss Aveline."

Miss Fleur, please answer the question.

The fluorescent lights buzzed and flickered. She sat up, feeling for her wig atop her head, but it was gone. The last thing she remembered was being remanded to the sheriff's custody. Then it all flooded back—her refusal to testify, Simon shouting at the marshals to arrest her. She must have been in a jail cell in the basement of the Lawministry.

When she saw the black-attired figure in the corner, sitting on an aluminum chair—the only piece of furniture in the cell—she nearly jumped out of her skin. It was Sister Morfyd in her habit, without her veil, but wearing a black silk mask over her nose and mouth.

"Come closer, Miss Aveline. Don't be afraid."

Aveline drew her knees to her chest. There was no way she was getting closer to that monster. Morfyd's green eyes seemed to absorb all the light in the room, glowing above her mask. They reminded Aveline of those eyes she had seen in the Great Central Forest, flashing menacingly in the underbrush.

"I'll tell you how I got into your dreams," said the Sister. "I hooked myself up to the same deep-brain stimulation machine. I lay on the floor next to your bed the entire night."

A chill ran down Aveline's spine. She could not believe that Morfyd had been just inches away the entire time—close enough to touch her.

"Don't be afraid," said Morfyd. "You have a gift, Miss Aveline. The gift of prophetic dreams. Sister Manánn told me about it." She paused. "I, too, have a gift. The gift of knowing how to use the machine to control others' dreams. I discovered that the machine not only stimulates the subconscious, but it also opens up a kind of portal for others to enter. When I show you how to do this, your power will be almost unlimited. You will be unstoppable. Will you let me teach you?"

"I won't let you teach me anything."

Morfyd's eyes brightened over the top of the mask. "That is your loss, Miss Aveline. There is only one other person in the world who knows how to manipulate dreams with the machine. But, alas, she happens to be on trial for high treason."

Aveline sat up a little straighter. "My mother?"

Morfyd nodded.

"How did she learn to do that?"

"She's clever, like you. Too clever for her own good, it seems. But I'm not here to talk about your mother. I'm here to talk about you."

Wiping her bleeding lip on her sleeve, Aveline slid a little farther away from the Sister, which was difficult because the cell was small. Her back was now up against the cold stone wall.

"What about me?" she said.

"I thought you had promised to be brave," answered Morfyd, "but you failed me."

"I would never testify against my mother! Ever! I *was* brave."

Snorting, Morfyd said, "That's not what I meant. You let your servant friends back at the Estate take the fall for you. That wasn't very brave of you, now, was it?"

"W-what are you talking about?"

The woman slid the chair closer, making an ear-splitting screech against the stone. "At first I wondered why I wasn't able to reeducate you. Your mind was just so *resistant* to the teachings of the Party, even after I had activated your subconscious with the machine. But then I realized it was because the cook had decided not to bake the drugs into your food as I had instructed. Your lady's maid conspired with them. You were only too happy to let them protect you. You all tried to play me for a fool.

"As soon as I realized your little secret, however, I decided to let you continue. I wanted to see how far you would take this charade of pretending to be 'brainwashed,' as you call it. Quite far, it seems. And look where it's gotten you." She gestured around the tiny cell. "By the way, in case you're wondering, I have taken Jossie and Mrs. Beauregard and her assistant Corey into my custody for your uncle to do with them as he sees fit."

Aveline reached behind her, gripping the wall with her fingernails. She wanted to spit blood at this revolting woman. But she had to admit that Morfyd was right. Aveline had put Jossie and the kitchen staff in harm's way. She knew how risky it was to disobey Morfyd's orders. She should have just told them to put the drugs in her food and allowed herself to be brainwashed, sparing their lives.

No. Everything she says is a lie. Don't you dare believe her.

The woman slid off her chair and onto the floor, sitting only inches from Aveline. The Sister didn't exactly pin her to the wall, but Aveline knew she couldn't escape her. There was nowhere to run.

Lowering her mask, Morfyd sniffed at her. "You smell like a sewer. Like human excrement. You know that, don't you?"

Aveline clenched her teeth.

"Face it, Miss Aveline. You knew you would end up in here. With me. Like this. You knew it when we were in Gholon's Pass together." Morfyd smiled broadly before she pulled her mask back up.

"That…that was just a dream."

"But dreams have power, don't they?"

Then Morfyd took something from one of the deep pockets of her habit, concealing it in her closed hand.

"Now I'm going to do something I should have done at the beginning." Opening her hand, she revealed a small syringe. Before Aveline could react, the Sister plunged the needle into her neck. "I told you I would break you, didn't I?"

****

Aveline awoke on a balcony in the courtroom, directly above rows upon rows of ministers and Party officials, with a clear view of the dais and the glass booth. She had no idea how she had gotten from her cell in the basement of the Lightministry all the way up here. She wore her black dress, smelling of lavender as if it had just come from the laundry. On her right shoulder she could see the end of her braided wig, the crimson loyalty ribbon tied in a perfect bow.

As she reached a hand up to touch her lip, she found that she could barely lift it; her arm seemed to weigh a thousand pounds.

It had to be the drug. Whatever Morfyd had put in that syringe made her feel almost giddy, yet weak at the same time. The way she'd felt at the care home. So weak that the Stam didn't even need to anchor her to the chair with zip ties or place a gag in her mouth. Though she could form coherent sentences in her mind, she wouldn't have been able to speak them. It was as if the connection between her brain and her mouth had been interrupted. A long string of drool fell from her lip, growing longer and spindlier until it nearly reached her collar.

Beside her, Morfyd took a black handkerchief from the pocket of her habit and patted her mouth. "There. All better."

At the trumpet's blast, the seven justices of the High Court entered the room and took a seat at the bench on the dais. Allyn, flanked by two officers, entered the glass booth soon after. Today, she was dressed not in cobalt but navy blue. This particular shade of blue was reserved for a prisoner on the day that his or her verdict was to be read.

"We the Justices of the High Court," began Magnus, "having heard all the evidence in *State of Alterra versus Allyn Monnag Fleur*, and having heard all testimony given against her, find the defendant guilty of the crimes of high treason, espionage, harboring of spies, embezzlement, seizure and mass destruction of State property, and attempted staging of a coup d'état against our Eternal Supreme Leader, Alfred Monnag Fleur, and our Supreme Leader, Simon Yrgess Fleur, and against the National Democratic Party."

Aveline's stomach dropped. She had known this was coming, but hearing the verdict read aloud suddenly made it real.

After clearing his throat, Magnus continued, "We hereby sentence you to six months of reeducation at the Rjellsfall Institute for Mental Hygiene in the Province of Frelimar."

No. It cannot be. Aveline thought for sure that Simon would sentence his sister to death by firing squad, not reeducation. This was the worst possible punishment he could inflict upon her.

"Any last words, Defendant Fleur?"

Calmly, Allyn rose to her feet and stood at the podium in the glass booth and looked out over the audience, lifting her chin ever so slightly. After a long pause, she began to speak into the microphone.

"When I was sixteen years old," she said in her rich Caladorian accent, "I stood before you, at the right hand of my father, and took the Sacred Oath. I promised to bear true faith and unconditional allegiance to Alfred Fleur. To support and defend the Constitution and laws of the State of Alterra against all enemies. To lay down my life for my Leader and for my country. The day I took that oath, I vowed to be your servant for as long as I lived.

"By taking that oath, I betrayed you.

"I was the architect of reeducation. I enlisted our country's top scientists to develop drugs to alter the mind and make it susceptible to my propaganda. I ordered the building of the Rjellsfall Institute for Mental Hygiene. I manipulated our justice system to ensure that Sandor Hayes would be sentenced to reeducation. I convinced you that we had his best interests at heart. That it was better to reform than to punish a traitor.

"The process was complete after three weeks. When we brought Sandor back, I was pleased with the result. More than pleased. I was overjoyed at how well it worked, this process I had designed. I spoke with my brother Simon about using reeducation as a tool to reform those who had committed treason against the State. And even to mold the minds of our youngest citizens so that they would remain loyal to us for their entire lives.

"But then I worked one-on-one with Sandor Hayes. I talked to him, saw him in action as an agent of the Stam. I realized that reeducation had taken away his soul, his self-consciousness—the spark of life that separates human beings from animals. I looked into his eyes and saw nothing there. This was my doing. I knew in my heart that I could never follow through on the plans I had made with Simon for reeducation on a massive scale.

"While ostensibly working with my brother, I joined the Resistance organization known as Manatha Dé. I diverted funds from the Ministry of Finance to the

Ministry of Health to develop drugs to reverse the reeducation process. I dispatched orders to Manatha Dé to raid the institutes and free as many prisoners as possible. I placed individuals who had been deprogrammed back into the Stam as double agents to actively work against my brother.

"I freely admit to all of this. And I am not ashamed. But neither am I proud. By taking the Sacred Oath, I betrayed you. And then, by breaking the oath, I have only begun to undo the damage I have done to Alterra and to our people, not only by reeducation but also by famine, poverty, and war. Without excuse or justification, I have destroyed my country.

"I accept the judgment of the High Court and shall not resist the sentence that they have passed on me. I take comfort in knowing that Manatha Dé, and my daughter Aveline, will continue my work when my mind is no longer my own. We will not stop until every institute is liberated and every citizen of Alterra lives free of the tyranny of their government."

She then spoke in Ebrian the motto of Manatha Dé: "*Dhe mina oslhù mina ta'slhendù kor.*" *From my darkness comes my greatest strength.*

Tears streamed down her cheeks. She did not wipe them away.

Aveline was also crying uncontrollably. She could barely voice the word "Mother" when the audience began to cheer. "All-*yn*! All-*yn*!"

Simon, who was sitting in the front row, leaped up and shouted to the officers in the glass booth, "Take her away!"

Allyn smiled at him, without any malice, and mouthed "I love you" up to Aveline in the balcony.

Then, graciously, she held her hands behind her back so that an officer could place the cuffs on her wrists.

Chapter 29

Like her mother, Aveline was remanded to her cell
in the Lawministry basement. Forced to hand over her
wig and change out of her dress and again put on the
blue jumpsuit.

All night, she cried, curled up in a ball on the cold
stone floor. She kept replaying Chief Justice Magnus's
words over and over in her mind. *We hereby sentence
you to six months of reeducation at the Rjellsfall
Institute for Mental Hygiene in the Province of
Frelimar*. She pictured her mother drugged and hooked
up to the machine, emerging three weeks later as a
carbon copy of Sandor Hayes. Allyn was right that her
mind would no longer be her own. It would belong to
Simon, to the Party. He would use her as a weapon to
ferret out the members of Manatha Dé and bring them
to "justice."

And he's going to do the same thing to me.

What was it like to no longer be yourself? she
wondered. Did Sandor miss the person he used to be?
Or did he not even remember?

Her whole body shook violently from the cold, and
from these thoughts. She wished that some kind soul
would throw her a blanket. Bring her a glass of water.
Her tongue felt as rough and dry as sandpaper.

She closed her eyes, imagining her mother at the
podium in the glass booth. How the audience had

cheered for her. *Making sedition fashionable*—wasn't that what Simon had once said? That was what had really upset him today. That the people were chanting *her* name, not his. After she had confessed to crime after crime. To betraying her own people.

Aveline felt a tiny ray of hope when she thought of how calmly her mother had accepted her fate. Maybe Allyn knew of a way to defeat the brainwashing. To resist it even if she were given the drugs. It was she who had designed the reeducation process, after all.

Through the stone wall Aveline could hear, faintly, the sound of crying. She slid closer to the wall and pressed her ear to the frigid stone. The crying became louder. It sounded like a girl's voice, or maybe a young woman's.

"Hello?" she said.

The sound stopped for a moment, then resumed.

"Can you hear me?"

When she did not receive a reply, she tried again. "Mother? Is that you?"

The crying turned to whimpering, and then trailed off altogether. Aveline couldn't imagine that the sheriff, or the Stam, or whoever ran this jail, would put the two of them in adjoining cells.

Teeth chattering, she lifted her head from the wall just as a cry issued through the stone. Aveline's heart thudded. She wanted to get up and slide the aluminum chair to the barred window at the top of the door so she might be able to see what was going on. But her muscles were still too weak from the drugs that Morfyd had given her hours ago.

She heard the heavy footfalls of guards in the hallway, boots squeaking on the freshly waxed tile floor. She could see movement when she looked up to the window. Followed by the jangle of keys and the heavy door of the adjoining cell creaking open. A tussle of bodies. The high-pitched scream of a girl.

"Let me go!"

Aveline froze. The voice belonged to Corey, the cook's sixteen-year-old assistant, who had conspired with Mrs. Beauregard and Jossie to keep the brainwashing drugs out of her food.

"Don't hurt her! Please!" said Aveline with all the strength she could muster. "Please! Take me instead!"

But her cries fell on deaf ears, as did Corey's. The girl's screams became fainter and fainter as the guards dragged her down the hallway.

Defeated, Aveline lay down again on the cold stone floor. She could hear the sound of water. Gurgling, dripping. This underground jail was probably close to the city's sewer system.

You smell like a sewer. Like human excrement. You know that, don't you?

She squeezed her eyes shut, focused on the sound of her own breathing. Moments later, instead of sewer sounds, she heard the lapping of waves. The cry of gulls.

She was back in the dream world, standing on the end of a long pier. A warm salt breeze played over her face and lifted her hair, which had grown long again. Turning her face to the sea, she saw that it was full of ships of all sizes, headed for the port. She couldn't make out any markings or symbols on them and didn't know the direction from which they came. Or the name of the city or even of the sea on which they traveled. But she could feel their power, and she knew that it was good.

****

She awakened inside a fluorescent obelisk. The iron door of her cell was open, and two men in black stood before her. One tapped her ribs with the toe of his boot.

"Get up."

Simon's face crystallized into view. His dark hair was parted on one side and slicked back from his forehead, the way Alfred had worn his when he was young.

He tapped her again with his foot, only this time it was more of a kick. "I said, 'Get up.' "

Swallowing, Aveline placed her palms against the stone and sat up painfully. Her head throbbed.

Simon crouched down at her eye level. "I have news for you."

"What news?" Her throat was dry.

"Your mother is dead." He said it as coldly as if he were reporting the weather.

"What?" For a moment, her heart stopped beating. "That…that can't be. You're lying to me!"

"Oh, how I wish I were."

Aveline shook her head. "H-how did she die?"

"She took her own life. With a draught of hemlock, it seems." He stood, brushing off the knees of his black uniform slacks. "I ought to have killed her myself when I had the chance."

Then, in a fit of rage, he picked up the aluminum chair and hurled it at the back wall of the cell. Aveline cowered with her hands over her head as the chair bounced off the stone and landed on its side right in front of her.

S. J. Carson

Simon stormed out of the cell and into the hallway, where he punched a hole in the opposite wall. As he pulled his bleeding fist away, he swore more foul oaths than Aveline had ever heard in her life. Oaths against Allyn, against himself, against God. She had never seen him in this attitude before, so full of fury.

"Don't touch me," he said to the guard who reached out to see the damage he'd done to his hand.

Simon clutched his wounded right hand and gritted his teeth, breathing heavily. Then he returned to the doorway of Aveline's cell. His Mark of Yrgess glowed like an ember. "If you want to see the traitor, you had better come quick before they take her away to the potter's field."

The potter's field. He was going to have her buried with the unnamed poor. There would be no motorcade down Heritage Way. No public viewing of her body in its glass coffin at Armand Fleur Park. No legions of citizens dressed in white with their flowers and tears. Simon would see to it that all vestiges of the Lightminister were erased from the Fleur Estate, from the history books. It would be as if she had never existed at all.

Before Aveline could open her mouth to say something to her uncle, he was gone. All that remained when he left were the fist-sized hole in the wall, the crumbling plaster. Drops of his blood on the tile floor.

The guard stepped into her cell and grabbed her arm, yanking her up to a standing position. He led her down several corridors until they reached the infirmary. A young Sister of Monnag in a black habit and veil unlocked a steel door to reveal a small room where Allyn's body lay on a stretcher. Aveline gasped. She was still dressed in her navy-blue suit. She had died a prisoner of the State of Alterra.

"I want to say goodbye to my mother," Aveline addressed the guard and the Sister of Monnag. "Alone."

The two adults nodded and left the room. She heard the door close behind her, and a wave of stars passed before her eyes. But her veins were so full of adrenaline that she did not faint. Slowly, she approached her mother's body.

Allyn's eyes were closed, her skin as white as the sheet beneath her, but her lips still held the faintest hint of color. She looked at peace, as though she were only sleeping. With a trembling hand, Aveline stroked her thick, dark hair.

"Mother," she whispered. Hoping that, at any moment, Allyn would open her eyes and tell her that this was all just a bad dream.

But she lay still.

Aveline began to weep. Although taking one's own life was the ultimate crime against the State and against God, Allyn had been brave to make that choice. She had not allowed Simon the opportunity to brainwash her. In death, she had eluded him.

Allyn had also sacrificed her own life for Aveline's. To use her connections within Manatha Dé to rescue Aveline from brainwashing at the care home. And yet, Aveline was still not safe from Simon. As soon as she returned home, Morfyd would begin feeding her the drugs and hook her up to the machine as she slept. In three weeks' time, the deed would be done. Aveline would become another Sandor Hayes. A mere instrument for her uncle to play however he wished.

"Mother, why does it have to be this way?"

Aveline lifted Allyn's cold hand, still soft and mobile. Rigor mortis had not yet set in.

She looked down at her mother's face. Her serene expression. Heard Allyn's voice from deep within: *We can't let them win, my darling. We are stronger than they are.*

Chapter 30

Although she was afraid to eat the food the guard had brought her, Aveline knew that she had to keep up her strength for whatever was going to happen next. Besides, she was starving. She sat cross-legged on the stone floor, gobbling down two slices of thinly buttered bread, with a tiny portion of sour-tasting stew containing only a few hunks of tough, stringy meat. Washing down her meager dinner with a glass of water, she knew it probably contained the brainwashing drugs. But what choice did she have?

After her meal, she began to feel sleepy. And weak. Pressing her palms together, she lay her head down atop them, a poor substitute for a pillow. Her body shook from the cold and from crying for her mother. She tried to clear the images from her head of Allyn's lifeless body, dressed in blue. The potter's field where she would soon be laid to rest among the paupers and the criminals.

Aveline had felt lonely in the past, but now she was truly all by herself. Everyone she cared about was either missing or imprisoned or dead. There was no one around her that she could trust anymore.

"I promise to be strong for you, Mother," she whispered. "I promise to do everything I can to carry on Manatha Dé's work in your memory. For as long as I can."

She didn't realize that she had fallen asleep when she awakened suddenly to flashing lights. The blare of an alarm. The overpowering, acrid odor of smoke.

Sitting up, she shielded her eyes and coughed. The door to her cell was now wide open and she could see a melee in the hallway—thick plumes of smoke, prisoners in blue running and screaming and tumbling to the ground, soldiers in sienna uniforms with rifles drawn, black-clad prison guards firing their long-barreled pistols at the soldiers. The *thwpt thwpt* sound of silenced guns, so recognizable to her now. Soldiers shouting in Ebrian.

Ebrian? What on earth was the Ebrian Army doing here?

Her stomach sank. Those ships she had seen in her dream—they were Ebrian ships crossing the Shinar Sea. They must have invaded Alterra, seeking revenge against their enemy.

Just when I thought my life couldn't possibly get any worse, I'm about to become a prisoner of the Virolannens.

With nowhere to run, she got to her knees and crawled behind the heavy door, hoping to shield herself from the bullets.

"Aveline!" called a man's voice. He pronounced her name the way an Alterran would. The voice sounded vaguely familiar, though she couldn't place it.

It grew more insistent now. "Aveline! Tell me where you are!"

Peeking her head around the door, she saw a tall, well-built man in Ebrian uniform. He had sandy blond hair, blue eyes, a nose wide at the bridge.

Christopher Llewellyn Fleur.

"Father?" she asked timidly.

"My sweet girl."

He reached behind the door and pulled her toward him and lifted her up. She touched his hair, his face, the tears that fell down his cheeks.

"No." She shook her head. "You're not real. This is only a dream."

At any moment, she expected him to vanish and to see Morfyd standing in his place. But the evil Sister did not appear. A bomb detonated somewhere down the hall, causing a deafening explosion and flash of fire just outside Aveline's cell.

Still clutching her, Kit ducked and called out a name that Aveline recognized. "Balthazar!"

My rescuer? He's alive?

"Commander Fleur!"

The burly Dagkorodh, in sienna fatigues like Kit's, charged into the cell and took Aveline from her father's arms. She was so relieved to see her friend that she no longer cared whether this was all a dream. She hugged him tightly.

"Father!" she shouted over Balthazar's shoulder as he carried her out of the cell and down the hallway, stepping around fallen bodies and burning debris.

Kit was gone. Lost in the crush of people. In the thick smoke and haze of pulsating strobe lights from the alarm system.

Balthazar continued to run, down one corridor and the next, a labyrinth of hallways lined with jail cells that comprised the subterranean Lawministry complex. They were moving so rapidly that Aveline lost track of where they were. As they got deeper into the complex, it became quieter. Less smoky. Still, occasionally,

Balthazar would pause at a blind corner and shoot his pistol. Once, he hit a Stam officer who fell backward with a strangled cry and a thud, a bullet hole between his eyes spouting blood. The rescuer leaped gracefully over his body and kept running.

At the end of the hallway was a dull steel door. Balthazar tried the handle and found it locked. Putting Aveline down for a moment, he backed up and ran into it with all his might, breaking the lock. As it opened, the door made an ear-splitting screech across the cement floor. Then the Dagkorodh grabbed Aveline's hand and pulled her inside, slamming the door shut behind them.

The room smelled musty, with a hint of cleaning solution. Balthazar slid a small, red-covered flashlight from his belt and shined it on their surroundings. They were in an old maintenance room, with a boiler, racks of tools, ladders, brooms, a mop in a bucket of foul-smelling water. He performed a quick sweep of the room, calling out in Alterran, then in Ebrian, for anyone who was in there to make themselves known.

But there was no response. No voices, no movement.

He walked over to the right-hand wall and shined his flashlight up on a large crimson batik bearing the Leader's face in white. Aveline was startled to see an image of her deceased grandfather staring back at her.

Tearing down the batik, Balthazar revealed a large, round hatch just above the floor, like that of a bank vault. She had seen one like it on a school tour of the Ministry of Finance, except this one was much smaller. At the center of the hatch was a wheel, which he turned first to the left, then to the right, until it popped open. A stale breeze assaulted their faces.

Aveline coughed, then crouched and followed the beam of the rescuer's flashlight. Before them was a dark, round passageway of sorts. She could hear water gurgling, echoing somewhere within. Scrunching up her nose, she wondered whether this was the sewer she had heard through the stones of her cell.

"Are we going in there?"

"Yes," he said. "We have to. It's our only way out."

"But remember the last time we were in a tunnel?"

He smiled gently in the dim red light. "There is no high tide, no falling river. Nothing like that. I will bring you to safety. You have to trust me."

She nodded. "I trust you."

"Follow me."

He crouched on his hands and knees and began crawling into the passageway.

"What if the Stam follows us?" she whispered.

She realized that it was impossible to turn around and pull the hatch closed.

"Don't worry. I've got my pistol."

She had never been so worried in her life.

Trembling, she followed the rescuer into the dark passageway. She cringed when her hands touched the cold, slimy surface. Because Balthazar took up nearly the entire space, she could see nothing before her. She crawled blindly until, moments later, they crashed down into a puddle.

"Eww," she said to herself, wishing she wasn't barefoot right now. When the prison guards had made her change into the blue jumpsuit, they had taken not only her dress but also her shoes. A barefoot prisoner, of course, was less likely to escape.

Wiping her wet, slimy hands on her jumpsuit, she looked back over her shoulder to check for Stam or the sheriff's men or whoever might be following them. She heard nothing, saw nothing. The passageway was so dark that she couldn't even see the maintenance room from which they'd come.

Balthazar shined his flashlight around. They stood in a long, wide tunnel that reminded her of the catacombs in the legends. It was as if they had crossed a portal into another world.

"W-where are we?" she asked.

"In Ebrian we call it *Ta'azmayù. Great maze.* A system of tunnels that connects all the buildings in the city. We have one in our capital city, Rehebeth."

Aveline had not heard of such a thing before. How had she lived in Calador for the past fourteen years and not known of this system of underground tunnels right beneath her feet?

"Do you think the Stam knows about this place?"

"I doubt it." His hand closed around the pistol on his belt.

While she took comfort in knowing that Balthazar could defend them, she thought he might be underestimating the secret police. Simon may not have been a straight "A" student at university, but he was as crafty as a fox. He'd probably learned of the system of underground tunnels from Alfred, who had designed the city of Calador himself.

They began walking through the tunnel. All was quiet except for the *drip-drop* of water falling on her head, and the burbling of what sounded like a stream close by.

Pretend you're in Wildweir.

But it was much too dark to be Wildweir, even on the darkest night in the dead of winter. Here, it was pitch black as it had been in the Great Central Forest. The only light came from Balthazar's flashlight. She braced herself to see green and yellow and red eyes blinking at her through the darkness.

As they advanced into the tunnel, splashing through puddles of standing water, a faint wind blew in their faces. The same wind she'd felt when Balthazar had first opened the hatch. Though it wasn't fresh, it didn't exactly stink of a sewer, either. It smelled more like air that had been trapped in a cave for hundreds of years.

Slender beams of sunlight fell across their bodies as they walked under a manhole. They were beneath a city street, she realized. She couldn't tell what time of day it was, but she guessed it was still morning. Maybe early afternoon.

The ground above them shook, causing her to cower. Was that the sound of cars? Of tanks rolling into the city? She heard people clamoring above. Bullets flying. Screams.

She sensed that the country was at war, although she couldn't be sure who was fighting whom—the Ebrians against the Alterrans, or the Ebrians and the Alterrans against Simon and the Stam and his Armed Forces? There was no way to tell. Everything was chaos.

Once they had passed the manhole, Balthazar turned down another part of the tunnel. It was quieter here. She could no longer hear anything on the street above. Not even the sound of running water. Only the skittering of cockroaches, or maybe rats, along the walls. She shuddered, gripping Balthazar's arm for support. Perspiration trickled from under her arms, dampening her jumpsuit.

This tunnel led to a dead end, a brick wall. The next tunnel they took ended similarly, but instead of a brick wall there was a giant fan inside a rusted iron cage, stirring the fetid air. Pushing it toward their nostrils.

When Balthazar shined his flashlight around the cage, Aveline noticed the source of the stench. A decomposing human body lay at the base of the fan. It was dressed in a blue prison jumpsuit just like the one she wore. An escapee who hadn't been so lucky. She could not even tell whether it was male or female, its face florid with mushrooms.

She began to scream. The rescuer clapped a hand over her mouth.

When he released it, she sputtered, "I thought you said there weren't any Stam down here."

"Yes. But that doesn't mean we're alone. You never know what enemies may be lurking in the shadows. We have to be very careful, Miss Aveline. And very quiet."

At his mention of enemies in the shadows, she started trembling again. Violent chills shook her body.

"We're lost," she whispered. "Aren't we?"

Balthazar didn't answer her; instead, he cast the beam of his flashlight around. "I memorized a map of this *Ta'azmayù*. I swear by the ancestors I did. I know this tunnel runs all the way under Marie Fleur Place. It doesn't come to a dead end. They must have changed something."

Aveline's mouth felt as dry as cotton. "Can you get us out of here, Balthazar?" She realized that she didn't even know where they were going. Was anywhere even safe when the country was at war?

"I will try my best, Miss Aveline."

Just then, she heard footfalls somewhere in the distance. Boots splashing through puddles. A male voice echoing off the walls of the tunnels.

"D-do you hear that?" she said.

He fell silent as the two listened.

"Yes," he whispered.

He switched off the flashlight and told her to keep quiet and not to move. They huddled together in the darkness, Balthazar's back pinned against the cage of the fan, his big arms around her. She wondered whether he could feel her heart thudding in her chest. The fan blew the stench of the corpse right into their faces, and she breathed out of her mouth so she wouldn't gag and give away their hiding spot.

As the footsteps inched closer, her heart picked up speed.

It's the Stam. We've come this far just for them to find us here. We're done for.

The footfalls stopped about twenty feet away from where she and Balthazar were crouched. She could see two roving white beams of flashlights. Could hear two voices, one male and one female. They weren't Stam; the Stam did not allow women to join their ranks.

Then who are they?

Coming closer, they shined their flashlights directly into Balthazar and Aveline's faces. As she screamed, the rescuer drew his gun.

The man chuckled nervously and held up his

hands. "At ease, soldier." Then he spoke Ebrian. *"Chlhundrù wa koren."* We come in peace.

The voice belonged to Thorsten Fenschel, the Lightministry's head librarian.

"Thorsten?" she said cautiously. "How did you get out of jail?" She remembered that the marshals had arrested him on the witness stand at her mother's trial.

"God bless the Tigers. They sprang us out this morning."

She was so relieved that it was only Thorsten, and that he was free, that she could have cried.

"Who are you?" she said, pointing to the woman.

"This is my assistant, Jennaen." Thorsten shined his beam on her. She was short and slender, in her early twenties, with a long, dark maiden braid and spectacles.

"Do you know the way out of here?" said Aveline.

"Yes. Come with us," said the head librarian. "The maps can't be trusted, you know."

The maps.

She remembered that all maps were made by the Lightministry. The maps of Alterra that omitted Rakan Fo, King Reuel's last stronghold, and the fractured land between southern Lystra and the Great Central Forest. And the maps of the *Ta'azmayù*.

Of course Balthazar hadn't been able to find his way out of the great maze! The Lightministry's job was to confuse. To rewrite history and alter geography. They claimed to tell you the truth, but it was only the truth they wanted you to hear.

"Does the Stam use the Lightministry's maps?" Aveline whispered to Thorsten as they walked.

"Oh, yes. I'm sure they're wandering around right now under the Avenue of the Acacias, looking for you.

But not to worry. They're a good two or three miles in the opposite direction."

She could feel the mirth in the older man's words. His delight in confusing the secret police.

If there was one positive thing that came out of the Lightministry's lies, she thought, it was that the Stam was traipsing around in the dark like a pack of confused idiots. Had the situation not been so desperate, she might have laughed.

She stayed close to Thorsten and his assistant as they guided her and Balthazar through the wending tunnels. At last, they reached a passageway similar to the one she had passed through to enter the *Ta'azmayù*. Crawling on their hands and knees through the same wet, slimy substance, they tumbled out through a circular opening into a large room with low ceilings and bars of fluorescent lights overhead.

As she stood wiping her hands on her already-wet jumpsuit, she watched Thorsten close the vault door and click the wheel back into place. He wrinkled his nose, a familiar tic, his salt-and-pepper mustache twitching.

Looking around, she recognized this room. It was the basement of the Lightministry, where they kept the Forbidden Books under lock and key. Although the room still smelled strongly of old leather and vellum, the rows upon rows of bookshelves all stood empty.

"What happened to all the books?" she asked, knowing that they weren't burned at the Cultural Purification Ceremony. "Did the Stam take them?"

Behind her spectacles, Jennaen's beady eyes sparkled. She wiped her hands on the skirt of her long gray dress and nodded. "Oh, they took them, all right,

Miss Aveline. But they weren't Forbidden Books. The Lightminister knew the Stam would be coming for them, so she had us ship them all to a secure location up north, in Corinthia."

Aveline furrowed her brow. "So, what books did the Stam take, then?"

The assistant's lips broke into a grin. "Party-sanctioned books. Hundreds of thousands of them."

Aveline clapped a hand over her mouth in disbelief.

"You see?" said Thorsten. "I was right about what I said on the witness stand. Nobody checks these things. Nobody sees what they're not looking for."

Aveline laughed to herself, thinking of the Stam burning stacks and stacks of books that had been approved by the Party. By Simon.

"Your mother is very clever," added Jennaen. She gulped, realizing her mistake. "*Was*, I mean. I'm so sorry for your loss, Miss Aveline."

"A loss for all of us," added Thorsten.

Aveline tried not to think of her mother on the stretcher in the prison infirmary. She wished she hadn't seen her like that. She wanted to remember her as she had looked on the day she came to collect Aveline at the stables, her long chestnut braid over her shoulder. Beautiful, proud. The most powerful woman in Alterra.

Aveline did not realize that tears had started to slide down her cheeks until Jennaen handed her a handkerchief. She thanked the assistant and wiped her eyes, then unfolded the handkerchief and saw that it was one of Allyn's, embroidered with her monogram and Monnag's head encircled by the fleur-de-lis. This only made Aveline weep harder.

She hiccupped. "I wish…I wish I'd had a chance to say goodbye."

"We always wish we had more time." Thorsten leaned down to her. "But your mother knew how much you loved her. And that you will carry on her work. With us."

Jennaen took the wet handkerchief from Aveline and slipped it back into the pocket of her dress. "And you have your father back."

My father.

She had seen him, touched him, so briefly, that she still wondered whether he was an apparition. Whether she was going to wake up to Sister Morfyd standing over her in her cell, saying, *I have finally broken you, child.*

"Where is he?" she said. "Balthazar, do you know where he is? Will you take me to him?"

The rescuer shook his head. "He told me that he would come to see you soon as he could. I told him that I would bring you here."

"But…there's a war going on, isn't there? I heard it while we were in the maze. What if—" She did not even want to voice the thought. "What if he doesn't make it?"

New, hot tears sprang to her eyes. She had lost nearly all her family: her grandfather, her mother, her stepfather. She couldn't bear to lose her father. Not again.

Balthazar knelt before her. "I won't let anything happen to him, Miss Aveline. I promise. I have sworn to protect him. Even if it costs me my life."

Chapter 31

At the center of the room, between rows of empty bookshelves, was a wooden table where they sat drinking the bergamot tea that Jennaen had made for them in her old copper kettle. The head librarian and his assistant regaled Aveline with the tale of how they'd smuggled the Forbidden Books up to the far-northern Province of Corinthia, in garbage bags and laundry sacks and shoeboxes. Aveline was so engrossed in the story that she almost forgot that they were in the middle of a war. Until the building shook from the blast of nearby artillery fire.

"Do you think this building is going to collapse?" she asked shakily.

"It won't," said Thorsten. "It's never been tested against shells or cannons or whatever they've got up there, but I do know one thing—we're in the basement. Deep in the basement. Even if the building falls, we'll be safe down here."

"What about the Stam? They used to guard this place, right? Wouldn't they still have a key?"

"You're right," replied Thorsten. "But I have a gun. Don't worry, Miss Aveline."

She wanted to trust him; he had been her mother's associate, after all. A fellow member of Manatha Dé. But still she was afraid. Thorsten's lone gun was no match for the Stam's myriad pistols and rifles.

Hours passed. To distract herself from her mounting anxiety, she told Thorsten and Jennaen about her escape from the care home. The flight down the coast in the Ebrian powerboat. How the boat had gotten stuck in the cave, and then how they were blasted up the tunnel to the land above. Their trek across the riven land from Caelmorden to the Forest. As she talked, she realized how unbelievable the whole thing sounded. Like a legend from one of the old books that she and Bruno used to read as children.

Jennaen pushed her glasses up the bridge of her nose. Her small eyes glittered behind the lenses like a mouse's. "What an adventure you've had, Miss Aveline!"

She shook her head. It hadn't been some fun adventure. It had been painful and arduous. All her friends were now prisoners of the Stam. Bruno and Quintana, Ben and Catherine. The Dagkorodh. The other children. She didn't know whether they were alive or dead, but if they were alive, she imagined that they had been taken to one of the institutes. They were probably half-brainwashed by now. It was too painful to think about.

Another bomb or artillery shell exploded in the street above, causing the fluorescent lights to sway on their long cables. She flinched.

The librarian's assistant reached across the table and squeezed her hand. "It's okay."

Aveline smiled wanly.

"Are you hungry?"

"Not really."

Fear had turned her stomach into a rock. Still, Jennaen offered her a wrapped piece of dried beef, probably from the Lightministry's store of rations. "You've got to keep up your strength."

She peeled off the wrapper and nibbled at the corner of the strip of beef, relieved that whatever food they gave her would not be laced with any brainwashing drugs.

She forced herself to eat the whole strip, to drink more tea. She wanted desperately to stay awake to greet her father when he returned.

But, as time wore on, exhaustion overtook her. Stifling a yawn, she found that she could barely keep her eyes open. From a supply closet Thorsten took down a big wool blanket emblazoned with the symbol of the Lightministry: Monnag, his wings spread, a sprig of laurel clutched in his tail.

"Sleep now, Miss Aveline." Thorsten spread the blanket over the tile floor.

Sliding from her chair, Aveline obeyed, lying on her back on the blanket. It was so large that Thorsten was able to fold it in half to cover her body.

As the librarian and his assistant talked at the table in hushed voices about people and places she had never heard of, she continued to force herself to stay awake. Silently, she recited the Alterran alphabet backward. Recited the words of poems and songs that had been drilled into her head by the Party since childhood. Hoping that her disgust at these little vessels of propaganda would keep her alert. Not knowing what visions she would have, she did not want to fall asleep and dream. Her worst fear was ending up in the forest again with Morfyd, or back in the rapids, struggling to keep her head above water. She didn't know if she had the strength to survive the river this time.

Eventually, though, she could no longer resist the pull of sleep. She did not know what time it was when she heard a knock—rather, a series of knocks that seemed to form a pattern. A secret code of sorts.

"It's the hatch," said Thorsten.

As she bolted upright, her stomach leaped. *The hatch.* Balthazar and her father were back!

Throwing off the blanket, Aveline jumped to her feet and followed the others around the empty stacks until they stood before the entrance to the *Ta'azmayù*. Thorsten spun the wheel, and the hatch popped open with a pneumatic wheeze. Both he and Jennaen shined their flashlights into the dark.

Their beams landed on a woman, crouched in the passageway, shielding her eyes.

"Madam Lightminister?" they cried in unison.

Jennaen extended her hand and pulled Allyn into the room. Aveline could not believe her eyes. Standing before her was her mother, dripping wet, her face and navy-blue suit streaked with blood, a holster around her waist with a Stam-style gun and a *saya* with a dagger.

"Mother!"

"Aveline!"

The two ran into each other's arms. Aveline grasped her mother tightly, touching her arms, her face, her hair, to make sure that she was real. That this wasn't some terrible apparition orchestrated by Sister Morfyd.

"Mother, how on earth…? Simon told me you drank hemlock. I saw you lying there in the infirmary. I thought you were dead!"

Allyn laughed. "Good. That's what I wanted him to think. I actually took an elixir of *Atropa belladonna.*

341

Nightshade. It can mimic a coma, so you don't appear to have a heartbeat. But its effects last only about eight hours. If the Ebrians had come a minute too late, Simon would have been in for quite a surprise when I awakened on that stretcher."

Mother outsmarted Simon after all. The thought made Aveline giddy.

Jennaen rushed toward Allyn with a towel and handed it to her. "Are you hurt, Madam Lightminister?"

Allyn accepted the towel. "No, Jennaen. I'm fine." Streaks of blood came off on the towel as she wiped her face. Aveline could see that the blood was not hers. "I had a bit of a tussle in the viaduct, that's all."

"With the Stam?" said Aveline.

"With one of the reeducated."

Aveline's eyes widened. "One of Simon's spies?"

She nodded. "He's got a corps of them now."

"Where are the Stam? Are they still wandering around under the city?"

"Perhaps some of them are. The Stam and the Army have put up quite the counteroffensive, but we've just about driven them to the district wall." Allyn rubbed her wet hair with the towel, then handed it back to Jennaen. "And we've just taken the People's Assembly."

Thorsten and Jennaen regarded her with awe. The young woman's jaw looked as if it might hit the ground.

"Are you our Leader now?" asked Jennaen.

She laughed, shaking her head. "Ask me tomorrow. I don't have the faintest idea what I am at the moment."

"Come, Madam Lightminister." Thorsten touched her arm. "You must be exhausted."

He led her to the table, but instead she chose to sit on the blanket with Aveline, holding her, caressing her short, frizzy blonde hair; kissing the top of her head.

Aveline closed her eyes, silently thanking God or whoever had come to her mother's rescue. It was surreal to have her back. To feel the warmth of her body. Her heartbeat. Aveline felt as though she had ascended into the Beyond, as she did the night of her mother's wedding, when the guests had released hundreds of paper lanterns onto the darkened pond.

"You'll never believe this," said Aveline, "but I saw Father today. In the Lawministry prison. Did you know he's alive?"

Allyn smiled. "Yes."

"Why didn't you tell me?"

"I would have, my darling, but I didn't know myself until very recently. Not until after Simon had stolen you away to Gilsevain."

"Where has he been all these years?"

"Living in Ebria. In the city of Rehebeth. Everyone thought he died when his plane went down during the war. But his body was never found. As it turned out, he was wounded but had survived the crash."

Aveline frowned. "If he was alive, why didn't he come back home?" She remembered the dream she'd had at Caelmorden. Her father expressing his doubts to Benjamin about Allyn's love for him.

"I'm sure he wanted to, but he couldn't. He was working with Manatha Dé. It's taken twelve, almost thirteen years to build an army large enough to invade Calador and overthrow the Party." She lifted Aveline's hands, enfolding them in her own. "Remember, for most of that time, I was his enemy. He couldn't have told me without compromising the mission. The mission was far more important than I."

"More important than me, too?" She looked into Allyn's eyes.

"You were always the most important thing to him, Aveline. You were—you *are*—his world. He did this for you. So you wouldn't have to live in a country like the one your grandfather and uncle and I had created. That's how much he loves you."

A tear fell from Allyn's eye down her cheek. Aveline reached up and wiped it away, unused to seeing her mother cry.

"What's going to happen now?" she whispered.

"Well, if all goes according to plan, we take back the city, remove Simon from power, and begin building a new government."

"You and Father?"

She nodded. "If he'll still have me."

Aveline wrapped her arms around her mother. Nuzzled her head under her chin the way she did when she was a little girl. Beneath the blood and sweat and grime of the *Ta'azmayù* on Allyn's clothes, she could detect the faintest hint of gardenia perfume. The only things missing were Allyn's pearls, which Simon must have taken from her. He had taken everything from her. Except her life.

"Do you still love Father?"

"I've always loved him."

The two stayed like that, holding one another, for a long time. Despite the artillery fire that shook the building and caused the fluorescent lights to tremble sickeningly on their wires overhead, Aveline had never felt so safe in all her life. Although Allyn was the most dangerous woman—the most dangerous *person*—in all of Alterra, Aveline thought that nothing bad could happen when she was in her mother's arms.

"Do you know where Bruno and Quintana are? And Benjamin and Catherine and the kids? Are they still alive?"

"They're with Manatha Dé."

Aveline let out an enormous breath as if she had been holding it for weeks.

"After the Stam captured you in the Forest, the Dagkorodh fought off Simon's men. Sadly, Balthazar was the only one who survived. He led our friends to the stronghold at Mt. Segog before returning to Calador to meet the Ebrian Army."

Relief flooded Aveline's body. Her friends were safe. But she wished it hadn't cost the other rescuers their lives. The rescuers whose names they could no longer speak.

Jennaen briefly disappeared into the head librarian's office and returned with a steaming cup of tea, which she handed to Allyn. Aveline liked the way her mother's staff took such good care of her. Allyn had always insisted that she could do everything herself, but sometimes it helped to have people around you who looked after your basic needs.

"Rest, Madam Lightminister," said Thorsten. "You deserve it."

"Thank you, Thorsten, but I couldn't sleep now even if I wanted to." She gestured beyond the walls of the Lightministry, then held her hand to her heart as if in the loyalty salute. "Not while my city is burning."

Aveline remembered the huge sign on the side of a tall building in the City Center that read *I AM*

ALTERRA. Allyn *was* Alterra. She *was* its capital city. All of the country's successes, and its failures, were her own. Aveline could not imagine taking on such an immense responsibility.

"*Our* city," Allyn corrected herself.

"You will rebuild it," said the librarian. "I have faith in you."

"No, Thorsten. We will rebuild it together. I no longer believe that one person, or one Party, should hold all the power. You will see—the new Alterra will look very different from the old. Everyone will have a voice."

Aveline stared at her incredulously, unable to imagine a country where there was more than one Party. Maybe even more than one Leader. The possibilities were dizzying.

She was so very tired. So many things were changing all at once. She didn't know whether she was ready for this new world. This new Alterra. She clung to her mother. All she wanted now were the comforts of home. Her room with its soft, familiar bed. The luxury of sleeping as long as she wanted without bad dreams. Though she didn't even know whether the Fleur Estate still stood.

"My sweet girl," said Allyn, gently lifting her head. "I only came for a moment, to make sure you were safe. But I have to go now. Your father needs me."

"No! You can't go, Mother." She grasped the soiled lapels of Allyn's suit. "I can't lose you again. I need you here with me."

"We will be together again soon, I promise." Allyn stood and wiped Aveline's tears away with her thumbs.

"You are a very brave girl. Standing up to Simon the way you did. I'm proud to call you my daughter."

Chapter 32

A week later, Aveline sat between her mother and father on the dais formerly reserved for the High Court. Both she and her parents wore the sienna fatigues of the Ebrians. But instead of the Virolannens' roaring tiger sigil on the left breast, they all wore the Fleurs' dragon sigil outlined in black.

Aveline looked from her mother to her father, unable to believe that her family was together again as in the dream she'd had at Gilsevain. She felt the same tension, the same urgency, between her parents as when they'd sat across from each other in the groundskeeper's cabin, speaking the Ebrian battle language.

She glanced out at the courtroom. Television cameras were stationed at all four corners of the room, although there was no live audience. The only other people present were Simon and Morfyd, their hands cuffed behind their backs, flanked by two burly Ebrian guards.

Simon stood at the table below the dais, his right hand in a cast and sling from when he'd punched the prison wall. He wore his white Party uniform, though without his medals or Monnag pin. But he still wore his Mark of Yrgess on his left pinky, now the least valuable piece of jewelry in all of Alterra.

Next to him, Morfyd was also dressed in white, a

satin pantsuit with winged shoulders. Her newly cut hair was slicked back from her forehead, her eyes darkly rimmed in kohl, the green irises glowing from within the black.

A trumpet sounded from backstage, behind the dais, signaling the commencement of the proceedings. From stage right, another sienna-clad guard appeared and descended a short flight of stairs. Standing before the defendants, he said, "Please state your names for the record."

Simon lifted his chin haughtily. "Simon Yrgess Fleur. Supreme Leader of the State of Alterra."

Then Morfyd. "Lady Aleitra Ravenelle. Daughter of Duke Brydon Ravenelle. Chatelaine of the Sovereign State of Rakan Fo and Commander of the Bhorowan."

Aveline gasped. She had long since figured out that Morfyd was no Sister of Monnag, but she was stunned to discover her true identity. Duke Brydon Ravenelle had been a beloved peer and confidant of King Reuel IV. That was why Lady Aleitra spoke with the *clain*. When Alfred came to power, he had changed the guttural *clain* of the noblemen into the lilting, mellifluous accent of Calador.

Aveline looked from her mother to her father, but neither seemed surprised at Lady Aleitra's revelation.

"I demand a State-appointed barrister," interjected Simon. "And a fair trial."

"A fair trial?" Allyn's voice boomed in the empty courtroom. "Like the one you gave me?"

"You are a convicted traitor, Monnag. You should be serving your sentence at Rjellsfall right now."

"Oh, really? If I am a traitor, then I have no power to give you a fair trial."

"Even illegitimate governments bestow that courtesy on their prisoners of war. Even your Ebrians bring their prisoners before Kirtje Virolannen."

"Yes. And not a single one has survived the guillotine." Allyn paused. Smiled. "But I will not be deciding your fate today. I am leaving that decision to my daughter Aveline."

Aveline nearly choked. "Me?"

Allyn nodded. "As I said before, everyone will have a voice in the new Alterra. Especially you, my darling. These two defendants have caused you the most pain and suffering. It is only fair that you get to decide what to do with them."

She wasn't sure that *she* was the one who had suffered the most at Simon and Aleitra's hands. After all, they had imprisoned Allyn, put her in a glass cage, and sentenced her to brainwashing. To escape, she'd had to fake her own death. What Aveline had suffered—even the beatings in her cell—seemed slight in comparison.

Taking a shaky breath, she stood, looking down on her uncle and his partner in crime. In her mind she ran through the possibilities. She could sentence them to death by firing squad, or hanging, or drowning, or any method she chose. But she couldn't bear to order them killed. She did not want that on her conscience.

She considered sentencing them to six months at Rjellsfall or Stellenkirk or Gilsevain Landing or one of the other Institutes for Mental Hygiene. That seemed like the right thing to do. To punish them in the exact same way they'd tried to punish her and her mother. And countless other citizens of Alterra, like Sandor Hayes and Edwena Page, whose only crime had been to speak out against the Party.

Then she remembered something her grandfather used to say—an eye for an eye makes the whole world blind. Sending her uncle and Lady Aleitra to one of the institutes might make her feel as though justice were being done. But, in the end, it would solve nothing. It would only create two more human robots…to do what? Spew propaganda all day long? Spy on other citizens? Perhaps if there were a way to reeducate them in the new Alterran ideals, then it might make sense to send them to an institute. But she didn't yet know what those ideals were, and she doubted that her mother and father had worked them all out yet.

No, she would not sentence Simon and Aleitra to reeducation.

The last option was to send them far, far away so they could never harm anyone ever again.

But where? She wracked her brain. She could not send them anywhere else in Alterra, even to the far-northern province of Corinthia; it would be too easy for them to come back. And she would not send them to Ebria, now that the Ebrians were no longer the enemy.

Then it came to her. That night when Edwena had come out of the brainwashing, she had described a strange dream she'd had. Of being enslaved by the Prophet Elignon in a distant land many thousands of miles beyond Alterra's farthest reaches.

Aveline pointed to her uncle. "Uncle Simon, I hereby exile you to the city of Abaddon in the Tormen Badlands."

To her surprise, he began to laugh. A bitter, hollow laugh.

"That's the best you can do?" He addressed the

cameras more so than his niece, as if wanting to bring the whole country in on the joke. "You little dolt, don't you realize that you've sent me on holiday?"

Aveline trembled, frustrated. Bit her bottom lip so she wouldn't start to cry. She looked to her mother for guidance, but Allyn only nodded, encouraging her to take the punishment one step further.

Again, she raised her arm and pointed at her uncle, willing the words to flow. "I hereby sentence you to serve the Prophet Elignon." She remembered what Catherine had said about Elignon being not a religious figure but a dictator in disguise. "To...to scrub his floors, and the pots and pans in his scullery, day and night, without a moment's rest. To chop wood and fetch water and obey his every command like a common servant."

As she spoke, her uncle's face tightened with anger. Finally, she had provoked a reaction in him. The worst blow to his ego was to be stripped of his power and forced into servitude.

He spat on the ground.

"Save your water, Simon." Aleitra turned to him. "They are not worthy of it. You are royalty. Never forget that. You must conserve your strength for the battle ahead of you."

Aveline pointed to her. "And you, Sister Morfyd, or Lady Aleitra Ravenelle, or whoever you are, I hereby sentence you to return to Rakan Fo, and be locked behind the iron gate for the rest of your life."

The woman turned to meet Aveline's stern gaze. But her green eyes were lit from within. Amused, playful. "As you wish, Miss Aveline." She lifted her eyebrow as a slow smile played across her lips. "I trust you will sleep well from now on."

Goosebumps cropped up all along Aveline's arms. Then she straightened her spine.

You are no longer the girl at the bottom of the dumpster, covered in slops, she told herself. *No one— not Simon, not Aleitra, not any bullies you might run into at school—will ever make you feel afraid again. You will not give them that power.*

"Guards," she commanded. "Take them away."

****

When the family returned to the Estate, Jossie greeted them at the door. Aveline ran into her arms.

The Ebrian Army had freed Jossie and the cook, Mrs. Beauregard, and her assistant Corey from the Lawministry jail. Allyn's friends at the Ministry of Health had then administered the antidote to flush the brainwashing drugs from their systems that Lady Aleitra had begun to feed them while in captivity.

Upon returning to the Estate, Allyn had gathered together all the servants and given them a choice. They could either remain here and continue to serve, or they could return to their home cities, whether in Illyria or the other provinces. She would do nothing to stop them. Not even try to convince them to remain.

Jossie had chosen to stay and to serve.

"I left my village, Gallinveil, so long ago," she confessed to Allyn. "I don't have any family left there anymore. My parents and sister died years ago from the fever. You are my family now."

Jossie did not yet know what her role would be in the new Alterra, but Allyn promised her that she would not always be a lady's maid. She could go to university if she wanted, train for a new career. Marry and have children if she desired.

Aveline could see that all the change was as overwhelming for Jossie as it was for her, even down to the smallest details. The serving staff were no longer required to call their bosses "Miss" or "Mister" or any kind of profession-based honorific, but Jossie continued in the old ways out of habit.

"My Leader," she addressed Allyn that evening when she walked into Aveline's room with a tea tray. Allyn did not correct her.

Jossie bowed her head, set down the tray, and quietly left the room, closing the door behind her. Allyn walked over to where Aveline sat on the stool before her vanity brushing her hair. When Allyn extended her hand, Aveline gave her the brush, and she began gently running the horsehair bristles through her daughter's hair.

"Your hair is getting longer," she mused. "Not yet long enough to braid, but long enough to tie back with a ribbon."

Aveline caught her mother's eyes in the mirror. Studied her. Since being freed by the Ebrians, she had lost weight; Aveline noticed the bones of her chest becoming visible once more, her cheekbones and jawline becoming more pronounced.

"The loyalty ribbon?" asked Aveline.

Allyn smiled. "No. You never have to wear that again. Haven't you got one in a different color in your drawer?"

Opening her jewelry box, Aveline slid her finger under the pink satin backing and pulled it forward, revealing the little silver key to the vanity drawer. She rolled back the stool and unlocked the drawer, pulling it out. Inside were ribbons in various colors—aqua, lavender, cerulean—as well as a small onyx ring.

Aveline grasped it and picked it up. Her mother's sigil ring. She had completely forgotten that she'd locked it in here to hide it from Lady Aleitra.

Leaning over her shoulder, Allyn said, "My ring! I thought it was lost."

Aveline handed the ring to her mother, who put down the brush and slipped the ring onto the fourth finger of her left hand. "Do you know, Aveline, that your father gave my ring to Ben Cachtice for safekeeping before he took his final flight? Ben returned it to me after the war. I never thought I would give it to anyone ever again."

"Until Jem," said Aveline quietly.

"That's right."

Aveline swiveled on her stool to face her mother. "Did you ever love Jem? Or was it all for show?"

Allyn took a long time before answering. Looking off into the distance, she started to say something, then changed her mind. She appeared almost agonized.

She turned to Aveline. "It wasn't all for show. I married him for political reasons, it's true. I've done a lot of things I'm not proud of. But I did love him. How could I not? He was kinder to me than I ever deserved."

"Is he still in Uria? Imprisoned in a tower?"

Allyn's eyes widened. "How could you possibly know that?"

"I saw him in a dream. I've been having these weird prophetic dreams lately. I think it was the brainwashing drugs. Whatever they gave me at the care home, that's when it all started."

"You are right, my darling. Jem was in a tower in

Uria, but he wasn't imprisoned. I sent him there because I didn't know if I could protect him from Simon or the Stam once I began working with Manatha Dé."

"But…aren't the Urians our enemies?"

"No." She shook her head. "There never was any war between Brixia and Uria. We never sent any of our troops to fight the Urians. The Party—" She stopped, correcting herself. "*I* invented the war. My goal was to distract the public from the corruption in their own government. The corruption for which I was responsible."

"Where is Jem now?"

"Back in Ede's River. Before I sent him off to Uria, we decided together to speak the words to dissolve our marriage. It was one of the most difficult things I ever had to do—to say goodbye to someone I loved. But he knows that I will take care of him and his family for as long as I live."

"Can I see him again?"

"Certainly. You are free to write to him. I'll give you his address. I'm sure he would love to hear from you." Allyn passed her fingers over the onyx, making it glow like an ember. "You know, I was thinking about what you said about your dreams. It wasn't the drugs. They had given you very little before you were rescued from the care home. I think there is something else behind your dreams. Something hereditary."

Aveline frowned. "What do you mean?"

"Well, when I was about your age, I started having the same kinds of dreams. Prophetic dreams."

"You *did*?"

She nodded.

"Mother, why didn't you ever tell me?"

"It's not the sort of thing you tell your child. 'Oh, Aveline, guess what? I have prophetic dreams. Do you, too?' And besides, you know that dreams aren't taken very seriously here in Alterra. Not the way they are in Ebria."

"Did you dream about any of this? I mean, the things that would happen with Grandfather or Simon or my father...or me?"

"Not completely, but I had glimpses of it. In one of my dreams I saw a fleet of ships crossing the Shinar Sea."

Aveline leaped from her stool. "So did I!" She couldn't believe that she and her mother had shared the same dream, maybe even at the same time. Then she remembered what Lady Aleitra had told her about the deep-brain stimulation machine. "Aleitra said that you were the only other person on earth who knew how to use the machine to manipulate dreams. Is that true?"

"I don't know whether I am the only person on earth, but I can use the machine for that purpose. When we were testing the machine at the Healthministry, I discovered a sort of gateway into others' dreams. The machine was not designed that way. I think it was an unintended effect of stimulating the subconscious mind. There is so much we don't know yet about the way it works."

"Will you teach me how to use it? To get into other people's dreams?"

"Only with their permission," said Allyn. "Otherwise it's a violation of their free will. No better than reeducation. But, yes, I will teach you what I know. Perhaps you can figure out a way to use it as a means for gaining knowledge from others from afar, or as a tool for self-discovery. Who knows?"

Aveline hugged her mother, excited to begin their experiments on the machine. To travel in their minds to distant lands. To fly together in lucid dreams over the rooftops of Calador.

"I know I haven't always been there for you when you needed me." Allyn tousled her daughter's hair. "But I want to change that."

"I would like that very much, Mother." Aveline beamed.

"Come. Let's go downstairs. Your father is waiting for us."

Down in the Great Room, Kit Llewellyn Fleur stood by the fireplace, smoking his pipe, the scent of vanilla tobacco perfuming the air. He wore a black three-piece suit, the kind he wore at university when he had met Allyn over a decade ago. Aveline marveled that he still looked very much like his picture hanging above the mantel. His almost thirteen years in Ebria had hardly aged him. Glancing at his portrait, and then at her father, she realized that the painting was no longer an homage to a fallen hero but the likeness of a living man.

"Kit," said Allyn. "There is something I'd like to give you."

Kit set his pipe on the mantel and exhaled the sweet-smelling smoke. She walked over to him and instructed him to hold out his hand. In his palm she placed her sigil ring, then closed his fingers around it. As he smiled down at her, Aveline thought that no other world existed except the one that they were creating together.

As her parents embraced, Aveline wandered over to the window, sat on the chaise longue, and looked out on the darkening pool deck and lawn. The month of Frost was coming to an end, bringing with it the months of Snow and Sleet and Wind. The coldest, cruelest months of the year.

But now, a light snow fell across the Estate, over the pool and the meadow and her grandmother Marie's hamlet with its hedge maze with forty-two solutions and one null set. Dusting the tops of the trees in Wildweir and the spikes of the iron fence that ran along the low hills and displayed the head of Monnag, and beyond, over the seven provinces of Alterra, flurries driven by wind from the north, soon to cover everything in the deep, white, endless forgetfulness of snow.

Chapter 33

"Hurry up!" cried Aveline. "We're going to be late!"

The school bell had already rung, and Aveline and her two best friends took off running down the hall on their way to their new class called Mastery of Dreams. Quintana ran so fast that she tripped over her untied shoelace and toppled onto the freshly-waxed tile floor, her books flying from her arms. Other children in the hallway began to giggle and point at her.

Aveline stopped. Crouching beside her friend, she began gathering up her books while Bruno glared at the onlookers, staring them down until they lowered their eyes and kept walking.

The three friends were all nearly fifteen years old, in the tenth grade. And they were dressed in street clothes, no longer in the uniforms of old. Gone were the tartan skirts and starched white shirts for girls; the black woolen pants and penny loafers for boys.

In the months since the Ebrians had marched on Calador, much had changed. Allyn had opened Belfort Academy to all children in the capital city, regardless of income or class. There was now no more distinction between the children of the wealthy and the scholarship students. Everyone was welcome, and education was free, funded by the Ministry of Education.

The maps that now hung on the school walls

reflected the correct geography, even the unsavory regions like Rakan Fo. And the school library was filled floor-to-ceiling with books—not just Party-sanctioned books, but Forbidden Books returned from the Province of Corinthia where they had been stored safely. The children could now read freely from books about science and medicine and the political structures of other nations—knowledge that the Party had kept secret for more than fifty years.

They could now listen without fear to the symphonies and concertos and string quartets of Milo Fresenius, who had given his first concert in Calador since being exiled to Ebria more than two years earlier. Aveline and her parents had sat in the front row of the concert hall, her mother rapt with passion, tears streaming down her cheeks. Fresenius had dedicated his Symphony No. 14 to her; it was now called the *Monnag*.

Even the Sisters of Monnag were freed from their religious order. Although they still taught at Belfort Academy and served as nurses and aides in the ministries, they were no longer required to wear the black habits and veils, or to be called "Sister" or "Mother." Allyn and Kit were in the process of dismantling the State religion. Any reference to "God" was no longer to the State God who favored the Fleurs but to the God of the Universe, a deity who watched over and protected everyone.

Allyn and Kit had also dismantled the Ministry of Civic Enlightenment. The film studio in the City Center and the country's newspaper, *The Egregor*, were now privately owned. Other competing newspapers, and television and radio stations, had since opened for business. People were allowed to criticize their Leaders on television, in the media, in the city streets, without fear of being arrested.

The Stam no longer existed, either. In its place was the Federal Police. One of the first tasks of the Federal Police had been to visit every building in Calador and remove the bugging apparatus from every room in every home. Citizens' private lives were to be private. Although everyone still looked over their shoulders or lowered their voices out of habit, no one was watching or listening any longer.

But, for as much progress as had been made in the last few months, there was still so much to do. An entire city to rebuild. Each morning, on her way to school, Aveline passed the burnt-out shells of buildings. She passed other buildings, too, whose sides had once displayed Party advertisements, that were now painted over. Long gone was the dark-haired girl biting into her piece of white bread slick with Party margarine. Long gone the young airman in his gray uniform holding his hand over his heart, with the caption *I AM ALTERRA*. Whether there would continue to be one Party or two— or more—was still a subject of heated debate in the People's Assembly.

Aveline handed the books back to Quintana in a neat stack. Her friend smiled and blushed, accepting the books with one hand and tucking a strand of hair behind her ear with the other. Quintana's lush dark hair was starting to grow back. It was now long enough to curl over her earlobes.

"Let's go," said Aveline. "We're already late."

"I think she'll wait for us…don't you?" Bruno grinned, showing his dimples.

The three friends hurried to the end of the hall and up the stairs to the second floor. Cautiously, Aveline opened the door to the classroom in which Mastery of Dreams had already started. At the head of the classroom stood Allyn Fleur in a black pantsuit, arms crossed over her chest.

"I'm sorry we're late, Mother," said Aveline, casting her eyes down to her scuffed tennis shoes.

"Do you know what the punishment is for latecomers?" Allyn's mouth twitched up at the corners. "You get to go first."

Aveline gulped. She and Bruno and Quintana took their seats up front. Except these were no ordinary classroom seats; they were reclining leather chairs. Each was fitted with an adjustable metal head-ring. The wearer leaned back and placed the ring on his or her head, which then created a field of electrical stimulation, inducing delta waves in the brain and causing the wearer to fall into a deep sleep. The rings were all connected by wires, allowing multiple wearers to join the same electrical field and access the same dream. Allyn was teaching them how to navigate and master the dream world. None of the children were very good at it yet, but they were all fast learners, especially Aveline.

No sooner than she and her two friends had settled themselves into their chairs and adjusted their head-rings, they began to dream. Bruno took control this time. Aveline knew it because she soon found herself in an ancient stone temple in the middle of a jungle—the beginning of his favorite adventure.

"Feel the weapon at your side," guided Allyn in a soothing voice. Aveline knew she was watching an image of their dream, transmitted from the machines to the television set at the front of the classroom. "Lift it from its holster or its *saya*."

Aveline reached down and felt a rough leather belt take shape around her waist. Felt the handle of a dagger in its *saya*. She pulled it out and examined its pearl handle, the sharpness of the blade.

When she leaped forward, she found that she was levitating above the stone floor. As if the rules of gravity had been suspended for a moment, she was as light as she would have been on the moon.

Sliding her dagger back into its *saya*, she jumped into the air and turned a somersault.

"Hey!" said Bruno with mock sternness. "This is *my* dream, you know!"

"Catch me if you can!" she taunted back and levitated to the top of the temple.

Easily, she lifted her arms and pushed through the roof, which vanished under her palms, revealing the afternoon sky above. The higher she flew through the air, the smaller the temple grew beneath her.

"Wait for us!" cried Quintana.

But Aveline was already soaring high above Calador.

"Bruno! Quintana!" she called to her friends below. "You're never going to believe this!"

She could see the City Center, the Victory Bridge, the Avenue of the Acacias. The frail spires of the Church of the Monnag. The tall building that had once been home to the Ministry of Civic Enlightenment. From this vantage point, all the people and the cars looked like they belonged in a trainset.

So this is what freedom feels like, she said to herself, as she continued upward through the clouds.

A word about the author…

S.J. Carson is a YA fantasy author and poet based in Las Vegas, Nevada. She holds degrees from Stanford and Boston Universities. A two-time Pushcart Prize nominee, her poems have appeared in both online and print journals. *Aveline* is her first novel.